Jan Butlin has written ~~for~~ television, including ~~such~~ *at Forty*, *No Strings*, ~~Time Lucky~~, but *Grace* ~~is her first novel~~.

Her interest in herbalism began when she was writing and researching the series *Let's Face It*, and she has tested all her heroine's recipes in her own kitchen.

Jan is married to broadcaster Martin King and they live in London's Covent Garden in a flat that used to belong to Errol Flynn, but unfortunately does not seem to be haunted . . .

Grace

Jan Butlin

KNIGHT

First published in Great Britain in 1990
by Michael O'Mara Books Ltd

First published in paperback in 1991
by HEADLINE BOOK PUBLISHING PLC

This edition published 1997 by
Knight an imprint of Brockhampton Press

10 9 8 7 6 5 4 3 2

ISBN 1 86019 6012

Typeset by Medcalf Type Ltd, Bicester, Oxon

Printed and bound in Great Britain by
Mackays of Chatham PLC, Chatham, Kent

Brockhampton Press
20 Bloomsbury Street
London
WC1B 3QA

**For Martin
with my love and thanks**

CONTENTS

PROLOGUE: VALERIAN

GRACE 1990

THE HERB VALERIAN

'Excellent for those burdened and for such as be troubled'
Culpeper

'So runs my dream; but what am I?'
Alfred Lord Tennyson

Last night I had the dream again.

And when I awoke, vulnerable and afraid, there were no strong arms to comfort me. 'Give in to memory. Don't fight. Don't allow it to lie in the recesses of your mind, festering, waiting to bring you down. Face it. Welcome it. And let facing it cleanse the memory of the terror.'

And yet I lay rigid. I could hear the 'roaches scuttling over the floor, and I knew, beyond doubt, that if I reached out my hand and turned on the light, I would see their squat, black forms hurrying towards the cracks in the crumbling plaster walls. I could hear a rat below the floorboards of the room above. And worse, much

viii

worse, I knew that tomorrow I would go to school, and that on my way home, somewhere on the stairs that smelt of urine and unwashed bodies and stale cooking, *he* would be waiting.

I reached out and turned on the bedroom light. No 'roaches scurried at the sudden intrusion of light into their night-time world. No rats above. But the dream haunted me, filled my mind.

My hand shook as I reached out and lit a discreetly monogrammed cigarette. I looked at the initials. G.L. Grace Laure. Beccy Mandel, the skinny, frightened little kid from the Lower East Side, was now known as Grace Laure. But who was I really?

I got out of bed and crossed to the dressing table. The soft light was kind to my face as I looked into the mirror. Forty-seven years old. A lifetime away from my dream . . . My dream.

My face was tense and, as I looked deeply into the mirror, the eyes that looked back at me did not belong to Grace Laure. They were Beccy's and they were frightened.

'Don't fight the memory,' Dr Schulman had said. 'Don't fight . . . welcome it. Remember . . .'

THE HERB

CITY AVENS

'It is governed by Jupiter and gives hopes
of a wholesome, healthful herb.'
Culpeper

THE WOMAN

PART ONE: CITY AVENS

BECCY 1955–1959

'I am the family face;
Flesh perishes, I live on.'
Thomas Hardy

CHAPTER ONE

I stood at the bottom of the stairs, the sound of my heartbeat louder than the noise of New York's traffic outside.

I would count up to ten and then I would run. On thin, young legs I would run, two steps at a time, towards our apartment on the fifth floor.

Sometimes I'd get there. Sometimes he'd catch me.

'I'll tell . . .'

'Tell and you're out. You, your ma, and that snotty-nosed kid are on the street. Your ma's four weeks behind. Wanna be out on the street?'

'No, but . . . please.'

'Shut up. I ain't hurting ya!'

But he is. He is hurting me. One hand inside my dress, reaching for my unformed breast, crushing my nipple between his fingers. His other hand is in my panties, his fingers probing, hurting, finding. He is pushing me against the wall. He smells of sweat and garlic and beer, and something else, something animal that I neither recognise nor understand. Then, suddenly, a shudder and it's over. He turns abruptly away. I sag down on my knees, not crying but feeling sick and unclean.

'Tell and you're out, kid!'

He has gone. Then up to our apartment. My mother is at the stove, her back to the door. I open my mouth to speak.

'Tell, and you're out.'

I say nothing. I am twelve years old and I am street-wise.

My mother had once been good looking, small-boned with fine features. Poverty and disappointment changed her. By the time I was twelve, lines of discontent were etched deeply into her face.

There had once been a framed photograph on our sideboard, taken on my parents' wedding day: my father, handsome and assured; my mother laughing up into his face, her eyes full of love. The day my father left us my mother took down the photograph. I don't know if she destroyed it, it just disappeared. She didn't weep. She simply never spoke my father's name again. If my brother and I asked after him, her lips tightened and she would ignore the question. Start speaking of something else as if she had not heard us. Eventually we stopped asking.

'Beccy . . . Beccy!' I had gone into the little cubicle that I shared with her. Just room for a double bed and a wash-stand, screened from the main living area by faded print drapes.

'Beccy!' My mother's voice was not really even exasperated by my lack of response. Not so much from good nature as from an emotional laziness. No, that wasn't fair, an emotional lassitude. Life had numbed my mother. I know, at least I think, she loved my brother Aaron and me, but somewhere along the line life had destroyed her ability to show emotion. By the time I was old enough to get to know her, my mother was a shell.

'Beccy!' This time I answered her.

'Yes, Ma?'

'Go find your brother. Supper's ready.'

'But . . .' It was much too early for supper, we usually ate much later when the light had gone and my brother

3

came in from the street. My mother anticipated my protest.

'Go find your brother: I got a job pressing at Goldman's tonight. You want me to be late? We don't need the money?'

Goldman's was a laundry that prided itself on fast service. About twenty women worked through the night, washing and ironing, so that someone could put on a clean shirt first thing the next morning. My mother hadn't been able to get regular work there, but if one of the women went sick they sometimes sent for her.

'He'll be in soon.' I couldn't, wouldn't, face those stairs again.

My mother sighed. I can never remember her slapping us but she was expert at sighing. All her cares, her sorrows, went into those sighs. They echoed with despair, of looks and a husband lost, of poverty, and of the bleak, grinding knowledge that tomorrow would be just the same as today. That there would be no silver lining in her clouds, just rain.

I heard her sigh, and knew I couldn't refuse her. 'Okay.' I walked from the room on to the landing.

I looked down the stairs. They were empty. I stood there and the sounds of the tenement closed in on me. A baby wailing. A man's voice raised in anger followed by a slap and the sound of a woman crying. Radios. On one louder than the rest, Deanna Durbin was waltzing, waltzing, high in the clouds. The sound was coming from the Janowskis' apartment, next door to ours. I was only twelve years old but I sensed the irony of old Mrs Janowski sitting in her stinking room, spilling gin down her front and dreaming of Hollywood and Deanna Durbin.

Mike Janowski was my friend, a small fierce boy my

own age. His parents were what my mother called Show Folk, endlessly on tour or in stock. Not successful, just earning enough to stay in that hard profession and send a little money home to keep Mrs Janowski in booze in return for looking after her grandson. In the three years we lived next to the Janowskis I never saw Mike's parents, although he received the odd postcard, so I guess they had virtually abandoned him.

Now I knocked at the Janowskis' door. I knew it was a pretty long shot that Mike would be there. It was summer and at that time of day most of the kids would be on the stoop or the fire escape, or playing baseball or gutter hockey in the dry, dusty street. But if he was there, I'd ask him to come find Aaron with me. I wouldn't have to walk down the stairs alone.

A moment later I heard Mrs Janowski shuffling to the door. It opened a few inches and a faded, bleary eye peered through the crack.

'Oh, it's you, Beccy. What you want, kid?'

She took the chain off its hook and opened the door. I suppose Mrs Janowski was only in her late fifties then, but when you're twelve even twenty seems old, and she seemed to me to be older than the Ancient Mariner.

Perhaps in her youth she had been softly pink and pretty. Now she was grotesque. Maybe someone once told her that she looked like Jean Harlow. There must have been some rational explanation for her appearance. Her hair was bleached to a startling shade of yellow, and tortured into tight waves and curls. I never saw her without a heavy, white make-up, finished off with rouge and fire-engine-red lips. She probably slept in it. Tonight, she was wearing a wrapper trimmed with ancient, soiled ostrich feathers, the whole ensemble finished off by a pair of heavily scuffed men's slippers. Mrs Janowski had

5

trouble with her feet. She smelt of gin and cheap perfume. At that time I couldn't understand how Mike could bear to live with her, but that was before I knew her for the good soul she was. Before I recognised the great gift she had: to love and show that she loved.

'Is Mike in?'

She stared at me vacantly, her mind grappling with this apparently difficult question.

Finally: 'What day is it?'

'Tuesday.'

'Then he ain't in. He's at the drug store.'

Mike had a job washing dishes at the soda fountain on the regular guy's night off.

'That's Thursday. He goes there on Thursdays!'

'Don't get clever with me, Missy. The guy changed his night off, see?' And with that she shut the door.

For a brief moment I considered going back into our apartment and telling my mother I was afraid to go downstairs, and why. But the janitor, my tormentor, was right — what would that achieve other than eviction?

I started to run down the stairs, then stopped. I forced myself to walk slowly. I'd had enough of terror and humiliation. I'd had enough of being a victim. If he caught me, so be it. I would endure it as I had on countless other occasions, but I wouldn't run. I reached the bottom of the first flight of stairs; three more flights to go. It was a hot night and I was sweating, but my body felt cold beneath the sweat. I forced myself to walk slowly on. Another flight of stairs. I was going to make it! Then a door slammed and he was standing at the bottom of the stairs, grinning up at me.

I could have turned back, but I had made a decision at the top of the stairs and I wouldn't go back on it. I was poor, a kid, a kike, but at that moment I found a kind of dignity. I walked on. I saw his expression change to one of puzzlement, and realised that part of his kick in abusing me was to experience my fear. My change of attitude unnerved him. For a moment I thought he was going to turn away, then he shook his head, like a dog shaking water from his coat, and started to climb the stairs towards me. 'Oh, God! Please, God, don't let him hurt me.'

I heard footsteps on the stairs behind me. The clip, clip of high heels on the steps.

'Hi, Beccy! Where you going? Got a boyfriend yet?'

It was Rosie Hartman from the second floor. She was about four years older than me, and confident of her own attractiveness. She wore a full skirt under which were at least three petticoats, a tight sweater and a wide belt. That year all the girls were trying to look like Lana Turner.

'Boys are stupid,' I said as I walked with her down the last flight of stairs, past the man I had grown to hate. I forced myself to look into his face. 'Good night, Mr Salvatore.'

I could feel his eyes following me as I walked out into the street. I was saved! The humid heat of a New York summer evening hit me in the face as we left our building. Rosie tripped off towards the subway on her ridiculously high heels. Some of the boys whistled as she walked past and she tossed her head, pretending to be annoyed but loving every admiring glance.

I looked around for Aaron, but couldn't see him. I had a hunch where he might be. Further along the block was a boarded-up building. Two years ago it had been a small bar and restaurant with a rooming house above. The old couple who ran it leased the bar and a couple of rooms in which they lived. It was hardly a roaring success, but it did okay. The kind of place where the old men from

7

the block could make a glass of beer or a coffee and a bagel last two hours while they played checkers. I guess old Mr and Mrs Shoaff made a few bucks out of it, enough to keep body and soul together. Then a new landlord bought the building and put a smart young lawyer to work, looking for loop-holes in the Shoaffs' lease. He found them. A new, astronomical rent was to be asked.

The Shoaffs packed up and went to live with their son and daughter-in-law in Detroit. They had been on the block for thirty-two years. Three days after they left, a fire devastated the building. There were people who said they had seen Mr Shoaff in the neighbourhood that night. But they didn't say it to the cops or to the fire department. The block always closed ranks against the authorities. Hell! Neighbours had raised the alarm, the roomers had been got out unhurt, the fire hadn't spread. Serve that bastard Uptown landlord right!

With the usual limited logic of the poor they didn't reason that whoever fired the building probably did the landlord a good turn. He might even have arranged it himself. He could collect the insurance and redevelop or keep the money and let the building rot. But revenge makes a better story than commerce and so the legend of Mr Shoaff grew and was nurtured on the block.

In spite of signs threatening dire consequences to anyone trespassing, some of the local boys met in the old building and, when they could get one, smoked a cigarette. Today, when the forbidden fruit is usually heroin or cocaine, how innocent that act of daring seems.

I slipped down the alley by the side of the building. I approached cautiously, partly because the structure really was dangerous, and partly because girls were banned from this masculine hideout. I pushed aside a piece of loose planking that hung on one rusty nail and entered the back yard. It was piled high with rubble and debris and stank of mould and decay. I crept to the rear of the building and called into the dark interior.

'Aaron!' Silence. Then again, 'Aaron! It's me, Beccy.'

A pause, and then from inside his voice, hostile at my daring to interrupt him when he was with his buddies.

'What you want?'

'Ma says you're to come home. She's working at Goldman's tonight and we're eating early.'

'Ah, shit!'

A moment later my brother Aaron came into the yard, blinking at the light after the gloom of the building.

'You shouldn't go in there. It could fall and kill you.'

'Ah, shit!'

He pushed past me and scrambled through the loose planking. I followed.

My brother was three years younger than me and I loved him fiercely. I knew, even then, that he could be greedy and lazy and deceitful, but I closed my mind to it. I guess because he had charm. Even as a kid, people sought to be with him. From the time he was a toddler and our father left, I had cared for him, looked out for him and, I suppose, spoilt him. A young girl child can have an astonishing well of maternal instinct and I lavished mine on Aaron.

He walked towards our building a few paces ahead of me, whistling tunelessly to himself, seemingly unaware of my presence. At nine years old, girls, especially sisters, are not to be fraternised with.

'I found him, Ma,' I called as I walked through the door.

My mother did not answer. She was sitting on a chair by the stove, her head leaning back against the wall, her face twisted by pain. One hand was pressed against the centre of her thin breast. Before that day, I never remember my mother being ill. I think perhaps a child grows up the first time it realises the mortality of its parents.

'Ma! Ma! Don't die!' I ran to her, tears streaming down my cheeks.

Aaron was standing in the doorway, white-faced. I put my arm around my mother's shoulders. 'I'll get you to bed, Ma.'

'Don't move me! Be . . . all right . . . minute.'

'Aaron, run to the drug store. Tell Mr O'Brien Ma needs a doctor. He'll know who to phone.'

'No! Money . . . don't need doctor. Money . . .'

She opened her eyes and looked at me. 'Don't, Beccy, please.'

The worst of the pain seemed to be passing, but she looked terrible and I was still frightened.

'But what is it, Ma? What's wrong with you?'

'Just a pain. Something I ate, I guess.'

'Can I get you anything?'

'Just a sip of water.'

'Aaron, get Ma a glass of water.' He ran to the sink.

'I'll be all right in a minute . . . got to get to Goldman's.'

'You crazy, Ma? You can't work when you're like this!'

'We need the money, Beccy.'

'I'll go. Well, why not? I can press. I press our clothes. You say I do it real good!'

'But . . .' I lifted the glass of water to my mother's lips. 'But nothing! You can't go. We need the money, so I'll go.'

'You're just a child, Beccy. They won't like it. It's hard work and there's school tomorrow.'

'It won't kill me to stay up one night! Besides, I'm skinny but I'm tall for my age. I'll tell them I'm fourteen.'

My mother continued to protest, but the pain had exhausted her and finally she gave in.

'All right. I guess you know what you're doing. And can you drop off my skin stuff to Mr O'Brien? I promised them for tonight.'

My mother made a few dollars by making up face creams, cleansers and tonics. The recipes came from my grandmother and her mother before that. Some of the recipes my mother couldn't make because they required herbs readily available in Central Europe but not in a New York ghetto. Elder flowers, linden flowers, comfrey . . . The names held a kind of magic for me, and I had secretly vowed that one day I would obtain them. The simpler mixtures my mother made up on our kitchen stove and Mr O'Brien sold them for her at the drug store. I used to love helping my mother on the evening she prepared her 'skin stuff' as she called it. A large pudding basin would be placed in a saucepan of boiling water on the stove. I would stir the bees-wax and lanolin until it had melted and then we would add honey and almond oil. The previous night my mother would have poured boiling water on to flower petals or herbs. Cups would stand ranged along the dresser that night and all the next day. While I stirred in the honey and oil, my mother would strain these infusions and set aside the water that remained. We would add lavender if the lotion was to be used to soothe the skin, rosemary if it was to be a night cream, parsley for an oily skin.

There were three things wrong with my mother's products. They weren't packaged, they contained no preservatives so wouldn't keep longer than three or four months, and they sold too cheaply. Mr O'Brien had a few customers who swore by my mother's creams and lotions, but most people simply couldn't believe that something in a plain brown pot that sold for thirty or forty cents would be any good.

When I knocked at Mrs Janowski's door for the second time that evening, I was wearing a dress of my mother's and my hair was no longer in braids. The tight braids had put waves into my thick hair, and so I had parted it in the middle and drawn the sides back from my face with two combs. I thought I looked like Hedy Lamarr.

I had made Aaron promise to sit with my mother and to seek help from Mr O'Brien if she was taken ill again. The one thing that troubled me about my appearance, that stopped me looking older, was the fact that I wore no make-up. My mother never used it, and I was too young to have given any thought to buying it, even if we had had the money. But from the look of Mrs Janowski, make-up was in plentiful supply in her apartment.

My mother was sleeping fitfully as I crept from the living room on to the landing, carrying the jars and bottles of creams and lotions for the drug store in an old shopping bag. I knocked at the Janowskis' door and once again waited for the sounds of Mrs Janowski shuffling to open it. The eye that appeared at the small opening that the chain allowed was even more bleary and bloodshot than last time.

'Yeah? Who the hell are you? And what the fuck do you want?'

I felt conflicting emotions: fear at her aggression, and pleasure that my changed appearance was convincing, albeit to a drunk.

'It's me, Beccy, Mike's friend from next door.'

'Huh? What yer do to yourself?'

I quickly explained about my mother having been

12

taken ill, my deputising for her, and my need to look older.

'. . . and, you see, I thought I should wear some make-up.'

'So you thought you'd use something from Doll's bag of tricks? Okay, kid, come in.' She undid the chain.

The apartment she led me into had exactly the same layout as ours — a living room, a kitchen, a screened-off alcove for a bed, and the use of the shared lavatory on the landing. Mike, like Aaron, slept on a day-bed in the living room.

Mrs Janowski pulled back the curtains that screened her bed from the living area, and gestured towards a dressing table. It was the kind that nowadays, stripped and polished, would fetch a high price in a fashionable junk shop. It had a central mirror flanked by small drawers, then two large drawers below that. Every drawer was open, its contents spilling out. The top of the dressing table was strewn with a collection of used and half used cosmetics, both ancient and modern.

'Help yourself, kid,' she said, sweeping a hand expansively over the dressing table. 'If I ain't got it, it ain't worth having!'

She picked up a block of mascara and absent-mindedly spat into it. Then she picked up a small brush and rubbed it along the spit-moistened block. I was seated at the dressing table by then, and she stood behind me, peering into the mirror and brushing mascara on to her sparse, spiky eyelashes.

'Mind you, this is a load of shit compared with eyeblack.' She caught sight of my bemused expression in the mirror.

'Don't know what that is, do you?'

I shook my head.

She pulled out one of the small drawers and turned it upside down. Its contents spewed out over the already unbelievably cluttered surface.

'Here somewhere . . .' She scrabbled among her treasures like a squirrel seeking a particularly luscious nut.

'Ah!' She held up a small block of what looked like black shoe polish.

'You melt this a little, just a little, over a candle. Then you take a spent match-stick, dig it in and blob, blob, blob on the end of every lash. Gives you eyes like the Queen of fucking Sheba! Always used it on stage . . . Didn't know I used to tread the boards, did you?'

'No!'

Was it true or some fantasy that had suddenly appealed to her befuddled brain?

'Burlesque! Yes, sirree, I had firm tits and a great little ass in those days!' She slapped her behind enthusiastically.

'Then I married Mr Janowski and . . .'

A pause. She wandered over to the gin bottle and poured herself a generous slug.

'And?' I prompted.

'And he wanted my bumps and grinds all to himself!'

She slumped into a chair and stared morosely into her glass. Suddenly, disturbingly, she gave a shout of raucous laughter. She drank, then — 'All to himself.' It was almost a whisper. She took another swallow of gin then seemed to remember my presence. She pointed towards the jumble of make-up. 'Help yourself, kid!'

As I looked into the mirror I could hear her muttering to herself, 'Yes, sirree! All to himself! Mr R. Janowski. Know what the "R" stands for? Rat! R for Rat. A two-timing rat! Rat Janowski . . .'

Against the background of her mutterings I picked up a pot of rouge and began to make up my face.

I had never used make-up before. Never seen my mother use it. But I instinctively painted my face with subtlety. I had never considered that I might be pretty, but as I lightly rouged my cheeks, outlined my eyes, mascaraed my lashes, my face came alive in the mirror.

My eyes had always seemed too large for my small face, but the rouge on my cheeks brought out the delicate strength of the bones and gave definition to my features. I searched through the mess on the dressing table for a lipstick but they were all such violent shades of red that I settled for a very little rouge rubbed over my lips with my finger, then powdered to tone down the colour.

I felt grown-up as I rose to thank Mrs Janowski. I never spoke my thanks because she was sleeping deeply, a faint smile on her lips. I wondered what her dreams were about. Perhaps in them she still had firm tits and a great little ass and good times with Rat Janowski. I let myself out silently.

Once again I forced myself to walk slowly down the stairs. I wouldn't run. This time, thank God, there was no sign of him.

I hurried along the two blocks to Mr O'Brien's drug store. To my surprise one or two boys whistled after me. It had never happened before and I decided that I liked it. But I knew the rules of the game and, like Rosie Hartman, tossed my head and looked disdainful.

I entered the drug store and looked around for Mr O'Brien. He was serving a customer at the drug counter and so I crossed to the soda fountain to say hallo to Mike.

The soda fountain was a popular hang-out with the more affluent kids in the neighbourhood. Mr O'Brien had recently installed a juke box, and a few couples were jiving in front of it, but it was a strict rule of the house that if you wanted to play the juke box you had to buy something to eat or drink from the fountain. I looked on enviously as the soda jerk prepared a Knickerbocker Glory for a pretty girl seated on one of the high stools. Her boyfriend sat on the next stool, his arm loosely around her shoulders. 'One day,' I thought. And that truly was the limit of my ambition at that moment. That one day I'd have a nickel to put in the juke box and forty cents to squander on a tall glass of peaches, four different flavours of ice cream, chopped nuts, whipped cream and raspberry syrup!

Mike was at the far end of the counter, his shirt sleeves rolled up and his arms in a sink full of hot suds. The fountain was busy and he had to keep the clean glasses coming. He washed up with the same serious intent that he brought to everything in life. He was small for his age but with an arresting face even then. His face, with its high, broad cheek-bones and slightly slanting eyes, spoke of his Slavic ancestry and he had the unusual colouring that one sometimes finds in Poles − a fair skin, blond hair and yet brown eyes.

Why is it that the Fates point a finger at one member of a family and decree that they will have the will to succeed, the ambition to fight their way out of a ghetto, and then the talent to fulfil their dreams? Neither of us could have guessed at that moment, Mike washing up, me on my way to work through the night in a laundry, that we were to be the chosen ones.

'Mike!' He glanced up as I spoke to him. He was only twelve years old and looked tired.

'Jeez, Beccy, what you do to yourself?' he asked in amazement.

'Grew up a little, I guess.' I touched my face and hair. 'Don't you like it?'

'Jeez! I don't know. You look, you look kinda . . .' Suddenly his face lit up with a warm smile. 'You look great!'

The soda jerk glared down the counter at us. 'Stop yabbing, kid! You're being paid to wash glasses, not to shoot your mouth off. Get back to work. Go on!'

He started washing glasses again. 'One day . . . one day I'm coming in here with money in my pocket. I'm going to order a double nut chocolate with maple syrup, heavy on the whipped cream, I'm going to watch him make it, I'm going to pay, then I'm going to walk away and leave it on the counter . . . one day!'

He looked so fierce that I believed him totally.

'Sure you are, Mike!'

'You can bet on it,' he said, throwing another smouldering glance at the soda jerk.

'Well, see you around, huh?'

Mike nodded and I crossed to the drug counter and left my mother's latest brew of skin foods with Mr O'Brien.

Goldman's was another three blocks from the drug store. As I walked I could feel my dress beginning to cling to me with the heat. It was well after nine o'clock but the night was sticky, with the smell of gasoline hanging on the humid air. But the discomfort I felt hurrying through the hot, crowded streets was as nothing compared to the hell hole that was Goldman's laundry.

That night I looked around at the other women working there, and I discovered ambition. Some of the women were only a few years older than me, some were grandmothers, but they all had one thing in common — they were losers. They were born losers and they would die losers. On the road between those two events they would struggle and scrimp and save to make a few dollars to keep their family together. They would struggle to keep themselves and their loved ones clean against all odds, living in stinking, over-crowded tenements. They would be brave and resilient, but they would never escape their environment.

I looked around me and I resolved that somehow I would get out. I wouldn't be married at seventeen, pregnant at eighteen and old before my time at thirty. I wouldn't have a care-lined face and rough hands scarred by work.

That was the only thought that sustained me through that terrible night. It was piece work and Mr Goldman was a hard task-master. Five beautifully ironed shirts he threw back at me and made me do again. And at six o'clock, I had grown to hate him. Just as I was leaving he called me over.

'Hilda Schultz's old man called. She'll be back this evening so I won't need you or your ma. So long, kid.'

We needed the money but I was glad, glad that neither I nor my mother had to go back there. And I pitied the women who worked there regularly.

I ran nearly all the way home. I wanted to see how my mother was, and I wanted to give her the three dollars I'd earned. I'd never tell her how much I'd hated it. In my excitement at getting out into the cool morning air, in my haste to see my mother, I actually forgot about Mr Salvatore. I had just started up the last flight of stairs when his hand closed around my ankle. He'd crept out on to the landing below then shot his hand through the banisters and caught me, like a snake striking at its victim.

I froze. I was frightened but I was calm. I knew in that instant that I would never submit to his abuse again.

Anything, even being homeless, would be better than living with this terror, this humiliation.

He mistook my immobility for submission and released my ankle.

'There's a good girlie. I ain't going to hurt you.'

He walked a couple of paces along the landing and started to climb the stairs behind me. I judged that after a couple of steps his face would be level with my foot. I swung around and kicked him hard between the eyes.

He was so astonished he didn't even cry out. He fell back against the banisters, heavily. They were old and rotten and the wood cracked under his weight. Still without making a sound, he fell to his death.

I couldn't believe that it had happened. My motive had been escape, I hadn't meant to kill him, but when I forced myself to look down to where he lay, I couldn't be sorry. He would terrify no more children.

The sound of his fall must have been heard by some of the tenants but they were used to ghetto life and they kept themselves to themselves. No doors were thrown open. There were no screams of horror or cries of accusation. Later someone would find him and call the cops. Later still some politician, who wanted to get his name in the papers, would call upon City Hall to do something about the scandal of lack of maintenance in tenement buildings. It was a tragic accident. Who was to say otherwise?

I was twelve years old and I had brought about a man's death. It was a secret I would take with me to the grave.

CHAPTER TWO

It was cold in our apartment.

So cold that I could see my breath hanging on the air as I worked in the kitchen. But it was not the cold that edged my mother's lips with blue and chilled her so that she shivered, even though I had wrapped her in the blankets from our bed.

There had seemed a kind of desperation in her desire to supervise while I made up one of her recipes, and so I had helped her from the bed I shared with her. Now she sat in a high-backed chair in the kitchen. It was winter, mid-winter, and the old people on the block swore that it was the worst in living memory, but maybe they said that every year. One thing was for sure, it was the worst in my young life. My hand could hardly feel the pencil as I wrote my mother's recipe for chapped lips into my notebook. Lately, she had made me make a record of all her various recipes for lotions and potions and creams.

'You'll need to go on making these, Beccy. You and Aaron will need every dollar and dime you can lay your hands on when . . . when . . .'

The 'when' hung heavily between us. We both knew that she was dying. We both knew it but neither of us dared voice our fears.

'Yes, Ma.' I kept my head bowed over the notebook in case she saw the tears that had suddenly stung my eyes. I kept writing.

My mother's voice went on: 'Two drachms of cloves, finely powdered. You remember what a drachm is, Beccy?'

'About an eighth of an ounce, Ma. Kinda like a pinch.'

'Good girl. I guess I could say a quarter of an ounce instead of two drachms, but I like to tell it just as my mother told me. And one day, when you tell your daughter, tell it like it is. No ounces, mind!'

I smiled at her. 'No ounces, Ma.'

'Better see if the bees-wax has melted.'

I crossed to the stove. 'Nearly!'

With the wind seemingly blowing straight down from Alaska, there were plenty of chapped lips on our block and Ma's remedy was selling well. The ingredients for this recipe were expensive, and some were difficult to get. So much so that Mr O'Brien at the drug store had to get his cousin who worked in a big pharmaceutical firm to send them specially. But the remedy really worked and often that winter I stood over the stove late into the night making new batches. After two months of bitter cold and vicious winds we were showing a profit of six dollars and forty cents, and we'd paid off most of the back rent.

My mother shivered and pulled the blankets more tightly about her thin body.

'All right. Now, do you remember what you do next?'

'Of course I do, Ma! I can practically make this in my sleep!'

I had the ingredients in a bowl on the kitchen table, waiting to be added to the molten bees-wax. A large juicy apple, finely chopped. A small bunch of black grapes, bruised. A quarter of a pound of unsalted butter. A quarter ounce each . . . No! . . . two drachms each of gum-benzoin, storax and spermaceti, courtesy of Mr O'Brien's cousin! Two drachms of finely powdered

21

cloves. Once I'd added the bees-wax I would simmer all
the ingredients on the stove for about three hours. I'd
see that they were well blended then press the mixture
through a sieve. After that they'd simmer for another
hour. Great-grandmother's recipes might have been
effective, but they were also labour-intensive!

I'd already mixed up an egg white with some flour and
now I carefully smeared this over a piece of clean linen
rag. The bees-wax was now a creamy golden liquid and
I carefully poured this into the bowl and stirred. Next,
I placed the rag on which I had smeared the egg white
and flour over the bowl and pressed the edges tightly
around its sides. Another clean piece of rag was placed
over this and tied into place with string. The next stage
was to steam the bowl in a saucepan of boiling water.

I carefully carried the bowl over to the stove and stood
it in a large saucepan, starting to add boiling water to
the saucepan. My mother's voice broke in: 'Only halfway
up the bowl or it will spoil.'

'Yes, Ma, I *know*! You don't have to keep telling me!'

'No, I see I don't. You're a bright girl, Beccy. I guess
you get that from your father.'

I put the kettle down and turned and looked at her.
It was the first time she had mentioned my father's name
since he had left us.

'Ma, do you know where he is?'

'I don't want to talk about it!'

'Not even now?' The words were out before I could
stop myself.

A pause. Then: 'No, Beccy, not even now.'

Her eyelids drooped and she seemed to fall into a light
sleep. I turned back to the stove.

'I hope you never learn to hate, Beccy.' Her voice was
almost a whisper. 'It eats you away and it don't do no

22

good . . . I hope you never learn. But if you do, maybe you'll understand.'

Her head nodded down on to her chest. I crossed and stood by her for a moment. Her breathing was laboured but her sleep seemed natural enough.

I felt so desperately sorry for her. She was young still, barely forty, but she looked like an old woman. Uptown, sleek matrons of my mother's age would be coming home from shopping trips, mixing a jug of martinis and putting them into the ice box. Uptown! Oh, God. How I longed to be part of that world. But most of all I longed for my mother to be part of that world. To be loved and pampered. To have three meals a day.

I laughed, but there was no humour in it. I'd suddenly thought that those Uptown bitches' poodles were probably better nourished than my mother. 'I hope you never learn to hate,' she'd said. But at that moment I hated. I hated our mean lives. I hated a society where the Have Nots were on a downward spiral to less and less, and the Haves got fatter and fatter. People say that you have to be tough to fight your way out of a ghetto. I know better. You have to be even tougher to stay in it. Survive in it. My poor, downtrodden mother never had a ghost of a chance.

I crossed to the window and opened it. The cold air seemed to grip me by the throat. I quickly pulled in three bottles from the window ledge and, without thinking, slammed the window shut. I looked anxiously across at my mother, but she hadn't stirred.

I crossed into our living room with the bottles. They were so cold they nearly burnt my fingers. What our kitchen cosmetic factory lacked in sophistication, it made up for in ingenuity.

Ideally the remedy for chapped lips should be made

23

up as a lipstick. But there was no way we could make lipsticks then. The trouble was that the consistency, once set, was too hard to be sold in jars. And so my mother and I devised a way of using old bottles as a mould. Aaron scavenged them from the neighbourhood trash cans. We would scald the bottles, then keep them warm by the stove. We poured the bees-wax, butter and fruit mixture into the warm bottles and left it to set. We then carefully broke the bottles and prised the glass away from the mixture. After that we could cut it into slices and wrap it in paper. Our method was primitive but it worked.

As we didn't own an ice box we could never make the recipe in summer, because the humid heat of New York would have stopped the wax from setting. But then, there's not much call for a remedy for chapped lips on the Lower East Side at that time of year!

I was kneeling on the floor, the bottles wrapped in an old piece of blanket, ready for me to break them, when the door burst open and Aaron dashed in.

'Jeez, it's cold! How's Ma?'

'About the same.'

He nodded. We had both given up the hope that she would get better. We simply prayed that she would stay with us a little longer.

'Got any soup?'

I usually tried to keep some sort of soup, however thin, heated ready.

I shook my head. 'I'm using the stove.' I crossed to the mantelpiece and took down an old biscuit tin. Carefully I counted out twenty cents. 'Here. Go get yourself something warm.' We couldn't afford it, but he was only a kid.

'Hell, I've got money. I just don't want to go out there again. It would freeze the . . .'

'Money? You've got money? Where did you get it?'

Aaron sighed, then shuffled his feet. He had said too much.

'I said, where did you get it?'

'Oh, it's no big deal. If you must know I just ran a little errand for Toni Rossi. He gave me two dollars. No sweat!'

'Give it to me. I SAID, GIVE IT TO ME!'

Aaron glared at me defiantly. 'What you making a fuss for?'

'You know darned well! You want to go to reform school, is that it? You think Ma hasn't got enough troubles?'

'Oh, Jeez, Beccy, everybody . . .'

'Oh, sure! Everybody helps Rossi run his numbers racket! But not every cop on the beat is on the take, and what happens if you're the one who gets caught? I mean it, Aaron, give me the money.'

I held out my hand, in truth unsure whether he should do as I asked. There was a pause then he reached into his pocket and drew out the two dollars. I snatched them from his hand.

'Don't you ever take money from him again, understand?'

He nodded. Then, 'But I don't see why . . .'

'Yes, you do! You're not stupid! You do see why! They're dagos and we're kikes! There's no love lost either way and if they want someone to toss to the cops to keep the local Precinct happy, they'll choose *you*, Aaron! So stay away from them, you hear me?'

I had crossed to the door and was pulling on my coat. I tied an old wool scarf of my mother's around my head.

'Where you going?'

'Where do you think?' I waved the two dollars at him. 'To give this back to Rossi, of course!'

He looked so crestfallen − oh, yes, Aaron was good at tugging on your heart strings − that I crossed to him and hugged him to me.

'I'm sorry, Aaron. I'm sorry. But I couldn't bear it if you got into trouble. Okay?

'Okay!' he said reluctantly.

'Keep an eye on Ma, and don't let the water in the saucepan boil away. You know how to top it up?'

'You think I'm a kid or something?'

I grinned at him affectionately. 'Yes!'

I went out on to the landing. Since Mr Salvatore's tragic 'accident', the stairs held no terrors for me. Janitors came and went. The current incumbent was a morbid-looking Pole, who, according to Mike, was the only member of his family to have survived the Holocaust. Still he clung to a desperate hope, spending most of his nights drinking and writing to various Jewish agencies, longing to find that somewhere . . . maybe . . . someone still lived. I shivered as I passed his door. His was a dimension of suffering that my mind simply sheered away from. It couldn't encompass the thought of such horror. Such terror.

I went out into the street. If only the weather had been merciful and it had snowed. The remnants of the last fall had been swept to the edge of the sidewalk and were now piles of dirty-coloured ice. But it was too intensely cold for another fall, and the wind blew so cruelly through the winter-bound city that it seemed to cut into my face as I walked along the street to the bar where Toni Rossi hung out. The cold was absolute.

The neon that winked at me should have read 'MARIO'S', but the 'I' and the 'O' had long since given out

26

and so the bar carried the strange legend, 'MAR 'S'. I went inside. The bar was nearly empty. Only the very intrepid or the very lonely would venture out on a night such as this. Or, as in my case, the very desperate.

Toni Rossi was sitting at a table at the back of the bar, drinking and playing cards with four or five of his henchmen. I'd never spoken to him before, but everyone on the block knew him. In our neighbourhood you would be very unwise not to recognise a Soldier of the local Family.

Looking back, I don't know why I wasn't frightened. Perhaps sheer cussedness sustained me. I walked to Rossi's table.

'Mr Rossi?'

He ignored me.

'Mr Rossi, this belongs to you.' I threw the two dollars down in front of him. 'You gave it to my kid brother, Aaron. We don't want your money, Mr Rossi, and I'd be grateful if you didn't ask him to work for you again.'

Slowly, Rossi put down his hand of cards.

'You've broken my concentration, kid. If I lose this game you owe me!'

'If you lose this game, Mr Rossi, it will be for the simple reason that the cards you hold aren't good enough to win with!'

'Is that so, kid? Ever heard of bluff and double bluff? Ever heard of skill?'

'You're not playing poker, Mr Rossi. And maybe that's just as well, your eyes give too much away. Now, you've got your two dollars back. I'm asking you, as politely as I know how, not to get Aaron to run errands for you because you know, and I know, they're errands that could land him in a lot of trouble. And I'm not having that!'

One of the men at the table laughed. 'You his sister or his ma?'

'I care for him. Will you give me your word, Mr Rossi?'

'And how much do you imagine that's worth?' He smiled when he said it, but the smile didn't reach his eyes.

'Only you know the answer to that, Mr Rossi!'

He lounged back in his chair. 'And if I refuse?'

'Then . . .' I stared at him. I looked straight into his eyes, and in that moment I knew him for the petty bully he was. I felt a kind of power. I held the pause.

'Then, Mr Rossi, you'll live to regret it!'

'Oh, yeah? What you going to do to me?'

'I rather imagine, Mr Rossi, it's more a case of what you're going to do to yourself.'

We looked at each other. We both seemed to sense that his death would be violent. Ignominious. Not many Soldiers die in their bed.

He was suddenly angry. 'Get out of here!' he yelled.

'Take it easy, Toni, she's just a kid.' This was from one of the older men at the table.

'I don't care what she is! She oughta know better . . . coming in here . . . talking to me – me! – Toni Rossi – like that. Get out!'

I turned and walked towards the door, willing myself to walk slowly, praying he couldn't see that I was shaking.

'And tell that kike kid brother of yours to stay away from me! I don't want him hanging around me no more. Understand?'

I didn't look back. 'I understand, Mr Rossi,' I said at the door. 'Oh yes, sir, I understand!'

Once outside, I hurried away into the night. Round the corner of the block, I practically fell into the first doorway. There, in the dark, away from the biting wind,

I could give way to the fit of shaking that had been threatening to envelop my body ever since I'd turned my back on Toni Rossi. I knew he wouldn't forgive my insult but I had seen so many neighbourhood kids sucked into petty crime and worse, and always it had started by just 'running an errand'. First the numbers racket, then, 'Deliver this message, will you, kid? Deliver this package, will you, kid?' I was determined that Aaron wasn't going to be caught in that trap. Firstly because I loved him, but also because in the little time my mother had left I wanted there to be no more grief for her.

The shaking passed and I ventured back on to the street. As I climbed the last flight of stairs that led to our floor I saw that the door to our apartment stood open. For a moment I was puzzled.

Then: 'Ma!'

I ran up the last few stairs and into our apartment. Mrs Janowski was sitting on the day bed, her arms around Aaron. She looked up as I came in. I knew the worst had happened and felt strangely calm. The tears would come later.

'Ma?'

Mrs Janowski nodded. 'Mike's gone for the doctor but it won't do no good, Beccy. The poor soul's gone.'

'Where is she?' I could see through the archway into the kitchen. My mother's chair was empty.

Mrs Janowski nodded towards the curtained-off area. 'It didn't seem dignified . . . leaving her in the chair.'

'She just gave a little gasp,' Aaron sobbed, 'and slumped over. It's not fair! It's not fair! I don't want her to die!'

'There, there, honey.' Mrs Janowski cuddled him.

I crossed towards the curtains.

'Better not, sweetie. Tell you what, why don't you and

29

Aaron come next door to old Doll's? Nice cup of hot coffee . . . plenty of sugar, eh? How about it? Mike'll see to everything.'

'Thank you, Mrs Janowski, but I want to see her to say goodbye. Take Aaron, will you? I'll be through in a minute. You're very kind.'

'Kind, nuts! We're neighbours, ain't we? Besides, my Mike thinks the world of you, Beccy. Come on, honey – ' this to Aaron – 'come on, lovey. Old Doll'll take care of you.'

She led Aaron from the room, and I was alone with my mother. I shut the door after them, then crossed to the curtains. So this was death. I'd read that when people die the lines of care and age on their face fall away, and they look at peace. This is a lie. My mother looked as careworn in death as she had in life. The only difference was, she was no longer breathing. Would never breathe again.

I sat on the edge of the bed and took her hand. 'Where are you, Ma? Somewhere nice? Or is there just a void? One long night? I love you, Ma.'

I bent and kissed her, then rose from the bed and walked into the living area of the room, pulling the curtains behind me.

I remember walking towards the door. I was going to Aaron. Then, there was a strange sound in the room. As if all the windows had been flung open and the wind had swirled in from the street. I felt suddenly hot. Then very cold. The room seemed much lighter than usual. Then dark. Very dark. I remember my surprise when I realised that I was lying on the floor. Then nothing.

Mike found me, and the doctor who had come to write a death certificate found himself tending to a living patient instead. I say living, but I drifted for nearly a fortnight in a kind of half life. I had brief moments of lucidity, then lapsed back into a strange world peopled by men and women whose voices were always far, far away. I remember Mike holding my hand. I remember Mrs Janowski sponging down my feverish body. Somewhere, in the distance, I heard a child crying. Aaron, I suppose. I finally rejoined the living ten days after my mother had been buried.

When I realised this, my first feeling was of guilt that I hadn't been there, aggravated by the sense of relief I felt at having missed the pain of the occasion. Then, a new thought: where on earth had the money to pay for the funeral come from? In our neighbourhood, undertakers worked on a strictly cash-only basis. The Janowskis lived from hand to mouth, so I knew it couldn't have been them. I briefly wondered if the tenement had contributed, but that was unlikely. There was barely enough money there for the living. None to spare for the dead.

On one of my first days up I asked Mike to come with me to the undertaker's to find out. I was back in our own apartment. While I had been ill I'd slept in Mrs Janowski's bed. She had slept on Mike's day-bed, and the two boys had stayed in our apartment. How could I ever repay the Janowskis for their kindness?

'Are you kidding, Beccy? You've only been up a day and it's freezing out. You want to be ill again?'

'But I must find out! Ma's funeral and I don't know who paid for it. You must see how important it is to me.'

Because I was still weak, tears started to run down my cheeks. I rubbed them away angrily.

'Now don't upset yourself. I'll go.'

'But . . .'

'But nothing! Hell, Beccy, you almost died! You had pneumonia, real bad.'

He looked so young and so fierce that I almost laughed. He had grown into a striking young man. Not tall, just a few inches taller than me, but then I was lanky for my age. But with his fine, fair hair, cut very short as was the fashion then, his high cheek-bones and brown eyes, his looks were arresting. I knew quite a few girls on the block had already set their cap at him. He didn't seem to notice them and that was my fault. Well, no, not my fault exactly, because I couldn't help how Mike felt for me. I was grateful and I loved him, but as a brother.

At fifteen I had started to take an interest in boys, enough to know that when I looked into Mike's concerned face, I couldn't return the kind of love he wanted from me.

'The undertaker's might not tell you who it was.'

'So I'll take Aaron with me. Tell 'em I'm a cousin or something.'

I looked him up and down, then smiled.

'Hell, don't be so spiky, Beccy. There must be some fair Jews!' He suddenly grinned. 'I'm your Norwegian cousin twice removed. Second son of your Norwegian great-aunt who married a Pole somewhere on Ellis Island.'

'You can't get married on Ellis Island.'

'So I'm illegitimate!'

I laughed. Mike was good for me.

'Go! Just go! But if he won't tell you, I'm going round there tomorrow.'

'He'll tell me . . . have faith, sweet Beccy!'

And with that he was gone.

Although I was anxious to know what Mike found out, my illness had left me ridiculously frail and soon my eyelids started to droop. I fell into a light sleep.

I was woken by the slam of the door. I opened my eyes to find Mike standing before me, white-faced.

'Beccy, tell me the truth. Have you ever done anything to be ashamed of?'

'Mike, whatever is it? I don't understand!'

'Yes, you do. You're not a fool, Beccy! I know you're only fifteen but lots of girls around here are real grown-up by that age. And they've, well . . .'

'I'm still a virgin, if that's what you mean!'

I had suddenly realised what he was getting at. A lot of boys of Mike's age would have been embarrassed by my bald statement. He just stared at me for a moment then dropped to his knees by the side of my chair.

'Forgive me, Beccy. Forgive me! I didn't want to think anything bad of you but . . . I was jealous, I guess.' He handed me an envelope.

'A man paid for your ma's funeral. He left this for you.'

I was bewildered. I couldn't believe that my father would take an interest in his family after all these years.

I had no uncles. My grandparents were dead.

I opened the letter. Unfolded the note inside. It read simply: *'Whatever I may have said, I like guts. Keep fighting, kid! Toni Rossi.'*

CHAPTER THREE

The day after Mike brought me the note from Toni Rossi, I felt my strength starting to return to me. I was young and I was resilient, and although I had been ill, very ill, I knew I'd recover. I also knew I was broke.

No cosmetics had been made in our kitchen. The six dollars and forty cents had been spent and we were four weeks behind with the rent. It was obvious that I would have to leave school and find a job. I was determined to keep our home going for Aaron and me. Determined that he should not be taken from me. Determined that he should finish his schooling. But above anything else, I was afraid.

My world then was encompassed by a few blocks. Perhaps, whatever the thrust of nature, a butterfly feels a moment of dread before it breaks free from its chrysalis. I knew that survival depended on my breaking free from my sense of belonging to the place where I had grown up. But there was a tribal reassurance within our ghetto. There were also very few jobs for an unskilled, untrained girl of fifteen.

I was reasonably schooled, although barely educated. The classes at our school were large and unruly, and there was a limit to what even the most dedicated teacher could achieve in those circumstances. And there were few dedicated teachers to be found in our midst. True, we occasionally had a young teacher fired by the desire to educate the children of the slums. But it didn't take long for them to look into the faces of their colleagues and see their resignation to failure. Usually, those young teachers moved on while they could still get a post elsewhere.

I could read. I could write. I could add and subtract. But at that time my mind had never been stimulated. Never been inspired to discover how a phrase in a piece of music, a line in a poem, an idea in a book, can open a door through which, for one brief moment, one can glimpse the stars.

Briefly I considered prostitution. But, possibly because my body had been fumbled with, used to satisfy a perverted lust when I was only a child, I was afraid of sex. Which hardly fitted me for a career in the world's oldest profession! And although Mr Salvatore's fingers had probed and pawed between my legs, he hadn't made me bleed, and so I assumed that I was still a virgin. I wasn't so naive that I didn't realise that if one was young, as I was, somewhere there would be a buyer prepared to pay a high price for virginity. But it would be a once-only sale and afterwards I would be irrevocably soiled while still sexually inexperienced. In any case, my whole being revolted against the idea.

I spent the next couple of days working all day and into the night making beauty preparations. Mr O'Brien, looking quite unrecognisable without his white cotton drug-store coat, called to offer his condolences. He also, kind man, offered to give me five dollars as an advance against future sales. I asked if he could make it ten. We finally settled for seven dollars fifty on the understanding that I deliver twenty-four of my mother's remedy for chapped lips by the following Monday. When he left, I realised that I had enjoyed the bargaining.

I picked up my notebook. A large, juicy apple, finely

chopped . . . a small bunch of black grapes, bruised . . .
a quarter of a pound of unsalted butter . . . two drachms
of cloves, finely powdered. Suddenly, I heard my
mother's voice, as clearly as if she had been sitting in her
high-backed chair beside me: 'No ounces, mind!'

'No ounces, Ma!' I whispered. And the tears that I had
been unable to shed on the day of her death, was too ill
to shed at her burial, coursed down my face. I had cried
before, sobbed even, but this was like nothing I had ever
experienced.

I simply sat with my notebook clutched to my chest
and let the tears flow down my face. They were
uncheckable, but in any case I made no attempt to stop
them. I cried for my mother, for her hard life and, yes,
for my own sense of loss and loneliness. I don't know
how long I sat there but I noticed that the room was
growing dark. Aaron would be home soon. Still I couldn't
stop the tears. He came in an hour later and found me
asleep at the kitchen table, my hands still clasping the
notebook to me.

Over the following few days I made the twenty-four wax
tablets for Mr O'Brien. I also scoured the Situations
Vacant columns in the newspapers. There seemed nothing
that I was suitable for. While holding the paper I
happened to notice my hands. They were red from the
cold and the skin, especially along the side of my
forefinger, was rough and cracked. I had never been a
vain person but the sight of my hands horrified me.
People notice hands and if I was to get a job other than
the most menial, I couldn't afford a slovenly appearance.

I turned to my mother's recipes. She'd made me write
down a recipe for a hand cream, although we'd never
made it. I glanced quickly through the ingredients. A

quarter of a pound of butter . . . Rose water . . . I still had some left from the batch I had made in the summer. Yolks of two large eggs . . . Honey . . . Oatmeal . . .

I pulled on my coat and then crossed and took a dollar from the tin on the mantelpiece. I needed oatmeal and eggs. I had a recipe for a toner that was fairly popular at the drug store. This required egg white, so if I made this at the same time as the hand cream the whites wouldn't be wasted. Both recipes used rose water and honey so that was all right, but I'd need to buy a cucumber and yoghurt for the toner. I took another fifty cents from the tin.

Earlier in the day, I'd put some beef flank that was good and, most importantly, cheap, on to stew. This was the first stage of a stew my mother used to make, which I now realise was goulash, another recipe my great-grandmother brought out of Hungary! I could cook this slowly in the oven for our supper, and leave the top of the stove clear to make the hand cream.

By the time Aaron came home from school I was happily immersed in making the hand cream. I don't know why, but I always felt a sense of well-being making Ma's recipes. Perhaps because I knew them to be unique and, in a strange way, they gave me a feeling of family. Of continuity.

I made the toner quickly and easily. I'd made it often. One crushed peeled cucumber mixed with a teaspoon of witch hazel, a teaspoon of rose water, the egg whites and a quarter of a teaspoon each of honey and yoghurt. An electric blender would have been a boon making this. Instead I had to beat the cucumber to a pulp with a wooden spoon, then whisk the whole mixture with a wire egg beater until my arm felt as if it was coming off. Once it was a smooth, runny cream I bottled it and put it on the window sill to cool. Cool! In fact, as it was still the depths of winter, it was like an ice box on our window sill.

The hand cream I had to concentrate on because I'd never made it before. I read the recipe from my notebook. A quarter of a pound of unsalted butter, which has been washed in spring water . . . I smiled at this. Ma telling it like it was! She'd certainly never seen spring water in her life, and neither had I. Tap would have to do! I couldn't really see how you were supposed to 'wash' butter, so I interpreted this as 'rinse'. I held the butter under the tap and rinsed it thoroughly. Then, according to Ma's recipe, you washed it again in rose water. I certainly wasn't going to let my precious rose water go down the sink, and so I beat the rose water into the butter. I knew from other recipes that rose water was good for softening the skin, so I couldn't see that it would do anything but good leaving it in the mixture.

I had already beaten the egg yolks and had them in a pudding basin standing in a pan of hot water, off the stove. I added the butter and rose water to the beaten eggs, then a large spoonful of honey. I put the pan on the stove on a low heat and kept stirring the mixture until it was well blended. I then took it off the stove to cool. While I was doing this, Aaron came in, or rather put his head around the door.

'Hi, Beccy! Whatcher doing?'

'Making hand cream. One of Ma's recipes.'

'Oh!' At twelve, he found that thoroughly boring. 'Listen, I'm going out with some of the guys.'

'Aaron, you'll freeze out there!'

'Oh, Jeez! I'll be okay!'

'All right . . . but be in by seven.' He was already on his way out. I called after him, 'And stay away from Toni Rossi!'

He put his head back around the door and grinned at me. 'Know what? You're turning into a real nagger!'

I laughed as he closed the door, but as I heard him running down the stairs I suddenly felt overwhelmed by what I was trying to do. How the hell could I bring up a ten-year-old boy? I was only a kid myself! I felt so young. So vulnerable. But was there any alternative?

I shrugged and turned back to Ma's recipe, putting the larger problems to the back of my mind and turning the wooden spoon in the mixture.

The next step was to add the oatmeal. As much as the mixture will take, the recipe said. I added it carefully and slowly until I had a smooth, firm paste.

The mixture was about blood temperature by now so I spooned it into jars, setting aside one for myself. I rubbed the cream well into my hands. I'd expected it to be sticky because of the honey but the oatmeal seemed to counteract that. It must sound strange but until then I'd never used any of my mother's preparations. From then on I did. I have much to thank my ancestors for.

Within a week my hands were looking much smoother and had lost their rough, red, chapped look. The next time I took some preparations along to Mr O'Brien I took some jars of hand cream also. To my amazement and annoyance he wouldn't sell them.

'But, Mr O'Brien, why not?'

'I've never sold it before, Beccy. How do I know that it works?'

'A few years ago you didn't know if any of Ma's things worked! Anyway, it *does* work, I tried it myself. Look! My hands were real rough. Now they ain't so bad, are they?' I held out my hands to him.

'I'm sorry, Beccy. It was different when your ma was alive, she knew what she was doing.'

'So do I,' I interrupted fiercely. 'So do I! I made all Ma's recipes with her and . . .'

'Did you make this one with her?' It was his turn to interrupt.

'Well, no, but that don't mean . . .'

'I'm not selling things in my store that I'm not sure about, and that's final, young lady!'

I turned away from him angrily and started to leave the store. As I got to the exit a woman I knew used Ma's products came in. I thrust the jar of hand cream into her hands.

'This is a gift, ma'am, it's for softening your hands. Would you be so kind as to use it night and morning, and if it works − ' I looked back at Mr O'Brien behind the counter − 'TELL MR O'BRIEN!'

With that I flung out of the shop, leaving Mr O'Brien as angry as I was and a very surprised customer clutching a jar of hand cream.

When I got home, I was still angry. Surely he could have trusted me! Gradually I started to cool down. Mr O'Brien was my one outlet for selling Ma's remedies, and I couldn't afford to offend him. Then I started to consider how foolish it was to limit myself in that way. If Mr O'Brien decided to stop stocking the remedies I made, our one source of income would be gone. I *must* get a job. And I must stop limiting the sale of Ma's recipes to Mr O'Brien's drug store.

I felt grateful to him for the advance he'd given me, but to be honest I have always had a streak of hard-headedness in my nature. I told myself that his generosity was after all part of a business transaction and, albeit in a small way, Mr O'Brien did very well out of our beauty products, marking the price up by at least one hundred per cent . . . I started to think what Aaron and I could do with that extra hundred per cent. I also started to wonder how much a stall at the Sunday market, held a few blocks away, would cost.

But first — and by now my need was desperate — I needed a job.

CHAPTER FOUR

As so often in my young life, Mike Janowski was my saviour.

The Janowskis seemed to have an inexhaustible supply of cousins. One of these, a stocky, tow-haired young man named Rudi, worked as a packer in the exclusive department store on Fifth Avenue, Kimberly and Lanting.

All Mike's cousins had been alerted to the need to find me a job. Rudi was the one who came through.

At least, he knew that there was a job going in the packing department. It was an unskilled job, and not at all well-paid, but then what else was I suited to? In any case it was better pay, even allowing for my subway fares, than I could hope to bring home if I worked locally. He got me an interview.

According to Rudi, Kimberly and Lanting was always known simply as Kimberly's. I suppose once there must have been a Mr Lanting, but the store was now part of the vast Kimberly business empire, with not a Lanting in sight. He also told me, much to my amusement, that at Kimberly's the men in the packing department handled the heavy goods, and products destined to be bought by gentlemen, while women were engaged to unpack anything that would be sold to ladies. This conjured up for me the wondrous notion that the gently reared, female clients of such a bastion of polite shopping as Kimberly's would faint should they discover that their hand-embroidered, lace-trimmed French knickers had been carefully folded and packed by rough, hairy male hands!

I dressed carefully for my interview. I had to appear neat and responsible, but at the same time look at least two years older than I truly was. My choice of clothes was extremely limited. The best I could hope for was to look clean and tidy and not too threadbare. I tried pulling my hair back into a severe bun, but this made me look as if I was auditioning for a high-school production of *Jane Eyre*. My hair was thick and long and tended to be unruly. I finally settled for tying the very end of my hair with ribbon then turning the hair under itself and tying the ribbon neatly around my head. It gave the effect of a kind of page boy. I wore an old navy blue suit of my mother's that I had sponged and pressed, and a white blouse that I had worn to school, freshly laundered and so starched that the collar rubbed the back of my neck. It was still bitterly cold so I had to wear my old coat, but resolved to take this off the minute I got into the building.

Even the staff entrance to Kimberly and Lanting's was impressive. The store had been built at the turn of the century and was a hymn to Mammon. Architecturally it was a mess, and yet at the same time magnificent. Victorian Gothic fought Egyptian Revivalism, so that one almost expected to see Queen Victoria and Cleopatra strolling arm in arm through the Haberdashery department!

Rudi was on the look-out for me just inside the entrance.

'Miss Connors, the Head Packer, is waiting for you. If she don't like you, you won't never get as far as Personnel.'

'What's she like?'

'Sour! A real sour old maid. The guys reckon she needs a good scr – .' He remembered my youth, glanced sideways at me and blushed. 'Anyways, she's a real tartar. She even scares the sh – Er, scares the older guys. Let's hope this is one of her good days.'

'What makes the difference between a good day and a bad day?'

'Her indigestion! She suffers from gas, real bad!'

We turned a corner and then passed through double swing doors. The packing room was vast. I stood just inside the doors with Rudi, over-awed by the size of the room and the hustling activity within it. As we entered, a tall, thin woman in her early fifties looked up from her seat at a desk in the corner of the room. She rose and walked towards us and I noticed the severity of her black clothes, relieved only by a lace tippet around her neck, held in place by a rather fine jet mourning brooch.

I assumed from her name that she was of Irish descent. Even in America where, at least in New York, so many races can be observed within a few square miles, there are entrenched notions about racial characteristics. The Poles are stupid, the Italians are volatile, the Jews are crafty, the Irish are feckless and happy . . . And yet my overwhelming impression, when I looked at Miss Connors, was of sadness. Nevertheless her face – although wary, possibly even hostile – had a liveliness and intelligence about it. There were tiny lines of pain beginning to show around her eyes that spoke of a rather more mortal enemy than indigestion.

For some inexplicable reason I smiled at her. I heard a little intake of breath at my side, Rudi's reaction to such lunacy.

Miss Connors stopped a couple of feet away from me and looked me up and down. She held the pause so long and so well that she should have been a tragedian. Then: 'Well, don't dawdle, girl. Come over to my desk.' She turned her back and walked briskly away. Rudi was apparently dismissed, I was to follow. I followed.

She indicated a chair beside her desk, then seated herself. Another searching look. Another pause. If the purpose of all this was to make me feel uncomfortable, she had scored a success. But I forced myself to sit calmly, my hands folded neatly on my lap. I stared back at her.

'You smiled at me just now. Why?' I hesitated. 'You may as well tell me the truth — when it comes to twigging a lie, I'm the bee's knees!' Her homely, old-fashioned speech belied her forbidding manner. 'Because if you were trying to ingratiate yourself, you sure as hell were barking up the wrong tree, miss.'

'Miss Connors, I need this job. I need it real bad but it ain't in my nature to crawl for it. And if I smiled at you . . .'

'Which you did!'

'Then I did it . . . I did it kinda on the spur of the moment. I suppose . . .' I shrugged, ' . . . I suppose I liked the look of you.'

There was a moment's silence. Then Miss Connors gave a shout of laughter that fleetingly brought the packing department to a standstill. I discovered from Rudi later that no one could remember hearing her laugh before.

'Then by heavens, girl, you're the only one in thirty years who has!'

Merriment surged up in her at this thought and she laughed again. She reached into a drawer of her desk and took out an old-fashioned crocodile purse. She searched in it until she found her handkerchief. It was lace-trimmed and beautifully laundered. With it she dabbed the tears of laughter from her eyes. Then, all humour gone, she dropped her purse back into the drawer and slammed it shut.

'Rudi must've told you . . . the job stinks, the pay's low, the hours are long, and I'm the very devil to work for. You still want it?'

It was my turn to pause.

'No, Miss Connors, I don't *want* the job. As you so rightly say, it don't seem much. Speaking frankly, ma'am, I'd rather be the Queen of England! But as that ain't likely, I'd be grateful if you'd employ me. I know how to work hard, real hard. You won't be sorry, I promise you. So, please, please, ma'am, will you take me on?'

I felt that I could almost reach out and touch the silence that hung between us. 'If she has to think about it, perhaps I'm in with a chance,' I told myself.

But Miss Connors' cool, appraising look gave nothing away. Then, slowly, 'You know, I think I'll return the compliment and say that I rather like the look of *you*!'

She suddenly seemed amused again, although I couldn't fathom why. 'Take this note along to Mrs Johnson, Personnel.' She wrote neatly on a memo pad. 'She'll ask you all the right questions,' Miss Connors smiled thinly, 'and don't worry too much if you give all the wrong answers. If I say I want you taken on, you'll get taken on. Why, this crazy place would come to a standstill without me!' She handed me the note. 'Now, scoot!'

'Thank you, Miss Connors! Oh, thank you!'

I took the note and headed excitedly towards the door. Her voice stopped me.

'And, Rebecca . . .' I turned. It seemed strange to hear my full name. 'Don't let me down!'

I shook my head. I recognised the finality of the

statement. There was little room for whims in Miss Connors' life but, on the spur of the moment, perhaps because I'd made her laugh, perhaps because she'd seen the desperate need in my eyes, she'd taken a chance and given me a job. She would not forgive easily if I failed her.

'Yes, ma'am . . . No, ma'am . . .' As Mrs Johnson's voice droned on through the ritual of employment, I silently added, 'Three bags full, ma'am!'

I didn't like Mrs Johnson. For a start, she'd kept me waiting outside her office for three-quarters of an hour before she saw me. And as no one had gone in or out of that office in that time, I assumed that this was a strategy to put me in my place. Once I was inside her sanctum, she didn't ask me to sit and so now I stood in front of her desk like a school child waiting to be disciplined.

She was a small, bird-like woman, very well groomed. How often have I found this type of woman to be spiteful! My conscious mind was listening to her, agreeing with her, but at the same time I was excitedly day-dreaming about what I would do with my first pay. I'd cook Aaron and myself a really good supper. Then I'd go to Schindler's store and make a down payment on a new pair of trousers for him. He was growing fast and I could no longer let down the pants he wore to school. What I really meant was 'nearly new'. But although Schindler's sold mainly second-hand clothes, they were always in good condition and had been thoroughly cleaned.

'Is that understood?' Her words brought me up sharp.

'Yes, ma'am!'

'Very well, Miss . . . er . . .' she referred to her notes.

47

'Miss Mandel.' Was it my imagination or did I detect a slight note of distaste as she spoke my name?

'We'll expect you here on Monday, 7 am sharp. You will, of course, always wear black.'

''But I haven't got . . .'

'Then if you wish to work here, I suggest you acquire some suitable clothing! Over the years Kimberly's has established certain standards of dress and of behaviour.

'As to that,' she went on repressively, 'you will never, never use any entrance to the store other than the staff entrance. Whatever the circumstances, to use the same entrance as our customers is unthinkable. Also you will never, never shop in the store.'

As a pair of leather gloves at Kimberly's cost approximately half my week's wages that wouldn't be very difficult to comply with!

'Any further questions?'

'No, ma'am. I guess not.'

'Very well. Welcome to Kimberly's.' She made it sound about as inviting as jumping into a snake pit. 'You may go.'

In spite of Mrs Johnson, I was so excited that on my way home I wanted to shout out to everyone on the subway: 'I've got a job! I've got a job!' By the time I got off at the station a few blocks from home, some of my euphoria was beginning to evaporate. Aaron and I had to live for ten days before I got paid. Well, I reckoned we'd manage somehow. But a black dress! There had been a black dress of my mother's at the back of the closet, but it was so old and so worn it was actually rotten in places and I'd had to throw it away. I'd toyed with the idea of asking Mrs Johnson for a small advance against my salary, but my pride had stopped me. And in any case, I'd been sure the answer would have been negative. For a decent dress I'd need to put down at least four dollars with Mr Schindler.

Of course there were money lenders in our neighbourhood, too many of them. But I was terrified of travelling that road. Would Mr O'Brien advance me more money? After my outburst over the hand cream, I doubted it. I wondered, briefly, how difficult it would be to dye something. But common sense told me not even to attempt it. I could simply ruin a dress that had a couple more years' wear in it. I couldn't turn to the Janowskis again. In any case, gin wasn't that cheap, and Mrs Janowski's fondness for it meant there was never any money to spare. Who then? Who could I ask? I wasn't about to lose a job through lack of a suitable dress.

I was nearly home by then. I retraced my steps and turned into the street in which stood Mario's bar. As I walked towards it, the 'MAR 'S' winked out through the gloom of the winter's day.

Once again I went into the bar. Once again, Toni Rossi was there. This time he was eating. I felt a pang of hunger and realised that it was well after midday. Two of the men I recognised from the card game were eating with him. I guess if you were Toni Rossi you never went anywhere alone.

'Mr Rossi . . . sir?'

'Jeez, Toni, it's the kike kid again! Got any more brothers we've got to stay away from?'

'Mr Rossi . . . ' I began again.

'That's me, kid!' he said, through a mouthful of food. Whatever it was, it sure had a lot of tomato sauce on it.

'I left a note here for you . . . thanking you . . .'

'Yeah, yeah!' He waved his fork impatiently.

I thought what a strange man he was. Clearly, I'd underestimated him when we'd met before. Because for all his bullying, he had a kind streak, and yet he seemed ashamed of it, wanted to deny it almost. After I learnt that he'd paid for Ma's funeral, I'd thought of offering to repay him over as many weeks, months or years as it took, but I quickly reasoned that he would be deeply insulted if I suggested this.

'I'll come straight to the point, sir. I need a black dress.'

'Whatser matter? Someone else in the family croak?'

I bit on my lip to stop myself reacting to such insensitivity.

'You go ahead and say it, kid. That's what I like about you . . . you ain't the meek type!'

'I won't say it, Mr Rossi, because I owe you. I need a black dress because I've got a job, in the packing department at Kimberly's. We have to wear black, you see, and . . .'

He put a ten-dollar bill on the table. 'I'll want fifteen back!'

As most money lenders charged a hundred per cent, sometimes even a hundred and twenty per cent if they sensed their victim was desperate, this wasn't as extortionate as it seemed.

'I only need four.'

'So buy yourself a little something extra!'

'Not at that interest rate!'

'You're playing on the wrong team to buck the rules, and you're giving me indigestion! Look, kid, I ain't no crapping money lender. Take the ten dollars . . . my terms . . . and then get out. Or just get out! Your choice!'

I picked up the ten dollars. 'You want me to sign something?'

He smiled. 'I promise you, we're real good at collecting

our debts. A piece of paper don't make no difference! Now, fuck off!'

My hand closed around the ten-dollar bill that was now safely in my coat pocket. 'Good day to you, Mr Rossi!' Then I added as sweetly as I knew how, 'You know something, sir? Your table manners stink!'

I turned and walked towards the door. I heard him chuckle, then he shouted after me, 'Like I said, kid, don't ever be meek. It wouldn't suit you!'

And so, the following Monday, at 6.50 am I once again walked through the staff entrance of Kimberly's. I was neatly and soberly dressed in a black woollen dress that nearly fitted, and I hated it.

How can I describe the two years that followed? Aaron and I ate, if not well, adequately. We had a roof over our heads. I paid back Toni Rossi and gradually cleared the back rent. I have known times of greater despair, times of much greater hardship. But, oh God, I have never experienced such boredom as I knew in that packing department! Twenty-four silk blouses . . . check! Thirty-six grey kid handbags . . . check! Ten beaded evening bags . . . check! The catalogue of goods was endless and once the pleasure of handling beautiful things had worn off – well, at least beautiful things that *other* women would wear – the routine was so consistent that it was numbing. I once asked one of my colleagues if she was bored and she looked at me as if I was mad, so I guessed the fault was with me. I'd force myself *not* to look at the clock because always I'd think an hour must have passed only to discover I'd only lived through another ten minutes.

Only two things sustained me during that time. I still made Ma's recipes, and Briony Connors became my friend.

I still only sold through Mr O'Brien. I'd enquired about a market stall, and was trying to put money aside in order to take one, but it was impossible. My wages, which would have been adequate for a single girl living at home with her parents, had to support two of us. It was always a struggle and we needed the extra money I could earn through Ma's recipes. I had to swallow my pride and go cap in hand to Mr O'Brien. I apologised. He was grudging, then gracious.

The reason for his acceptance of my apology was soon revealed. His stocks of my products were very low and his regular customers were getting anxious about new supplies. Also, and it really cost him to tell me this, the woman I'd given the hand cream to swore by it and had recommended it to her friends. He'd like to order twenty-four jars. I agreed but privately resolved that as soon as I was well and truly back into his good books, we'd renegotiate terms!

And so my evenings and Sundays continued much as they always had, making Ma's recipes. And I was happy doing it. One or two of the boys at work had asked me out. They were pleasant enough, but I was wary of falling into the sexual trap that I so feared. I always declined. I had the example of the tenement before me daily. Rosie Hartman, she of the clickety high heels and swishing full skirts, the prettiest girl on the block, had married three years previously when she was just seventeen. She was unrecognisable from the joyous girl I used to meet on the stairs. Maybe she was happy, I don't know, but she looked worn down with the care of her two babies and I'd heard that her husband had lost his job in the rising wave of unemployment. The war had been over for thirteen years and already people spoke with nostalgia about the wartime boom that had brought full employment. How quickly they were forgetting the tears and the pain and the bloodshed!

My friendship with Briony began because I was going to make a batch of Ma's recipes one evening and would be using the stove. Aaron was staying on after school as he was now in the baseball team and they had a practice session. I'd thought that I'd have a coffee and a quick meal at the automat opposite the subway station. You could get a hot meal for not much more than it cost me to cook for one at home. After a day in that packing department I was always hungry.

I got my meal and a coffee and looked around for a seat. The place was crowded but there was one seat vacant by the window. I was just sitting down when I realised I was about to sit opposite Miss Connors. I was appalled. The junior and senior staff never fraternised. And in any case, Miss Connors was renowned in the department for her acid tongue. She surely wouldn't take kindly to my sitting at the same table.

Miss Connors was drinking a coffee and had just finished eating. She was reading a book. She looked at me over her reading glasses.

'For heaven's sake, child, sit down!'

'I'm sorry, Miss Connors, I didn't realise it was you at the table. It was the only seat you see.' I looked around wildly. 'I'll try and find . . .'

'Sit down!' I sat. One didn't argue with Miss Connors when she used that tone of voice.

'Thank you, ma'am.'

'It's a free country, Rebecca. We are no longer within the hallowed halls of Kimberly's.' She waved at my plate. 'To use a colloquialism, "Enjoy!" '

I started to eat and immediately her hand came across the table and touched mine for a moment.

'Oh, my dear!' Her voice was full of concern. 'I do hope you didn't think . . . I used that expression without thinking and I realise it could have sounded sarcastic. Racist even.'

'I didn't take it that way ma'am.'

'Good! I have never been able to understand racism. I see it everywhere I look, but we are all God's creatures. How insecure a section of our community must feel if they can only bolster their egos by looking down on others.' She took a sip of her coffee and returned to her book.

'Money helps!'

She looked up and across the table at me. 'I beg your pardon?'

'I reckon if you've got money, you might still get looked down on . . . but not to your face!'

She laughed. 'My word, we've a philosopher in our midst!' It could have sounded like a put-down, but she said it with such unaffected amusement, I couldn't take offence.

'You've a good mind, Rebecca,' she went on. 'How do you use it?'

'Beg pardon, ma'am?'

'However good one's mind, it needs oiling, rather like an automobile. Without oil an automobile seizes up. Without ideas, without stimulus, the mind atrophies . . . I should know! Without books, without the theatre, our packing department would have driven me mad long ago.'

I looked at her in astonishment. 'You feel like that too?'

'All the time.'

'I hope you won't be offended, Miss Connors, you giving me the job and all but, you know these training schemes the store has, to be a shop assistant . . . well, I've applied.'

Her face took on a closed expression. At the time, I interpreted it as her reaction to my ingratitude in wanting to leave her department. I went on hastily, 'Nothing personal. It's just that . . . well! Anyway, I've applied! But I ain't heard nothing yet!'

'You haven't heard anything yet.'

'Pardon?'

'And you beg my pardon! You're a bright girl, Rebecca, it's absurd to be chained to your class for lack of a little effort with your speech!'

I thought about this for a moment. I knew I was ambitious, but until then I hadn't really thought my ambition through. I intended to achieve a better life through struggle and hard work, but I hadn't perceived the improvement in personal terms. I immediately seized on what she was saying. Enough doors would be closed to me because of my race; to compound that rejection through illiteracy was absurd.

'Thank you. Thank you, Miss Connors, you've just said something very important to me.' I was still taking it in. 'And I guess you're right!'

She smiled. 'We'll pass that as an Americanism! "I imagine you're correct" would have been more pleasing!'

She returned to her book and her coffee. A few minutes passed.

'Excuse me, ma'am . . .'

'Yes?'

'I kinda . . . er . . . I just wondered what you were reading.'

'*The Crucible*.' I obviously looked blank. 'It's a play. A very fine play by Arthur Miller. Have you ever been to the theatre?' I shook my head. 'Oh, Rebecca, it's so fine! I come alive when I'm sitting in that darkened auditorium. No matter if the play is trite, the acting second-rate − the theatre holds a mirror up to the world, and then lets you pass through that mirror, if you have the imagination. The curtain goes up and both audience and actors are in a sort of time capsule. And until that curtain falls it's something unique that they share together.'

She held the book out to me. 'Here! Read it and tell me what you think. It's about Salem, but more importantly, about some rather more recent witch hunts. Senator McCarthy,' she added grimly, 'will achieve his ambition to be remembered by posterity, but rotten fish, my dear, will smell sweeter!'

'Thank you.'

'Ah, well!' She rose. 'I must get back to the Aged Parent. I'd like to know what you make of the book, Rebecca. You have a mind that cuts through to the bone, and I'll be interested to see how Mr Miller survives your scrutiny.' I felt she was laughing at me again. 'Indicate to me, discreetly if you would, lest we shake the very foundation of Kimberly's, when you've read the play, and perhaps we might meet here for a coffee and discuss it. That is . . .' She suddenly seemed vulnerable and I realised that, like me, she was lonely. 'That is . . . if it is agreeable to you?'

'I'd like that very much.'

She nodded and then was gone. Oh, Briony, even now, I miss you so much! And I can still feel angry that someone who enriched my life as she did should have been taken from me so soon. I know that must sound selfish. Well, so be it! But I'd never really had a friend before. I'd certainly never had a 'dear terrier', as Briony became, in my life. She worried at me, not to 'improve' but to enrich myself. And, as I read more and more, and increasingly not only the books that Briony gave me but also books that I borrowed from the public library I had joined, ideas and arguments ricocheted around our table at the automat. It was a new world for me, and I revelled in it.

What puzzled me, as our friendship deepened, was Briony's lack of support for my applications to join the store's trainee schemes. I soon realised that her spirit was too generous for her to resent my longing to move on from her department.

'What's the matter, Rebecca?' were her first words when we met one evening.

'My application for the trainee scheme . . . I've been turned down again!'

'Oh, my dear, don't you *know* . . . ' she began impulsively, then stopped.

'Know what?'

'I'm sorry, Rebecca, I've said too much!'

'No, please. You can't just . . . Please! What is it you know?'

'I didn't want to hurt you . . . I thought you'd realise. But gradually . . . You're so young, Rebecca, and you seem to have a knack of taking life head on.'

'Please, Briony, come to the point.'

'Have you never looked around at the Kimberly staff who meet the public? Have you never looked around the locker room and seen a divided nation?'

I stared at her for a moment then the truth dawned on me. 'What a fool I've been! And how that bitch Johnson must've laughed at me!'

'Don't take it too much to heart, Rebecca.'

'How can you say that? You! You who've taught me to think, to express myself! Being Jewish isn't something

I'm going to grow out of, you know, and I'm damned if I'm going to spend the rest of my life being patronised.'

'I don't know what to say to you, my dear, how to comfort you.'

'I don't want to be comforted,' I replied angrily. 'I want to get even! Oh, Bri, I'm sorry. I don't mean to take it out on you. I just . . . just feel so wretched. I think I'll go on home now if you don't mind. I won't be very good company this evening.'

'Will you be all right?'

'Oh, yes.' I smiled at her. 'Didn't you know, Bri, I'm as tough as old boots!'

Brave words, but all night I drifted in and out of sleep, and each time I emerged from dreaming to awareness I was overwhelmed by a sense of misery.

In the morning despair and self-pity gave way to anger. Whatever the cost, I was going to challenge Mrs Johnson about her constant rejection of my applications. When the time came for my coffee break, instead of going to the staff canteen I went straight to the Personnel office. When I got to the outer office Mrs Johnson was just entering her room with a well-dressed, middle-aged man.

'Excuse me, Mrs Johnson.' I only had fifteen minutes and as I assumed she was about to interview the man for a post, I desperately wanted to see her first.

'Really, Miss . . . er . . . ?'

'Mandel . . . Rebecca Mandel. I wonder if you could see me for a moment. It's very important.'

'If you need to see me, and I can't imagine why that should be, you must make an appointment with my secretary. In any case, surely you can see that I am busy right now?'

Before I could reply, the man by her side spoke to Mrs Johnson. 'That's quite all right. I really don't mind waiting for a few minutes . . . this young lady seems very anxious to speak with you.'

Mrs Johnson thought for a moment. 'Oh, very well!' She turned and walked into her office. The man smiled at me and indicated that I should follow. I went in and, to my surprise, the man followed me. But once inside he crossed to the far side and looked out of the window, discreetly leaving us to pursue our conversation. Mrs Johnson sat behind her desk. Once again she didn't invite me to be seated.

'Well?' Her manner was icy.

'Mrs Johnson, I've applied six times in the last two years to go on a staff training scheme . . . I'd like to work in the store as a shop assistant. Other people from the packing department have been taken on but I always seem to be turned down. I wondered if you'd tell me why.'

'And this is why you've rushed along here without making an appointment?'

'Yes! In terms of education and deportment there seems very little difference between me and the successful applicants. I wondered if there was some other reason for rejecting me.'

'It was considered that you were unsuitable. That's all you need to know.'

'I think not! In what way was I unsuitable?'

'I will not be interrogated like this. If you value your position at Kimberly's, I suggest you leave now!'

Goodbye job. Goodbye the rent being paid up. Mr Schindler would have a long wait for the next instalment on the jacket I was buying for Aaron. I stood my ground.

'I'm sorry, Mrs Johnson, but as I'm sure you never do anything without a reason, I am staying until you tell me exactly why I am unsuitable! Could it by any chance be because I am Jewish?'

'You're being ridiculous!'

'Am I? I looked at the women shop assistants in the locker room this morning, Mrs Johnson. There was not one Jew, one Negro, one Italian. That's just a coincidence, I suppose?'

The man turned from the window. 'Is this true, Mrs Johnson?'

'Of course it isn't, sir!' But she was clearly flustered. And she'd called him 'sir'. Who on earth was he?

'Perhaps you would introduce me to the young lady.'

'Yes, of course. Rebecca, this is Mr Kimberly. Mr John Kimberly.'

Well, I thought, if there was ever the slightest doubt that I'd be fired, my fate was now sealed!

Mr Kimberly walked across the room towards me and held out his hand.

'How do you do?'

'How do you do!' I echoed. His handshake was firm and assured.

'You do realise that you've just made a very serious allegation against this store?'

'Yes.' There seemed no point in my denying it. The damage had been done.

'Absolutely outrageous! And quite untrue!' Mrs Johnson was practically jumping up and down with indignation. 'Just because you are not considered good enough to . . .'

'Mr Kimberly.' I cut straight across Mrs Johnson's diatribe. 'If you doubt what I say is true, may I suggest that you walk through your store, sir, and see for yourself? When I say "your" store, I take it that you are . . .?'

'Oh, yes, I'm one of *the* Kimberlys. Merchant adventurers who got respectable after supplying both the

British and the Americans during the War of Independence. We weren't above selling boots to both the Confederates and the Yanks either. Perhaps you, Miss Mandel, and you, Mrs Johnson, would care to accompany me through the store?'

'I have a great deal of work to do, Mr Kimberly, and I really don't think that I . . .'

Mr Kimberly cut short Mrs Johnson's protestations. 'I framed it, out of courtesy, as a request, Mrs Johnson, but if it would salve your conscience as to whether or not you should leave your work, I can always make it an order.' He smiled politely when he said this, but it didn't take the sting out of his words.

'Well, if you put it like that . . . ' she said huffily.

'I do! Shall we go?' He turned to me. 'I don't concern myself with the day-to-day running of the store. In fact, I haven't set foot in the place for nearly a year. And I never shop here!'

'You don't, sir?' I grinned in spite of myself. 'I'm sure they'd give you very good terms!'

Mr Kimberly laughed and I heard a noise rather like a chicken being strangled coming from the direction of Mrs Johnson's desk.

'Shall we go?' He held the door open for Mrs Johnson and myself. I stood back to let her past, and as I saw her venomous expression I told myself that it was just as well that looks couldn't kill!

We walked through the outer office and along a winding corridor. Then we went through two heavily carved, oak swing doors, and entered Kimberly's.

I'd never been inside the store before. I'd gazed longingly at the beautifully dressed windows on my way home from work. But they had not prepared me for the hushed opulence of the store itself.

There was a huge marble staircase rising from the main shopping hall to the mezzanine floor. Mr Kimberly crossed to the staircase and indicated that we were to follow.

'I think this gives us a good vantage point.' I stared across the hall. 'Well, Rebecca, can you see any of your own race?'

I looked around, then shook my head.

'Neither can I!' He turned to Mrs Johnson. 'Only White Anglo-Saxon Protestants by the look of it − at least on this floor, Mrs Johnson! Shall we go up to the next?'

'Mr Kimberly, sir,' I blurted out. 'I'm sorry, I really didn't mean to . . .'

'Didn't you, Rebecca?' He turned on the stairs and looked at me. 'Didn't you?'

I sighed. 'Yes, sir, I'm afraid I did!'

'I'm glad to hear it! I would have been disappointed if you'd gone mealy-mouthed on me.'

We started up towards the next floor. But Mrs Johnson could stand no more of this.

'Mr Kimberly, this really is not fair! You surely must know, sir, that it has been a policy of Kimberly's . . . an unwritten rule . . . that persons of, shall we say, ethnic minorities were not to be employed.'

'No, I did not know, madam! If I had I would have stopped it immediately! And I don't look too kindly on anyone perpetuating such discrimination.'

'But your grandfather always insisted . . .'

'Good God, my grandfather has been dead for twenty years! Fourteen years ago, Mrs Johnson, I fought against Fascism, and I didn't fight alongside Jews and Italians and Poles − I fought alongside Americans!'

He was desperately angry and one or two shoppers had

started to glare at him. One simply didn't behave like that in Kimberly's!

'Excuse me, sir,' I said tentatively.

'Yes?' He turned from a white-faced Mrs Johnson.

'Well! Forgive my saying this, sir, but this really isn't the kind of shop where people shout!'

He looked at me for a moment and then smiled.

'It isn't, is it? I'm afraid it's also the kind of shop where fewer and fewer people come to buy things! Mrs Johnson, I'll see you in my office in half an hour, please. Rebecca, follow me!'

He walked briskly up the stairs.

'You'll be sorry for this!' Mrs Johnson hissed at me as I passed her. I ignored her but privately thought: 'But not as sorry as you will be!' Whoever had said 'Revenge is sweet' knew what they were talking about!

At the next floor we took the elevator to the top. Mr Kimberly didn't speak to me as we got out but simply indicated I should follow him.

We walked along a plushly carpeted corridor then through a door that had 'John Kimberly' printed on it. A secretary rose from her desk as we entered his outer office.

'Mr Kimberly, sir. We weren't expecting you today.'

'That's all right, Marjorie. Oh, this is Rebecca Mandel. She's going on one of our training schemes.'

From the startled look that Mr Kimberly's secretary gave me, it was clear that she was thinking, 'Over Mrs Johnson's dead body!'

John Kimberly smiled sadly at her. 'Et tu, Brute?'

He opened the door to his office and I went in. I'd never seen anything like it. It was sumptuous, huge and panelled in dark oak. A large leather-topped partners' desk stood at an angle to the window. Deeply buttoned armchairs and two chesterfields were grouped around the room.

I must have gasped because John Kimberly smiled and said, 'It is beautiful, isn't it? The panelling is Elizabethan. My grandfather had it shipped from England.'

'I wonder what happened to the house it came from?'

'Are you accusing my grandfather of being a vandal?' He laughed. 'Well, perhaps you're right!' Then, seriously, 'He certainly was the most terrible old bigot. I do hope you'll believe me when I say I had no idea that Kimberly's practised discrimination . . . Oh, I know that's no excuse. The store belongs to *my* family and I should have involved myself more in the running of it . . . but, well, we have quite a few other businesses and I haven't really interested myself much with this side of things. How can we make it up to you?'

'If you meant what you said about my training to be a shop assistant, you've already made it up.'

'Of course I meant it . . . is that really all you want, Rebecca?'

'It's what I want at the moment, sir.'

'And then . . . ?'

I thought about his question for a moment.

'I have a friend, a dear friend, Briony Connors. She's taught me so much. She's encouraged me to read, to try to speak properly . . . And I find that I love learning. I want to go on with it. I don't mean to sound ungrateful, but I don't see myself as a shop assistant all my life. I like to think I have a future.'

He looked at me and then smiled. 'I like to think so too! I asked you up here so that I could apologise. Now I think we should have a drink. To your future.' He looked at his watch. 'Eleven-thirty. A glass of champagne would be civilised, I think.'

He crossed to a door in the panelling, and when he opened it I saw that it led to a cupboard that had been equipped as a bar.

'Grandfather liked his comforts,' he said as he took a bottle of champagne from a small ice box. He opened it noiselessly and poured the wine into two flute-shaped crystal glasses.

He crossed to me, gave me a glass and lifted his in a toast. 'To your future, Rebecca!'

'Thank you.' I took my first sip of champagne. It was delicious.

He watched me as I drank. 'Well? No giggles? No bubbles up your nose?'

I shook my head. 'This is the first time I've had champagne. I feel that I should take it seriously.'

'Oh, you should, Rebecca. You should. It's a very fine vintage. And what do you make of it?'

I took another sip. 'I think, Mr Kimberly, that given the opportunity I could grow to find it an indispensable part of my life!'

He laughed, then looked straight into my eyes, seeming suddenly grave.

'Oh, you'll get the opportunity, Rebecca. I think that's something we can both count on!'

He was right.

THE HERB

CHAMOMILE

'To comfort and strengthen'
Parkinson

THE WOMAN

PART TWO: CHAMOMILE
BECCY 1959–1961

'Tomorrow do thy worst,
For I have lived today.'
John Dryden

CHAPTER FIVE

Although I had been incredibly grateful to John Kimberly for championing my cause with Mrs Johnson, it had never crossed my mind that I would see him again. Then Briony and I decided to try to get in to see *A Raisin in the Sun* at the Ethel Barrymore Theatre. The play had been the dramatic hit of the season and had won the New York Drama Critics Circle Award. Briony had talked with me about the theme of the play. It told the story of a Chicago black family which bought a house in a white neighbourhood, and the ensuing bigotry they had to endure. The play sounded fascinating but, to be honest, the main reason I wanted to go to see it was because it starred Sidney Poitier, returning to Broadway after great success in Hollywood. An incredibly handsome, dignified and passionate actor, he had been the first black to become a star leading man and I was a little in love with him.

It was February and the weather was truly miserable. We knew we'd have to get to the theatre a good two hours before curtain up to have any chance of getting a gallery seat. When I'd met Briony at the automat, after the store had closed, I was concerned for her. She looked unwell and seemed to be starting a cold or even flu. I'd tried to persuade her to go home and postpone our visit to the theatre, but she would have none of it. After an hour in the relentlessly drizzling rain, though, she was coughing badly and I tried to reason with her again. By then, her innate common sense was coming to the fore and she admitted that she would be much better off at home in bed. But she wouldn't hear of my leaving the queue.

'My dear girl, after queuing for an hour in this deathly weather I positively forbid you to leave. I can see the play some other time.' I opened my mouth to protest. 'No! I won't go if my leaving spoils your evening.' She smiled at me. 'Though it will be on your head if I spend the rest of my life reclining on a chaise longue, gently coughing my lungs away like a modern-day Elizabeth Barrett Browning. Mind you, if the reward was to marry the man who wrote, "*Escape me? Never — Beloved! While I am I, and you are you*", it might be a fate to be embraced!'

Then raising her hand she admonished me with a forefinger as if I were a half-trained puppy. 'Stay!' With that she was gone. I thought of following her to see if she was all right, but one thing I had learnt during my friendship with Briony — she meant what she said!

Another three-quarters of an hour passed, each minute more miserable than the last. Although there was a canopy over the area where those wanting gallery seats queued, the wind drove the rain in on us. But at least I was fairly near the front of the queue and knew that when the doors opened I'd get a seat.

'Miss Mandel? . . . It is Miss Mandel, isn't it?'

At that very moment the doors leading to the gallery box office opened and the crowd surged forward.

'Mr Kimberly! Oh, hallo, sir! . . . Excuse me! Goodbye!'

As grateful as I was to John Kimberly, after two hours spent waiting for that precise moment when I might get a seat in the gallery, I wasn't going to miss my chance.

As I was pushed forward by the crowd behind me John Kimberly kept pace with me. 'Are you here by yourself?'

'Yes.'

'Then will you . . .?' I was jostled by two people behind me and nearly fell. 'Will you . . .? Oh, for heaven's sake!' A strong arm slid around my waist and I was pulled clear of the crowd.

'Oh, no! I've lost my place.' I tried to rejoin the queue.

'Miss Mandel!' I was busy elbowing my way past the two theatre-goers who had nearly pushed me over, but they were larger than me and, once again, I needed to be rescued.

'Mr Kimberly, I don't want to be rude but I really do . . . desperately . . . want to see this play!' I turned from him again, but he held me.

'As do I. I'm asking you to join me.' He smiled at me. 'Well, at least I'm trying to! But I see you come from fighting stock!'

'Join you? I don't understand,' I said rather foolishly.

'It's quite simple,' he said, leading me towards the theatre lobby. 'I have two tickets. My daughter was to have come with me but she made her excuses.' He smiled indulgently. 'I rather suspect she's fallen in love again.'

'Mr Kimberly, wait! Please stop!' He halted, then turned and looked at me. 'I'm sorry. I've been very rude. In my anxiety to stop you being crushed to death, I didn't give you the opportunity to say you'd rather not sit with me . . . although I hope that isn't the case.'

'Of course it isn't! It's just that . . . well. . . look at me! I must be giving a very good impersonation of a drowned rat. I'd seem . . .' I hung my head, 'I'd seem out of place in the better seats.'

A finely shaped, tanned hand gently lifted my chin. 'Miss Mandel, I cannot believe my ears. I had you marked down as someone who knew themselves to be as good as, or better than the next man. Are you to be defeated by a wet overcoat?'

I suddenly grinned. 'Even when it's dry, it's two years old and second-hand! But you're right, Mr Kimberly, the play's the thing!'

In spite of my concern about my appearance, I had a wonderful evening. I'd never sat in the stalls before. Never even been in the main lobby of a theatre. There was such a sense of occasion. The play was a hit so there was a feeling of excited anticipation among the theatregoers. This was the first time I'd been in a group of people who were all, seemingly, very affluent. Feelings of being out of place were suppressed by the sheer pleasure of admiring the beautiful clothes, furs and jewels the women were wearing. They looked so groomed, so poised, and when they brushed past me I could smell their expensive scent.

Out of the corner of my eye I saw John Kimberly watching me, an expression of kindly amusement on his handsome face.

I grinned. 'I must look as if I've got my nose pressed up against a shop window. It's all so new to me, you see.'

'It's wonderful to see someone enjoying themselves so much. Come on, let's find our seats.' This because the bell for curtain up had just rung.

We had perfect seats. Front centre stalls about ten rows from the stage. The play was everything I had hoped for and more. The black family not at all stereotyped, the theme strong but not preaching revolution, and I was enchanted by the power and beauty of Sidney Poitier. At the curtain call the audience spontaneously rose to its feet to applaud.

As we edged our way through the crowd and out on to the sidewalk, I said, 'Oh, I can't thank you enough. I never wanted it to end!' I was practically dancing with pleasure and excitement.

'The evening doesn't have to end yet, does it? Will you dine with me?' I glanced at my watch. 'Please, please don't think me ungracious . . . ungrateful . . . but someone is keeping an eye on my young brother for me. I don't want to abuse their kindness by being late.' I was surprised by how disappointed this rich and influential man looked, and so I added impulsively, 'Would . . . would you consider eating somewhere where they can serve us quickly? I don't know . . .' I shrugged '. . . just go to a little place for a pizza or some pasta? Or is that just not your style?'

'My dear Miss Mandel,' he laughed, 'I haven't come from another planet. Not only would I consider eating pasta, I *love* it! And I know where we can get the best in the world.' He flagged down a passing cab and gave the driver an address just off Lafayette Street. We were heading for Little Italy.

Hostaria Romana was a little café situated in a semi-basement. It was exactly as an Italian restaurant should be. Red-check tablecloths, candles in Chianti bottles with the remains of their predecessors dried on the glass and raffia. We were greeted warmly by an elderly woman dressed in unrelieved black. I was introduced to her and to her two sons who waited at table. The atmosphere was totally unpretentious and the food out of this world. We started with *insalata di fagioli e tonno*, which was tuna fish with haricot beans, garnished with slices of onion and parsley and dressed with olive oil and vinegar. As I ate I realised how ignorant I was of real Italian cooking. But then, I thought philosophically, I was ignorant about so many things. This was followed by *spaghettini alle vongole* . . . spaghetti with a red clam sauce. With this feast we drank Soave Classico. One of the sons, Mario, served the wine flamboyantly, talking lovingly of the hills of Verona where the wine came from and assuring us that it was young. This totally bemused me as I thought good wines were supposed to be old.

'Not all good wines. Even at three years old Soave loses its freshness. My God, I'm beginning to sound like a wine snob. What could be more hateful? Here!' John Kimberly refilled my glass. 'The most important thing to remember about wine is to enjoy it and to hell with the vintage!'

'Ah! But perhaps,' I teased, 'for some people it's impossible to have one without the other!' He laughed and our meal continued in companionable, easy conversation.

I glanced across the table and thought how astonishing this evening was. Not only was I dining with the man who owned the store in which I worked, I was having fun! He was so easy to talk to. He, as did Briony and I, loved the theatre. I told him, with great affection for that indomitable lady, how she had refused to come to see *My Fair Lady* with me because the right to perform *Pygmalion* had been withdrawn. We discussed the items that were appearing in the gossip columns, speculating that Richard Burton was going to play the lead in Lerner and Loewe's new musical, *Camelot*.

Looking at John Kimberly as we talked, I thought how strange it was that I hadn't noticed before how attractive he was. Or perhaps I'd been so in awe of him when we met at the store, I hadn't let myself think something so human. He was tall and moved with the easy grace of someone who is a natural athlete. I discovered that he was a keen yachtsman, which must account for his healthy-looking tan. His hair was very dark with flecks of grey running through it, which was hardly surprising as I judged him to be in his mid-forties. His face was finely featured and, in repose, could look rather forbidding. Then it would become alive with humour, and the warmth behind his hazel eyes combined with a slightly lopsided, wryly amused smile to devastate you with the sheer charm of the man. And yet this charm was never used self-consciously or to impose his will on others.

I dragged my thoughts away from the attractiveness of my host and reluctantly looked at my watch. He was instantly apologetic. 'Oh, I'm sorry. I've kept you too long. How selfish of me. I'll see you home.'

'Oh, no! Thank you, but I can get home by myself. If you could just drop me at the nearest subway . . .'

'You can't imagine I'm going to let you go home alone at this time of night?'

'It won't be the first time,' I interrupted.

'Maybe, but this time I know about it,' he said, grimly. 'I'd never forgive myself if . . .'

I lifted my chin defiantly. 'I can take care of myself.'

'Yes! Yes, I'm sure you can. But tonight you are not going to be given the opportunity.' He swiftly paid the bill, then phoned for a cab. While we were waiting I said, 'All right, I'll go home in a cab. But I'd rather . . . well, in my neighbourhood . . . On the block that is . . .'

I floundered, not knowing how to explain that if I was brought home by an expensively dressed older man my reputation would be in tatters.

'Look,' he said gently, understanding my dilemma, 'I'll see you into the cab, give the driver the fare and assume you'll arrive home safely. Is that a fair compromise?'

I hesitated. I could, after all, stop the cab a block away from our apartment building, walk the rest of the way, and no one need be any the wiser that I hadn't ridden home on the subway. Because there would certainly be speculation about how Beccy Mandel could afford a cab ride to the Lower East Side!

'Thank you, Mr Kimberly. You're very kind.'

'Thank *you*, Miss Mandel,' he replied gravely. 'But now that we've broken bread and drunk wine together, do you think I might be permitted to call you Rebecca?'

I smiled. 'My friends call me Beccy.'

'And *my* friends call me John.' At that moment a horn sounded out in the street and through the window we could see the cab pulling up outside. I therefore had no opportunity to explain that the prospect of addressing the owner of Kimberly's department store as John seemed to me to be incredibly presumptuous. Rather like asking God if he had a first name!

Ah well, I thought as the cab drove through the darkened streets, I was hardly likely to have to face the problem of how to address John Kimberly again. That evening had come about by a series of chances. Briony being unwell, John Kimberly's daughter cancelling her visit to the theatre with her father at the last moment, the simple fact that we had chosen to see the same play on the same night. It was unlikely that we would ever meet again.

Three weeks later a note was delivered to me at the store. It read, '*My recalcitrant daughter has, once again, let me down! I have first night tickets for* Sweet Bird of Youth. *Would you care too join me? Please do. John.*'

The first night of *Sweet Bird of Youth*! Starring Geraldine Page and Paul Newman, it was the most fashionable theatrical event of the season. The sheer glamour of it took my breath away. What would I wear? What could I possibly wear? Everyone who was anyone would be there. In that case, I told myself sternly, no one would notice *me*! Even so, I couldn't let Mr Kimberly down. To be a victim of circumstance and sit in the stalls damp and bedraggled just once was forgivable. But to accept an invitation to such an occasion and not be at least moderately well-dressed was unthinkable!

I was too excited by the invitation to question John Kimberly's motive in asking me. I think I simply accepted it at its face value. His daughter was unavailable, he knew of my love for the theatre and the incredible pleasure that sitting in the stalls to see *A Raisin in the Sun* had given me, so where was the harm? I truly believed that he had rationalised the invitation in the same way. A stage-struck young woman was being treated kindly and charitably. Where, indeed, was the harm?

I desperately wanted to accept John Kimberly's invitation, but I dare not without first resolving what I was going to wear. My salary at the store had to support both Aaron and me. There was no way that I could buy a new dress, and my existing wardrobe was hopelessly inadequate. There was also no point in my buying a secondhand evening dress, because when would I ever wear it again? To hire from one of the established dress agencies was too expensive. I wished that I had talent as a needle woman, but beyond letting down or putting up a hem or sewing on the odd button, I didn't even know how to start to make a dress. In any case, I'd have to buy the material.

Then I hit on a plan. The money I made from O'Brien's drug store I was saving in case of an emergency. Aaron and I were young and healthy, but we might need money for a doctor if there were an accident. And if, for some reason, I lost my job, we would need money to tide us over until I could get another. So far I had saved twelve dollars and forty-five cents. I could use that to buy a dress from Schindler's second-hand clothing shop. Wear it one night, then sell it back to Mr Schindler the next day. Obviously he would buy more cheaply than he sold, but

CHAMOMILE

even so I would have the use of the dress for much less than the cost of hiring.

The last customer I served before the store closed that evening was so difficult I could have hit her. I desperately wanted to close down my counter, then, on the way home, telephone the number on John Kimberly's notepaper and accept the invitation.

As a trainee I was working in a number of different departments. Since the showdown with Mrs Johnson, quite a few new trainees had joined who were from races previously unacceptable at Kimberly's. Even so, the bulk of the staff were from the old regime, and they resented the changes. I knew that I dare not put a foot wrong as nothing would delight the manageress of my department more than to give me a good dressing down. And so I gritted my teeth and did my utmost to cope politely with the woman dithering over the huge range of embroidery silks I was showing her. How I longed to shout, 'I'm going to the most glamorous first night of the season, and I don't give a damn if you think the rose umber silk is a little too bright, and the strawberry a little too pink!'

At long last she selected what she wanted, changed her mind yet again, and left without buying anything. The store was just closing and so I quickly tidied my counter and started to leave. The manageress, Mrs Watson, called me back. She was a tight-lipped woman with a waspish tongue who bitterly resented the changes in the store's attitude to staff recruitment. She was constantly finding fault with me and I found it difficult to hide my dislike of her. However, I did hide it because I wanted to keep my job.

'Miss Mandel, if only you were as enthusiastic about serving customers as you are about leaving for home!'

This was terribly unfair as I was keen to learn and to get promotion at Kimberly's.

'I'm sorry if you don't find my work satisfactory, Mrs Watson. I do my best to give good service.'

'Then clearly your best is not good enough!' she replied tartly. 'Really, I don't know how I'm supposed to maintain standards with the type of girls they're sending me nowadays. Not at all suited to a *high-class* establishment.' And with that she walked away from me.

'You old cat,' I thought, as I watched her go. Then I grinned to myself. What would she say if she knew that the owner of the store clearly didn't think me low class? I hugged my secret to me, and was warmed by it.

On the way back from the subway to our apartment building, I stopped at a phone booth and dialled John Kimberly's number. I was totally disconcerted when the telephone was answered: 'The Kimberly residence.' I'd had no idea that people answered the phone with such formality!

'Oh . . . er . . . excuse me . . . I'm phoning Mr Kimberly.'

'Who shall I say is calling?'

'Beccy . . . Beccy . . . Mandel. Please, sir,' I added idiotically. In a moment John Kimberly's voice came over the line. It sounded warm and friendly.

'Beccy! I'm so glad you called. How are you?'

'Very well, thank you, Mr Kimberly.'

'Now Beccy, I thought we agreed I was "John". Don't make me feel even older than I am,' he added with a laugh. The sound relaxed me. I really did like this man.

'If there's any danger of that, I'll most certainly call you "John"! I was phoning about your invitation.'

'Do say you can come.'

'I'd love to. Thank you. It's very kind of you.'

'Not at all. I know how you love the theatre. Can I pick you up?'

'Oh, no! I won't have time to go home. I'll come straight from work. I'll . . . I'll meet you at the theatre.'

'Fine. Tell you what. There's a rather smart cocktail bar two doors down from the theatre. Why don't we meet there for a drink . . . say . . . half an hour before curtain up?'

'I'd like that.'

'That's just great. Six-thirty at Dominique's then. I'll look forward to it.'

'Oh, so will I! Until next Friday then. Goodbye.'

'Goodbye.'

As I hurried home I didn't stop to ask myself whether I was so excited because I was going to a Broadway first night, or because I was seeing John Kimberly again. I simply knew that I couldn't wait for the next four days to pass.

Our apartment was empty when I got in. Then I remembered that Aaron was playing baseball after school that evening. He'd be home shortly. I couldn't wait to go to Schindler's and see what dresses they had in stock. I knew there wouldn't be anything wonderful but, with luck, hoped I'd find something pretty.

I kept our savings in an old biscuit tin which I hid at the back of the food cupboard in the kitchen. Now I took the tin out of the cupboard. A lot of the twelve dollars forty-five cents was in nickels and dimes and therefore I couldn't understand why the tin was so light. I had only to open it to know exactly why. It was empty!

At that moment the door to our apartment opened and Aaron sauntered in. He saw me standing in the kitchen holding the empty tin. From his expression I immediately knew who had taken the money. I was angry, really angry. I loved Aaron fiercely. Anything he wanted that was in my power to give, I'd move heaven and earth to get for him. But to *steal* from me!

'Gee, Beccy, don't look like that! Hell, I just borrowed it. I'll pay it back!'

'How?' I asked, coldly.

'Pool . . . I'm real good at it.'

'I've told you to stay away from the pool rooms.'

'Yeah, yeah! But guys don't always do what their big sisters tell them! Ah, come on, it's not the end of the world!'

'It is for me. I was going to buy a dress.' I was near to tears. 'Someone asked me to go to the theatre . . . now I can't go!'

'You been to the theatre before . . . you didn't buy no new dress. What you want a new dress for?'

'BECAUSE I HAD A CHANCE TO DO SOMETHING GLAMOROUS!' I shouted at him. 'A CHANCE TO GET AWAY FROM THE DRUDGE AND THE ENDLESS SCRIMPING AND SAVING . . . A CHANCE TO BETTER MYSELF!'

Aaron hung his head and then looked up and gave me a shy smile. I surprised myself by thinking, 'Here it comes. Here comes the charm.' I suddenly felt tired. Tired of our way of life. Tired of Aaron's deceit and lies.

I sat down abruptly at the kitchen table. I knew I couldn't contain my tears much longer. 'Go away, Aaron. I'll get supper a bit later . . . Just go away for now!'

'Gee, Beccy, I'm sorry.'

'Just go.'

He paused for a moment then shrugged, turned on his heel and left. As soon as the door closed behind him, I gave in to my disappointment. I put my head in my hands and wept. I was so bound up in my own misery that I didn't hear the tap on the door. Mrs Janowski came into the living room.

'Beccy, you home? Beccy! What's the matter, love?' She moved to my side. I found a handkerchief in my pocket and started to scrub at my face.

'Nothing!'

'Oh, sure! I know you well. I got you marked down as a cry baby for years! Now come on. Tell old Doll all about it.'

She sat at the kitchen table and took my hand. Her sympathy was too much for me and tears started to run down my face again. I blurted out everything to her. Her immediate reaction surprised me. 'This guy . . . the one who's taking you to the theatre . . . he on the level?'

'On the level?'

'I mean, is it going to be the theatre, a bite to eat, and then bed?'

'No, of course it isn't! He's just being kind to me!'

'Oh, yeah?' she said cynically.

'I promise you it's nothing like that. He just knows that I'm mad about the theatre and . . . well . . .' I shrugged. 'But, oh God, I was looking forward to it!'

'I could kill that kid brother of yours!' She stood up, reached out and took my hand, jerking me to my feet. 'Oh, well! No use crying over spilt milk. Come on, Cinderella. You're going to the fucking ball!'

She started to lead me to the door. 'Where are we going?'

'Where do you think? To find some mice and pumpkins, of course! We're going next door. Don't dawdle.'

As soon as we entered her apartment she crossed to a trunk and started to rummage through it. From the very bottom she took out a dress box. The cardboard was practically grey with age. She pulled off the lid and carefully took out something wrapped in layer after layer of tissue paper. She placed the package almost reverently on the table, then started to unwrap it. From the folds and folds of paper she took out an exquisite cream lace dress.

'Can't think why I kept it. Who'd want to remember marrying Rat Janowski?' She came and held the dress against me. 'Hard to imagine now, but I wasn't much bigger than you in them days! All the rage, ain't it? Nipped waist, and loads of petticoats under the skirt. Well, here we are! We'll cut out the sleeves and make the neckline a little lower. Shorten the skirt to mid-calf and everyone will think you're one of the Rockefellers.'

'But I can't let you cut up your wedding dress!'

'Why not? Should've done it years ago. Should've shredded it the first time I found Rat humping a chorus girl! It would make me happy for you to have it, Beccy,' she added seriously. 'Take it and have your night out.'

'Oh, you dear!' I hugged her. 'The lace is so beautiful, and the dress looks like new.'

'Yeah, well. I ain't had much call for wedding dresses in my life. Once and then mothballs. And that was once too often!'

I was terribly nervous as I walked into Dominique's the following Friday. Mrs Janowski had transformed her wedding dress. I had done a great deal of the hemming and sewing but she had been bold enough to cut and shape the new dress. When I complimented her, she winked a heavily made-up eye and said, 'I ain't just a pretty face!'

One of her friends in the tenement scraped a living as a dressmaker, and Mrs Janowski had persuaded her to part with her precious current copy of *Vogue* for an evening. We read through it avidly. From it we discovered that Dior's A-line and Jacques Griffe's 'Sack' were *out*. To be honest, I'd never noticed they were *in*!

Mrs Janowski was right. The 'look' for spring 1959 was a nipped waist, with a full skirt over many petticoats. The neckline was low but cut square and the sleeves were also squared off just at the top of the arms. Skirts now weren't quite so long as during the days of the New Look which had taken the world by storm in the late forties.

With the material left over from the shortened skirt we'd made a stole. I thanked God that the weather had moved from a miserable February to a warm March. My old overcoat would have looked ridiculous over Mrs Janowski's wonderful creation!

As I entered Dominique's, the *maitre d'* glided forward to greet me. I was too inexperienced to know that, so long as a customer was well dressed and reasonably presentable, a good *maitre d'* always greeted them as a long-lost friend. Much safer than giving offence by forgetting a well-paying face!

'Good evening, madam. So good to see you again!'

I was about to succumb to honesty and point out that I'd never been there before, but he continued: 'If I may say so, madam is looking particularly beautiful tonight.'

'Thank you. I'm meeting Mr Kimberly here . . . Mr John Kimberly.' I was starting to play the same game!

'Of course.' He smiled an ingratiating smile. 'Is there another Mr Kimberly? Follow me, please, madam.'

I followed him across the deep-piled carpet. As we entered the main body of the cocktail bar, John rose to greet me. He was impeccably dressed in a beautifully cut evening suit, and I thanked God for Mrs Janowski's wedding dress. He stretched out both arms and took my hands in his. 'Beccy, good to see you!' He led me to a deeply buttoned banquette seat. The *maitre d'* hovered behind us.

'I can't tell you how glad I am that you were free this evening. Now, what will you have to drink? A dry martini? No! I remember. You're in training to acquire a taste for champagne! Two champagne cocktails, please, Alain.'

The *maitre d'* inclined his head and moved silently away to give the order to the barman.

'Do you think they have to train to walk as smoothly as that? Tiptoe over broken glass without making a sound or something?'

'It's a delicious thought,' John laughed.

The cocktails were served. We sipped them and chatted. I don't know why we were so easy in each other's company, but not once did I think about the age difference between us. Perhaps the key to the whole mystery of chemistry and attraction is laughter. A moment of keenly observed humour can strike such a chord in another human being. That moment encapsulates a person's outlook on life in a way that hours of searching conversation cannot. Of course it was exciting to be with such a rich, good-looking and powerful man, but above all I think it was the discovery that we both looked at the world with the same wry sense of humour that made us enjoy being together. John offered me another cocktail, but I wanted a clear head to enjoy the play and so we left for the Martin Beck Theatre.

A hundred flash-bulbs seemed to be exploding as the Press jostled to get photographs of celebrities arriving. Police were holding back the fans and the autograph hunters. Stretch limousines queued around the block.

Inside the theatre lobby it was almost worse, because the world and his wife wanted to make sure that everyone knew they had tickets to the theatrical event of the season. I thought I caught a glimpse of Katherine Hepburn and Gregory Peck and I practically had to pinch myself to believe I was really there. The audience seemed to be made up of the theatrical *Who's Who*. John was delighted by my enjoyment of the occasion. He smiled down at me as we moved into the auditorium.

'No one could ever feel tired and jaded when they're with you, Beccy!'

The performance was utterly thrilling. A triumph for the play and for the actors. Afterwards, to my total joy, John took me to Sardi's on 44th Street. Sardi's! The very name is synonymous with New York theatre.

To my surprise, the restaurant itself wasn't particularly grand. Banquette seating, white tablecloths, nothing exceptional until you looked at the walls. To someone as stagestruck as me it was like a dream come true. The walls were totally covered with signed photographs of the stars, dating right back to 1921 when Sardi's was first opened.

When we had nearly finished our meal the cast of *Sweet Bird of Youth* arrived and the whole restaurant rose to its feet and applauded. I was in my seventh heaven. John told me that the producers of the play were giving a party in a private room and that usually everyone stayed up until the dawn when the first papers hit the street with the notices, good or bad.

After dinner, John once again wanted to take me home, but understood my unspoken reasons for refusing. And so I took a cab ride back to the slums, back to the real world.

In the days that followed I found myself longing to

hear from him again. I tried to analyse my feelings. I knew that he liked me, found my company amusing, but surely that was all. Except in greeting or parting he had not touched me. Why should he find me attractive? He moved in an Uptown world full of elegant, desirable women. Beccy Mandel, a shop assistant from the Lower East Side, could be no match for them. And yet . . . and yet . . .

Ten days after the first night of *Sweet Bird of Youth* there was another note. This time there was no mention of his daughter, it was simply an invitation to visit Hostaria Romana again.

We started to see each other more and more often. After a while I stopped asking myself what did he see in me, why did he seek out my company? I simply lived my life a day at a time. Although I found him very attractive, John always behaved impeccably towards me. I had no reason to believe that our relationship would develop beyond friendship. Then a strange thought occurred to me. I was lying in bed after an evening spent with John when I suddenly became aware that for the first time in my life I was conscious of being really happy.

CHAPTER SIX

Since I'd stopped working in the store room, I no longer saw Briony daily. In fact, we met much more rarely since I had started to see John. At first I didn't want to tell her about him and simply made excuses not to meet her for a meal after the store closed or to go to the cinema or theatre as we sometimes did. Then I realised how much I must be hurting her by the apparent cooling off of our friendship. I called into the store room during my lunch break and asked her if she was free that evening. We arranged to meet at the automat.

She was already waiting for me when I hurried in. John had left a note asking me out to dinner and so I had had to telephone and leave a message with his manservant that I was unable to meet him. I got a coffee and joined her.

'How are you, Beccy? You're looking very well.'

I looked at her well-loved, gaunt face across the table and unthinkingly blurted out: 'Bri, you're not! What's wrong? Are you ill?'

'No, my dear! You've simply forgotten what a plain old maid I am. Now, tell me your news. You've obviously decided to tell me about your friendship with Mr Kimberly.' She laughed. 'Don't look so astonished. A romance between the owner of our store and a young trainee sales assistant is hardly likely to go unnoticed!'

'I've done nothing wrong, Bri,' I said defensively.

'By that, my dear young friend, I suppose you to mean you haven't slept with him — yet! Well, I've just described myself as an old maid. I was brought up to believe that men "only wanted one thing" and that nice women always denied it them. But just because a young woman is plain, as I was, doesn't mean she doesn't have the same desires . . . the same longings . . . as her more beautiful sisters. Looking back, I wish heartily that some young man had asked me to do "something wrong", because I suspect I would have enjoyed it hugely!'

I shook my head, smiling. 'Oh, Bri, dear Bri. What would I ever do without you?'

Her face seemed suddenly grave and for a brief moment I looked into her eyes and saw death there. Then, briskly, she told me, 'That's something I don't intend you to find out, young woman. So! What's to become of you and Mr Kimberly?' More kindly she added, 'He's married, Beccy. I suppose you know that?'

'He's never been dishonest with me. I know the situation, and I believe him when he says his relationship with his wife is dead. Am I being very naive?

'Oh, Briony, he's so wonderful to be with! — He's my teacher, my friend.' I looked across at her. 'I've been very lucky with my friends, haven't I?'

'He's going to want more than friendship, Beccy. You have to face that. I don't see you as a gold-digger, my dear, but ask yourself . . . is he going to go on taking you to dinner, buying you gifts, without asking something in return? And I know you too well to think you'd be dishonest about any bargain you entered into. Does that sound crude? But it seems to me you must either stop seeing this man or realise it will lead to an affair.'

Three days later Mike's cousin, who worked in Kimberly's store rooms, got a note through to me. If this sounds a little like getting a message through enemy lines, the simile is totally accurate. A huge department store is rather like an empire. A rather corrupt empire. You have your rulers, your administrators, your spies, your informers. And, lastly, you have anarchism, the bond between worker and worker – rare at Kimberly's in spite of John's reforms – which unites store men and women, cleaners, caterers and the actual shop staff and managers. Mostly we anarchists were young. Without exception our backgrounds were less than Ivy League. And although we had no political aims, we were as one in our failure to understand why a floor walker should not speak to a man or woman who unpacked the goods on sale in their department.

The note simply read: '*Your friend, Briony, rushed to hospital. St Joseph's. Seems critical.*'

I sought out my department's manageress. The ease with which I got leave to go to the hospital confirmed Bri's statement that the store knew of my friendship with John. Well, what the hell? If getting to Briony as soon as possible was the price I had to pay for a certain notoriety, so be it!

At St Joseph's I rushed straight to Reception. A well-starched, dour-looking nurse was on duty.

'Please . . . my friend.' I gave her Briony's name. 'I understand she's been brought here. Can I see her? See her doctor?'

'Are you next of kin?'

'No! I've told you . . . I'm a friend.' As far as I knew Briony had no living relatives, her old and extremely difficult and demanding father having died the year before. Even then, I thought with affection, Briony's sense of humour and passion for literature had lightened the burden, for she had always referred to her father as the Aged Parent.

'We are trying to reach her next of kin.'

'Then you're wasting your time. I'm sure she has none. Please, please, tell me how she is.'

'I'm sorry. Standard procedures must be obeyed.'

'You mean,' I said angrily, 'you won't let her closest friend know how she is . . . see her? She could be asking for me! Until you have established what I'm telling you . . . she has no next of kin!'

'Precisely.'

I was desperate. I had already feared for Briony's health. And now . . . How would she understand that I wasn't with her only because the rules were being inflexibly applied by this uncaring fool of a nurse?

I looked around for a telephone and saw one across the lobby. I had never asked John for anything, never abused our friendship, but now I knew he was the only person who could help me.

I did what I had never done before. I telephoned the head office of his company, the store being a very small part of the Kimberly empire. I doubted that I would be put through, but John, dear John, had obviously told his secretary that if ever I called I was to be put straight through.

He came on the line.

'John? I'm sorry . . . I'm so sorry to call you there . . . I wouldn't have done it, only I'm desperate! Oh, John, it's Briony!' I struggled against the tears that were pricking my eyes.

'Just tell me where you are, darling, I'll come for you.'

I explained that I was at St Joseph's and that I wasn't being allowed to see Briony or know how she was because I wasn't a relative.

'But she has none, John. I'm sure of that! Oh God, she might be dying and I'm not with her.'

'Beccy, just sit tight, darling. I'll make a couple of phone calls to the hospital's administrators then I'll be there. Trust me?'

'You know I do!'

'That's my girl!' And he had gone.

I waited. I sat in the lobby and waited. Staff in white coats bustled by, clipboards under their arms. Relatives, clutching fruit and flowers, wandered in looking bewildered, seeking wards, loved ones.

But above everything else there was the smell. That terrible all-pervading smell of disinfectant that engulfs you as soon as you enter a hospital building. Can no one, I thought angrily, create a disinfectant that doesn't reek of coal tar and carbolic? That doesn't conjure up images of the deserving poor having their heads deloused before entering the workhouse?

In what seemed like a lifetime, but was in fact only about thirty minutes, John arrived. Yes, the word privilege did spring to mind, but I didn't care. I cared only for Briony. John spoke to the doctor who was looking after her, then came and sat beside me.

'Beccy, it's gone too far. They can't operate and . . .' He shrugged, hopelessly.

'How long?'

'Hours . . . days . . . They can't tell. She's a critically sick woman. I'm so sorry, my darling.'

'If only she'd gone to a doctor! It's my fault,' I said wildly. 'I should have *made* her!'

John took my hand. 'From all you've told me about your Briony, I respect her decision to avoid months of painful treatment and go out with the dignity I think she desired.'

I nodded. I couldn't speak. Briony meant so much to me. Oh, I know there must have been those who suspected her motives in befriending me. What a sad world when two women cannot be friends without giving grounds for suspicion! For a number of reasons her own life had been unfulfilled. I didn't know what she saw in me, and, at that moment, I felt so unworthy, but she chose to give me her friendship and to open my heart and mind to a better world than the Lower East Side.

'Will they let me stay with her? I don't want her to be alone when . . .' I forced myself to say the words, '. . . when she dies.'

'I've already arranged for her to be moved to her own room. They'll let you stay with her for as long as you wish. Do you want me here with you?'

I shook my head. 'You've already done more that I can ever thank you for. You have your work, your own life.'

'This isn't the time to tell you. Even so, *you* are my life, Beccy. My whole life.'

Holding my hand, he put my palm to his lips and kissed it. 'Whatever you want, whatever I can do, I'm only a phone call away. I'll keep in touch with the hospital.' Then he was gone.

I telephoned Mike at work. He had a job as gofer/dogsbody at a television company in the city. I arranged that Mrs Janowski would take care of Aaron.

'For as long as you need, kid.'

I couldn't help smiling at the 'kid'. Mike was only a little older than me, but he was suddenly very aware of his status as wage earner and man about town.

I went back to Reception to find out where Briony was. The previously forbidding nurse was now totally unctuous.

'Room 214 on the second floor, Miss Mandel. I'm so sorry about your friend.'

I nodded and turned away to the elevators.

'Oh, and Miss Mandel . . .' I turned. 'Whatever you need, you've only to ask. Mr Kimberly has arranged everything.'

So John's wealth has waved a magic wand and we're all transformed, I thought, as I took the elevator to the second floor. If only the same magic could stop Briony being taken from me. But life isn't something money can buy. The rich may sometimes postpone death but it is as inevitable for them as it is for the rest of us. And, I suddenly thought irreverently, if there truly is an after-life and we are all equal there, how they must hate it!

A nurse was sitting with Briony when I entered her room. She lay so still I thought for a moment that death had already claimed her. Then I saw that she was breathing. Very shallowly, but breathing. I crossed to the bedside and took her hand. The nurse said something to me but I didn't really hear her. I don't know whether Bri had slipped into a coma or whether she was heavily drugged. She was asleep and yet it didn't seem a normal sleep.

I started to talk to her. I talked about anything. Everything. About the plays we'd seen. The books I'd borrowed from her and, yes, how much I loved her. It seemed to me that by talking I might penetrate that half world she was in and bring her back to me, however briefly.

Day and night blurred. I dozed then awoke guiltily in case I had missed her passing, or not been there had she managed to speak to me.

About eleven o'clock on the second day she opened her eyes and was totally lucid. She was very weak but she gently squeezed my hand. She smiled at me, then said, 'If that man isn't good to you I'll come back and haunt him!'

Then she closed her eyes and drifted into what seemed a more natural, gentle sleep.

An hour later the new day took her from me. The nurse tried to lead me away but I wouldn't let go of Briony's hand. I couldn't bear the thought of her being by herself. I didn't cry, I just clung to her hand. Somewhere, a long way away it seemed, I could hear the doctor and the nurse whispering. But it meant nothing to me. I cared only for my loss. I don't know how long I stayed there with her before I heard the door to her room open and suddenly I was in John's arms.

Then I started to cry. I cried for Briony, for my mother, for the terrible hopelessness that seemed to engulf me. I was too young to have another person I loved so much taken from me. Then I sobbed out how I hated my selfishness for thinking only of my loss and not Briony's pain.

I felt a sharp sensation in my arm and then, as I slipped into a merciful sleep, I felt John lift me and carry me from the room.

CHAPTER SEVEN

Softness, warmth, darkness. These were the first things I was aware of as I slowly awoke. No, not darkness. Not complete darkness, because across what seemed to me a room as vast as a cathedral, a fire glowed.

I stretched out my arms and felt the fine linen sheets. Unlike the sounds in our apartment, the city seemed hushed, remote, as if it dared not intrude. Then the events of the past few days flooded my mind. I sighed at the memory.

A figure rose from a high-backed armchair by the fire. It was John. Of course, he must have brought me to his home.

'Beccy? Darling? Are you awake?' he asked quietly.

'Yes, just! What time is it?'

'About seven.'

'Seven? But it was midnight . . . and . . . seven? Why is it so dark?'

He sat on the edge of the bed and took my hands in his. He smiled at me.

'Because it's seven in the evening. You've slept the day through. It's what you needed.'

'And you've stayed here with me?'

'Yes. How could I not?'

A sudden thought came to me as I fully regained my senses.

'Aaron . . .' I started to struggle from the bed. John pushed me gently back.

'For once you are not going to take the troubles of the universe on your young shoulders! Mrs Janowski is taking good care of Aaron. A very discreet older woman in my employ called on her and explained about Miss Connors' illness. I had authorised her to offer payment . . .'

'Oh, no!'

'I think we can say that she quickly recognised Mrs Janowski's independence, also her loyalty to you . . . something I can well understand.'

'I never pay her . . . not in money, she wouldn't take it. I make it up to her by buying her . . . gifts.'

I'd hesitated before the word 'gifts' because the fact that what I gave her, what she wanted, was gin seemed a private matter between that dear, odd old woman and myself.

John grinned suddenly. 'She sent you a message: "For as long as it takes, lovey. If there's one thing old Doll can manage, it's boys!" '

I smiled at that, it was so like her, and relaxed back against the pillows. I was sad still, but a great sense of contentment seemed to wash over me. I realised that although I had been blessed in my friends, this was the first time in my life someone had taken total care of me. The years of worrying about money, of taking care of my mother, trying to make a home for Aaron, slipped from me. This beautiful room filled with antiques, a fire glowing in the hearth even though we were in the middle of the city, was as far from anything I had known as was possible, and yet I felt at peace. As if I had come home.

'Are you hungry? I didn't know when you'd wake, so I arranged for something simple to be left out for us. I thought we could dine by the fire in the library. Serve ourselves, if that's all right.'

I laughed, not unkindly but with genuine amusement at our different conceptions of life.

'Forgive me, John. I'm not laughing at you. Never at you. It's just the notion of doing anything but serve myself!'

He leant forward and, for the first time, kissed me on the lips. It was a light kiss which spoke more of affection than of love.

'Don't ever change, Beccy. I'd never forgive you! Now, my dearest girl, what's it to be? Do you want to rest or are you ready to dine? Oh, by the way, my housekeeper had your clothes pressed and laundered. She also lent you that rather voluminous nightdress!'

I inwardly shuddered at the thought of anyone in this splendid household caring for my somewhat utilitarian cotton underwear . . . to say nothing of my Kimberly stores regulation black dress.

'I'd like to get up. Could I possibly have a bath before dinner?'

'Of course. There's a bathroom through here.'

He indicated a heavy mahogany door leading from the bedroom. 'You'll find a robe — everything you want, I think — but if not, simply ring. I'll come back in about an hour, shall we say? Take you through to the library.'

He moved towards the bedroom door, then turned back. 'Try not to be too sad, darling.' He closed the door quietly behind him.

I lay in bed for a few more moments, savouring its opulent comfort, then rose and went through to the bathroom. I was like a child. Only my fear of smelling like a tropical garden after a heavy rainfall stopped me from using bath oil, bath essence, salts *and* a foaming bath gel! I settled for the oil and felt its subtle fragrance ease my limbs as I lay in the huge marble bath.

Afterwards I washed my hair and towelled it dry as best I could. My hair was long and after this treatment simply refused to stay in a neat bun as befitted a young sales assistant in Haberdashery.

I dressed and waited for John. There was a knock at the door. 'May I come in?'

I opened the door.

'Beccy! Your hair. I'd no idea . . .'

'I'm sorry. I washed it. I tried to put it up but it keeps falling down. Do you mind very much?'

'Mind? My dear girl, you look beautiful! You are positively forbidden ever to drag it back in that Plain Jane hairstyle again!'

I smiled. 'I think Miss Howes of Haberdashery and Fancy Goods . . . she's our manageress . . . might have something to say about that!'

John laughed. 'Is the whole store run by dragons?' I nodded. 'Then we'll just have to slay them, one by one! Madam, your arm!'

He offered his arm to me, then led me through to the library. It was a truly magnificent room. A table had been laid in front of a huge malachite chimney piece. Again a fire roared in the grate.

'Where on earth do you keep the fuel for all these fires?'

'I'm told there's storage space in the basement.'

'Told! Don't you *know*?'

He looked a little apologetic. 'I've . . . er . . . taken it on trust.'

He pulled back a chair for me and I sat down. Everything seemed so unreal. The room, this immense apartment, being here alone with him.

Food had been left on a side table. John poured soup from a large thermos jug. It was a thin, clear soup tasting

a little like beef broth but with a hint of sherry. I asked
what it was.

'Well, my dear, my old nurse would have called it beef
broth.' I was right! 'But my cook adds sherry and would
leave me if I called it anything but consommé!'

'Consommé.' I repeated the word. It was new to me
but I was eager to learn. 'Whatever it is, it's delicious!'

This was followed by a galantine of chicken, another
word to remember, with an assortment of salads. We
finished the meal with a mouth-watering soft cheese,
wedge-shaped and with a strong yet subtle flavour. John
said it was French and called Brie. We sipped a white port
as we ate this strange but delicious cheese. Apparently
a ruby would have been too heavy, a tawny too tangy.
He had a wonderful gift for imparting information
without sounding pompous or as if he were lecturing. He
simply, charmingly, and with great ease, made my
discovery of all these new things part of our conversation.
So that although, yes, I was a pupil in lifemanship, I was
never made to feel so.

A pot of coffee had been left on a hot plate. John
moved the table and we sat on either side of the fire in
comfortably worn armchairs. We sipped our coffee, both
occupied with our own thoughts. Mine were with Briony.
I no longer felt the deep, searing grief of yesterday.
Perhaps nature is merciful and when we have reached the
very zenith of agony, of grief, our bodies tell us we can
stand no more and memories of the loved lost one crowd
the mind and offer comfort. It was as if Briony stood
by my shoulder and said, 'Go forward.' I felt as if she
was telling me that I could not endlessly be a pupil. That
I had to be my own woman. Briony had gone from my
life but I could build on what she had taught me, and
make it my own. And I realised that if I was to have any

true relationship with John, it must be as man and woman, not as pupil and teacher.

For as long as I live I will love firelight. Its life, its changing patterns, its reassurance. Dim the lights and sit by a real fire and you can speak your heart.

Is it because it was the first tangible thing that separated man from the beasts? Something primeval that spells safety to us? Or is it simply a sentimental notion that hearth goes with home? All I can say is that from that moment in John's apartment, wherever I've lived, wherever I've created a home, an open fire has always been part of it.

We sat in companionable silence and then: 'I can't tell you how often I've sat here by myself and imagined you with me. It always seemed too much to hope for.'

John rose abruptly and went to the drinks tray. 'How can you ever forgive me, Beccy?'

'Forgive you? What do you mean?' I was bewildered by his change of tone, of mood.

'I've been so selfish. I fooled myself that there was no harm in seeing you, that I was simply taking an interest in an extremely bright employee.' He laughed bitterly and took a drink of his Scotch. 'My God, I'm old enough to know better, aren't I?'

He turned to me and his face softened. 'You were so different, you see. So enthusiastic, so hungry for life . . . It seemed that for as long as I could remember I'd been surrounded by people who knew everything, had seen everything . . . then I went into the store that day, and there you were. Standing up to that bitch. Looking so scared and being so brave. I think I started to fall in love with you that moment. And now . . . well, I've always thought of myself as an honourable man – at least I've hoped I was – so I'm bitterly ashamed that I sought you out, pursued you.'

'Why?'

'Why! Good God, I'm a married man. All right, not a happily married man, but still tied to my wife . . . and I'm old enough to be your father.' He turned away from me.

'And that's the secret of human relationships, is it? Like a chemistry formula. You get the age difference just right. The man can be a few years older than the woman, but never more than that. A woman must never get involved with a younger man. Then we put the same race, the same class, into the melting pot and — Eureka! you have automatic love, happiness, fidelity. Is that what you're saying, John?'

'You're only a girl, Beccy.'

I rose and joined him. 'I'm a woman, John. I've been a woman since my mother died. I've had to be. Look at me, please.' He turned back to me. 'Don't you see that I'm a woman? A woman who wants to return your love.' I put my arms around him.

'Oh, Beccy!'

'Kiss me, John. Please kiss me.'

'Oh, darling girl, I want you so much but . . .'

I reached up and put my lips on his. I wanted this dear man to love me. I felt desire. I felt ready to become truly a woman.

A brief moment and then he returned my kiss passionately.

'You've taught me so much, darling. Teach me this too,' I whispered.

Then I was in his arms. He lifted me on to the deep sofa that faced the fire, murmured words of love, of passion, as he undressed me. He kissed my eyes, my lips, buried his face in my hair. Then we were both naked in the firelight.

'Oh, my love, my little love!'

As he caressed my nipples I felt them harden with desire. His hands were stroking my thighs, gently opening my legs. I felt his tongue and heard myself moan with excitement and pleasure. Only momentary pain when he entered my body and then the two of us were locked in an age-old rhythm. An exquisitely prolonged moment of ecstasy and we lay still in each other's arms.

'Don't ever leave me, Beccy. I couldn't endure it . . . not now, my darling.'

'Shhh, dearest.' I held him in my arms and as the logs on the fire crackled then burnt down into glowing embers, we fell asleep.

When I awoke I was still naked but in bed. I turned my head and saw John beside me. As I turned to him, he smiled. 'Pleasant dreams?'

I stretched languorously. 'Remarkable dreams! Is it daytime?' He nodded. I moved my body against his. 'I've always believed in day-dreams . . . or is that hoping for too much?'

He laughed. 'No, you young minx, it's certainly not!'

We made love again. Blissfully. Passionately. And this time, although I was not skilled, I returned John's lovemaking. Giving as well as taking. Matching his desire.

Afterwards we lay in each other's arms and John tried to talk about the future. Our future. I silenced him with my kisses. Although we had made love, I wasn't ready to assume the role of mistress. There was so much to consider. Aaron. My job. What I wanted to do with my life. I knew that whatever happened John was a part of that, but could I make him my whole life? I knew that if we lived together there would be times when he would have to be with his wife, his family, and I would be lonely and, however much I fought it, surely jealous. Could I commit myself to a life with a man who, however much he loved me, would always have obligations that would come before me? I decided to wait. To give myself time to judge my true feelings. Before that the day must be faced, and plans made, for Briony's funeral. How I dreaded that.

I spent one more day with John. One more extravagantly happy, feckless day. Servants came and went so discreetly that we hardly noticed them. We ate, laughed, drank fine wines and made love. In the evening he started to teach me how to play chess and I gave him lessons in how to shoot craps. We must have looked an incredible pair — John casually but elegantly dressed while I had only my cheap, black store dress to wear. But my hair was down and my feet were bare as we knelt on the fine Aubusson rugs in the drawing room and flung dice against the silk-covered walls.

The next morning I crept from bed and watched the dawn come up over the Park. Tomorrow was here with its decisions to be made. I knew that I wanted to be with him. I was honest enough to admit that I wanted to be with John the man, but I also wanted the world he had to offer me. But how would I fit into that world? We couldn't live in an ivory tower forever. I would have to adapt to his life style, and the social gulf between us was enormous. I smiled bitterly: social and racial gulf. There were still many establishments that would not welcome a Jewess. And what of Aaron? I couldn't abandon him.

I was so deep in my thoughts that I didn't hear John cross the room to me. A robe was slipped around my shoulders and his arm gently drew me to his side.

'A penny for them, darling.'

I smiled and shook my head, replying lightly, 'Oh just putting the world to rights!'

'My world would be forever right if you stayed with me.'

I put my finger to his lips, to stop him saying any more. 'A little time, that's all I need. A little time.'

He took my hand and kissed it. 'I'd like to say take all the time you need . . . but I want you with me too much for that. Forgive a selfish old man.'

'Old!' I stood on tiptoe and kissed him. 'Come back to bed and show me what an old man you are! Then I'll believe it!'

John laughed and lifted me into his arms. And as the dawn crept on into the golden light of morning, we made love.

As I walked from the subway back home, through the filthy, rubbish-strewn streets, past the graffiti-daubed walls, I thought wryly that now I knew exactly how Cinderella felt when the footmen turned to mice and the coach back into a pumpkin. John had wanted to drive me home but I'd refused. Even a cab caused comment on our block; John's Mercedes would have started a riot. Or worse, the word would have gone out that Beccy Mandel, for all her quiet ways, had gone the way of so many other girls and was now earning her living on her back.

I stopped briefly at Mrs Janowski's apartment to tell her I was home and to thank her.

'Any time, Beccy. Any time. But . . . not at work?'

'No. My boss arranged that I could be away until after Briony's funeral tomorrow.'

She whistled. 'That's some boss you've got there, kid!'

'Yes. He's . . . very kind.'

Mrs Janowski looked at me shrewdly. 'You don't say?'

'Well, the store gives time off when a relative dies and Mr Kimberly knew how close I was to Briony.'

'How'd he know that?'

I looked straight into her eyes. I felt I'd nothing to be ashamed of, I simply hadn't wanted to confide in her until I'd had time to consider my feelings. Time really to think through where my relationship with John was heading.

'I told him.'

'Uh-huh! Well, you've always had an old head on young shoulders, Beccy love, so I guess you know what you're doing. But let old Doll give you one bit of advice . . . and, boy, do I know the truth of this, kid! Men,' she spat, 'men can be fucking tricky! You remember that.'

I smiled. 'I'll try.'

'Ain't no smiling matter. You take care!'

'I will.' I kissed her painted cheek. 'And thanks for everything. See you!'

I let myself into our apartment. Put the coffee pot on to boil. Tidied a few things. But the apartment was so small and our possessions so few there was really nothing to do. Later I'd slip out and buy something for our supper. I'd cook something nice, one of Aaron's favourites to make up for having left him alone these last few days. Perhaps some *tsimmes* with dumplings . . . that's a kind of Jewish hot pot made sweet with syrup or fruit. My grandmother had shown me how to make it when I was a little girl, and Aaron loved it.

I was restless. Partly because I felt cooped up in so small a space after the splendour of John's apartment, and partly because it seemed so strange to be at home on a weekday. My mind was in a turmoil. Because of John. Because of Briony. I reached out and took down the book in which I had written my mother's recipes. I would undertake a task from it, knowing instinctively that soon the familiar rhythms of stirring and blending, of melting bees-wax and crushing herbs, would soothe me. The concentration needed would calm my thoughts and clear my mind.

I sat in my mother's high-backed wooden chair at the kitchen table and turned the pages of the book. For some reason I wanted a different task. To try something new. After the problems I'd had selling Mr O'Brien the hand cream I knew that this was rash, but I didn't care. And perhaps, as the hand cream was now one of my best sellers at the drug store, this time Mr O'Brien would give me the benefit of the doubt.

There was no recipe for a moisturiser as such in the book. I'd noticed in the Cosmetics Hall at Kimberly's that moisturisers were now more popular than face creams. I'd talked to one of the sales girls and she'd told me that they were lighter and more easily absorbed than creams and therefore could be used under make-up during the day time although she felt that the creams were better to use at night. Now that I had a lover, I wasn't so sure. What man wants to see his beloved's face on the pillow looking like a basic cake mix?

And then I came upon it: 'A Lotion to Soften and Preserve the Skin'. I quickly read the recipe. It used glycerine rather than lanolin, and I knew that glycerine would make the mixture lighter. I read on. Honey . . . Almond oil . . . I had both. Rose water . . . I had that too . . . And an infusion of chamomile in oil . . . I only needed to buy glycerine from the drug store and I could get started! I'd made a number of herb oils a couple of weeks earlier. We had an old iron mincer, the kind that clamps on to the table and you fit in a disc for how fine you want the mince. Using the finest disc I'd mince a number of herbs. You then placed the herbs separately in a mixture of one and a quarter cups of vegetable oil plus a large spoonful of wine vinegar. After that, you put the infusion in a light place such as a window sill for at least two weeks. I noted with a smile that one could also use marigold petals. Not much chance of those in the Lower East Side!

I pulled on my coat and hurried to the drug store for the glycerine. While I was out I went to the butcher's and the grocery store to shop for supper. Only hours ago I'd stood with my lover's arms around me, looking out across Central Park from the bedroom of one of the richest and most sumptuous apartments in town. And yet here I was, picking up the threads of my old life as easily and as naturally as a chameleon changes the colour of its skin.

Back home I quickly got to work making the moisturiser. I was pretty certain that that was what I would end up with.

As I made my preparations I felt excited about trying something new and, in spite of the events of the past week, absorbed in the work.

I melted the honey and almond oil in a basin over boiling water and I also added a little white wax to give the mixture some body. This was the first time I'd experimented by making a small change to the original recipe, but the recipes in my book must have been the result of trial and error, and I felt that the time had come for me too to be courageous.

The glycerine and chamomile oil had only to be warmed. When the mixture in the basin had melted, I removed it from the heat. Then, slowly, carefully, I beat in the warmed glycerine and chamomile oil. Finally, I added the rose water. Because I was so obsessed with the need to win the battle against the vermin and pests that plagued our building, our apartment always smelt strongly of carbolic and disinfectant. But, as I blended the rose water into the mixture already scented by chamomile oil, a luscious smell pervaded the kitchen. One day, I thought, I'd go to Provence and walk through sweet-smelling fields of lavender, of thyme and meadowsweet. As I spooned the mixture into jars before sealing, it did seem finer and lighter than the creams I usually made. It would need a couple of days to settle before I could be sure. But for at least a couple of hours I had occupied myself and had been able to tear my mind away from thoughts of John, and of course, the grief I felt at the loss of my dear Briony.

CHAPTER EIGHT

As they lowered Briony's coffin into the open grave, I closed my eyes and let thoughts of her flood my mind. What was happening on this cold and windy day in Brooklyn had nothing to do with the Briony I'd loved. It was a necessary ritual, a mark of respect, but it had no religious significance for me because I knew that Briony totally rejected the idea of God and positively disliked the thought of Eternity: 'All that sitting around on cold marble. Not for me, my dear!'

I wanted to believe that her spirit lived on in some way, but for the time being I sought comfort in my memories.

Mike reached out and took my hand, and I felt John's eyes on us. Although I'd told him about the Janowskis, neither of us could have anticipated Mike's presence here at the funeral. I'd just seen Aaron off to school when there had been a knock at the apartment door. It was Mike. He'd grown lately and his one and only suit was too small for him. But its worn shiny material had been freshly sponged and pressed and from somewhere or other he'd got an ancient black tie. And yet this gangling young man had a quiet dignity about him that was impressive.

'I couldn't let you go alone, Beccy. On a day like today you should have a man to take care of you, and . . . well. I guess I'm the nearest thing to family you've got!'

'There's no need, Mike.'

'Yes, there is,' he interrupted firmly. 'There's every need! Now get your coat like a good girl.'

After the service I introduced Mike to John. I explained that he had not wanted me to come alone. John nodded his approval. He had said exactly the same thing but I had felt that Briony's funeral was neither the time nor the place for us to be obviously together.

While we were talking, an elderly man approached us. 'Excuse me, gentlemen, but could I have a word with Miss Mandel? It is Miss Mandel, isn't it?'

'Yes, but . . .'

'Excuse us, please.' He took my arm and led me a little away from John and Mike.

'I'm Henry Castleman, Miss Connors' attorney.' He handed me his card. 'I wonder if you could call at my office before you return home? It's only a few blocks away. In fact, if it is convenient, I could drive you and your friend there.'

'Thank you but I don't understand. . .'

'It would be more appropriate to explain at my office.'

'Very well, if you'd just give me a moment.'

'Of course.'

I went back to John and Mike and told them that Mr Castleman had asked me to go to his office and could give us a lift. John smiled. 'How very intriguing. Well, goodbye, Miss Mandel. I hope to see you soon. Good to meet you, Mr Janowski.'

I solemnly shook hands with the man whose arms I'd left little more than twenty-four hours ago, and then watched his tall, stylish figure walk briskly to his waiting car. His chauffeur opened the car door for him and he was gone.

'Nice guy! Kinda human too . . . for a boss!'

'Yes!' I slipped my arm through Mike's. 'Come on, let's see what Mr Castleman wants.'

What Mr Castleman wanted took my breath away. I had never given any thought to Briony's financial situation. I knew that she had lived with and cared for her elderly father, and had stayed on in the family home after his death. The family home had, in fact, been a very substantial Victorian rowhouse in the Park Slope neighbourhood. Mr Castleman anticipated that when it was sold it would fetch a considerable sum. There were also bonds and shares that had been left to her by her father.

'But I don't understand . . . why on earth did she go on working at Kimberly's? She hated the place!'

'I think Miss Connors came from a generation where the work ethic was very strong,' Mr Castleman replied dryly.

'Even so . . .' I shook my head.

The bulk of Briony's estate was to be used to set up an award which was to be given annually to the most promising woman writing for the theatre. Apparently, a few months before her death, Briony had been in touch with the Writers' Guild of America and they had agreed to help form a trust to administer the award. I thought this a wonderful idea. So that was how my friend's spirit would live on! I remembered the first time I had met her and how her plain features had lit up when she spoke of her love of the theatre, and wondered if, secretly, that was the career Briony had wished to pursue.

She had left me all her books and, astonishingly, five thousand dollars. It seemed a fortune to me. I sat, stunned, then realised that Mr Castleman was asking me a question.

'Miss Mandel . . . Miss Mandel!'

'Oh! Yes! I'm sorry . . .'

'I was asking if you had a bank account?'

'No. I haven't really ever needed one.'

'Well, perhaps you could open an account and then telephone me so that I can make all the necessary arrangements. My number is on my card.'

'Yes. Thank you.'

'Any advice you need, I'll be happy to oblige. Miss Connors thought a great deal of you, young woman . . . and I found her to be an unfailingly good judge of character!'

He rose and escorted me to the office door.

'The books . . . where would you like me to have them sent?'

'Knowing Briony, there must be quite a number . . .'

He smiled. 'There are!'

'Then may I leave the arrangements for a little while? I have a very small apartment, you see, and . . .'

'They can stay where they are for the time being. I'll have them crated, and if the house is sold quickly they can be stored until you know where you want them sent. Well, my dear, goodbye . . . for the time being.'

Mike was waiting for me in the outer office. He rose as I entered. 'Everything all right, Beccy? There's no trouble is there?'

'No! Goodbye, miss.' This to the secretary. 'No trouble! COME ON!'

I virtually dragged Mike from the office and down the two flights of stairs into the street. Then I stopped and faced him.

'You and I, Mike Janowski, are going to find the best, the finest restaurant in the neighbourhood. I've still got most of last week's wages in my purse and we're going to

112

spend it! We're going to have a splendid lunch . . . with wine . . . and we're going to lift our glasses and drink to a wonderful woman and a true friend: Briony Connors!'

I took his hand again and started to walk quickly along the street.

'You gone mad, Beccy? Last week's wages? On lunch!' You gone mad?'

'Yes! Wonderfully, marvellously mad!'

'Last week's wages! Jeez, Beccy, your rent.'

'I'll send them a cheque.'

'You have gone mad!'

We turned a corner and there it was: Café St-Pierre. Its entrance was so discreet, so chic, that it practically had a sign outside, shouting, 'We don't need to advertise'.

'This is it.'

Mike stopped and looked at the menu displayed outside. 'It's in French, Beccy. How will we know what we're eating?'

'We won't. We'll live dangerously.'

I moved towards the restaurant's entrance. Mike held me back.

'Come on, Beccy. A joke's a joke but this has gone far enough. We can't go in there.'

'Why not?'

'Oh hell, you know why not. We . . . we . . . don't fit!'

'Then we'll learn.'

'And, besides, I . . . I haven't got enough money to take you in there. God knows I wish I had but . . .'

I clasped his hand. 'Look, do this for me, Mike. I'll explain in a minute. Let me pay, *please*. I want to do this . . . We're good enough to go in there, because people can only make you feel little if you let them. Come on, let's show them! We may be Dead End Kids but we've got style!'

Mike looked at me for a moment, then threw his head back and laughed. 'Jeez, you've got cheek, Beccy! But I'm with you all the way, kid. Here we go.'

He held open the door for me and we entered the elegant gloom of Café St-Pierre.

The *maitre d'* hurried forward then stopped as his experienced eye took us in. But I'd been to a few restaurants with John and I'd quickly realised that you could fool all of the people some of the time if you were only confident. Before the *maitre d'* could speak, I attacked.

'Good afternoon. I'm afraid we haven't booked but we'd like a table for two.' I turned to Mike. 'I think we'd like our aperitifs at the table rather than at the bar, wouldn't we?'

Mike barely concealed a grin, and nodded. The *maitre d'* still hesitated.

'Is there some problem?' I asked innocently, and then continued, 'If you're fully booked, please say so and we'll go elsewhere.'

Another hesitation. Then, totally dropping his Maurice Chevalier manner, he winked at us and said, 'Okay, kids, you're in!'

We were given the worst table in the restaurant. Cramped and too close to the swing door to the kitchen. But, what the hell, it didn't seem the moment to quibble!

After the triumph of getting a table, our next hurdle was actually to order a meal. Neither Mike nor I could speak a word of French! We stared hopelessly at the menu for a few minutes.

'Why don't we just ask the waiter?' Mike said.

'No! That would be giving in. This is an adventure, remember! I just wish I knew the French for frog!'

'Why?'

'Because I don't want to eat their legs!'

Mike shuddered, then grinned. 'Soup! We'll stick to soup!'

'What about the main course?'

'I don't know . . . Gee! They don't even have french fries on this menu.'

'Point at something . . . anything . . . and say we'll both have it. Same with the wine.'

'Wine? We're going to have wine, Beccy?'

'Sure! Why not? This might be a once in a lifetime experience for us!' For us but not for me, I thought. Not if I go to live with John. A new world beckoned and I was suddenly afraid. I glanced across at Mike to see if he'd noticed my sudden change of mood, but he was studying the menu intently.

'*Soupe à l'oignon*,' he read. 'Pretty safe bet that's onion soup, eh?'

'I reckon. Do you like it?'

Mike shrugged. 'Dunno! I've never had it. But at least we'll know what's in it!'

Now I too was grappling with the menu. 'There's a lot of *Boeuf*. Do you think that's beef?'

'Steak! I just found steak! *Steak au Poivre*.'

Just then the waiter glided to our table. 'Mademoiselle . . . monsieur . . . you are ready to order?'

Mike suddenly became very dignified. 'Thank you. To start with, *Soupe à l'oignon*.'

'An excellent choice, monsieur, we are renowned for our onion soup.'

Mike's eyes danced. 'They're renowned for their *onion soup*, Beccy! Then we'll both have *Steak au Poivre*.'

'Just a moment . . .' If Mike could be grand, I wasn't going to be left out, '. . . I'm toying with the idea of *Pieds*

115

de Contrebandiers.' I had no idea how to pronounce it and so I pointed to it on the menu just to be sure.

Suddenly our waiter lapsed into a decidedly Brooklyn accent and hissed out of the side of his mouth: 'I wouldn't, kid! It's pig's trotters. You like pig's trotters?'

I paused. I dared not look at Mike because I knew we would both burst into laughter. 'Perhaps, after all, the *Steak au Poivre!*'

The waiter slipped effortlessly back into his former suave self. 'Thank you, mademoiselle. And how would you like the steaks?' This to Mike.

'Like them?' Mike shrugged. 'On a plate, I guess!'

I saw the waiter's lips twitch. Another moment and all three of us would have been helpless with laughter at the absurdity of the scene. 'Rare? Medium? Or well done?'

'Oh . . . er . . . ''medium'' sounds pretty safe. Right, medium!'

It was a wonderful meal and, as we left the restaurant, the *maitre d'* gave me a beautiful, long-stemmed red rose. Out on the street, I clutched Mike's arm. 'Would you mind, Mike? I want to put this on Briony's grave!'

'Mind? Anything you want, kid!' He covered my hand with his. 'Anything.'

We started to walk back towards the cemetery. 'I suppose,' I said slowly, 'I should feel all wrong about us having lunch, and a great time, and laughing on the day that Briony was buried . . . but I don't! Briony's money paid for the lunch and I feel I've celebrated her life, her generosity. She always encouraged me to take a step forward, and then again, forward. I think . . . I hope . . . she would have approved of our adventure because nothing can change how much I loved her. How much I'll miss her.' My voice broke when I said that, and Mike put his arm around me and drew me close to his

116

side. The boy was becoming a man, and was offering me a man's strength.

In the subway on the way home we were silent. Both lost in our own thoughts. Then Mike suddenly said, 'It was real good of your boss to come to her funeral . . . you must have appreciated that.'

'Oh I did, but then he's an exceptional man . . . I mean, he owns Kimberly's and all sorts of other businesses but he still took an interest in me. When I couldn't get on the training scheme . . .' My heart was so full of love for John that it came as a great relief to say his name out loud, to talk about him, even though I was careful not to mention my relationship with him. I suppose I rattled on about him because I suddenly caught Mike looking at me in a strange way. I couldn't really read his expression. Sadness? Regret? Suspicion?

I quickly changed the subject, but afterwards I wondered if I'd given too much of my feelings away. But why should Mike mind about John? I knew he felt protective towards me. Had always looked out for me. Cared for me in a brotherly way. Therefore I reasoned that he would be concerned about my going to live with a married man. But nothing could have prepared me for his reaction when I finally decided where my future lay.

Whore, Hooker, Slut . . . these were the words that Mike flung at me when I told him and Mrs Janowski that I was going to live with John. I buried my face in my hands as he rushed from the apartment, crashing the door shut behind him. A moment later a hand touched my shoulder. 'He'll be good to you, this man?'

I nodded. 'I believe so. I truly believe so.'

'You in love with him?'

A momentary pause. 'No.'

'Good! Plays hell with a woman, loving a man.'

'But you don't understand . . . I *do* love him, I love him so much. He's a wonderful man. But you can love a man without being *in* love with him, can't you?'

Mrs Janowski smiled. 'I guess.'

I started to cry. 'But whatever I feel for John, I care about Mike. And now he hates me!'

'Aw, Beccy. Hates you? Hating you ain't Mike's problem.' I heard her move across the room. A glass was placed in my hand. 'Here, drink this!'

I drank, then choked as the neat gin hit my throat.

Mrs Janowski sat by me and took my hand.

'Don't you know, Beccy? Don't you know that Mike's in love with you?' I started to protest, but she pressed on. 'I know it was just brother and sister stuff to begin with. Then you grew into a beautiful young woman . . .'

I shook my head at the word beautiful.

'You should look in the mirror sometimes, kid. Okay, it ain't a pretty, pretty doll face . . . but you got something, Beccy. Why do you think this guy wants to take care of you? I take it he ain't the Salvation Army? No, he's like all guys. He sees something beautiful, something kinda different, and he wants to own it. The good thing is by the sound of it, this guy not only wants it, he can afford it!'

I took another sip of the gin. This time I didn't choke. 'You make it sound so sordid.'

'It ain't sordid. It's life! Tell me something. If this guy was a doorman, a janitor, you'd move in with him?'

I thought about this, but I already knew the answer. 'I guess not,' I whispered.

'Good for you, gal. Look life in the eye, and if you're going to bullshit someone, never let it be yourself. You're a good girl, Beccy. I know that. I know how you cared for your ma, how you've kept things going for Aaron. I ain't condemning you. I just want you to go into this with your eyes wide open. That way you won't get hurt.'

'I wouldn't be doing this if I didn't care for John, very deeply. He can't marry me. I wouldn't expect him to. I don't fit into his world — yet! But I'm going to, and I'm going to make him happy. Really happy. I'm not a tart! Hell, I've had offers but I've never even looked at another man.'

I rose abruptly and started to walk about the room, angry with myself.

'Who am I kidding? All right, I'm selling myself to the highest bidder! He happens to be a good man. I happen to love him. But that's the truth of it. Well, so what? Isn't that what all women do? Do we have a choice? . . . Oh, sure, you're supposed to marry for love, but don't tell me that women don't cast a more favourable eye on a man who has a good job, good prospects. Even now, how many women have careers? Can make their own way in the world? No! We're brought up by our mothers to be wives, and the bargain works both ways. I'll sleep with you, cook for you, bear your children. You provide a roof over my head and food on the table. And when you say a girl's made a "good" marriage you're not talking about the depth of her love, you mean that the husband's loaded. Well, I'm doing exactly the same thing.'

'Except you ain't got a wedding ring.'

I laughed then and flung my arms around Mrs Janowski.

'No, you darling old thing. I ain't got a wedding ring. And you know something? I don't give a damn! I've got my whole life before me, and I'm going to live it the way *I* want.'

'That's my gal.'

She hugged me to her and kissed me. She smelt of stale gin and cheap perfume. Her bizarre pink and white make-up seemed like a mask over her wrinkly old face, but I didn't mind. I loved her.

'You won't forget old Doll, now you're going to be Uptown?'

'What do you think?'

A pause and then she smiled. 'I guess we'll keep in touch. And, well, I guess you know, kid . . . we'll be here if you need us.'

I pulled away from her. '*You'll* be here, I know that. But not Mike. He'll never forgive me.'

'Never's a long time, Beccy. You'll see.'

Another embrace and then I left her. I took the key from my pocket and silently entered our old apartment next door. I stood in the centre of the living room, numbed by images of the past. Then I looked around. I couldn't be ashamed of our old home because it was the best we could do, the best we had. But, oh, the stink of poverty! By that I don't mean that there was a tangible smell, I'd kept the place spotlessly clean, but the very walls seemed to seep despair. And yet that was the wrong word, because despair was a strong emotion. The spirit that pervaded these few rooms, indeed the whole building, was resignation, acceptance of a lesser life.

There were only two things I'd take with me: my mother's wedding ring, and the book of her grandmother's recipes that my mother had dictated to me. Nothing else was part of me, of my family. This was the only home I could remember and I hated it.

A young couple, newly wed and barely a year older than me, were moving in that evening. They had been pathetically grateful when I'd offered them the few sticks of furniture, the threadbare rag rugs. Now I wished I'd asked John to refurnish the apartment. I wanted to take out these pathetic belongings and burn them. Or better still, throw open the windows and let wind and rain destroy.

I felt no ghosts, but I remembered. Was my mother's spirit here? I thought not. I hoped not. Because my love for her was within me, and where I was going she was going too.

I was young and the religion I believed in was myself.

'Come with me, Ma. Leave this dreadful place. Be young and fit and free. Live within me, because maybe that is the only eternity we can perceive.' As long as I lived, my mother would never be dead. All that was dead was the place where we had lived.

I had kept a cab waiting. He had been dubious when I had given him an address in the Lower East Side, but a twenty-dollar bill had, briefly, bought his allegiance. He whistled appreciatively when I gave him the address of John's apartment.

'You sure go from the ridiculous to the sublime, sister!'

No easy retort came to my lips. It was early evening, early fall. The men, those who had work, were coming home, their empty lunch boxes under their arm. Another day, another dollar. Kids ran errands or scratched a few dimes doing jobs after school. I saw myself, I saw Aaron, scurrying up front steps into teeming tenements.

I knew that whatever life held for me in the future, I'd never return to the Lower East Side. Oh, I'd keep in touch with Mrs Janowski, and Mike too if he could ever find it in his heart to forgive me. But I'd never return to that way of life, this I promised myself.

The city lay before me, seemed to hold out its arms to me. Millions and millions of lights. In the streets, in the office blocks, outside cinemas and theatres, they made an ever changing pattern against the inky sky. Never mind that there were mean streets out there: murder, lust, greed. The city shone out its magic and I was enchanted.

The cab turned into the street in which stood John's apartment block. It was handsome and solid, built about 1910. Human nature being what it is, no doubt within these vast, splendid apartments husbands hit wives, babies cried, tears were shed. But, unlike the tenement, you never heard a sound. The thick walls, the deep carpets and heavy drapes, completely insulated you from your neighbours. No old women gossiped on the stoop. Instead a canopy ran from building to sidewalk and a doorman was always on duty to ease the passage from limo to lobby. The rich might not be able to change the weather, but they could be endlessly sheltered from it.

John had lived there for ten years. He had bought the apartment when he and his wife had agreed to go their own ways. Madeleine, John's wife, loathed New York. Both she and John came from prominent Boston families. Both were Roman Catholic. Both were aware of family and social obligations so a divorce had never been discussed. There were two sons, both at Yale, and a daughter. Sophie was two years younger than me, and currently at a finishing school in Switzerland. There was a town house in Boston, where Madeleine mainly lived, and a country house at Martha's Vineyard. John and Madeleine presented a united front at Thanksgivings, graduations, family functions. It could have fooled no one but the situation was accepted.

If Madeleine had affairs, she was discreet. John had had a few brief affairs, he told me, but mainly he'd thrown himself into the creation of his business empire.

As the cab drew to a halt, the uniformed doorman

stepped forward and opened the door. I smiled my thanks, paid off the driver and hurried into the building as I knew John would be waiting for me.

A new life lay ahead of me. I was too young to be daunted by it. I knew I was moving into another world. John's world. And silently I thanked Briony for giving me a glimpse of that other world. A world where access to literature, the arts, the theatre was taken as a right. A world where no one had to struggle to remember to say 'isn't' instead of 'ain't', 'I did' instead of 'I done', because their life style and education predetermined their speech and grammar.

It may sound strange but the five thousand dollars left to me by Briony had made it easier to make up my mind about living with John. That amount of money was hardly enough to ensure an easy, comfortable life, but it gave me the kind of independence which meant that I was going to John because I wanted to and not for monetary gain. Of course, there was material gain: clothes, jewels, life style and, most importantly, Aaron's education.

CHAPTER NINE

At my suggestion, I had a small apartment on the floor below John's. Of course his servants knew that we were lovers, but they had all been with John for a long time and were very loyal. I wouldn't let him buy the apartment for me. Something in my nature shied away from the notion of being a 'kept woman'. Perhaps it was a rather pathetic sop to my conscience, but I was very young and the illusion of independence was somehow very important to me.

At first I was like a deprived child in a toy shop. Instead of scraping to make ends meet, I had *carte blanche* to furnish and decorate my apartment. It may seem incredible, but I found it difficult to spend money. My early years had conditioned me. We had bought some good but very dull furniture from the previous tenant. I was perfectly happy to make do with this but John wouldn't hear of it.

'My dear girl, I am not — repeat *not* — going to spend my evenings, weekends and nights in this mausoleum!'

'You know my background, John. You can't seriously imagine that I have the talent . . . the . . . the flair to redecorate and furnish this apartment. I'd just make a fool of myself!'

John looked at me or a moment and then shook his head. 'I'm disappointed in you, Beccy. You once took me to task for assuming that our age difference would stand in the way of our happiness. Well, now I'm saying to you: "Where's your guts?"'

'Style is something you're born with. Oh, you can polish it, sharpen it by experience or a keen mind, but like the song said, you've either got it or you haven't. Believe me, my darling, I've known people who are as rich as Croesus who have neither and never will have. And look at the arts. Do you honestly believe that every designer, artist or musician was born with a silver spoon in their mouth?'

I crossed the room and stood for a moment looking out of the window. Then I turned to John and smiled. 'You win.'

'That's my girl.'

'But, if you hate it when it's done, I won't change it.'

John laughed. 'I didn't for a moment imagine you would.'

Before I started I had one very important question to ask myself. Which colours did I like? Choice simply hadn't come into my life before. I'd had to wear black at Kimberly's and the rest of my clothes were make do and mend. Similarly our furnishings, rugs and drapes were there because they were there. You go through a pile of second-hand drapes on a market stall looking for the best bargain, not something to enrich your life. So, where to start? After John's challenge I was determined to make my own decisions, my own choices, and not to ask him for help.

'Look at the arts,' John had said when he was trying to persuade me to develop my own style. Well, although it wasn't what he had meant, I would take his advice literally. What better people to teach me about colour than the great artists of the world? The Metropolitan Museum of Art would teach me how to decorate my apartment!

The Museum was on 82nd and 5th Avenue, a pleasant walk away from our apartment building. John had taken me to the Museum of Modern Art, or MOMA as fashionable New Yorkers called it, I gathered. Now I wanted to visit the older museum, which housed one of the world's largest art collections.

What can I say about that day? I positively drowned in colour because on that first visit I discovered the Impressionists. In particular, I discovered Monet. Or perhaps he discovered me. I was so overwhelmed by the beauty of his work that I felt tears come to my eyes. My favourite was *Vétheuil in Summer*. 'Painting the Light' was how the Impressionists described their work. Layer after layer of colour captured the transitory effect of light and of atmosphere. Today, I can shudder at my simplistic and philistine approach to one of the world's greatest works of art. Then, I looked at *Vétheuil in Summer* and ignored, or simply didn't see, the multitude of secondary colours because in that moment of immeasurable pleasure as I first looked upon it I saw only the four main elements: blue, green, and warm beige against a subtle but rich rose. Those were the colours I wanted to live with. Now I had somewhere to start. Once I knew the effect I wanted to achieve I scoured New York for fabrics, furniture, and for the right colours. Not only the expensive shops on and near Madison and Fifth Avenue. I sought out little antique shops, specialist shops that would mix paint for me until I felt it was just right, even thrift shops.

My apartment, although by my standards vast, was actually very much a bachelor 'pad' compared to many of the grand establishments in the block. There was an L-shaped reception room, the main part of it for use as a sitting room, the smaller part of the L to be the dining room. I felt that both rooms, because they led into one another, should be decorated in the same colours.

The walls I had painted in a light viridian green, the woodwork in a warm beige. I wanted to find furnishing material with dominant colours somewhere between cobalt blue and smoke. The two principal themes fashionable in New York at that time were either a stark, rather cubist modernism, or what I would describe as Duchess of Windsor kitsch — silk damask upholstery on desperately uncomfortable fake Empire couches and a plethora of gilt-edged side tables. No doubt with the Windsors the couches were genuine, but the effect was definitely phoney.

I knew that John would feel let down if the apartment wasn't elegant, but at the same time I wanted to create a home not a show-piece.

I'd seen photographs of the sitting rooms in English country houses: a few good antiques mixed with large comfortable sofas and armchairs. The rooms seemed to reflect the taste of the owner but quietly, unobtrusively. They looked like good places to curl up and read a book in. And because I was still desperately sensitive about my origins, I too wanted a style that didn't overwhelm.

Then I made my find: a small interior design shop tucked away from the fashionable shopping areas around Madison. Its rather poky window had a display of designs that took my breath away. The materials were intensely romantic, lyrical almost, and in spite of their rather formal repeating patterns, so full of life. All the designs on display reflected nature. Birds, water-lilies, leaves. The fabrics' fairy-tale quality was utterly enchanting and I was bewitched. I entered the shop.

'Plonk yourself down, love. Won't be a jiffy. I'm just brewing up,' I heard a voice call from the back of the shop.

A wooden chair with an unusually high back was placed by a small counter. I sat down gingerly and was astonished to find how comfortable it was.

After a moment a figure bustled into the shop carrying a cup of tea. He stopped when he saw me.

'Liberty's circa 1905!' he said, indicating the chair. 'Utterly divine and rather camp, just like me! Bruno Barret at your service.'

He held out his hand and I shook it, replying rather hesitantly, 'I'm Beccy Mandel.' My training at Kimberly's had certainly not prepared me for this kind of shop assistant. His approach was totally friendly and disarming, with not the merest hint that there was a need actually to sell something.

'So, what can I do for you, dearie?'

'The fabrics in the window . . . I've never seen anything so lovely.'

'Ah, the girl's got taste! They're English, love. Whizzed across the Pond from dear old Blighty to yours truly. Got a book here somewhere.' He started to ferret around among a pile of sample books. 'Arthur Sanderson and Sons of Berners Street. They've got a lot of the original blocks, you see.'

'Original blocks?'

'Of William Morris designs — that's what you've been admiring, pet. All pre-Raphaelite and Arts and Crafts. You know, willowy ladies with long tresses hanging around lily-ponds . . . *Very* tasteful!'

While he dashed around the shop muttering encouragements to himself to find the elusive pattern book — 'Who's a silly then? You can find it, you know you can . . . Don't say that daft old queen at Bloomingdales didn't bring it back . . .' — I was able to take stock of Bruno Barret. I saw a plump little man of indeterminate age. He was startlingly dressed in bottle-green cords (I was to discover they were called Chelsea cords), a bright yellow vest (again Bruno would have corrected me here — a bright yellow *waistcoat*) over a checked shirt. Around his neck he wore a long and badly knitted woollen scarf. Bruno's mother sent these home-made horrors regularly from England apparently because he'd been 'chesty' as a child and she was convinced that America was damp! But the *pièce de résistance* was a bright ginger toupee which neither matched the remaining hair visible beneath it, nor sat quite straight.

I never discovered whether Bruno had a total blind spot about his own appearance, or if the crazy mismatch of colour and style was a private joke, the humour of which was known only to him. His flair and taste when it came to furnishings or other people's clothes were impeccable. In fact, I have never known anyone to rival him. But his personal appearance was at best eccentric and at worst utterly risible.

'Gotcha!'

A large pattern book was dragged from beneath an Ambrose Heal sideboard.

'*Voilà*, my little chickadee. Do you like W.C. Fields? I absolutely adore him!'

The book was plonked on the counter.

'I don't know about you, love, but I need something a bit stronger than tea after all that exertion! Glass of dry white?'

I had no time to reply.

'Good choice! Me too! Take a butcher's — butcher's hook, look — while I rustle up the necessary.'

And with that he darted back into the darkness at the rear of the shop.

I rose and started to turn the pages of the pattern book, feeling I had found exactly what I was looking for. I turned the pages and paper after paper, print after print, took my breath away.

Bruno bustled back into the shop carrying a bottle of wine and two glasses.

'It's Californian, pet, and marginally better than mouth wash, but it'll wet your whistle!' He looked over my shoulder. 'Lovely, aren't they?'

'Oh, Mr Barret, they're beautiful!' I took a glass of wine. 'Can you look for something . . . not know what it is . . . then find it?'

Bruno looked at me for a moment and then said, quite seriously, 'You can if the Good Fairy stood by your cradle and granted you the gift!'

'The gift? I don't understand.'

'Some call it style . . . some panache. I just call it the gift. A few chosen ones instinctively and unequivocally know what's right for them. There's no influence, no argument, they just *know*.' He suddenly grinned. 'And God help anyone who tries to change their mind!'

Suddenly there was a shift of gear, a change of attitude. Bruno was once again behind the flippant mask. He indicated the pattern book.

'Sanderson's will do you special printings if you think you can improve on good old Willy Morris. Cost an arm and a leg, of course, but if you can afford it . . .' he shrugged, 'why not?'

'Because it would be sacrilege! You didn't honestly expect me to try to change these wonderful designs?'

'Let's say I was hoping . . . hoping you wouldn't! I'd have hated to despise someone as pretty as you are.' He raised his glass. 'Chin chin, young thing.'

We drank. I rather think to each other.

I sipped my wine and gave myself up to the enjoyment of discovering William Morris's designs.

'Upholstery *and* curtains would be a bit too much, don't you think?'

'In every sense, duckie! These are sixty dollars a yard! Or . . .?'

'Yes?'

'Is money no problem?'

I smiled. 'Money's always a problem, isn't it? Too much or too little . . . although I'd prefer the former! But I can buy what I like for my apartment. I have a very generous allowance from a friend.'

'Oooh, don't talk to me about friends! Last one I had decamped . . . and I use the word advisedly . . . with the family silver so to speak. I thought, "That's it! I 'm getting too old for all this nonsense." Now I'm quite happy with two Siamese – cats, that is – and a good book at bed time. So, which ones take your fancy?'

'All of them! But to be serious I think it comes down to these two. I don't suppose . . . I don't suppose you'd call at my apartment and advise me? For a fee, of course,' I added hastily.

'No fee, pet, if you're going to buy the fabrics through my company. I'll settle for a very large, very cold martini.'

'Done! There's just one thing. I don't know how to make a martini.'

'Ignorant child! Take one glass jug. Place in the fridge – "ice box" to you colonials! – for a few hours. Add a large amount of gin, a twist of lemon, and let the vermouth bottle simply glance in the gin's direction. Back into the ice box – and you will never be forgiven if you add ice. Crushed or otherwise!'

I grinned. 'I can see you're going to be a hard taskmaster.'

'Oh, I am pet! I am! And once we've sorted out your

curtains, we'll start on your clothes. Where *did* you get that frock?'

I named an established designer.

'Him!' Bruno shrieked. 'An old poof who can't stand beautiful young women. Fat old dowagers go there, pet, not lovely young things like you. Anyway, first things first. Give us your address and I'll pop along tomorrow afternoon. Okay?'

'Okay!'

By five o'clock the next afternoon, Bruno was on his third martini and prowling around my apartment.

'Love the colour on the walls, duckie. Just right with the paint work.'

I explained to him about *Vétheuil in Summer*.

'Interior decorations by Monet! Now that would look good in *House and Garden*. Cecil Beaton, eat your heart out!'

We had a wonderful afternoon, arguing, discussing, getting excited about first one pattern and then another. By seven, decisions had been made. William Morris fabric for the upholstery; plain, very heavy linen drapes at the windows. But they would be hung on rings from poles rather than on runners.

The bedroom I wanted to keep simple and romantic, decorated in warm beige and rose. But I had seen two lamps in Bruno's shop that I felt would tie in with the style of the living rooms. I asked him about them.

'Tiffany, dearie, circa 1900. Your friend will faint when he gets the bill!'

'Not if he admires them as much as I do. He's . . . well . . . he's very rich.'

Bruno looked at me shrewdly. 'And that makes you feel uncomfortable?'

I thought for a moment. 'I suppose I just can't get used to it. All my life I've had to scrape and save. I didn't try to ensnare John for his money. I didn't try to ensnare him at all . . . it just happened! And now . . . well, look at this apartment. Look at my clothes,' I laughed. 'Even if you do hate them, they're expensive. My brother, Aaron, is being educated privately. I can have anything and everything I want. It's like a dream but . . .' I shrugged. 'I suppose I just don't know how to cope. I can't look ahead and imagine there ever being a time when I'll be used to all this.'

I smiled. 'Sorry, that was a very long answer to your question and somehow I imagine that in your book the most unforgivable sin is being boring!'

'In my book, the most unforgivable sin is being pretentious! Just be yourself, lovie, and it'll all come right in the wash!'

He drained his martini and stood up.

'Well, mustn't outstay my welcome.'

'You haven't. You couldn't! Look,' I said, impulsively, 'are you busy this evening? John's dining at his club with his sons and I wondered if you would you like to stay and have supper? It would be such fun . . . for me, anyway!'

Bruno hesitated for a brief moment, then grinned. 'For me too, doll! Lead on to the kitchen. I'm a whizz with a salad!'

I had such fun that evening. Bruno was caustic, outrageous, very sophisticated and yet utterly homely. I'd made no friends in my new life. And, however much I'd fought to get out of the ghetto, I missed the day to day contact with the Janowskis. The chats on the way home from work with the old ladies on the stoops. Aaron and his friends crashing in and demanding to be fed. The beggar girl had been turned into a princess, but sometimes the palace could be terribly lonely. Especially when John wasn't there. However much I'd warned myself against it, I found it so hard not to feel isolated and rather lost when he was with his family.

We had an omelette and salad, followed by cheese, and drank two bottles of John's very good claret. It was marvellous for me to be with someone so utterly Uptown but at the same time so down to earth. Bruno made no apologies for his humble origins. In fact, he nearly flaunted them. But at the same time he felt confident about his talent. His flair.

He told me how he'd come to New York as the set designer for a fashionable West End play that had transferred to Broadway. 'Well, I could see the writing on the wall, pet. I designed exquisite sets mainly for Binkie at Tennant's. I wanted them to look lovely, but I cared about the play . . . I didn't want anyone coming away from a musical I'd designed whistling the sets!

'Once Director's Theatre shacked up with Subsidised Theatre they were on a right old wank! And no one gave a toss about the written word or whether the costume designs hid the fact that the leading lady had a big arse. Start yelling for truth in the theatre and everything looks ugly. The wheel will turn, of course, and we'll be back to creating wondrous illusions, but I've never felt the need to be unfashionable and that was just around the corner . . . so! A lifelong passion for Art Nouveau led me to your feet, fair damsel. "For man is man, and master of his fate." That's one thing I've got in common with Queen Victoria, pet, I just love Tennyson!'

Bruno left at midnight. I hadn't laughed so much for ages, if ever. I went to bed happy and content, even though I wasn't in John's arms that night.

CHAMOMILE

I lay in the dark and thought about my meeting with Bruno. 'Be yourself,' he had said. In many ways I was unsure of who I really was. I'd been so influenced by Briony, then by John. But at the edge of my mind there was a growing feeling that at long last I'd graduated. That I had started to become aware of my own style. I was on the edge of becoming my own woman.

CHAPTER TEN

I had said to Mrs Janowski that I hadn't been in love
with John when I started our affair, although I loved him
deeply. I suppose I had made that distinction because I
had had a girlish notion of romance. Or perhaps Briony
had lent me too many nineteenth-century novels where
the heroine had to suffer deeply before she found true
love. I knew now that I was giddily, marvellously, in love
with John. Yet, as I had anticipated, there were many
times when I was alone, many times when I longed to
change my status from mistress to wife so that we could
truly share our lives. John had broached the subject of
getting a divorce a number of times. But why hurt so
many people when we were happy as we were? I felt that
at least until his daughter, who was engaged to be married
to the eldest son of a very devout Roman Catholic family,
was happily settled, we should not even discuss the
possibility of John's seeking a divorce.

In Europe we were discreet but lived more or less
openly as a couple. In New York our relationship was
an open secret but we did everything possible to avoid
embarrassing John's family. And, so far, the gossip
columnists had kept their claws sheathed. On very public
occasions such as a first night or a gallery opening we
were careful to be among a party.

But it hadn't all been glamour and first-class hotels.
In fact, the very happiest time had been spent in England.
John rented a rambling old rectory in a small village in

East Anglia: Moreton-Juxta-Mare . . . Moreton near the Sea. The village consisted of a church surrounded by a huddle of cottages. The vicar lived in a new redbrick house on the outskirts of the village, the rectory having been built in the days when servants were two a penny and most churchmen had some private means.

The rectory was on the other side of the village street from the church and stood in its own grounds. The original house had been Elizabethan and in that part there was a library with massive beams, and an enormous brick fireplace. Even though the evenings were comparatively warm John would light a fire and we would burn driftwood we'd scavenged from along the shore. The fire hissed and smelt of salt and tar and I would sit before it looking into the flames, John's arms around me, utterly content.

A wealthy and ambitious rector of the late eighteenth century had added on to the old house. But although the Georgian part was exquisite, it was much more formal and we rarely used it.

We found a couple of old bicycles in a shed in the grounds and spent whole days exploring the countryside on them: stopping at isolated little pubs for a lunch of bread and cheese and cider; swimming in the muddy, cold waters of the estuary; walking for miles along the deserted sea wall, the salty river mouth opening into the sea on one side, on the other marshy land with tall reeds and, as far as the eye could see, fields of ripening corn.

Of course, we both knew that it couldn't last. That we would have to return to the real world, where John was an internationally respected businessman not a madcap beachcomber. Where we must avoid being seen too often in public, and where sometimes we had to be apart. But for those brief weeks in summer, nothing could mar our happiness. We had been going to arrange for Aaron to join us in his school holidays, but the parents of his closest friend at his new school were renting a house in Bermuda and had asked him to stay. Whereas I had found it difficult adjusting to my new style of life, Aaron had made the transition effortlessly. But he had always had charm, a knack for making friends. Of falling on his feet. I loved my brother too much to envy him for this, but I was aware how different we were.

An added richness to our time in Moreton was the fact that the rectory had a herb garden. All those years I'd read my mother's recipes and longed to smell and to touch herbs that weren't available to me! The herb garden was laid out in a circle, the plants divided by ancient bricks arranged in a herring-bone pattern. The tallest plants were near the centre, the outer part of the circle filled with low-growing varieties. Thyme, chamomile, parsley, old English marigolds, sweet myrtle, chives . . . As I weeded the garden I memorised the names. I had found an illustrated book on herbs in the library and was determined to learn everything I could.

I couldn't tear myself away from John long enough to make many recipes, but when I washed my hair, the final rinse was an infusion of newly picked rosemary steeped in boiling water, left for twenty or so minutes and then strained.

I asked John if he thought it would be all right for me to pick and dry some of the herbs. He laughed and said, 'With the rent the owners are charging, you can pick the whole garden!'

I picked some of the herbs that featured in my recipes and, not knowing how to deal with them, tied each bunch with string and hung them in the sun to dry.

I couldn't have done anything worse. I know now that,

for cosmetics, it's the oil in the herb that's vital. If you even bruise the leaf some of the herb's effectiveness is lost. But during that golden, happy summer in the early sixties I knew none of those things. I simply felt the greatest pleasure that at long last I was actually handling herbs, and that in doing so I was forging a link with my heritage.

The night before we left the old rectory I cooked supper for us both, simple but the kind of food I love. Fresh Dover sole bought early that morning from the fishing boats at Aldeburgh, and a green salad cut from the kitchen garden only minutes before I was going to serve it. John had champagne on ice, and after our meal we sat on the terrace looking across the darkening garden to the meadows and the estuary beyond, sipping our wine.

Then, as the moon came out and the tide ebbed, we went to bed and made love, slowly, exquisitely. It was so beautiful that at the peak of our ecstasy tears came to my eyes. John held me close.

'Darling, what's wrong? I didn't hurt you, did I?'

'Far from it! I've never really believed that people cry from happiness but obviously they do. I love you so much!'

'Oh, Beccy! My little Beccy . . . don't ever leave me.'

'Never. Never . . . do we really have to go from this enchanted place?'

'Sorry, my love. Sadly the Kimberly empire can't run itself. I must be at that board meeting in Paris.' He sighed. 'Perhaps when the boys come into the business . . . if they do. Still, we'll have a few days at Cap d'Antibes before we fly back to New York. Say, I've got a great idea! You love it here, don't you?'

'Oh, yes, you know I do!'

'Then shall I see if I can rent the house for Christmas?' His arms tightened around me. 'I'm sorry, darling, I'll have to see the family at Thanksgiving but Christmas will be ours. It probably won't snow, there'll be a howling wind and pouring rain and the chimney will smoke . . . but would you like to be here?'

'I'd love it.'

'Then we'll make it a date. Christmas at Moreton!'

After a few hectic days in Paris we flew to Nice. A car was waiting for us at the airport and in the warm autumnal sun we drove along the coast to our hotel.

John had booked us into the legendary Hôtel Cap d'Antibes. There was a wonderful Gallic opulence about the place. It had been built at the end of the Second Empire and the style was as voluptuous and full-blown as the great bowls of roses that decorated the marble-floored reception hall. If I had to chose one word to describe the hotel it would be 'sensuous'. The marvellous tapestries, the marble bathrooms, the sight and sound of the sea, the smell of azaleas, all combined to a perfection that would please even the most demanding hedonist. This was the original for the Hôtel des Étrangers in Fitzgerald's *Tender is the Night*. Here, while Scott sipped champagne in the Eden Roc restaurant, poor mad Zelda Fitzgerald dived from the rocks into the magnificent pool. Here high society rubbed shoulders with the *demi-monde*. Here the passwords were wealth and glamour. The first attribute would certainly secure you a suite but only the second could make you part of this dazzling establishment.

When I had started my relationship with John, I had no concept of the pleasures that were available to the very rich. Yes, I knew there was a better world than my

140

desperate existence on the Lower East Side but I'd had no idea that the better world could encompass style, grace, beauty, and time to appreciate, to play, to enjoy. And even though, in many ways, the Hôtel Cap d'Antibes was a memorial to a vanished Riviera social set, there one could not escape the deeply satisfying sense of luxury that a more uncaring modern world had forgotten how to enjoy.

We were to spend five days at Cap d'Antibes before flying back to New York. I would miss the freedom we had in Europe and surely, eventually, the strain of constant discretion which was so much part of our life in the States would affect our relationship? But I pushed that thought from my mind. Just being with John was enough for the time being. And the future? Hang the future, and bask in the happiness of the present!

We lazed away the days and at night made passionate love. John was a wonderful lover. His fingers caressing my body . . . fondling me . . . penetrating me until my need for him to be inside me was almost painful. I would feel the warmth and the moisture between my legs and he knew that I was ready. Then we would be as one, giving, loving, until we both cried out with the joy of our climax.

Afterwards I would sleep in his arms, the soft balmy breeze blowing into the bedroom from the Mediterranean, caressing us as we slept.

On the third morning there was an invitation among John's mail. 'This might be rather fun, darling. We've been invited to lunch in Cannes. Susan Brownlow's yacht is moored here. I know her manager quite well . . . we met in Paris and I said I was staying here. Would you like to go?'

Susan Brownlow, superstar. I had queued in all

weathers to see her films — when I had the price of a
ticket. She was my favourite. Her producers had cleverly
manipulated the public's taste for living vicariously so
that her private life blurred into her screen persona. Most
of her movies were trash but women all over the world
identified with her heartbreak, her love of men, and
ultimately her betrayal by them.

'I'd love to,' I replied. 'But forgive me if I'm
starstruck!'

Her green eyes were legendary. True, now the whites were
flecked with red and the famous aquiline profile blurred
by too much booze and too many pills, but the heart-
stopping beauty was still there, and before her next movie
a few weeks in an exclusive clinic in Lausanne would
restore her to near perfection. How long the see-saw of
excess and abstinence could last was a matter for her
many physicians. But right now it was party time.

The invitation had said, 'Dress casual'. But, of course,
that meant designer casual. I was wearing a deceptively
simple pair of yellow silk trousers the price of which
would have kept my mother, myself and Aaron for at
least two years! With them I wore a white sweater of fine
jersey. It had been made in Italy but sold on the Rive
Gauche. Around my neck I wore a single fine gold chain
from Tiffany's. Dress casual! Ridiculous, but this was
the world in which I now lived.

After lunch, I leant on the yacht's rail and looked
along the Quai St-Pierre and up into the old town of
Cannes. It was mid-afternoon. The light on the harbour
and the sea had softened to a warm gold. I reflected on
the two years I'd been with John. Two wonderfully happy
years.

'Menton's dowdy,
Monte's brass.
Nice is rowdy,
Cannes is class!'

My reverie was interrupted by Susan Brownlow's famous husky voice. She laughed. 'Great little rhyme, isn't it? I was taught it by one of those dusty-looking old Brits at the Casino. It's exactly how I feel about the Riviera! I never tire of Cannes. Well, perhaps when the Film Festival junket is in full swing. You're very pretty, you know, and you have the most gorgeous skin . . . I can understand why John is so besotted.'

I looked across to where he stood chatting to a group of men. 'I hope so,' I said. 'I certainly am! I was just standing here thinking how lucky I am. Thinking about the past.'

'Thinking about the past? At your age, kid! Take a tip from me, *never* think about the past. It's been lived through . . . gone! Today and the future's all that counts. Hell,' she chuckled, 'don't even learn by your mistakes because some mistakes can be a lot of fun! Look, don't give any secrets away if you don't want to but what salon do you go to, to have skin like that?'

'I don't. I make my own skin products. I used to make them to sell and then, when I met John and didn't have to any more, I still went on.' I shrugged. 'I just couldn't find anything to buy that was as good.'

'But where did you get the recipes?'

'My mother . . . her mother . . . her grandmother. I don't really know how far back the recipes go. When my mother knew she was dying, she made me write them down. She didn't want them to be forgotten. I suppose if I ever have a daughter, I'll hand them on to her!'

'Why on earth don't you market them? The damned things really work! You'd make a fortune!'

'Oh, it was one thing just selling to the corner drug store but I don't really see how you could sell on a big scale. Everything's made with natural ingredients, you see. Nothing will keep for more than a few months.'

'Hell, kid, all you need to do is buy a pot of Pond's cold cream. Take it to a chemist, get it analysed and find out what stops it going mouldy or whatever happens to your things. You're Jewish, aren't you, baby? Come on, show a little chutzpah!'

'Yes, I'm Jewish . . .' I began defensively.

But Susan interrupted. 'Don't get your hackles up. I know exactly how you feel.' She smiled. 'A nose job and a change of name can work wonders!'

'You mean . . .?'

'Sure! I figured if you can't beat them . . . join them. I was damned if I was going to spend my life being kept out of two-bit Country Clubs. You're lucky, you don't need a nose job, but a change of name would make it easier for John to take you to see the Pyramids. Think about it . . . and think about your mother's gift to you.'

I shook my head. 'I can't see John wanting me to.'

Susan interrupted me again. 'John may not always be around.'

'Oh, don't say that! I couldn't bear to be without him.'

'Life can be bloody mean sometimes. Believe me, I've got the scars to prove it. And on that merry note, I think I'll go in search of another drink. If you ever change your mind, I'll be one of your first customers. Toodle pip, as I said once in a ghastly British movie!'

And with that she was gone.

Life without John. The thought was unbearable. But all things being equal I supposed I'd have to face it one day. Nothing lasts forever and John was a good deal older than me. A slight breeze blew in from the Golfe de la Napoule, and I shivered. We were coming to the end of a long vacation which had been the happiest time of my life. What lay ahead for us? I wondered.

John's voice interrupted my thoughts. 'You're smiling. Pleasant memories or happy anticipation?'

I turned to him, leaning against the yacht's rail. 'Happy anticipation. I was looking forward to Christmas at Moreton.'

John laughed. 'You're standing in warm sunshine, on a luxury ocean-going yacht, moored at one of the most glamorous resorts in the world . . . and you're thinking about Moreton!'

'I know. I'll never make a jet-setter, will I?'

'How about we say our goodbyes to Susan? I thought you might like to drive back to Eden Roc via Grasse.'

'Grasse! Oh, you know I would!'

We looked in vain for Susan. Her current escort, a handsome middle-aged actor better known for his sun tan than for his dramatic ability, was getting noisily and bitterly drunk. He had obviously noticed, as had I, that not only had Susan disappeared, so had an extremely handsome young waiter. I could see why she'd said she didn't want to learn by her mistakes, she'd too much fun making them. But who was the mistake? The young waiter or the discarded escort? Only Susan knew the answer. Briefly it crossed my mind to wonder if I'd ever be like that, taking pleasure from sex but not caring about my partners, but that afternoon I was too young, too happy and too much in love to imagine it could ever be so.

The sun was still wonderfully warm as John drove the hired convertible up through the Old Town of Cannes which rises steeply from the harbour. The streets here are narrow but the scruffiness of the old quarter was camouflaged by its rakish, romantic atmosphere. Many of the houses were brightly painted and the dappled sunlight on their walls distracted the eye away from their peeling plaster. Even so, it seemed a world away from the glamour of the Carlton and the élitist shops of the Rue d'Antibes.

'If I can, I'll bring you back here after Christmas. Then you'll be able to see the wild mimosa. In January and February the hills behind Cannes are a mass of blooms. I'd like to show them to you.'

I reached out and lightly touched John's hand on the steering wheel. 'Never feel you have to take me to new places, give me things. I just want to be with you. I may be young but I'm not a fool, darling. I know you've another life, a life I can't share, but . . .' I shrugged, 'I know the score and I never want you to feel torn between your family, your business and me.'

'I wish to Christ things weren't as they are,' John said savagely. 'I'll make things work out for us, Beccy, if it's the last thing I do!'

I laughed, trying to lighten John's mood. 'Well, if it's the last thing you do, it won't be much use to me, will it?'

He smiled, but I could see he was still brooding about what he'd said.

We were driving up the hill known as the Californie. Blocks of luxury flats with marvellous views across the town to Les Îles de Lérins sat awkwardly alongside much older, distinguished-looking villas. The streets here were deserted at that hour, the windows of the villas still shuttered against the heat of the afternoon sun. I felt relaxed and happy. I was with John, I'd had a wonderful afternoon, and we were on the way to Grasse, a place

I'd always wanted to visit. God was in his Heaven and all was well with the world.

Suddenly the quiet of the afternoon was splintered by the incessant blast of a horn. I looked around to see where the noise was coming from. I heard John cry out 'What the hell . . .?' then saw a truck swing around the bend in front of us — travelling at a break-neck speed, and on our side of the road.

Then noise. Metal smashing metal. The screech of tyres on warm asphalt as John desperately tried to control the car. More noise. This time metal against concrete as the car crashed into the huge brick walls forged when the road was cut into the steep hillside. The sound of breaking glass. Then silence until John fell against the motor horn on the steering wheel. I thought I could hear someone screaming. I didn't realise it was me.

CHAPTER ELEVEN

It was Christmas. Christmas at Moreton. John was wrong, there wasn't wind and rain, there was snow. Snow and a Christmas tree and a log fire roaring in the grate. Everything was wonderful. There was only one thing wrong. I ran through the house, room after room, calling John's name but I couldn't find him. Then, strangely, I found Mike. He was there talking to my mother. In the Georgian drawing room I found Bruno and Mrs Janowski and Briony. But Briony was dead, wasn't she? John would tell me. If only I could find him! He wouldn't leave me by myself. Not at Christmas.

And something else was wrong. I was happy. I knew I was happy. Then why were my cheeks wet with tears?

I started to be aware that I felt pain. My head, my ankle, my ribs. Surely John was here somewhere? He wouldn't let me be left alone, hurting. I heard someone whispering but it was a long way off. How far I couldn't tell.

'I think she's beginning to come out of it. Thank God!'

A pause. Someone seemed to be walking towards me. But it was dark, very dark, and I couldn't see them.

'Beccy? Beccy, can you hear me?'

It *was* Mike. Mike talking to me. But it couldn't be. Why would he be at Moreton?

'Mike? . . . Why are you . . .?' It seemed so terribly hard to speak. I tried again. 'Mike?'

'I'm here, Beccy.'

'I don't understand . . . Why are you here for Christmas?'

Then the other voice. The voice I didn't recognise. 'She thinks it's Christmas. She's probably delirious. I'd better fetch Doctor.'

'I don't care where she thinks she is . . . just so long as she's coming back to us.'

Coming back? To where? To our old apartment? No, I couldn't bear that. Slowly, painfully, I opened my eyes. I didn't know where I was. Blinds shaded the windows. Even so the light hurt. Someone was holding my hand.

'John . . .?'

'No, kid, it's Mike.'

I turned my head a little. I was in bed. A hospital bed. Mike was sitting by my side, holding my hand. His face was grey with anxiety. For me? Still I couldn't comprehend what was happening.

'Mike, I can't remember . . . I can't remember!'

'Shhh, don't upset yourself. I'm here. I'll take care of you. I'll take care of everything.'

Why should Mike take care of me? Where was John? Then I did remember!

'Oh, God! We were driving to Grasse. He wanted to show me Grasse. There was a truck and then we . . . we . . .'

I paused. Because what I was going to ask next was too painful even to think about, let alone speak out aloud.

'John's dead, isn't he?'

At that moment the door to the small ward opened and a doctor and nurse hurried in. Mike moved towards them. 'She's come to, Doctor. She's asking about Mr Kimberly. I really think I should . . .'

The doctor moved to the bed. 'Now, now, Miss

Mandel. You've been ill . . . very ill. So let's not worry
about things. Just rest and . . .'

'I have to know! Tell me!'

'For God's sake, she has the right to the truth!' Mike
said angrily. He brushed aside the doctor's protests and
knelt by the bed. He took my hand again and softly
touched my cheek.

'Beccy . . . little Beccy . . . I'm so sorry. So very sorry.'

I closed my eyes. Images of John swam into my
consciousness. Drinking champagne at Kimberly's the
first day I met him. At the hospital when Briony lay
dying. His gentleness the first time we made love. But
mostly at Moreton. John running with me along the
beach like a schoolboy. John holding me in his arms
before the driftwood fire in the library. John laughing,
racing through the lanes on an old bicycle, looking tanned
and fit and so alive. So alive.

'It was my fault,' I whispered. 'He wanted to show me
Grasse.'

'It wasn't your fault! If it was anyone's fault it was
the mechanic who let that truck on the road with faulty
brakes. It was an accident, Beccy. A tragic accident. Try
not to be too sad.'

'Too sad!' I said bitterly. 'I'll never be happy again.
I loved him so much.'

'You'll be happy again, Beccy, I promise you that.
Time heals everything. Oh, I'm not saying you'll forget.
The next weeks, months, will be hell. But nothing will
bring him back, kid! You're just going to have to fight
it through.'

'I can't fight it through . . . I don't even want to. I
don't want to live without John.'

'Oh, that's great, kid! Just turn up your toes and die.'

'Mr Janowski, please!' This from the doctor.

'And how about Aaron? You going to leave him to fend for himself? You never have before, however tough it was. You've always taken care of Aaron. And how about me? Think I wouldn't miss you? How about old Doll? It'd break her heart if anything happened to you. Okay, John Kimberly died. But you lived and it must have been for a purpose!'

'Mr Janowski, I really must insist . . . Miss Mandel is too weak to . . .'

'Miss Mandel isn't weak! She's as tough as old boots. You should've seen her on our block. Any kid got rough with her brother, she gave em hell!' Mike squeezed my hand. 'You can lick this too, kid. I'm counting on you. Okay?'

I knew he was right. I didn't want to live without John but in my heart I knew I wasn't ready to die. From somewhere I'd have to find the strength to start afresh.

'Okay?' Mike said again, insistently.

Quietly, I started to cry. 'Okay,' I whispered.

The next few days were a confusion of pain, agonized weeping for the man who was gone from me, a drugged sleep that I longed for and then dreaded because the waking moments were so dreadful. I'd dream of John and wake up aware that something terrible had happened but unable to remember precisely what. Then reality would flood my mind and I'd know that he was dead.

Mike was infinitely patient. Always seeming to be there when I awoke. Holding me when I wept. Listening when I spoke of my life with John.

After four days in this half world I awoke in the early evening. Mike, as usual, was there. For the first time since the accident I felt coherent. Able truly to grasp the facts of my surroundings and what was happening.

Mike was sitting on the far side of the room reading

some typed pages. As I stirred he put them down and moved to my side. I held out my hand to him.

'You've forgiven me then?'

'Forgiven you?'

'The last time we met . . .'

'Don't let's talk about that. I didn't know what I was saying.' He smiled. 'I guess I was jealous . . . How do you feel?'

'A mess!' I smiled. 'But a slightly better mess.'

'That's my girl!'

'There are so many questions.'

'Fire away.'

'How long have I been here?'

'Twelve days. Broken ankle, cracked ribs, severe concussion, deep shock. You've been in a pretty bad way, kid.'

'And where am I?'

'A private clinic just outside Juan-les-Pins. The Anglo-American Hospital in Cannes recommended it. Once it was clear you needed nursing rather than surgery, I thought it best to whisk you away. There were quite a few reporters around. It's been a pretty sensational story, I'm afraid.' Mike shrugged. 'I just didn't want them to get to you. At least, not until you were stronger.'

'And . . . and . . . John?'

'His family flew him home. They obviously didn't give a damn about you . . . how you were . . . what you'd be feeling.'

'I can understand that.'

'Well, I can't! You and Kimberly had been together for two years. He obviously cared for you deeply. I think his family could've shown some sense of responsibility. God knows what sort of media circus would've been going on if I hadn't taken charge!'

'You always come to my rescue, don't you, Mike?'

'Oh sure, Lancelot's my middle name!' He grinned.

'I'm sorry to be asking so many questions. But you look . . . different.'

Mike laughed. 'You mean it's the first time you've seen me dressed in anything that didn't come from old Schindler's "hand-me-down" store.' He pulled his chair over to my bed and leant forward enthusiastically.

'I've cracked the Big Apple, kid. Me, Mike Janowski! The schmuck from the Lower East Side, who spent most of the time running about with the seat of his pants practically out, has finally made it.'

'But how . . . I mean, that's wonderful. But *how*?' A sudden thought. 'You're not in any trouble, are you, Mike?'

'Hell, do I look like a gangster? Television, baby. That's the gravy train. The movies are dying or dead. Television is big business, and it's a young man's game.'

'I knew you worked for a TV company in the city but I didn't think you got the kind of money that would buy a two-hundred-dollar jacket.'

'I didn't. I sure as hell didn't! You may find it kinda strange but, even when I was a kid, I used to listen to the comedy shows on the radio and I'd try to make up jokes for my favourite stars. It was one of the things that kept me sane wading through those mounds of dirty dishes at that damned drug store. It was a sort of private thing with myself. I never told anybody.'

'Not even me!' I interrupted.

'Not even you, Beccy. Perhaps I was a weird kid, I don't know.'

'We had a pretty weird childhood.'

'Yeah. But we didn't know it at the time, did we? I mean, it wasn't as if we'd come down in the world. That greasy, stinking apartment building . . . it was the only home we knew. What were our horizons? East of the Bowery and north of the Manhattan Bridge forged more than physical boundaries. Well, I'm out of it, Beccy. I've gotten free. And how? Jokes!'

'Jokes?'

'Yeah. The top shows on TV are comedies. Our studio makes one of the best, *The Sid Caesar Show*. I nearly drove the producer mad asking him to read my gags and sketches. Well, finally he did and he liked them. Sid liked them . . . I got on the team!'

'Hence the two-hundred-dollar jacket?'

'Hell, no, kid! Being one of the team pays but not that much. You hear of *One and One*?'

I shook my head. 'Should I?'

'You sure should! It's just about the hottest show back home . . . and I created it.'

'Mike!' I was truly dumbfounded. Since that bitter argument when I'd moved in with John, I'd kept in touch with Mrs Janowski but not Mike. She always said he was doing fine but we'd been abroad a lot the last year and although I'd sent postcards and letters, I'd had little news of the Janowskis.

'You see, I got to thinking . . .' by now Mike was pacing up and down the room in his excitement, 'everything seemed to me to be so middle-aged! Phil Silvers . . . Sid Caesar . . . George Burns . . . They're all great but what was there for people of our generation to watch? Then I got the idea for *One and One*.'

'Makes two?'

'Exactly! It's a show about newly weds but not sentimental. More like a younger version of Tracy and Hepburn. Very sharp. Very New York. The wife's feminine but she's not dumb like, say, Lucille Ball or

Gracie Allen. She knows how to stick up for herself. She's loving but kinda feisty.' He grinned at me. 'A bit like you, I guess. The husband's pushy. He works for a recording company and, although he wants his dinner on the table when he comes home, he knows that times have changed and his wife's life can't revolve around him. It's warm. There's a lot of conflict. And, oh boy, do the public love it! It's different, you see.'

'I'm so proud of you, Mike.'

'I wrote a couple of scripts to see how it would work out then I showed them to my producer. He wasn't sure, but I persuaded him to pitch them to CBS. The rest is history! Twenty-six episodes a year, Beccy! I co-produce and head a team of writers.'

'Is that . . .' I indicated the typed pages, '. . . what you were reading when I woke up?'

'Yes.' He came and took my hand. 'I'm sorry, Beccy, I've got to get back. I wouldn't have dreamed of leaving you even for a little while you were still so sick. But now . . .'

'Of course you must go. It was marvellous of you to come at all. I mean, how did you know what had happened?'

Mike looked sad. 'Oh, baby, you're such a kid still, aren't you? In spite of everything. Do you really imagine that what happened and the fact that you and John were together wouldn't have been splashed across the front page of every rag in the States? It's got all the ingredients. Multi-millionaire businessman . . . highly respected . . . not officially separated from his wife . . . young mistress half his age . . .'

'Don't! Oh, please, don't go on! It all sounds so sordid and it wasn't like that, Mike. It really wasn't. I . . . I truly loved John. At first, I was dazzled, flattered by his interest in me. I'll never understand why he found me attractive. Perhaps I was a novelty, I truly don't know. But afterwards . . .'

I thought for a moment, trying to convey to Mike even a fraction of my feelings for John. 'Afterwards the age difference didn't matter. Our backgrounds didn't matter. We were just . . . complete with each other.' We were silent for a moment. Both engrossed in our thoughts.

'I envy him,' Mike said softly.

I couldn't speak. There were no words that would adequately express my gratitude. But if Mike wanted something more than gratitude, more than loving friendship, sadly I had nothing to offer him.

Mike left for the States the next day. He intended to fly back as soon as I could leave the clinic and take me home.

'Perhaps your staying with us will make Doll move Uptown! I'm renting an apartment just off the Park. There's plenty of room for her but she refuses to move. She visits but she won't move!' He grinned suddenly. 'She says every old person she knows who has moved out of the old building dies within six months! I mean, hell! They'd probably have died sooner if they'd stayed where they were, but once Doll gets an idea in her head . . . Well, you know!'

'I sure do! Give her my love.'

He kissed me lightly on the forehead.

'See you soon, kid.' He gave me a card. 'My home number and my direct line number at the studio. Anything you want, you just have to call.' And with that he was gone.

I felt utterly lost and lonely after he left. It was selfish of me to want him back by my side. I knew from Mrs Janowski that at one time Mike had thought he was in love with me. His actions since the accident and his care of me indicated that perhaps she was right and he still felt the same. I loved him, but as a brother, a life-long friend, not as a lover.

I hadn't had the heart, or perhaps the guts, to tell Mike that I doubted I'd go back to the States when I left the clinic. I really didn't think I could bear to be in New York without John. And if as Mike said the Press were likely to hound me, I didn't want to make my misery public property.

An idea was beginning to form in my mind. A lot would depend on my finances. I'd had a very generous allowance from John, and Briony's attorney Mr Castleman had invested my five thousand dollars for me, so I knew I had some funds. What I wanted to do was to go back to Moreton for a while. Not the rectory. I could never afford that, but perhaps I could rent one of the small cottages dotted around the estuary. I wanted to give myself time to mourn John, to come to terms with my grief. In New York I knew I would try to shut his memory out. But I felt that at Moreton, where we'd been so happy, I could open my mind and my heart to him. To say, he may be dead but he's here . . . and here . . . and here. He would walk by me as I crunched across the shingle to the sand that was revealed as the tide ebbed. And when I sat, as we often had on the coarsely grassed banks that rose steeply from the shore, watching the sea birds flying low over the water, then diving for some small fish, I knew I would not be alone.

In the days that followed Mike's departure I had two further visits. The first visit was bizarre, the second deeply hurtful.

The weather was balmy and warm even though it was early October. The clinic was inland from Juan-les-pins, built among pine woods. Some of the trees had been cleared and the house was surrounded by well-kept lawns. I'd asked the nurse to take me outside. My ribs were no longer so painful and the blinding headaches that had plagued me were beginning to ease. My ankle was still in plaster and so I was helped into a wheelchair and pushed out on to the terrace. A few other patients sat basking in the Mediterranean sunshine. The nurse chatted to me as she wheeled me outside.

I was grateful that Mike had found an English-speaking clinic. I had started to learn French but my grasp of the language was still very elementary. My nurse was an Englishwoman from Bedford. I remarked that she was a long way from home and she told me how she'd fallen in love with a dashing soldier in the Free French army and after the war they had married and returned to his family home.

'I had a choice: stay with my family and friends and people I'd known all my life, or make a fresh start with the man I loved. I've never regretted it − although the food took some getting used to!'

I thought that a lovely put-down. With French cuisine world renowned, and all the wonderful seafood you could eat along the Mediterranean coast, this kind, bustling little woman was still missing roast beef and Yorkshire pudding!

I sat on the terrace for a while, glancing now and then at the magazine the nurse had given me. Then I heard footsteps moving towards me across the flagstones.

'Miss Mandel?'

'Yes.'

'May I join you?'

'Of course.'

I saw a tall, elegant woman of about forty, perhaps

a little older. She was stylishly dressed in a Givenchy suit. Her jewellery was expensive, very expensive, but discreet. She carried a garden chair over to my side and sat. I suddenly remembered where I had seen her before.

'But we've met, haven't we? Just briefly on Susan Brownlow's yacht. How kind of you to visit me. Although . . . how did you find me?'

'Ah! I have friends along the coast. They asked the right questions of the right people . . . and so, here I am.'

'I hope the Press don't have the same access to your friends.'

'Believe me, they don't.'

'Then all's well.'

'Is it? I do hope so. When I heard of the accident, I was concerned for you, dear. Forgive me, this is a delicate subject, but how are you placed financially?'

'I hardly think . . .'

'Oh, I realise how impertinent the question seems. But, believe me, I have only your best interests at heart. I've seen so many girls in your position, beloved mistresses or expensive playthings, discarded by the man involved or, as in your case, dealt a cruel hand by fate. But the long and the short of their dilemma is that they are left without a protector.'

I smiled. 'This all sounds splendidly Victorian. Are you, by chance, representing a charity for fallen women?'

'Well, not exactly a *charity*. I have a proposition to put to you. There are no witnesses and if you choose to repeat what I am about to say to you, I shall deny it.'

' "Curiouser and curiouser." '

' "Said Alice." Quite! I shall start by reintroducing myself.'

'Yes, I'm sorry. We met so briefly before and I don't quite remember . . .'

'Why should you? A great tragedy has happened since then. I'm surprised that you remembered that we had met before.'

'Forgive me. I noticed your dress. It was so striking, so different.'

'Oh dear! That means that Yves Saint Laurent was wearing me, not me wearing his design! However brilliant the designer . . . and in my opinion he is a very brilliant young man. Did you know he was leaving Dior and starting his own House next year?'

I shook my head. In spite of my life with John, and for all Bruno's coaching, I still felt the cost of couturier clothes to be a little immoral. But my visitor was continuing: ' . . . a successful woman should never look like a fashion plate. It lacks . . .' she thought for a moment, choosing her words carefully ' . . . flair! Now, my dear, to business.'

'Business?' I was, by now, totally puzzled.

'Yes.' She handed me her card.

'Mrs Clare Deveney,' I read.

'The "Mrs" is purely a flag of convenience. My clients find it reassuring. I have never married and never will. I dislike men intensely.'

'Isn't that a little sweeping?'

'Not really. Tell me, have you never been to bed with another woman?'

'You mean . . .?'

'Of course I do! I'm not talking about going to bed to sleep. I mean sex.'

I had felt myself to be at least a little sophisticated but now I coloured. 'No, I have not!'

'Oh, my dear, you've missed such a lot! What could be more natural than women understanding exactly what pleases? A number of my girls are lesbians. It makes it

CHAMOMILE

so much easier. You can please a man physically but not be involved emotionally. Sex becomes a simple business transaction.'

'Have you . . . have you come here to procure me?'

'I have come here to ensure that a beautiful and striking young girl does not return to being — what was it? — a shop girl.' She laughed. 'I don't run a brothel, my dear. I introduce a few well-chosen young women to rich men who are prepared to pay for their services. My girls are not prostitutes or call-girls, they are courtesans. And when the liaison is over there is money in the bank and no hard feelings.'

I struggled to keep my voice calm. To contain my anger. 'Mrs . . . *Miss* Deveney, two weeks ago the man I loved very much was killed. Whatever fine words you may use, you are inviting me to enter a life of prostitution. You mistake both my relationship with John Kimberly and my character.' I tore her business card in half and handed it to her. 'Good afternoon.'

Clare Deveney slipped the torn card into her handbag and then rose. She appeared unruffled by my reaction.

'Maybe you'll be lucky and meet another Kimberly. But if you don't, when you're worn down by a life of drudgery, your looks have gone and you're broke, you'll regret this. Goodbye, my dear. I doubt that we'll meet again. You see, I only move in the very *best* circles.'

I watched her elegant figure as she walked away from me. She could have passed anywhere as a successful businesswoman, the wife of a Senator, a woman of independent means. Instead she was a 'Madam'. I shuddered. Scratch the fashionable jet-setting world and you found men and women without pride. Ambition, yes, but no pride. Men and women not only willing to sell themselves sexually but in every conceivable way to satisfy the hedonistic cravings of the rich. Drugs. Procuring not only women but young children of both sexes. Accommodating voyeurism. Conspiring to gratify perverts. A vast twilight world existed to pander and to supply. Although it was impossible not to brush against it, John had despised that world. I was certainly not going to become a part of it now. If, and this was doubtful, I was ever to return to the life that he had opened my eyes to, then it would be because I had earned my place there and not as a piece of merchandise.

Three days later I had my second visitor. The sun was very hot that day and I had asked for my chair to be pushed among the pines, where there was a view of the sea. A slight breeze blew in from the Golfe Juan and for a while, sitting there, the pain and grief of the last two weeks seemed to slip from me and I was at peace.

My tranquillity was interrupted by my friendly little nurse bustling over from the house.

'Miss Mandel, you have a visitor. Do you feel well enough to see him?'

'Him?' I was surprised by the happiness I felt. 'Do you mean Mr Janowski's back already?'

'I'm afraid not, dear. It's a Mr Kimberly.'

I stared at her for a moment, not comprehending, and looked towards the house. My heart lurched because I thought I saw John standing on the terrace, looking across the lawns towards me. The nurse handed me a visiting card. It read, '*John Kimberly, Jr*'.

'Yes, I'll see him. Thank you.'

A few moments later John's elder son was walking towards me across the well-kept lawn. The resemblance between them was striking. The same build. Tall and loose-limbed with the walk of a natural athlete. But there was an arrogance in his son's bearing that was not John's.

He stopped in front of my wheelchair and looked at me for several seconds. He wasn't really like his father at all. John's eyes had been hazel. This young man's were a steely blue. At last he spoke.

'Well, well. I can see why my father made such a damned fool of himself over you.'

'I can't think what possible reply I çan make to that and so I'll simply say "Good afternoon." Although from your manner you obviously haven't come here as a friend.'

'I don't make friends with whores. I might screw them occasionally but that's all they're any good for.'

'Perhaps you would like to explain two things and then leave. How did you find me? And what exactly do you want?'

'I checked at Sunnybank . . .'

'Sunnybank?'

'The Anglo-American hospital in Cannes. As my name was Kimberly they saw no harm in telling me where Janowski had spirited you away to. By the way, is Janowski another lover? Exactly how many men were you two-timing my father with?'

'Mike Janowski is a family friend. I don't have to answer your stupid question, but I will. I was entirely faithful to your father. I loved him very much. He was a fine, intelligent, gentle man . . . I'm at a loss to understand how he could have produced such an uncouth son!'

His face flushed with anger at that. 'I didn't come here to make pretty speeches to my father's whore. I came to tell you that he left you one million dollars.'

'What?'

'And that my family intend that you will never get a penny of it. We'll go to court. Say that my father was a foolish man, obsessed with a scheming young woman of questionable morals, who exerted undue influence through sexual favours. We might not win but we'll drag your name through the mud.'

'And your father's name, too. Don't you care about that?'

'It'll be worth it to stop you getting your greedy little hands on my family's money.'

I stared at him for a moment.

'I pity you. If your father's memory means so little to you, *you're* the one motivated by greed.' I shook my head. 'John loved you. How could he had been so wrong about someone so close? The last thing I would ever do is let you besmirch your father's name. Do you have a notebook or diary with you?'

'Yes. Why?'

'I'm going to give you the name and address of my attorney.' I gave him Mr Castleman's name and address. 'I will instruct him to draw up papers renouncing any claim on your father's estate.'

It was his turn to be dumbfounded. 'Are you serious?'

'As we're discussing an inheritance of one million dollars I'm hardly likely to be joking! There is one condition: your father set up a trust fund to educate my brother Aaron. I very much doubt that the trust can be broken but I want written assurances from your attorney that the trust will stand until my brother has finished his education. At some time in the future I'll pay you back every penny, with interest! Do we have a deal?'

There was a pause while he looked at me. Then he shook his head. 'I just don't understand you.'

'You don't have to understand me . . . you simply have to agree or disagree with the offer I'm making. It will be open for forty-eight hours. After that . . .' I shrugged

' . . . I'll see you in court, as they say. If you want time to think about it, please do. If you're going to accept here and now, please do it quickly as I'd like you out of my sight as soon as possible.'

'I accept. I'll wire my attorney to contact your . . . ' he glanced at the note he had made, 'Mr Castleman. Castleman! Another Jew?' he sneered.

'He's an honourable man. That's all you need to know. Now, please go.'

The meeting had been a terrible strain and I could feel the tears start to well behind my eyes. I willed him to go while I could still hang on to my composure.

Mercifully, he turned on his heel and walked quickly away from me. I forced myself to sit upright in my chair in case he looked back. Strangely, halfway across the lawn, he did. He stopped, then turned and stared at me for a few moments, his expression puzzled. When eventually he walked briskly into the house, I held on for another few seconds then slumped in my chair and gave in to my tears. I tried to pull myself together. 'For whom are you crying?' I asked myself angrily. 'For myself! Just once I have the right to cry for myself!' I put my head in my hands and wept.

A sudden gust of wind from the sea blew my hair around my face. I heard John's voice so clearly telling me the first time he had seen me with my hair down: 'You are positively forbidden ever to drag it back in that Plain Jane hairstyle again!' And then he was there, his arms around me, comforting me. I felt his presence so strongly that if I could have taken my hands from my tear-stained eyes I must, I surely must, have seen him.

The wind died as suddenly as it had sprung up. A faint breeze ruffled the pine needles. Occasionally a cone dropped, or was it a squirrel leaping from tree to tree?

Otherwise silence. I was alone again. But I knew I hadn't been only moments before.

A week passed. I was getting much stronger. The headaches had virtually disappeared. In another day the plaster on my ankle would be taken off and, if all was well, I could leave the clinic.

I had made two telephone calls after the hateful visit from John's son. The first to Mr Castleman to explain the situation with the Kimberly family and to tell him of the agreement I had come to. He was outraged and urged me to fight but I was adamant. If the car crash had interested the Press to the extent that Mike had outlined, then any court case would be a sensation. Everything John had achieved, the way he had built up his business, his war record, his generosity to many charities, would be forgotten in the rush to titillate the Great American Public with stories about his love, or as they would call it – lust, for a young mistress.

I also arranged to have my possessions cleared from the apartment John had rented for me and put into store until I knew where I was going to live. I told Mr Castleman of my plans to return to Moreton. To give myself some space before I faced up to the future. He wired money to the clinic to cover my travel expenses and I promised to let him know as soon as I was settled in England.

A much more painful call was the one I made to Mike to tell him I wouldn't be returning to New York. He was disappointed but understanding. 'I was looking forward to having you around, kid. It would've been like old times. Still, I take it you're not going to bury yourself in that East Anglian marsh forever?'

I assured him I wasn't. I just had to be alone for a while.

'Any time you need me, Beccy, I'm just a phone call away. You know that, don't you?'

'Yes, I know that. How can I ever repay you? You've been the most wonderful friend.'

'Cut it out, Beccy. Want to hear a grown man cry? Keep in touch, won't you? I don't want to lose you again.'

I laughed. 'I'll probably be a millstone around your neck until we're both old and grey.'

There was a momentary pause and then Mike replied softly, 'I think I'd kinda like that.' Then he was his old breezy self again. 'Chin up, kid! I'll keep an eye on Aaron for you. Hey, this really *is* like old times.'

And, before I could send my love to Mrs Janowski, he hung up.

Mike had contacted Aaron as soon as he had arrived in France and knew how I was. I'd only had one letter from my brother, which surprised me, but then he was very young and, like so many young boys, totally self-absorbed. Even so, a small voice inside me said, 'You're his only sister and you nearly died.' But I brushed those thoughts aside. Aaron was, after all, Aaron.

The next problem to be faced was my bill at the clinic. My clothes and personal belongings were still at the Hôtel Cap d'Antibes, and my jewel case in their safe. I'd never wanted to wear or to own a lot of jewellery though I had some rather fine pieces that I loved. John had wanted to buy me more but I'd refused. I simply wasn't interested in hoarding gems that would have to be kept most of the time in a security vault. Looking to the future, it was inevitable that I would have to sell my jewellery though I hoped to keep perhaps one or two pieces of particular sentimental value. How soon I would have to start selling depended on the size of the bill presented by the clinic.

I'd had a private ward, excellent treatment and considerate nursing. I couldn't imagine it would all come cheaply on the French Riviera.

By then I was managing to hobble about with the aid of sticks and arranged to have a meeting with the business administrator of the clinic. To my astonishment I was told that they had been instructed not to present me with a bill. Mr John Kimberly Jr had arranged that he would settle the account personally.

After my meeting with him I simply couldn't believe that. 'Surely there's been some mistake?'

The administrator, a rather severe-looking woman in her mid-fifties, smiled thinly.

'I can assure you, Miss Mandel, the settlement of our accounts is something we do not make mistakes about. Mr Kimberly made the arrangements after his visit to you. We also received a wire this morning from Mr Janowski asking for your bill to be sent to him. It seems your friends are anxious to help you in this matter.'

Her manner made it clear that she thought me a young woman of low morals, with rather too many men in her life.

'Which gentleman would you like me to send the account to? I assume you have a preference.'

I thought for a moment. Although Mike was clearly enjoying great success, it had been very recent and I had no idea how well off he really was. Also, he was in a notoriously fickle profession where artists, writers and directors were only as good as their last show. What if his next project was a failure? He'd need every penny he had. On the other hand I loathed the idea of taking money from John's obnoxious son . . . And yet . . . there must be some good, some kindness in him to lead him to make such a generous offer. Or was it simply a guilty conscience?

The administrator started to drum her fingers on her desk in an irritated fashion. I was taking too long to make up my mind. Well, I was already committed to paying the Kimberlys back for Aaron's education; I might as well get further into debt to them and save Mike's money.

'Thank you. Will you arrange to send the bill to Mr Kimberly please? I hope to leaving tomorrow. I'm very grateful for the care I've had here. The medical staff have been so kind.' I gave a slight emphasis to the word 'medical', and the administrator flushed as she understood my meaning. However, I gave her no time to comment.

'Good morning.' I rose from the chair opposite her desk and, with as much dignity as I could muster, hobbled to the door. Not the best of exits but at least I'd had the last word.

Back in my room I moved to the window and looked out. Through the pine forest you could catch glimpses of the sea. It was very beautiful but how I wished with all my heart that we'd never come to France! If we hadn't, or if we'd driven straight back to Cap d'Antibes instead of taking the road to Grasse, perhaps John would still be alive. If . . . if . . . if . . . but there was no turning back. I was alone now and, if all went well tomorrow, I would soon be returning to Moreton.

THE HERB

BALM

'Is sovereign for the brain, strengthening the
memory and powerfully chasing away melancholy'
John Evelyn

THE WOMAN

PART THREE: BALM
BECCY 1961–1963

'. . . It lies
Deep-meadow'd, happy, fair with orchard lawns,
And bowery hollows crown'd with summer sea,
Where I will heal me of my grievous wound.'
Alfred, Lord Tennyson

CHAPTER TWELVE

And so I came to Munkyns. I'd spent a week staying in a comfortable but hardly grand pub in Baildon, the small market town near Moreton-Juxta-Mare. There were three estate agents in the town. None of them had many properties to let. The choice seemed to be between rather grand, well-furnished houses, which I couldn't afford, or tiny cottages out on the wind-swept marshes, so derelict that even the most dedicated Anglophile couldn't pass them off as 'quaint'.

I was beginning to think I must have been crazy to give in to my urge to come back to Moreton and its surrounds. Then one of the agents telephoned me at The Blue Boar to say that a property had just come on to his books that might be suitable.

The cottage was on the estuary just outside Moreton. John and I had walked every inch of the sea wall that stopped the wide rough waters flooding the fields along its banks. I knew exactly where the cottage was although I had only caught a glimpse of it through the unkempt hawthorn hedge that surrounded it. As the agent drove me out to view it, I prayed that this property wouldn't be in the advanced stage of dereliction that the other small houses had been in.

The road to Moreton was so familiar. The small villages, the farms with their grazing cattle and sheep. And always, through the fields, a view of the river that runs into the estuary and on into the sea.

We turned into the village street, the rectory on our right. Don't look back! Don't look back unless it is with gratitude and joy for those happy, happy days. The church stood opposite the rectory with, as always, a large sign outside showing the amount of money raised to restore its tower. Then we drove past The Cage, the old village lock-up where criminals were held until they could be taken to the gaol house in Baildon. The last person to be held there was a suspected German spy in the First World War. He, poor devil, simply turned out to be an elderly birdwatcher. After The Cage stood a low terrace of very old houses, said locally to have been a monks' dormitory offering shelter to pilgrims on their way to worship at the ancient chapel on the marshes.

Just before the unsurfaced track that led to the chapel, another turned off the road. It ran parallel with the sea wall and at the end of it stood Munkyns.

I asked the agent about the cottage's name. 'Supposed to have belonged once to the great priory at Colchester. The cottage is old, very old, that's for sure, but whether the story about the monks is true or not I couldn't say. Can't move hereabouts without coming across tales of monks and pilgrims. And smugglers, of course,' he added gloomily.

We bumped along the track which led into the large, desperately over-grown garden.

'I hope the interior is more prepossessing than the outside!' I said fervently.

'Oh, shouldn't be too bad. This place belongs to the farm, and is a tied cottage. The widow of one of the farm workers rented it. The garden got a bit much for the old girl. She's gone to live with her daughter and son-in-law in one of the new council houses, so the farmer's willing to let it until he decides what to do with it.'

The key to the front door was a vast piece of iron that looked as if it was meant to unlock the dungeons at the Tower of London. But the old oak door swung back on well-oiled hinges, which in itself was encouraging.

My first impression of the interior was that the former tenant had an unfortunate preference for peppermint-green paint.

'Was she colour blind, do you think?' I asked.

The estate agent grinned. 'Looks like it!' He started to wander around. 'But this really isn't too bad, you know. The beams haven't been boarded in, neither has the fireplace. That's quite something nowadays.'

I looked around and, apart from the green paint, liked what I saw. The front door opened directly into the living room, which was large and sunny. Heavy oak beams – probably ship's timbers from a wreck, the agent told me – covered the ceiling. The walls were roughly plastered with stud work left showing. The floor was flagstones with a few grubby rugs thrown down on them. But it was the fireplace that drew me. It was huge, taking up nearly the whole of one wall. The mortar between the brickwork was crumbling in places but even so the fireplace looked as if it would last for another few centuries. Over the hearth was an oak bressummer, intricately carved.

A door beside the fireplace led into a narrow passageway, one side of which was taken up by the depth of the fireplace. It must have been at least six feet deep. The passage led to another much smaller room, an inner hall really, and from here rather rickety old stairs went up to the upper floor. The agent thought that these two rooms would have been the original Hall House, possibly built as early as the twelfth or thirteenth century. From this inner room another door opened into the newer cross-wing. 'Newer' in the sense that it was probably added when Elizabeth I reigned over England! What must have been a long, beautifully proportioned room had been crudely partitioned to create a kitchen at the back. It was sparsely furnished and pretty dirty, but at least the cottage had been wired for electricity and so there was a stove and a rather dangerous-looking primitive water heater over the sink, which was deep and made of fire-clay. The whole effect was dingy and mean.

'Why on earth did they put this partition up? The whole room would've made a beautiful farmhouse kitchen.'

The agent shrugged. 'This was probably done about forty or fifty years ago. They had pretty big families then. Perhaps they needed the front part as an extra bedroom, or gran and granddad lived with them. Who knows?'

'Who indeed!'

We went through a low plank door to a fuel store tucked under the cat-slide roof in the older part of the building. A door from this led to an evil-smelling bathroom. Well, I thought, at least there's a septic tank! Most of the other cottages I'd seen had no bathroom and a chemical lavatory at the end of the garden. Although we'd had to share a lavatory with two other families in the tenement, at least it had flushed.

Upstairs there was further evidence of a large family. The rooms had been partitioned into a mass of little cubicles. The only saving grace was the large room in the cross-wing. This, mercifully, had been left alone. The ceiling was low and the floor sloped alarmingly, but there was a breathtaking view from the casement window across the ploughed fields to the sea wall and the estuary beyond.

Strangely, this room seemed to have been used as a storage room, the widow apparently preferring to sleep in one of the tiny, misformed bedrooms. I asked the agent why he thought this was. He looked apologetic, his desire to let the place struggling with a basic honesty misplaced in a member of his profession.

'You wouldn't think it on a lovely, sunny autumn day like this but when it blows in these parts, by heck it blows! Straight across the North Sea from the Russian steppes. Best to be cosy in winter.'

I thought for a moment. 'Look,' I said, 'you don't by any chance have another call to make in the area? I am interested, but I'd like to have, say, half an hour here on my own to get the feel of the place.'

'Well, I don't have any other business in the area but . . .' he grinned almost boyishly, ' . . . the publican who runs The Three Horseshoes in the village is a mate of mine. I could pop down there, wet my whistle and be back in half an hour or so. How would that do?'

'Just fine. Thank you.'

He set off with the jaunty step of one playing truant.

I watched his car bump off down the track, then went and sat in the living room. The cottage was being let furnished. Presumably the farmer had bought the widow's bits and pieces when she'd moved. The furnishings were pretty ugly but that's what I'd been used to until I met John. From rags to riches and back again, I thought wryly. If my limited resources could run to a few bright new rugs and some material to make new drapes the place, although not transformed, would be considerably more welcoming.

'What the hell am I doing here?' I asked myself. Apart from the time in England I'd spent with John, I'd lived all my life in intensely urban areas. I had never spent a day in the tenement without hearing some sort of noise from neighbours, whether it be laughter, a marital row or just the radio. The Jews had, by tradition, clung together in an alien land. I was a child of the ghetto. And yet here I was, planning to live a life of almost total solitude in a once beautiful, but now ramshackle, old house in one of the remotest parts of East Anglia. Was this what I really wanted?

And yet, as I sat there, the whole house seemed to welcome me. As I surrendered to its atmosphere I felt a sense of belonging, of peace, that I hadn't known since that dreadful day on the way to Grasse. Perhaps the house wanted me to live here. After all, only a couple of generations ago my family had lived a peasant existence. Was that what was calling me? And then I thought, 'This house needs to be loved. It needs someone not simply to eke out a day-to-day existence here, but someone to wash and scrub, help heal its wounds. Someone who will try to make it beautiful again.' Well, if the house needed to be loved, I needed something to love. Something to do with my life. A way of using my energies so that at night I'd go to bed exhausted, too tired to dream of John.

I walked across to the fireplace and touched the bressummer. 'Well, old house,' I said rather idiotically, 'you've won! I'm coming to live here!'

CHAPTER THIRTEEN

I struck a deal with the estate agent: a quarter's rent in advance with an option to rent for a further quarter. I asked him to get permission from the farmer for me to redecorate. I really didn't feel I could live with the peppermint-green paint. Bruno would have had a nervous breakdown if he'd seen it! I also wanted permission to remove the partitioning around the kitchen and make one large room again. The agent didn't think this would be a problem but would have to confirm it with the farmer.

I planned to move in almost immediately and more or less camp out while I cleaned up the house. I knew I wanted to use the large room in the upstairs part of the cross-wing as my bedroom, and hang the easterly winds! If I could make at least one more bedroom habitable that would be fine for Aaron if he could come over and stay. The air fare was a big factor though.

The next day I dashed about Baildon doing some basic shopping. Although the widow's old bedstead was a rather nice brass affair, I didn't fancy her mattress. So I bought the cheapest I could find and some bed linen. Cleaning materials I could buy from the cavernous shop in the village, that seemed to sell everything from cornflakes to bicycle repair kits. I also wanted to buy the basic ingredients I needed to start making cosmetics again. I'd no idea what my outlet would be, but I wanted to try to make some money selling my products.

Especially as I had, potentially, access to more herbal and plant ingredients than I'd ever had before.

I made a list of the things I would need to buy from the chemist's shop. In my mind, I kept calling it a drug store. Who was it who said the English and Americans were divided by a common language? Lanolin, almond oil, borax, glycerine, rose water, orange-flower water, bees-wax, oil of lavender . . . the list seemed endless.

The chemist's shop was in the oldest part of Baildon. It had quaintly bowed windows and, behind the counter, the original apothecary's drawers. Rows and rows of little compartments still with their contents' name painted on the front in gold. The chemist was a tall, thin, elderly man, rather forbidding in his manner but actually a dear. I was enchanted by his name which sounded as if it came straight out of Dickens – Archibald Crabtree. To my delight he had absolutely everything I wanted. He also agreed to sell me some plain brown glass jars and bottles.

'Forgive my asking, miss, but I am intrigued by your purchases. Dare I ask what you intend to use them for?'

I explained about my mother's recipes and how we'd sold to the drug store back home. I smiled at him. 'I don't suppose I can interest you in a similar deal?'

He thought for a moment. Then, 'I don't see why not. Back to nature seems to be all the rage nowadays, so why not herbal skin care? I'll try a few. You choose what you think are your best sellers. Strictly sale or return, miss. Anything I sell we'll split fifty-fifty. How's that?'

'Fifty-fifty? I do all the work.'

'I pay rent and rates on my shop.'

'How about forty-sixty in my favour? And I get the ingredients at cost.'

Mr Crabtree thought for a moment, then laughed. 'You drive a hard bargain, my dear, but I think I can accommodate you.' He held out his hand and we shook on the deal.

I warned him that the products would only have a shelf life of three months, four at the outside, as they lacked preservatives.

'Mmm. Perhaps we can work on that. Still, first things first. Let's see how they sell.'

I walked out into the High Street the happiest I'd been for ages. I had something to do and somewhere to sell. I went next to Baildon's one and only, but very good, book shop. I wanted to buy every book I could about herbs. Also anything they had about identifying wild herbs. I knew from the herb book in the library at the rectory that there were a number of interesting wild herbs growing locally. In particular I wanted to find marsh mallow as I had a recipe for a face pack that used its root. One of the things I was determined to do in the long winter evenings that lay ahead was to study the composition of the herbs in my recipes. I knew that the beauty products worked, but I didn't know *why*.

Apart from my experiment with making a moisturiser the day before Briony's funeral, I had simply followed age-old recipes, hardly giving thought to why a particular herb was good for a certain skin condition but not for another. The products I and my mother had made were simply a means to an end. We sold to earn money. Now I wanted to understand. I was privileged to have in my possession rare, perhaps unique, recipes but, since a little girl, I had been practising the ancient craft of herbalism without thought or knowledge.

I bought a number of books, practically everything they had on the subject. I also made a couple of 'finds' in their second-hand section: *Herbal Delights*, published in 1937, and *Herb-Lore for Housewives*, published in 1938. The latter had the most moving prayer from an old herbal in its preface:

> *'Whatsoever Herb thy power dost produce, give, I pray, with good will to all Nations to save them, and grant me this my medicine. Those who rightly receive these herbs from me, do thou make them whole.'*

Make them whole . . . that was, I supposed, what I was seeking from herbs. Not as the prayer meant but to give a purpose to a life that now had to be lived without John.

I dropped my purchases off at The Blue Boar and then made my last shopping call in Baildon. The landlord's wife had recommended to me an old-established grocers at the top of the High Street, Collins'. I could buy most of my food at the village stores in Moreton, but I knew from my time at the rectory that the cheese was definitely mouse-trap and the watery ham came from a large tin. So much for the myth of English rural life! I knew that for the coming weeks I would be virtually skivvying to make Munkyns in some way habitable, and I'd therefore have neither the time nor the inclination to do much cooking for myself. The kitchen was the first priority as it was unthinkable that I could make my skin-care products in such dirty surroundings. I wasn't seeking mouth-watering provisions, just something pleasantly edible to see me through the first days at Munkyns.

A quaintly old-fashioned brass bell tinkled as I opened the wooden, glass-panelled door to Collins'. I looked around and was enchanted. I was in an Aladdin's cave of groceries. It was as if I'd stepped back a hundred years in time. Large sacks of various dark sugars were lined against one wall. Jostling for space on the shelves above were containers of wild dried apricots from Afghanistan, Turkish sultanas, Greek currants, Muscatels from Spain. But, joy of joys, behind the wooden counter, row upon row of old-fashioned sweet jars containing every dried herb and spice you could imagine. Because the drying process evaporates the essential oils, I had only one recipe using dried herbs. The exception was for a face pack using dried elder flowers. Unsurprisingly I had never been able to buy that ingredient in our neighbourhood! But there it was. The herbs were sold by the ounce and the assistant must have thought me slightly mad when I bought a pound of elder flowers.

Then over to the cheese and bacon counter. There was a huge variety of cheeses. This counter was presided over by Mrs Collins herself, a plump, twinkling woman who looked rather like one of her cottage loaves. Any cheese I was interested in she insisted I try. 'Better safe than sorry, my dear!' After a very pleasurable time selecting cheeses, I bought local honey, cider vinegar and ground almonds for my recipes. Also free-range eggs and a locally cured bacon from Dunmow.

Mrs Collins asked me if I'd heard of the Dunmow Flitch. I hadn't. Every year, she explained, couples living in the village of Dunmow competed for a side of bacon, called a flitch. They had to prove that for the whole of the last year they had lived together in total harmony without even one cross word. Having heard the sound of marital disharmony coming from virtually every apartment, I cynically doubted whether any couple from our tenement would have made it even to first base!

That evening, my last at The Blue Boar, I wrote long letters to Mike, to Bruno and to Aaron, letting them know where I was going to be living and how I was. Physically

I was much improved. My ankle was still strapped and I'd had instructions from the clinic to arrange for physiotherapy. As soon as I was settled, I'd do that at Baildon's Cottage Hospital. Emotionally I was still devastated but trying to live one day at a time. Trying to fill every second of the day to ease the pain. But the nights . . . oh, the nights! Waking or sleeping, and then dreaming, I was obsessed by my loss. But I was determined that none of my anguish would creep into my letters, so I concentrated on writing, if not cheerful, at least positive letters to the dearest people in my life.

As usual I had a glass of cider and a light evening meal in the bar. The locals were friendly but never intrusive, for which I was profoundly grateful. At about nine o'clock the estate agent who had arranged the letting of Munkyns called in to give me the key and the tenancy agreement. He'd spoken with the farmer who owned the cottage and reported that he'd been totally indifferent as to whether or not I redecorated or knocked down the partitions. I was immensely cheered by the latter information as I knew I'd be spending a great deal of time in the kitchen and had found it a very depressing, bleak place. I'd no idea how you took down a partition but, as it had looked a pretty flimsy affair, I assumed you attacked it with as much brute force as it was possible to muster. I remembered seeing an axe in the fuel store, also a box of old but purposeful-looking tools on a shelf. I'd start with the axe and work my way through the box. If the partition was still standing after that, it wouldn't be for want of demolition attempts.

I'd arranged for the mattress to be delivered late morning. The rest of my purchases and belongings I packed into a taxi immediately after breakfast the next day. The driver helped me into the cottage with everything, then looked around with the seasoned mistrust of the town dweller.

'You going to be all right here, miss?'

'Of course I am!' I replied with rather more assurance than I actually felt. 'Why shouldn't I be?'

The driver gave me a look that I imagine would usually be reserved for inmates of Bedlam. 'Why shouldn't you be? Cos there's nothing bleeding here! Just water, fields, birds.' He shuddered. 'Nature!'

'I take it you don't think much of the country,' I said.

'You've said a mouthful there, dearie. I tried it once. Got a job on a farm, cottage and everything thrown in. Bloody hell! Nothing to do of an evening, and every morning at dawn you got deafened by ruddy bird-song. No, give me pavements any time.'

I prayed that he was wrong and I was right.

I have to admit that as I watched the taxi bump off down the track, I felt isolated. Then I shook myself. This was, after all, what I wanted. Or at least thought I wanted. I was extremely lucky, the weather was still holding. In fact, it was exceptionally warm and pleasant for November. I stood on my doorstep in the sunshine and looked around. I found my environment stunningly beautiful. Once again I was puzzled by my feelings for this place. Was it only because of the wonderfully happy weeks I'd spent here with John? Or was it that I'd hated the ghetto in which I'd been brought up so much, and this was in such total contrast, that I was inextricably drawn here? Then I thought about the chapel. It was well over a thousand years old. A place of pilgrimage and worship for centuries and centuries. Although I was not a Christian, one surely could not help being touched by such spirituality. Was there, perhaps, some rough magic here that was reaching out to me and offering comfort?

I turned and went into the cottage. Enough of daydreaming, of exploring my soul; my body needed to get to work. Last night in bed I had established my priorities. I needed a clean place to sleep, and a clean functioning kitchen. Also, while the earth was still warm, I needed to spend a certain amount of time clearing a plot in the garden so that I could plant herbs now for the spring. I had already begun to study my newly acquired herb books!

I looked around the living room and thought, 'What this place needs is a fire.' It was quite warm with the sun coming in through the windows but I felt a fire would give heart to the room. There were quite a few logs left in the fuel store, and the estate agent had said that I could buy more from the farm.

I felt heartened as the fire sprang into life and the flames from the kindling began to leap around the logs, which started to crackle as they caught alight.

I now felt ready to attack the ruined kitchen. The first priority was the partition. I went through to the fuel store at the back and picked up the axe. It was heavier than I'd anticipated but getting rid of that ugly wood partition had now become something of a crusade. I went into the front room in the cross-wing and swung the axe. There was a terrible noise of splintering wood. 'At least I'll have plenty of kindling,' I thought with a certain grim humour. I pulled the axe out of the wood with extreme difficulty. I was beginning to understand why my family had settled for life in a New York slum rather than the backwoods of America!

I was about to swing the axe again when I was interrupted by a laconic voice behind me.

'My God, it's Boadicea!'

I lowered the axe and swung around. I saw a good-looking, fair-headed young man in his late twenties leaning in the doorway, smiling at me. He was casually but expensively dressed for riding: tweed hacking jacket, checked shirt, jodhpurs and well-polished riding boots, carrying a cap in his hand. He was of medium build, almost stocky, but with the hard body of a sportsman.

'I'm . . . I'm sorry,' I said, a little breathless from my exertions. 'I didn't hear you arrive.'

He laughed. 'With the noise you were making, I doubt if you'd have heard the massed bands of the Coldstream Guards!' He moved further into the room and held out his hand to me. 'Hallo, there. I'm Kit D'Arcy.'

I transferred the axe to my left hand and then shook the proffered hand. His name seemed familiar to me.

'Kit . . . ?' I said, puzzled.

'Short for Christian. In a land dominated by the Church of England, such a name is a terrible cross to bear.'

'Thus Kit?' I said, amused by his irreverence.

'Also, it's shorter.'

'Kit D'Arcy . . . Now I remember. You're my landlord.'

He'd been a shadowy figure if I'd thought of him at all. The estate agent's constant use of the word 'farmer' had conjured up an image of a rosy-faced, rotund, old fellow with a pork pie hat and straw behind his ears. Certainly no one like Kit D'Arcy.

'Guilty as charged!' He looked around. 'I say, this is all pretty ramshackle, isn't it? I'm sorry. You see I only bought the farm . . . well . . . to be correct, my father only bought the farm for me a year ago and there's been a hell of a lot of work getting it into some sort of shape. I simply haven't had a chance to do anything about Munkyns.'

'It must have been a lovely old house once. And it suits me for the time being.'

He looked at me for a moment. 'Why on earth would a lovely young woman like you want to bury herself in a place like this?'

He must have caught an expression in my eyes. 'I'm sorry, that was damned impertinent of me. Why you're here is your business and none of mine. But at least let me help to make the place a bit more habitable.'

'There's really no need . . .'

'My dear girl, having seen your efforts with that axe, there's every need!' He laughed. His laughter was infectious and I joined in. 'Yes, I must look pretty ridiculous. I don't somehow think I'm cut out to be a handyman.'

'Tell you what, I'll send a couple of my chaps along to get this down for you, and then make good where it's been. And I'm sure I can get some women from the village to give you a hand to give the place a good clean out.'

'That's very kind, but I'm afraid I really can't afford to . . .'

'Who said anything about *you* affording it?'

I started to protest but he interrupted. 'I insist. Besides, I bet there's some Act on the Statute Books that would get me boiled in oil for letting a place in this condition. So you see, in my own interests I can't possibly take no for an answer!'

I hesitated for a moment, then shrugged.'Well, if you insist. I have to admit I've felt a bit daunted by what I've taken on.'

His eyes twinkled at me. 'You looked anything but daunted when I came in. My God, if the Saxons had you on their side the Danes would never have dared to land here! Well, I'd better get back to work.' He paused for a moment, then said sincerely, 'I do hope you find whatever it is you're looking for here.'

'Thank you,' I said, simply. 'So do I.'

I walked with him to the front door. He'd tied his horse to one of the old, gnarled apple trees in the garden. An elderly, chubby Labrador dog sat in the shade of the tree waiting patiently for him. It rose and wagged its tail as soon as Kit appeared.

'Goodbye. Thank you for your help.'

'Think nothing of it.' He smiled. 'I'm sure you're going to be a model tenant.'

He unhitched his horse's bridle and swung effortlessly into the saddle.

'When you're settled in, I do hope you'll come and have supper with me at the farm one night.'

'Thank you, I'd like that. As you say, when I've settled in.'

Then, with a wave of his hand, he turned his horse and rode away down the track. The old dog trotted gamely after him.

I turned and walked back into Munkyns. Well, old house, I thought, help is at hand.

CHAPTER FOURTEEN

The next week Munkyns hummed with activity. A couple
of hours after Kit D'Arcy had left, two brawny young
farm labourers, Fred and Eric, presented themselves and
informed me that 'The Guvnor' had sent them. I showed
them the partition and left them to get on with it while
I scrubbed out the room above that was to be my
bedroom.

By the time we stopped for a cup of tea that afternoon
− a very important interlude in England − the partition
was down and, although covered in dust and bits of wood
chippings, the main room in the cross-wing was restored
to its original proportions. Inspired by that success, I got
Fred and Eric to help me take down the boarding across
the old fireplace. We found a gem. An old, blackened
kitchen range and, to one side of it, the original bread
oven. So I had been right! This room had once been used
as the kitchen for the house. I had no illusions about
trying to cook on the range but, as my only means of
heating the house was by open fires, I could make the
new room cosy by burning logs in the fire box.

While Fred and Eric were bashing away, my mattress
was delivered and another delivery man drove away down
the track scratching his head at the insanity of my wanting
to live in such a place.

Before Fred and Eric left that evening they helped me
get the widow's old brass bedstead from one of the little
partitioned bedrooms and set it up in the upstairs room

in the cross-wing. At least I'd have somewhere to sleep that night.

As they were going I thanked them for their good-natured help, and tried to give them some money to have a drink on me in the pub that night. But they would have none of it. Eric turned in the doorway. 'We'll be back in the morning to clear up and do a bit of plastering. Pardon me asking, though, you going to be all right here by yourself?'

Would I never find one human soul who thought me sane to be living at Munkyns?

'Quite all right, thanks. See you tomorrow.'

He nodded and strode off after Fred. But he didn't seem convinced.

I spent the evening scrubbing and cleaning the living room. Looking at my hands, I thought ruefully that the first thing I'd better make was hand cream.

By ten o'clock I was utterly exhausted and ready for bed. I'd asked Fred if it was possible to keep an open fire in overnight and he'd told me to bank it down with wood ash and put one large log on to smoulder. 'That's what me gran always does . . . 'course me mum's got electric!' he added proudly. Well, I thought, if it's good enough for Fred's gran, it's good enough for me!

I lay in bed that night and thought back over the day. Was I in fact mad to come to Munkyns? I thought not. I knew my reasons for coming back to Moreton and they still seemed to hold good. Perhaps I was running away, but if in doing so I could make a bridge between my old life and whatever I could make of my future, was that such a bad thing?

I was terribly tired and my eyelids started to droop. The tide was turning in the estuary and the breeze it always seemed to bring rattled the casement windows. As

I drifted off to sleep, I knew I was alone but didn't feel lonely. Although the man I still deeply loved was buried in the family plot in New England, I could feel him near me. I fell into a deep, healing sleep. And if I had dreams that night, I awoke refreshed and unaware of them.

The morning was fine and sunny again — I was to learn by bitter experience how unusual such consistent weather was in England. Fred's gran proved to be right: the fire had stayed in. I put another couple of logs on. The fire was helping to rid the house of its unlived-in feeling. I made myself a coffee and wandered out into the garden. It was a sad sight, a sorry tangle of brambles and weeds and overgrown flowerbeds. I looked around. Given the age of the property, surely there must have been a herb garden here once. And, with knowledge gleaned from my herb books, I knew that even at that time of year rosemary, sage, thyme, possibly even mint in a sheltered position, should still be growing. At that moment, I happened to glance down the track that led to the road and was totally diverted by the sight of a flotilla of bicycles heading towards Munkyns.

In the lead, by a head, was Fred. He was closely followed by Eric. Then, a little way back, a tall, thin woman with hair an unlikely shade of red was wobbling along the track on an ancient, man's bicycle. Even with the wind against her, she managed to keep a lighted cigarette clamped between her lips. Bringing up the rear, pedalling furiously to keep up, was the female equivalent of the Michelin tyre man.

'Morning' . . . 'Morning' . . . 'Morning' . . . 'Morning' they chorused as they arrived. Fred made the introductions. The tall, thin woman was his Auntie Lil. The Michelin tyre lady was Auntie Lil's sister-in-law. Or, as Fred put it, 'My Auntie Ivy by marriage'. They'd come

191

to 'do' the old house. Auntie Lil swung her long legs over the cross-bar of her bicycle, displaying more than a glimpse of spotlessly clean, old-fashioned bloomers which were in surprising contrast to her bright red hair and dashingly made-up face. If it hadn't been for those bloomers, I'd have put Auntie Lil down as the village Delilah!

Within no time Munkyns rang with a cacophony of busy sounds. I couldn't believe that it was only a little over twenty-four hours since I'd left Baildon. On the way through the village, I'd stopped at the stores and bought cleaning materials and a large amount of white paint. Now everything was being put to use. Lil and Ivy were dusting, scrubbing, brushing like a pair of demons as if the dirt of centuries was a personal insult to them. I was determinedly obliterating the peppermint-green paint in the living room, and could hear Fred and Eric plastering and hammering, 'making good' the new kitchen.

I don't know quite what they made of me. There was a commune of sorts a little further up the coast, where Flower People tried to get back to nature. No doubt they thought me yet another barmy drop-out but their manner to me was friendly and kind. Mid-morning I made mugs of coffee, and we took them into the garden to drink. We laughed and chatted and teased as if we'd known each other for years. Why, I wondered, did I feel so at ease with these people? Then it came to me. However my life might have changed in the last two years, my roots were working-class. Although I had been totally at ease with John, I had found it difficult to adjust to mixing with the new people I'd met with him. People who, with the exception of Bruno, had such privileged backgrounds and life styles. Being with these people was like being back on the stoop, sharing worries, poverty and, yes, joys with each other, because we were all we had.

While we were in the garden I asked if they knew if marsh mallow grew thereabouts. They all fell about with laughter. Ivy was the first one to recover.

'Grow?' she wheezed. 'Bless you, your garden's covered in the blooming stuff!'

'Where?'

'There . . . there . . . over here . . . Oooh, you're going to have a job getting rid of that muck. Worse than ground elder.'

I didn't have the heart to tell them that the last thing I wanted to do was to get rid of it. I asked if I would find any other wild herbs locally. There was a fair amount of head scratching and argument about this.

'There's garlic mustard.'

'Jack-by-the-Hedge, gran calls it.'

'Basil and thyme . . . Next summer, early, they'll be.'

'Got more chance of finding them here,' Fred said, indicating the wild garden, 'than elsewhere. It's all the spraying, you see.'

'Keep on like this,' Ivy added gloomily, 'and there won't be nothing left . . . not even us!'

I asked if they knew anyone around there who had a herb garden and would sell to me. Once again, Fred's gran came to the fore.

'Just grows the usual stuff, of course,' he said. Then rattled off a collection of herbs that nearly blew my mind. 'Rosemary, sage, tarragon, basil, comfrey, lemon balm, dill, fennel, parsley, applemint, peppermint, chives, marigolds . . .'

'Marigolds? Them's not a herb,' Eric said scornfully.

'Gran says they are, and she oughta know.'

'Would . . . would your gran . . . ' I asked tentatively, trying to contain my excitement, ' . . . let me see her herb garden?'

' 'Course she would! She'd love it. She's been a bit on the lonely side since me old granda went to kick up the daisies. You say when, and I'll let her know you're coming.'

'Would tomorrow morning be all right?'

'Can't see why not. I'll pop up after tea and let you know.'

'Thanks. It'd mean such a lot to me.'

Fred and Eric returned to their work on the farm at lunch time. Before they went, I got them to carry a couple of armchairs through from the living room to the room in the cross-wing which I planned to be a combined kitchen and sitting room. The winter might be harsh and it seemed to me prudent to heat one room really well rather than the whole house. Also, my bedroom was above that room, and if I could keep the kitchen range in all the time, that would help to heat the room upstairs as well. In our apartment on the Lower East Side we'd always tried to keep the kitchen really cosy in winter so that there was at least one place of refuge. I saw no reason why the same principle should not apply to an ancient house in the east of England.

CHAPTER FIFTEEN

Within a week the old house, although still the worse for wear, was habitable. Lil and Ivy had done wonders. I was winning the war against peppermint-green paint. And, most importantly, I had access to an old-established herb garden.

Fred's gran, Martha, was a bird-like little woman of indeterminate years. But what she lacked in size, she made up for in character. 'Show me someone with a herb garden, and they won't have much wrong with their innards!' was practically the first thing she said to me. At that time of the year there were only a few fresh herbs but those there were grew profusely and I arranged to buy a supply of rosemary, sage and thyme from her. At first, she was very reluctant to take money from me, but when I explained that I , in turn, intended to make money from the products I made, she relented. Her window sills and a little lean-to conservatory were a mass of cuttings and seedlings. She showed me which herbs I could at least try to grow through the winter, as long as I put them in good light and a warm room.

I talked to Martha about my recipes. I was interested to know if she knew of any similar. But, apart from making a chamomile flower hair rinse for fair hair, and a rosemary one for dark, she had mainly used herbs medicinally. A catnip poultice for sores; a mixture of elderflowers, peppermint and yarrow boiled with honey and cayenne pepper for colds; celery seeds and dandelion root for arthritis — these were just some of the remedies she rattled off.

I asked her if she had the recipes written down and she said, 'Only a few. The others . . . well . . . I reckon I just remember what me mum and me old gran taught me.'

So, here again we had women passing down recipes and knowledge over the centuries. I thought how much must be lost to us because, for a number of reasons, the chain of knowledge had been broken. Families dispersed by war or emigration. People moving to the cities and no longer caring about the old skills. And I counted myself wonderfully fortunate that my mother had made me write down the age-old lore she carried in her head.

As I walked back across the fields carrying my seeds and cuttings — Martha had told me not to get the fresh herbs until the day I was actually going to make my skincare products, so that the oils wouldn't dry out — I was chilled to think that two hundred years ago, an old lady like her, living alone and plying her skills, would probably have ended up being burnt or drowned as a witch.

The day after my visit to Martha, I caught the early morning bus into Baildon. Ivy, Lil and I had to admit defeat with the electric stove. It would take a blow torch to remove the years of caked-on fat and grease, and only one ring was in working order. As I planned to make up as many of my recipes as Mr Crabtree could sell, and hoped to find other outlets, a clean, fully working stove was essential. I suppose I could have asked Kit D'Arcy to replace it, but he'd already been so good about offering help to clean up the house I was reluctant to do so. Mr Castleman had transferred my funds to a bank in Baildon and I realised I must now dip into my savings.

It took no time to purchase a new oven as I simply settled for the cheapest one on offer and arranged delivery for the end of the week. I then had three hours to kill before a bus would take me back to Moreton.

I wandered along the High Street looking in shop windows. Then into the maze of narrow, higgledy-piggledy streets that led off the main thoroughfare. I don't really know why, but I stopped outside a little shop specialising in model making. The window was a mass of rubber moulds and clay figures which had been made from the moulds. As I gazed in the window an idea started to form in my mind. I'd been giving considerable thought to the range of products I should make for Mr Crabtree, and I'd decided that I would initially concentrate on recipes that protected or soothed the skin. The combination of the English climate and the fine, fair skins that so many of the women had, seemed to make this a wise choice. One of the most obvious things to make was the recipe for chapped lips which had been so successful the terrible winter my mother had died. But I wanted to experiment with adapting the basic recipe to make lipsticks. There were two main stumbling blocks: adding colour, and finding some way to make the lipstick shape. The original method had been to pour the molten mixture into a bottle then, when it was ice cold, break the glass and slice the hardened ingredients. I needed something more sophisticated than that. Was there any way I could make the lipsticks from a mould?

I entered the shop. An intense, bespectacled man in his late thirties was seated behind the counter, painstakingly working on pulling up the sails on a model clipper, which was inside a bottle. I watched for a moment as he carefully pulled the mast and rigging upright with fine cotton.

'I'd no idea that was how it was done!'

'Mmmm . . . ' he said, without looking up. 'Got to get the scale just right or you're up the spout. Won't be a jiffy. There!' He pulled the last bit of rigging into place. I applauded. He looked up, flushed with pleasure at his achievement. 'Right, young lady, what can I do for you?'

'I think it's going to be a bit of a challenge,' I said, hesitantly.

'Good. Just the job. Fire away!'

I explained about the lipsticks. That I needed a mould so that I could make, say, ten lipsticks at a time. But that I'd no idea how to make the mould. It would have to take a basically hot wax mixture, then stay rigid while the lipsticks set.

'Sort of like a series of cow's udders . . . but not as pliable!' He grinned.

I laughed. 'Well, I've never got close to a cow's udder, but, yes, that's the general idea.'

'And how big do you want these lipsticks?'

I took my own from my handbag. It was a very expensive, exclusive brand that I'd bought in Paris. Now I looked at it the proportions seemed a bit mean. Also, a more generous size would make the hardened mixture easier to handle when prising it from whatever mould I might have.

'About an eighth of an inch wider and a quarter of an inch longer than this.' I handed him the lipstick. He placed it on a piece of paper and traced around it. He stared at the tracing thoughtfully for a moment and looked up.

'You're American, aren't you?' I nodded. 'Staying in Baildon?'

'No. I've rented a cottage at Moreton.'

'Got wheels?'

'Unfortunately, only the ones that belong to the Baildon and District Bus Company!'

'I'll need a few days to think about this. Tell you what, give me your number and I'll give you a buzz when I've come up with something.'

'No telephone yet, I'm afraid!'

'Cor, you are going native. Okay, give me your address and I'll drop you a card as soon as I yell "Eureka!" No, hang on. You're in luck. My local's darts team is playing The Three Horseshoes in your village on Friday. If I've got anything, I'll drive over a bit early. How's that?'

'You're being very kind!'

'Not a bit of it,' he said cheerfully. 'Like I said, I enjoy a challenge!'

I gave him my address and directions as to how to find Munkyns and went back out into the street feeling confident that something ingenious would come from the meeting.

The following Friday, although I'd certainly not forgotten about the mould I wanted, I was so exhausted by the time Ivy and Lil left, I virtually collapsed into a chair by the kitchen range. That day had been their last day at Munkyns. Ivy, surprisingly light on her feet for her size, had dashed up and down stairs with pails of hot water and scrubbed out the partitioned bedrooms.

'I know you're not needing them,' she said, 'but you don't want nothing breeding in there!'

'Breeding?'

'Germs!' she said darkly.

Even with the help of Ivy and Lil, setting Munkyns in some sort of order had been a mammoth task. How, I reflected, had I ever imagined I could achieve it alone?

I looked back over the week, astonished at how life had gathered me up and swept me along. I still felt such pain about John's death. But, as I slumped in the battered old armchair by the range, I had to admit that I had romanticised my attitude to my return to Moreton. I'd seen myself as some figure from a Brontë novel, wandering across the marshes, flinging the name of my lost love to the searching wind.

But I didn't want to lay John's ghost to rest, I rationalised. I wanted to draw his memory close to me. To live with it without sorrow. I'd wanted to shake off my melancholy and replace it with a celebration of our love. What I hadn't bargained for was the day-to-day involvement with local people! My reawakened fascination with my mother's recipes. The chance to use, and to learn about, herbs that grew to hand, rather than those bought off a market stall.

Was my fate then to be a survivor? Mike had shown me that, however much I might believe that I couldn't go on without John, the basic will to live was there. Emotionally or physically, I could never have submitted myself to suttee.

So what had I achieved by so stubbornly insisting that I return to Moreton? 'I suppose,' I thought slowly, 'I've given myself a chance to recover my own identity.' However much I loved John, with him I'd been basically a beloved pupil, under his protection. Mike had offered me a variation on the same relationship. He would have cosseted and cared for me. And, however much a part of my being cried out for that, another part rejected it. Until John had come into my life, I'd been a fighter. A she animal guarding her home and her family. My home and my fight might have been pathetic but they were real to me. They were all I'd had.

I think I must have dozed in my chair because I didn't hear the car coming slowly up the track. The first thing

I was aware of was an insistent banging on the cross-wing window.

'Anyone at home? Hallo there, it's me, Charlie Hessop. Model maker. Halloooo!'

'Hallo. Yes, I'm here. Sorry!' This as I scrambled to the front door. 'Hallo, there.'

Charlie Hessop was standing on my front doorstep. He carried a small cardboard box under one arm, and was looking as pleased as punch.

'I cracked it!' he grinned.

'Wonderful! Do come in.'

I led the way into the kitchen. 'I hope you don't mind coming in here, I more or less live in it.'

'Don't blame you.' He looked around him appreciatively. 'It's a lovely room.'

I laughed. 'You wouldn't have said so if you'd seen it a week ago! Now, what have you got for me?'

Charlie put the cardboard box down on the kitchen table and he opened it up rather like a conjurer, 'Ta ra!' He placed the mould on the table. 'I made it from fibreglass, 'cos I reckoned you'd need to be able to boil it out or something between batches . . . Neat, eh?'

It was indeed. The mould would make ten lipsticks and sat perfectly rigid on the table.

'I didn't box it in. Thought you'd probably want to dunk this in warm water to get the lipsticks out when they set, rather like a jelly.'

'It's marvellous. Just what I wanted. But how on earth did you . . .?'

He anticipated the rest of my question. 'Ah! Thought you'd ask that so I brought along the template. It's a real touch of the Heath Robinson's I can tell you, but it worked!'

What he put on the table was totally ingenious but so

simple it was breathtaking. Charlie had got ten pieces of wooden dowel, cut them to length, rounded the ends, then nailed them to a base.

'I rubbed olive oil on the wood so that I could ease it out of the fibre-glass okay. People eat olive oil, don't they? So I didn't think it could do any harm.'

'Oh, Mr Hessop . . .'

'Charlie,' he corrected me. 'No one local calls me by my surname.'

'Charlie then, thank you! And I'm Beccy. I can't thank you enough. It's *exactly* what I wanted. You are clever. Now, how much do I owe you?'

'Would a quid be too steep?'

'A pound! That's not nearly enough for all this work.'

'Go on with you. I enjoyed it.'

I took two pounds from my purse. 'Please, you must take this. I insist.'

'I'll take it but one of these goes in the lifeboat collection tin.'

I shrugged. 'In that case, put another one in for me as well. I can't tell you what this mould will mean to me.' I gave him another pound.

'I'll take the template back with me. You never know,' he grinned, 'you might want to expand your industry. Make twenty lipsticks at a time.'

I laughed. 'Or I might become a tycoon and make thirty or forty! While I'm planning to become a captain . . . or captainess . . . of industry, can I ask one more favour?'

'Ask away.'

'Well, you've solved how to make the lipsticks for me. Now I'll need something to put them in, a case.'

'Mmm . . . Metal or plastic?'

I thought for a moment. 'Better be plastic, because I'll

need to be able to sterilise them.' I laughed again. 'When I really hit the big time I'll order something fancier! I thought there might be some small factory in Baildon making sort of . . . bits and pieces.'

'I think the word you're seeking is components,' Charlie said, grinning as I floundered.

'I believe you!' I took my lipstick from my handbag. 'Do you know anyone who could make me something like this, but to fit around your wooden dowels?'

'There's a chap I know, got his own place on the new industrial estate. Just a little business but he supplies plastic parts to a big electrical company over Chelmsford way. Can I take this to bits?' he asked, taking the lipstick. It was my favourite, but what the hell? It was in a good cause. 'Be my guest.'

'Basically three bits, see. The case, the holder, and this bit that the lipstick goes in so you can push it up and down. Once we've got the moulds it should be a doddle. Leave it with me, I'll see what I can do. How many do you want? Shouldn't think this bloke would want to make less than a hundred.'

'Then let's make it a hundred. Should I pay you something in advance?'

'No. Let's see if I can get him to make the bits first.' He glanced at his watch. 'Must be getting on. Match'll be starting soon.'

I went with him to the door, thanking him profusely. Charlie brushed aside my gratitude and walked to his car. He was just about to get in when he turned back to me. 'You going out tonight?' I shook my head. 'Well, a pretty girl like you shouldn't be on her own of a Friday evening! Tell you what, why not come down to the pub? There'll be quite a good crowd down there . . . be a bit of fun. What do you say?'

I hesitated.

'Oh, come on, it'll do you good. I promise I won't pounce on you or anything. Happily married man, that's me. My missus would be with me, only we couldn't get a babysitter.'

'It's not that I don't trust you,' I said hastily. 'There's just such a lot to do still.'

'It'll still be there tomorrow! Come on, powder your nose or whatever you ladies have to do before you step outside.'

'All right. Won't be a minute.' I hurried inside and got a jacket and my purse. It would take too long to make up my face. The Three Horseshoes would just have to put up with me unadorned, I thought.

I don't think I could have felt more foreign walking into the pub that evening if I'd been a Turkish potentate! My speech, my colouring, my attitude to the pace of life. But Charlie took my arm and led me into a merry crowd of people. I was soon being introduced to the darts team and their supporters. There was much good-natured kidding about the fact that I was there and Charlie's wife wasn't, but I could tell from their tone that no one seriously believed that he was a philanderer.

We were in the public bar, which was crowded. Ivy and Lil were there with their husbands, to whom I was introduced. Then Eric came in with his very pretty girlfriend and there were more introductions. After a while we were joined by Fred, Fred's mum, and his gran, Martha. I was bought glasses of cider, bags of potato crisps, even a pork pie. I insisted on buying a round and, while I was at the bar, saw Kit D'Arcy in the saloon bar. He waved and mimed would I like a drink? I smiled and shook my head, indicating the glasses lined up in front of me.

I thought how ironic it was that the last social event I went to was lunch on Susan Brownlow's yacht. Now I was a spectator at a darts match at a pub tucked away in a tiny village in the depths of East Anglia!

As Charlie had brought me there I wasn't sure which team I should support: my newly adopted village team or his. I need not have worried. It quickly became clear that the darts match was simply an excuse for regulars from two pubs to get together and have a good night out. However, it rounded things off very nicely when Charlie made the winning score. The landlord called 'Time gentlemen, please', and the pub started to clear. Friendly goodnights were said and I walked out on to the village street with Charlie. I'd come to Moreton to sorrow, but events seemed to be forcing me to rejoin the human race.

It was a beautiful night, cold but with clear skies. The moon was very bright and the heavens a mass of stars. I decided that I'd like to walk home. Charlie would have none of it.

'I brought you here, I'll take you back. Supposing something happened to you . . . I'd never forgive myself!'

'Charlie, I'm a New Yorker! I've walked alone down streets that would make your hair curl. It's just such a lovely night and a walk would round off the evening perfectly.'

'Then I'll walk with you.'

'Oh, don't be ridiculous, you dear man. That would make you late and your wife would be worried. Honestly, I'll be all right.'

'Well, if you insist,' he said reluctantly.

'I do!' I held out my hand to him. 'Thanks for this evening, Charlie, it did me a world of good. And thanks for your invention.'

Charlie coloured with pleasure. 'Any time! Like I said, I enjoy a bit of a challenge. And you don't get many of them in Baildon! Well, goodnight. I'll be in touch as soon as I find out about the lipstick cases.'

Charlie drove off and I started to walk back to Munkyns. The village street had cleared while Charlie and I stood talking. Behind me I heard the landlord locking the pub doors. A solitary cat ran across the road but it was in shadow and so I couldn't be sure whether or not it was a black one to bring me luck.

I stopped by the churchyard and leant against the wall, looking at the old rectory where I'd known such happiness. The house was in darkness. No new tenants, or had they gone early to bed? I let my thoughts wander back to the summer, and found that I was remembering with gladness, with a sense of fulfilment, that I'd been so loved and so in love. At that moment, someone or something reached out to me and released me from my pain. I'd been allowed to look back and rejoice instead of regret. I was at peace.

CHAPTER SIXTEEN

The next morning I started work in the kitchen. It all felt so homely, so familiar. Saucepans of water boiling on the stove with basins of melting ingredients on them. I'd bought a number of food dyes from Collins' in Baildon on the basis that if you could eat it, you wouldn't come to much harm having it on your lips.

The lipstick recipe was blurred by my tears. I'd written this the day my mother had died and, although I hadn't cried then, re-reading the recipe some time later had broken my heart and I'd sobbed my sadness on to the page.

Now all the ingredients were lined up on my kitchen table at Munkyns. Powdered cloves, finely chopped apples, crushed grapes, unsalted butter, gum-benzoin, storax, and spermaceti. I'd decided that as soon as the bees-wax had melted I'd mix everything together, then divide the mixture into a number of smaller bowls and experiment with adding different colours. My main concern was that the basic mixture would 'take' colour and that I wouldn't be left with a lipstick that was good for chapped lips but had the colour crazed through it.

I'd decided to mix four different colours. I had cochineal, orange, raspberry and strawberry flavourings. I planned to vary the depth of colour by mixing the dyes with orange-flower water.

The colours seemed to mix in well with the basic

ingredients, but I couldn't be sure until they had set. There was a pantry under the cat-slide roof at the back of the kitchen. Ivy and Lil had scrubbed down the shelves, the walls and the floor and it was now spotlessly clean. It was also freezing in there, so it was an ideal place to put mixtures to harden. I placed the embryo lipsticks out there, then set to work with two new recipes — new in the sense that although my mother knew them, we'd never been able to try them because we'd lacked the ingredients. Both used marsh-mallow roots. Early the day before I'd pulled up some clumps of marsh mallow from the garden. The roots were long with a tapering end, the external colour yellowish brown, with a white flesh. I scrubbed the roots thoroughly, then chopped them finely and left them to steep in cold water for twenty-four hours.

Both recipes were fairly simple. The first was for a face pack. I strained the marsh-mallow water, discarded the roots and bottled the decoction which was left. Then I beat together an egg yolk, a teaspoon of honey and a tablespoon of the strong marsh-mallow water. This only really made enough for one pack, but as I'd never made it before, I wanted to try it on myself before making enough to take into Mr Crabtree's shop.

The second recipe was for a hand cream. Again it used a tablespoon of marsh-mallow water. I poured that into a mixing bowl, then added two tablespoons of ground almonds, a teaspoon of milk and a few drops of lavender oil. This filled one of the glass jars I'd bought from Mr Crabtree. Before I started on the other recipes I rubbed some of the cream into my rather battered hands. I liked the feel of it, but it would be a few days before I could tell how well it was working. I'd looked up marsh mallow in my newly acquired herb books. They all agreed that the roots were used to make a decoction that would soothe sun burn, very dry skin, and minor burns. In theory the recipes should work!

I washed out the bowls I'd been using, then put on my coat and set out to walk across the fields to Martha's cottage. I wanted to spend the afternoon preparing a number of the tried and tested recipes my mother had made for Mr O'Brien's drug store: cleansing creams, skin fresheners, a couple of different face packs. I'd also decided to make the moisturiser I'd experimented with the day before Briony's funeral. I'd been making it and using it ever since and, if Susan Brownlow's reaction was anything to go by, it had kept my skin in excellent condition.

The sky was low, and dark, and threatening. But still beautiful. The vast East Anglian skies, immortalised by Constable and the Norwich School of painters, are not a romantic myth. They dominate the landscape, the scudding clouds and changing light always dramatic. Halfway across the fields that led to Martha's cottage, I saw a horseman on the horizon. At sight of me, horse and rider broke into a gallop. As they drew nearer and I saw the old, black dog lolloping behind, I knew who it was. Kit D'Arcy.

I waved, and within moments he was by my side. He doffed his cap to me. 'Well met, fair lady.'

'Shouldn't you be wearing a riding hat?'

'Oh, I should, I should. The trouble is, it gets between you and your senses. Tell me anything you like doing that wouldn't be spoiled by wearing a lump of concrete on your head.'

'If that's a challenge, I pass!'

'Out here' — he looked around at the fields — 'we're still comparatively free. I don't want to be sensible . . . I want to be capricious, a maverick. I want to believe in

209

unicorns. I want to hold the twentieth century at bay for as long as possible, and be the exact opposite of the mythical person that the Welfare State is trying to care for. I want life to be a challenge, don't you?'

Before I could answer he smiled at me and said, 'You do! I know you do. Everything about you proclaims it. The line of your body, the set of your head. Don't tell me you're a conformist because I shan't believe you, Miss Mandel.'

I laughed. 'Well, whether I want it to be or not, life is a challenge. For me it always has been. I guess you either give in and go under, or pick up the gauntlet . . . although I'm not too sure about the unicorns!'

'Then I'll have to convert you. Where are you off to? Or am I being nosey?'

'To see Fred's gran, Martha. I'm getting some herbs from her.'

'Well, I won't hold you up. But I was going to ride over to see you sometime today. I wondered if you'd like to come over and have supper at the farm tomorrow evening? Do say yes. I've got a brace of pheasant hanging in my larder. I need someone to share them with!'

'All right. Thanks. You're very kind. What sort of time?'

'I'll drive over and pick you up. About seven all right?'

'Seven will be fine. But I can easily walk.'

'No! It'll be dark by then, and by the look of this sky we're in for some bad weather.' He grinned. 'I'm not sharing my pheasants with a drowned rat.'

'Okay. See you about seven then.'

It was just noon when I arrived at Martha's cottage.

'Just as well there ain't no sun about, or I shouldn't be picking these. Never pick herbs in strong sunlight,' she scolded.

'Why not?'

She thought about this for a moment. 'I don't rightly know . . . I just knows you mustn't! "To make your herbs a boon, Pick after dew and afore noon," that's what me mum always said. And gently! You've got to hold them gently,' she said as she gave me the freshly picked bunch of herbs. 'You bruise them, you take all the goodness out of them.'

As I walked back to Munkyns I thought how alike Martha and I were. We both had knowledge that we didn't fully understand. Immediately I got back to the cottage, even before I took my coat off, I put the herbs carefully down on the kitchen table and took down my herb books. 'After dew and afore noon.' I looked up harvesting.

Martha's herb-lore made total sense. When the dew evaporates from the leaves and the day becomes warmer, the essential oils rise into the leaves of the plant. But once the sun becomes really hot on them, the oils are dried out. If you bruise the leaves they start to sweat and again you loose the most precious ingredient, the essential oils. There was so much to learn.

I spent the rest of the day making herb oils and infusions. They'd be ready to use the following afternoon. If the colour in the lipstick mixture was still holding good, I would also make a selection of lipsticks to take into Mr Crabtree's shop. 'Now I know what they mean by a cottage industry,' I thought wryly.

That evening I sat down and wrote a long letter to Aaron. I hadn't seen him for just over five months, and I missed him very much. Could I possibly afford the air fare for him to come to stay during his Christmas holidays? I decided that, afford it or not, I wanted to see him desperately. My jewellery was being kept for me in the bank in Baildon. I'd sell one of the pieces and send the money to Aaron. After all, we only had each other, and I didn't want him to grow away from me. Or not to realise how much I still loved him.

As I lay in bed that night, I thought about my brother being here with me. To the best of my ability, I'd give him the kind of traditional Christmas that John had planned for us. A Christmas tree, carols, perhaps it really would snow. As I drifted off to sleep I thought, 'Never mind that we're Jewish, we'll have a holiday straight out of Dickens' *A Christmas Carol*.'

As I sat in Kit D'Arcy's comfortable, old-fashioned kitchen, sipping a glass of champagne, I thought what a strange mixture he was. Ostensibly a hardened countryman but sensitive enough to dream of unicorns. Now he was hugely enjoying cooking our supper. A large, old Aga cooker was set into a brick fireplace. Kit was basting the pheasants, which he'd cooked in Calvados on a bed of onions and apples. He'd asked if I'd minded having our pre-dinner drink in the kitchen so that he could put the finishing touches to our meal. I don't know what I'd expected really. Perhaps a housekeeper or at best a simple meal which had been partially cooked and only needed to be heated up. Instead the table in the dining room had been set with fine silver and crystal glasses and Kit was cooking an elaborate three-course dinner.

'If I'd known everything was going to be so elegant, I'd have dressed more formally . . . I think I was expecting a simple meal in your farm kitchen.'

I was in fact casually but well dressed. Camel slacks, a high-necked white silk blouse, and a finely knitted jacket.

'I'm not exactly dressed up like a dog's dinner, am I?

212

I just love to cook and this seemed a good opportunity. In any case, you must know that you look gorgeous! I don't know much about women's clothes, but I'm pretty damned sure that outfit wasn't picked up in the High Street!'

'I must admit you're right. When I knew I was coming to Europe earlier this year, a friend of mine dragged me round practically every chic little boutique in New York.'

'A boyfriend?'

I smiled and shook my head, 'No, just a friend.' However fond I was of Bruno, the thought of him as my lover was highly amusing.

Kit put the pheasants back into the cooker, then crossed to the fridge.

'We can start eating now if you like.'

'Can I help?'

'Certainly not! Pretty ladies are allowed in my kitchen on condition that they do nothing practical.'

He'd taken from the fridge two bowls of iced soup which was a delicate, rosy colour. I followed him through to the dining room. The farm house was a large, rather ugly Victorian building, but inside the rooms were well-proportioned and elegantly but comfortably furnished.

'You have a lovely home.'

'Thank you. I can claim some responsibility for the furnishings, but the high level of polishing is entirely due to Ivy and Lil.'

I laughed. 'The demon cleaners! Although I have to say I can't imagine how I could have coped without them.'

'Neither can I. Munkyns was in a terrible state. I am sorry.'

'You must come over and see it. It's looking a lot

happier now. Although I warn you, it'll be a casserole in the kitchen, not a sumptuous meal like this!'

It was a lovely meal. Iced tomato and orange soup with lemon thyme. To go with the pheasants, Kit had cooked game chips and a purée of Brussels sprouts. To finish the meal he had made something called Eton Mess, which was anything but!

'From *the* Eton?' I asked.

'So I'm told!' he laughed. 'When I was there we only ever seemed to have suet pudding with lumpy custard.'

So, Kit had been to Eton. He certainly was not a simple farmer.

'Apart from delicious . . . what exactly is it?'

'Meringues crushed in a raspberry fool. You can make it with shop meringues, but it's better to have home made.'

I smiled. 'And these, of course, are home made.'

'Of course! Would you like coffee in the drawing room or the sitting room? The sitting room's cosier. On the other hand, you have the look of a woman who fits naturally into gracious surroundings.'

'Oh, Kit, you couldn't be more wrong about me. Show me your drawing room but I'm sure I'll settle for your sitting room.'

The drawing room was exquisite. Kit was right, it was a gracious room. But too formal for me to be truly comfortable in. A huge, breakfront bookcase took up nearly the whole of one wall. Winged Hepplewhite walnut armchairs stood on either side of the fireplace. Opposite the fire was a Georgian giltwood settee with an arched back and rounded sides. The upholstery was in a beautiful damask. I crossed and touched it.

'It's Gainsborough silk, woven by a little firm in Sudbury. The silk comes from a village nearby —

Glemsford. A royal bride's wedding dresses are always made of Glemsford silk.'

'It's very beautiful. The whole room is absolutely lovely.'

'But you don't really like it?'

'I *admire* it. It's a marvellous room to display all these antiques. You're obviously an avid collector.'

'Not really. Some I'm very fond of. Mostly they're pieces my family no longer have any use for.'

'My God! If this is what they've thrown out, what on earth have they kept?'

Kit laughed. 'Enough to keep Sotheby's happy for a very long time. Come on! Let's have coffee. I can tell from your expression we're having it in the sitting room.'

He led the way back through the hall and into the sitting room. It was exactly the kind of room I'd tried to create in my apartment. Comfortable sofas with loose covers. Side tables piled with books that were obviously well read and well loved. The room had style, but it was casual and unselfconscious. A toasting fork and a chestnut roaster leant against the fireplace. In front of the fire was a large, rather chewed dog basket. Kit's old labrador, Rufus, thumped his tail as we entered. His master knelt and fondled his ears.

'I should really be training up another dog . . . but I can't bear this old chap to think his days are numbered.' He crossed to the door. 'Make yourself at home. Coffee'll only be a moment.'

I curled up in a large armchair by the fire. Rufus stood up stiffly, then came and pressed his muzzle into my hand, wanting more fussing. I felt very relaxed. At home even. Kit was an easy host. It would be tempting to slip into some kind of relationship with him. Tempting because I liked him very much, but totally unfair because

I had nothing to offer him. Although I was finding it easier to live on a day-to-day basis, I still mourned John and, in the foreseeable future, wanted no one to take his place.

I started to think about the beautiful furniture in the drawing room. What kind of a home could Kit have come from that could let those antiques go so easily? Then I had it! When John and I were staying at the rectory, we'd driven into Suffolk to see one of the jewels, if not *the* jewel, of Elizabethan architecture, D'Arcy House, the family seat of the Earls of Montacut. I remembered that the walls of the Great Parlour had been adorned with family portraits. The latest had been by Sir Alfred Munnings, an equestrian study of the present Earl, his Countess and their only son: Lord Christian D'Arcy!

If John and I hadn't argued over the portrait I'd never have remembered it. Munnings, an ex-President of the Royal Academy, had been vociferous in his condemnation of modern art. John thought him an old bigot and his paintings trite. I was totally uneducated about art but found the portrait graceful and striking. The name might, of course, be a coincidence, but I doubted it. Kit's furniture, his education, his knowledge of fine things, indicated a background such as D'Arcy House. Then what was he doing farming here? And why didn't he use his title?

Well, what was I doing here? We all have to find ourselves in whatever way we can. No doubt, in the fullness of time, we would admit our past, our reasons for coming to these beautiful but windswept marshes. But until Kit was ready to confide in me, I felt I should keep what I had guessed to myself.

CHAPTER SEVENTEEN

The next morning brought an 'in haste' but affectionate letter from Mike. His series was still topping the ratings. He was thinking of striking out in Los Angeles. Mrs Janowski was still refusing to leave the Lower East Side. How was I? *'Please, please come home as soon as you feel able . . .'*

In the afternoon, I had a long, amusing, gossipy letter from Bruno. I was touched that they both obviously made time in their busy lives to reply to my letters the minute they got them. I felt myself so fortunate to have two such true friends and I hoped for a letter from Aaron in the next morning's post.

I spent the day making batches of lipsticks although, of course, I couldn't actually market them until I had cases. I hoped Charlie was making headway there. Even without the lipsticks, I had a good selection of products to take in to Mr Crabtree. First thing the following morning, I planned to catch the early bus into Baildon.

There was a barn just by Munkyns. It was strewn with bits and pieces of old agricultural paraphernalia, and, from the junk, I rescued a large, battered but strong basket. Ideal for transporting my skin-care cosmetics. I laughed at the thought that I'd be getting on the bus looking like some old countrywoman going to market!

As I entered Mr Crabtree's shop he hurried forward to greet me. His surprisingly lively eyes glinted with suppressed excitement which was in strange contrast to his thin face and reserved demeanour.

'Miss Mandel, I've been hoping you'd call.'

'I'm so sorry I haven't been in before. It's taken me some time to get together the ingredients and . . .'

'No, no!' he interrupted. 'I was not admonishing you . . . simply anxious to see you. I have been doing some research.'

'Into what?' I asked, bewildered.

'Preservatives. You see, I started to think about what you said. That your products lacked shelf-life. Well, I was at university with a chap who has done rather well as a back-room boy for one of these big cosmetics companies. So, I rang him up and took him out to lunch. Simpson's in the Strand — a quite excellent roast from the trolley. I didn't ask him to do anything dishonourable, you understand . . .'

'I'm sure you didn't,' I reassured him.

'I simply declared my interest and asked his advice. Well, naturally he could not give me the exact proportion of contents but he was able to tell me that the two safest preservatives are methyll and propilparaban.'

'Safest?' I queried. I was now absolutely riveted by what he was telling me.

'This, to use an Americanism, is where we struck oil, Miss Mandel! My friend, whom I think at this stage should remain nameless, is experiencing certain difficulties with his employers. It stems from a quite irrational obsession with youth. My friend is a healthy sixty-year-old, and his company are trying to force him into early retirement. Nothing to do with his abilities. Nothing to do with his work capacity. Simply to do with his birth certificate! Nonsense, isn't it?'

'Oh, quite,' I said hastily. In fact, at the age of twenty,

sixty seemed to me as old as Methuselah! Although I could see that it was ridiculous to ask a learned, capable man to retire simply to suit corporate policy.

'His understandable bitterness moved him to divulge certain facts. Not formulae, you understand. Apparently there is growing concern among the medical profession about the very high level of preservatives used by the cosmetics industry. The danger is that they can be toxic and, in the long term, may destroy the balance of natural bacteria.'

'And therefore,' I said slowly, thinking my way through this fascinating information, 'the reason why my skin-care products work so well . . . is their very lack of preservatives.'

'It seems highly possible!'

'This is simply a hypothetical question,' I said. 'I mean, mass production is hardly my problem! But in terms of an industry, how could they manufacture and distribute enough goods without preservatives?'

'They couldn't! But they could keep them to the absolute minimum. Have a shelf-life of, say, six to nine months, and after that make a virtue of the fact that unsold products were withdrawn and destroyed.'

There was a wooden chair by the counter for the convenience of customers waiting for their prescriptions. I sat down on it abruptly. 'It's a wonderful idea. And so simple!'

'All the best ideas are. Now what I propose, with your permission, is that we should select a few products and vary the amount of preservatives until we find the very lowest amount that will give us the desired shelf-life. The two preservatives I mentioned occur naturally in the B vitamins and should therefore be the least harmful to your natural ingredients.'

'This is terribly exciting, Mr Crabtree. But, why? Why should you want to do this?'

There was a moment's silence before Mr Crabtree sighed and leant against his counter. 'I'm not a very gregarious man, Miss Mandel. My wife, whom I loved dearly, died three years ago. We had no children. Since then I have filled the lonely evenings with a good book, fine music, the occasional glass of port . . . but it is not enough. I need something that will occupy me totally. A quest even. In short, Miss Mandel, I have grieved for too long. Now I need to rejoin the human race. A chance remark by you has triggered off something, engaged my heart and my mind. At last I have something I *want* to do again.' He sighed once more. 'Forgive me. I have said much too much. You must think me a terrible old bore.'

'I think nothing of the kind! I too,' I added slowly, 'am grieving for someone. I came to this area to lay a ghost. Perhaps, Mr Crabtree, we could lay our ghosts together. I think we should at least try!'

We went through the various products that I'd brought in. I'd labelled them as to the skin types and problems for which they were suited. We set a selection aside for Mr Crabtree to experiment upon. He planned to ask his friend if there was a way of speeding up the time process as we were both anxious to get results as soon as possible.

After leaving the chemist's shop I walked along the High Street then turned off to Charlie's model shop. I waited until he had finished serving a customer, then received both good news and bad. We could get the lipstick cases made in Baildon, but the small manufacturer Charlie had been in touch with would only do a run of two hundred cases.

'For how much?'

'A shilling a case. The price will come down if you order more.'

'Order more! I only want fifty per cent of what he's offering now.' Then I thought for a moment. 'There is a time and tide . . .' I suddenly had a compelling feeling that it had to be *now*. If I was going to make something of my life, I had to be brave, to play my hunches. It was like looking through a kaleidoscope and discovering that the patterns had been fixed, predestined even. Whichever way the coloured pieces fell, they held a meaning for me. Charlie, Mr Crabtree and I were strangely linked. We latter two by our need to escape from the pain of our immediate lives. And Charlie? I remembered him saying that there weren't enough challenges in Baildon and thought that Charlie was, perhaps, trapped in a way of small-town life that, however loving and reassuring, gave him no scope for his true ambitions. Charlie was essentially a creator, an innovator. He could, possibly would, jog his life away in Baildon. But . . .

But. That word that spans an abyss of forgotten desires, hopes and dreams. And all because a small voice inside once said, 'Success is too tough.' 'Okay, two hundred at a shilling apiece. And we'll screw him when we want five thousand!'

Charlie laughed. 'It's a deal! Oh, Christ, Beccy, I feel alive! I think you're as mad as a hatter. Two hundred lipsticks sold by old Archie Crabtree. Two hundred! Purgatives and pills, that's all he knows about. But lipsticks, two hundred of them! Oh, well, might as well be hung for a sheep as a lamb.'

'For a what as a what?'

'It was a quaint old British custom. Steal a sheep and you were for the high jump. Steal a lamb and you still danced at the end of a rope. So what would you rather

steal if you were trying to feed a hungry family? There's
more meat on a sheep. And if you were caught, sheep
or lamb, the path still led to hell!'

After I left Charlie I went to a travel agent to check
the air fare for Aaron, then on to the bank. I saw the
assistant manager and asked if he could recommend a
trustworthy jeweller. He suggested an old-established
shop in the High Street then arranged for my box of
jewellery to be brought from the vault. He discreetly left
me alone in his office while I opened the box and selected
a piece to sell. It was very painful because everything I
took out reminded me of John and our life together. I
forced myself to be rational. I wasn't wearing the
jewellery. I had a responsibility to Aaron and I truly
believed that John would have wished me to honour that
rather than be sentimental.

I selected the piece I thought was possibly of the least
value, a tear-drop single pearl on a gold chain. There was
a knock on the door of the office.'

'Have you finished, Miss Mandel?'

'Yes, thank you. You've been very kind. When I've
sold this . . .' I held up the pendant, '. . .. I'll deposit
the money in my account and then I'd like to arrange
to send some to my brother in the States. A bank in New
York handles a trust fund for him, for his school fees
and a small allowance. Is it possible to have money
transferred to his account and changed into dollars?'

'Yes, of course. Ask for me when you return and I'll
put all the necessary wheels in motion.'

Later, as I sat on the bus going home, I thought back
over the day. There was plenty of time for reflection as,
although Moreton was only about twelve miles from
Baildon, the bus took over an hour to do the journey.
There were countless stops. Detours up winding country

lanes to serve a remote village, then back the same way to rejoin the main road. Sometimes people would give the driver parcels to drop off further along the route. Once I was on the bus and the driver was even given a mug of tea with instructions to return the empty mug on the way back! I leant back in the uncomfortable seat, my now empty basket on my lap. Strange to be so happy and sad in just one day. Happy because of Mr Crabtree's willingness to work on my recipes so that we could add a small amount of preservatives. Happy because Charlie seemed to feel so much part of my venture. Happy because I'd sent Aaron money and in only a few weeks I should be seeing him. But so sad to part with my pendant . . .

I'd got a very fair price for it but, however hard I tried, I couldn't fight off the memories of the last time I'd worn it. I could even remember the date, September 16th, 1960 . . . John Kennedy and Richard Nixon debated for an hour in a television studio in Chicago. The debate was broadcast all over America. John was fiercely Democrat and had asked a few friends, who knew of our relationship and either approved or were indifferent, to watch the debate at his apartment and then stay on for an informal supper party. It was the first time I'd played hostess for him and I was terribly nervous. I confided my fears to Bruno.

'My pet, you're going to look gorgeous and be brilliant! Trust your Uncle Bruno.' Then, his ginger toupee more askew than ever, he'd whirled me around a number of boutiques until we found what he declared to be just right. It was a silk shirt-waister dress the colour of rich double cream with very slightly darker tiny suede buttons and a wide matching suede belt. It was simple but stunning. To complement it I'd worn only one piece of jewellery – the pearl pendant. At the end of the evening I could tell that John was proud of me and . . . and . . .

A hand was shaking my shoulder.

'Come on, miss. Last stop, unless you want to turn around with me and go all the way back to Baildon!'

It was the driver. I must have dozed off.

'Oh, I'm sorry! Thank you!'

I clambered down the bus steps and started the half mile walk from the village to Munkyns.

When I arrived back at the cottage I was disappointed to discover that there was still no letter from Aaron. Perhaps tomorrow. That evening I sat at the kitchen table and wrote a long letter to him, telling him of my life at Munkyns since I'd last written and explaining that I'd arranged for money to be sent to his bank to pay for his trip so that we could spend the Christmas holidays together.

A week passed and still there was no letter from Aaron. I brushed my anxiety aside. He probably had exams to contend with, I thought. Any day now I'd hear from him.

I was busy painting Munkyns, making my skin-care products, trying to clear some of the garden. I had a good number of herbs in pots on the window sills that faced the sun, but it was a race against the weather to clear enough space for a good herb garden. The days were drawing in and I couldn't work outside much later than half past four in the afternoon. On the Saturday I worked until the last glimmer of light had gone, then went inside, drew the curtains against the night sky and made up both fires. There was a chill in the air and I had a feeling that we might be in for a cold night.

My limbs ached from the gardening and so I soaked in a hot bath. Then, because it seemed as if most of the fine top soil that had been blown around in the wind from the estuary had ended up in it, I washed my hair. By now it was early evening. I towelled myself dry and put on a lovely, warm cashmere dressing gown that John had bought me the previous Christmas. It was a dark navy blue with my initials monogrammed in a rich golden silk thread on the single pocket. I partly dried my hair and left it hanging loose to finish drying. I made myself a cup of coffee then sat at the kitchen table. My herb books were spread out on the table with a chart I had started to make. I planned to cross reference all the herbs that contained the same vitamins, and the properties they were enriched with that would help different skin problems.

I worked for a while but felt strangely restless. Was I lonely? Yes, I had to admit that I was, and yet I had sought solitude. Or was it simply that it was Saturday night, and that was a night for dancing, for dining, for being with the one you loved? I rose from the table angrily, telling myself not to be so childish. I crossed to a second-hand radio I'd bought in Baildon and tuned in to the BBC's Third Programme. They were broadcasting a concert from the Festival Hall on London's South Bank. I glanced at my watch and cursed that I'd missed the start of it. Vaughan Williams' *Fantasia on a Theme by Thomas Tallis* filled my kitchen. It was haunting, beautiful. Normally I would have curled up in one of the ancient, cracked leather armchairs by the fire, given myself up to the music and been sustained by its grace. Instead I paced the kitchen, my mood desperately at odds with the sweep of sound coming from the radio. I leant my head against the bressummer over the range. Why was I suddenly feeling so damned lonely?

I stood there for a moment, trying to fight off the bleak mood that threatened to engulf me. Then I heard a car coming slowly up the track. It stopped outside. A single door slammed. I drew my dressing gown tightly around me and crossed from the kitchen, into the hall, then through to the front door. As I arrived, there was a knock on the door. The New Yorker in me cautioned me to call out before opening it.

'Hallo?'

'Beccy It's Kit.'

'Kit, hallo.' I opened the door, then remembered how I was dressed. 'I'm sorry, I've just had a bath and washed my hair.'

'I can see!' He reached out, lightly touching my hair. 'You remind me of a poem by Eliot . . .'

'Oh, Kit! Dear Kit,' I laughed, 'Don't let's stand on the doorstep discussing Eliot! We'll freeze. Do come in!'

'May I bring Rufus inside? He can't bear to be left behind so he's in the back of my old heap.'

'Of course! I might even find him a digestive biscuit.'

Kit and Rufus entered Munkyns and followed me through to the kitchen. The dog immediately made himself at home and settled in front of the glowing range.

'You've done wonders here.' Kit warmed his hands at the fire. 'You know, when I was a kid I used to love going into my nanny's sitting room. It was so safe and snug. So . . . human!' A shadow crossed his face. 'It was the only room in that damned house I liked!' Just as suddenly his mood changed. He turned to me, urbane and charming once more.

'I've been terribly presumptuous calling like this. You see, I saw your lights across the fields and wondered if you were alone this evening. Are you? Or am I being a nuisance?'

'Never that! It's strange that you came to see me. I was feeling . . . oh, I don't know . . . stupidly restless. Rather lonely. Isn't that silly?' I added lightly.

Kit didn't reply. From the radio now, the wonderful sweeping strings of the orchestra played *Fantasia on 'Greensleeves'*. It was so utterly British, encapsulating everything I felt about Munkyns . . . About the marshes . . . About the timelessness of the estuary . . . The chapel . . . And I felt, so strongly, the rough magic, the part pagan, part Christian call of the earth from that wild landscape.

Then Kit spoke. 'Beccy, all I ask is your friendship . . . at least for now. I promise I'll never ask before you're ready to give. Never trespass. Please trust me.'

'Of course I do.' I held out my hand to him. 'Friends?'

Instead of shaking it, he lifted my hand to his lips and kissed it. 'Friends!' Then he was at the door. 'Look, are you free this evening? Throw me out if you're not. Otherwise, I brought a picnic.'

'A picnic? In mid-winter! Oh, Kit, thank you. That's exactly the kind of heart-warming nonsense I need.'

'Good! I'll go and fetch everything in from the car.'

'And I'll go and get dressed.'

We both left the kitchen, Kit in the direction of the front door, I towards the stairs. Rufus opened one eye but was too lazy to follow either of us.

'Beccy.'

'Yes?' I turned at the bottom of the stairs.

'Leave your hair down.' Then he was gone.

CHAPTER EIGHTEEN

We built up the fire on the range and dined at the kitchen table.

'I just grabbed a few things from the larder.' I looked at the spread that Kit had set out. Cold game pie, salads, a variety of English cheeses, home-made chutney. I laughed. 'Then your larder is much better stocked than mine! I was going to dine on baked beans tonight.'

He had also brought wine with him. We sat a long time over our meal, chatting, laughing, sometimes arguing. I was absurdly relieved that I wasn't spending the evening alone. After our supper, I made coffee and we sat on either side of the range toasting our legs. Rufus stretched out, head on paws, snoring between us.

We sat in silence for a while, staring into the leaping flames from the log fire. Comfortable with each other. I was thinking about what Kit had said about 'that damned house' and wondering if one day he'd confide in me. His thoughts must have been running on similar lines because he suddenly said, 'You know, Beccy, I'm a good listener if you want to tell me . . .'

'Tell you?'

'What's troubling you. Why you're here.'

'I have a hunch I could say the same thing to you.'

There was a pause, then Kit sighed. 'Yes, you're right. I suppose we all have our secrets.'

'I'm not hiding anything, Kit. Well, I suppose that's not strictly true. Let's say I am avoiding something.

Running away, if you like . . . I don't know! The Press have probably lost interest by now. I was in the same car as John Kimberly when he was killed a little over two months ago.'

'John Kimberly . . . the American millionaire?'

'Yes.'

'Just a minute . . . he rented the rectory here in the summer. I was too busy with the harvest to take much interest but the village was fairly agog.'

'Was it? Yes, I suppose it would be.'

'Were you with him here too?'

'Yes. We lived together for two years. We were wonderfully happy but the very happiest here. We were going to come back this Christmas.'

Kit was silent for a moment, then said, 'Poor darling. You poor, poor darling. It must have been a hard decision to come back here without him.'

'No, that's where you're wrong. This was the only place I *could* come. You see, the time we spent here was the only time we had together when we could forget our different backgrounds, the fact that he had family ties, family responsibilities. I felt that perhaps I could . . . well . . . I suppose find him again here. And the strangest thing is that in looking for John, I've started to find myself. I don't know what's going to happen, but I shall never be sorry that I came back.'

'Neither shall I, Beccy. Neither shall I.'

A wind blew up and rattled the windows. It was good to be indoors, safe by the fire. 'And how about you, Kit? Do you want to tell me about the damned house you mentioned?' I paused, then remembered Charlie's phrase. Might as well be hung for a sheep as a lamb. 'It's D'Arcy House, isn't it?'

'You know?'

'I guessed. You see, John and I visited it when we were staying at the rectory.'

Kit rose and went to the kitchen table. He poured himself a glass of wine. 'Good! A few more shillings towards the fight against the deathwatch beetle!' Then he was instantly contrite. 'Hell, that sounded rude, Beccy. I only have to think about that great mouldering pile and it brings the worst out in me.'

'It's one of the most beautiful houses I've ever seen.'

'Oh, yes, it's beautiful. It's also an avaricious monster! Every bloody penny the family has ever had has gone into that place. We can't maintain it, we just fight a constantly losing battle to stop it falling down. Can you imagine the cost! There's miles of timber-framing. Hundreds of thousands of clay peg-tiles, all slipping. Priceless tapestries that are fading. Countless paintings and works of art that need cleaning, restoring. The list is endless. And by an accident of birth I'm doomed to spend the rest of my life trying to shore up a museum!'

'But surely you must be proud of your heritage?'

'Proud?' Kit sighed. 'Yes, I suppose so. But by nature, or because for as long as I can remember "The Family" has been drummed into me? As if every earl only existed to pass on the title to his son, and every countess was nothing more than a brood mare.

'But, yes! A D'Arcy won his spurs at Agincourt. The earldom was created by Charles II as payment for the D'Arcys' loyalty during the Civil War . . . And so what? Every living human being has ancestors. It's only the noblemen who make such a damned fuss about it!'

I smiled. ' *"When Adam ploughed and Eve span, Who was then the gentleman?"* '

Kit laughed, his bleak mood banished for the moment.

'An American who quotes John Ball?'

'Have you never read Mark Twain or Emily Dickinson?'

'Not quite the same thing is it?'

And so I told Kit about Briony, my friendship with her, the books she'd left me. Also about the five thousand dollars. How grateful I was. How I missed her.

'I've been so fortunate in my friendships.'

'It takes two to make a friendship, Beccy. I expect your friends also count themselves lucky. I know I do, because I am right in saying, aren't I, that we *are* friends?'

'Of course we are!' I smiled. 'Only good friends would sit in front of a fire in a draughty old kitchen on a Saturday night, and pour out their troubles to each other.'

There was a slight pause, and then Kit said, softly, 'Lovers might.'

'Yes, they might,' I said slowly. 'But my lover is dead. It would clearly be foolish of me . . . life denying . . . to say that I'll never fall in love again. But right now I can't look forward and see a time when my heart doesn't belong to John.' I felt tears blur my eyes and turned away so that Kit wouldn't see them.

After a moment he was by my side. He gave me a glass of wine. 'Have I spoilt everything, Beccy? Please say I haven't. It's been such a special evening.'

'Of course you haven't spoilt it, Kit! I just felt I had to set the record straight. Don't let's talk about it any more.' We sat watching the fire fade to embers, talking about nothing in particular. Comfortable with each other again.

On the Sunday, although as far as I knew Mr Crabtree had not made one sale, I spent the day making more beauty preparations. I felt that if we had even the smallest amount of success it would be disastrous to keep customers waiting for further supplies.

The following morning did not bring a letter from Aaron, and by then I was getting very worried. Christmas was only a couple of weeks away. Flights had to be booked, arrangements made. I resolved to leave things one more day then cable the school. What did arrive in the post was a card from Charlie, simply saying '*Colour*?', and a letter from Mr Crabtree. Would I telephone him as soon as possible?

As I pulled on my jacket, ready to walk to the telephone box, I reflected that it was probably a self-defeating economy not to have a phone installed. Telephone lines went to Kit's farm and so surely it couldn't be that difficult or expensive to extend them to Munkyns.

I walked along the track which led to the road and considered the problem of choosing the right colour for the lipstick cases, as I assumed that's what Charlie was asking about. So much cosmetic packaging was 'feminine', in pretty but anaemic pastel colours. Or sometimes a more sophisticated black on white, such as Chanel and her imitators used. Then I remembered my dressing gown. How the gold monogram on the rich dark blue had a lush, baroque feel to it, and I decided then and there that was the positive, stylish image I wanted. Of course, there was no chance of gold lettering on the blue cases. But at least it was a start. And who knew? One day . . .

I telephoned Charlie first and arranged that the cases would be as rich a navy blue as possible. Then I dialled the number of Mr Crabtree's shop. After a few moments his shop assistant answered. I explained who I was, and then Mr Crabtree came on the line. 'Good morning, Miss Mandel. How are you?'

'I'm fine, and do please call me Beccy.'

'Thank you, Beccy. Now, I wanted to talk to you . . . On Friday I had a letter from my friend, the one I told you about. I'm afraid his fears were accurate and he is being forced to take an early retirement. He is very despondent about it.'

'I'm sorry.'

'Thank you. Yes. Well, . . . he lives, as do I, alone. He was divorced from his wife a number of years ago. A most unsuitable woman with hair a very unlikely shade of yellow. Not blonde, you understand, yellow.'

'I get the picture,' I said. And then couldn't help smiling at fond memories of Mrs Janowski's brightly coloured curls.

'I thought that he might like to come and stay with me for a while. It would ease my loneliness, and perhaps, help him through a difficult time in his life. The point is this. If he came to stay, he would be an ideal person to help me on my work investigating the use of preservatives in your recipes.

'But, Beccy, you have entrusted me with exact knowledge of the ingredients. If my friend helped me, I should have to pass that secret on to him. I can't possibly do that without your permission.'

'Yes, I understand that. Mr Crabtree, when we last spoke you described your friend as an honourable man. A man who, in spite of an understandable sense of resentment against his employers, would only give you the name of the preservatives he recommended, nothing more. I feel that you trust him. Why shouldn't I? Do, please, write to your friend and ask him to stay. By the sound of it, it will do you both good. By the way, what's his name?'

'Josiah. Josiah Beere. Joss to his friends.'

'I'm glad to hear it!' I laughed. 'I'd find Josiah much too biblical on a day-to-day basis. Any luck with selling my products, Mr Crabtree?'

'If you are to be Beccy then I insist on being Archie! No, only a few sales as yet. But, you know, it's early days.'

'Early days, yes,' I said, trying not to sound too disappointed. 'Well, goodbye. I'll be in touch soon, Archie.'

'You know, my dear, it's good to hear a woman's voice speaking my Christian name again. Goodbye.'

The following morning I heard at last from Aaron. It was a cable and simply read: 'IN DEBT STOP NOTHING SERIOUS STOP MONEY RESCUED ME STOP THANKS STOP SORRY SKIING THESE HOLS STOP P.S. WHAT'S YIDDISH FOR CHRISTMAS?'

I found my hands shaking with anger as I read it. If Aaron was in trouble, of course I would have sold the pendant to help him. But to take the money intended for his air fare, without a letter or any proper explanation! And why was he in debt? His allowance from the trust fund was not excessive, but it was generous. I was worried but didn't know how to cope with my worry. I simply couldn't ask Mike or Bruno to involve themselves further in my problems. In any case, would Aaron confide in them? And, yes, I had to face it, would he even tell them the truth? I paced the kitchen, absolutely furious with him. Then suddenly, I stopped and simply had to laugh. However rotten his behaviour over the money I'd sent him, he had scored a point with 'WHAT'S YIDDISH FOR CHRISTMAS?' Although it was something I'd wanted to give him, how ridiculous it was for two Jewish kids from the Lower East Side to have a Dickensian Christmas! And I could understand that Aaron preferred to spend his holidays with his friends, rather than his sister. If he wanted to go skiing, so be it. I'd spend Christmas alone. With John.

CHAPTER NINETEEN

I sat outside the buyer's office and waited. I'd been there for four hours but I was determined to see her. She was the buyer for the cosmetics department of one of the most distinguished stores in the world. If I could persuade her to carry my range of cosmetics it would be a giant leap forward. I'd telephoned several times to make an appointment but was always either brushed off by her secretary, or told to write in. I knew what that meant. My letter would go directly into a waste-paper basket. And so I'd decided to sit outside her office for as long as it took for her to agree to see me.

I'd planned my assault carefully. There seemed to me to be no point in giving her the whole of our now quite extensive range of products. But if I could convince her that my herb-based cosmetics really worked I must have a chance of interesting her in stocking them. The best way to do that surely was to get her to actually use them. What I desperately needed to know was her skin type. And to do that I must see her. But how? At that stage I didn't have a plan, but I had determination.

It was fall again. I'd been nearly a year at Munkyns. And, in the past six months, from morning to night the house had throbbed with activity. Three girls worked with me full-time. We'd exhausted the village's supply of perennial herbs which were a major part of our most popular cosmetics, and I was buying from herb farms the length and breadth of East Anglia.

What had started quietly, with a few respectable sales at Archie's shop, had, in the New Year, suddenly burgeoned. From a slow start, I found that in the weeks running up to Christmas it was practically impossible to keep up with the demand. Although it would have been totally unfair to place my products in another shop in Baildon, it appeared to me that our sales area could be extended.

I discussed this with Archie and arranged that, for a percentage of any new business, he would contact independent chemists in the area. I wanted to leave the chain stores until I could be sure we could supply increased demand. I'd bought a fairly decrepit old van which gave me mobility, however inelegantly. I drove myself through the region, mainly doing deals at craft shops and centres. The products, still only packaged in pharmaceutical brown glass containers, were simply labelled 'NATURAL INGREDIENTS' with beneath that the skin type or skin problem they were aimed at.

After I'd placed the products, there was always a lull while customers bought then tried them. After about four weeks, and strangely this time stayed constant, there would be a sudden surge in demand.

By midsummer I lacked only two things before attempting national marketing. Although Archie and Joss had proved conclusively in laboratory conditions that the preservatives worked for at least nine months, I wanted to be sure in terms of actual time. I also wanted to find a visual identity for the products.

A gold logo on blue was my cherished ambition. I'd been walking to Charlie's model shop, and by then had felt bold enough to try to take a short cut through the maze of little lanes that lay between the High Street and the shipyards and tiny port. Tucked away in a lane made up of ancient, timber-framed terraced houses, I came upon an antique shop. The items in the window were mainly bric-à-brac but a piece of vivid blue glassware caught my eye. It was exquisite. The colour was a deep, rich blue. At first sight dense, but when the light caught it, it seemed that every blue in the universe was encapsulated within. The glass encased a small spoon. A card in front of this enchanting object stated, '*Bristol glass. An étui, containing lady's snuff-spoon. Circa 1744*'.

I knew I'd found the glass I wanted. Was it possible to obtain a modern equivalent? I entered the shop. It smelt of bees-wax, old dogs, linseed oil, wood varnish, and the odd, over friendly cat!

As I entered the shop and the bell over the door tinkled, three Jack Russell terriers bounded towards me, each one trying to outdo the others by the insistence of its yappy welcome.

'QUIET, DOGS!' was roared from the depth of the shop.

A large, dishevelled young woman crashed her way through to where I was standing.

'Ooops!' said the proprietress. 'Breakages must be paid for. It costs me a fortune!'

I patted the dogs, then asked about the étui. Could one still buy Bristol glass?

'Not as such. One or two glassmakers are still making blue glass. They use a cobalt base. Most of the blue stuff you see around nowadays comes from Czechoslovakia though.'

'As good as this?'

'Ah! You've said a mouthful there, m'dear. No. It's good, but it hasn't got this depth. See!'

She held the exquisite piece of glass up to the light. The effect was quite breathtaking. I knew I had to own it. I could kid myself that, in fact, I wanted to use it as a model, but the truth was I'd just fallen in love with it.

'Look, I want to buy this but I don't suppose you know of anywhere in England, preferably in this region, where I could get blue glass made or blown or whatever you call it?'

'You haven't asked the price of the étui, you know.' She smiled. 'Just as well I'm an honest woman!'

I laughed at my own stupidity. 'I'm usually quite businesslike. You can tell I just fell in love with the damned thing.'

'It's £5, I'm afraid. You see it's eighteenth-century and . . .'

'£5 is okay!' I said, mentally berating myself for my extravagance. I couldn't afford it, but what the hell! The young antique dealer started crashing around again, searching for wrapping paper. I saw what she meant about breakages.

'Think there's some chap up by Kings Lynn who's started a small glassworks. You might try there. Not sure of his name but there's a Glassmakers' Federation, you know. They'd tell you. Got their number here somewhere.'

Bits of paper flew in all directions as she rustled through the drawers of her desk.

'Ah!' She jotted down a London telephone number on a piece of paper. 'Give them a buzz. I've always found them pretty helpful.'

'Thanks.'

And so my trail led to Stanley Upton-Smith. He'd started a small glassworks in a flint barn at a village outside the ancient town of Kings Lynn. I'd tracked down, through the Federation, a factory in Derbyshire which could make me a range of blue glass with a good depth of colour. But I needed to place a minimum order of fifty thousand! If I placed an order for that quantity I could get a price of 1s 3d per pot. I couldn't understand why I had to place such a huge order, but the factory manager I spoke to explained that every time they changed the colour of the glass they had to let the furnace cool, which meant a considerable loss of production time. Although the business was doing well, I was a long way from being able to place that kind of order.

The only alternative was to have a craftsman glassmaker hand blow the pots for me. Stanley Upton-Smith was the only glassmaker in the whole of East Anglia known to the Federation.

I telephoned and made an appointment. It was a long but fascinating drive to Kings Lynn. To Ely, where the great eleventh-century cathedral sits high above the vast, hedgeless fields of the Fens, then up through the dark, brooding Brecklands. Finally, after skirting Kings Lynn itself, I drove up into the saltings of north-west Norfolk, and arrived at the tiny village of Castle Mere.

In the manner of so many ancient villages, the cottages and houses were built right on to the village street. Many of the buildings were terraced. Sometimes an imposing brick-fronted Georgian house was attached to a small timber-framed cottage built centuries before. The terraces were broken by occasional cart tracks leading to gardens and outbuildings at the rear. Nailed to the side of a building was a sign pointing down one of these tracks. It simply read, '*Castle Glass*'.

I parked my van, and walked down the track to the flint, stone and pebble barn. As I neared it I could hear music. I recognised it as Mozart but was not well informed enough to identify more than that. From further down the village street I could hear a radio blaring out pop music, in strange contrast to this timeless setting.

The inside of the barn was warm from the furnace, which was closed. At the far end a tall, almost skeletal young man was carefully packing glass paper-weights. They were beautiful — clear glass with a centre of twisted, multi-coloured shapes.

'Mr Upton-Smith?'

'Yes? Oh, you must be Miss Mandel.' His tone totally lacked enthusiasm. He was treating me as an annoying disturbance rather than a customer. He was well spoken, but his voice was thin and reedy as if it wasn't used very often.

'A moment, please.'

While I waited for him to finish the packing I looked around the barn which doubled as workshop and gallery. Although Stanley Upton-Smith had what seemed to me a less than charming manner, he was clearly brilliant, his use of colour and form bold but with a delicacy within that boldness. After a few minutes, he joined me as I looked at a single wine glass. The drinking part of the glass was a simple flute shape, but the stem was twisted and coloured on a high conical foot.

'It's quite lovely,' I said.

'Yes. Isn't it?' the maker replied. No false modesty here! I decided to be as straightforward as he. I took out the thick brown glass pots and bottles which we used for the skin-care products and placed them on his desk. Then I took out the Bristol glass étui. A gasp of appreciation escaped from Mr Upton-Smith's thin lips. He reached out and touched the glass lovingly. As I looked at his entranced face, I realised that he wasn't unpleasant, simply totally absorbed by his art. Glass, for him, took precedence over everything else in life.

'I make cosmetics, Mr Upton-Smith. At the moment I market them in these plain brown pots and bottles. I want to make up a presentation of a few of my products, and I want it to be in blue glass as near to Bristol blue as possible. I'd also like a logo in gold on the glass. Just two letters. Could you do that?'

'I can do anything, Miss Mandel.'

'Except be modest,' I replied tartly.

To my astonishment he burst out laughing. 'Yes, anything but that! Think how much energy we expend pretending that we don't believe in ourselves. And why? Because some idiot once conned the northern races into believing that humility was a virtue. Bullshit! Humility simply makes you governable. Do *you* believe that the meek will inherit the earth?'

'Well,' I said slowly, 'they might *inherit* it . . . but only after the pushy bastards have finished with it!'

'A woman after my own heart.'

'Now hang on! That doesn't mean that I approve of the pushy bastards. I simply recognise that they're there. And having the best of it!'

'Mmm . . . yes. I have to tell you I'm on the side of the pushy bastards, not the angels. My father was a vicar. Strong on guilt, weak on love. Now, to business! How many? How soon?'

'How soon? Yesterday! How many? Two small bottles. Two medium pots. One small pot.'

'I'll have to hand blow them, free hand, for such a small order, you know. Cool the furnace. Set up the colour. There's no way I can do them for less than a pound each.'

'If I wanted to mass produce them later, could you do that?'

'Good Lord, no! Wouldn't even want to. I'll make

wooden moulds for you, though. We can agree a fee for the design after I've blown the pots and bottles. Have you a design for your logo?'

'Not really. Just two letters.' And, for the first time, I passed on the letters that were to give a name to my products – G.L. 'I want the feel to be baroque. An italic script perhaps. Not so fancy that you can't distinguish the letters, or how will people remember the product?'

'Like this?' With the confident, bold strokes of an artist, he drew the initials on a piece of scrap paper. It was exactly what I wanted. The line was dashing, even challenging. It made a statement.

'That's perfect! Oh, yes!' I smiled. There was no sting in my words. 'But you don't believe in compliments, do you?'

'If you believe in compliments, Miss Mandel,' Stanley Upton-Smith replied gravely, 'you have to believe in criticism. I'd rather trust myself, and the people who buy my glass.'

'Then I think you're an enviably sane man!'

'As a matter of curiosity, what does "G.L." stand for?'

'Grace Laure.'

'And who is Grace Laure?'

'I'm not sure,' I answered slowly. 'Possibly my alter ego.'

He smiled, and the smile illuminated his thin face. 'That sounds intriguing! What does it mean?'

And so I told him, with amusement, about the evening that Grace Laure had been born.

I'd decided to try a London store and thought I might as well start at the top. But I needed to package the product and to establish a name for it. In spite of the

success of Helena Rubenstein, Rebecca Mandel didn't
sound right to me. Possibly it was because I knew only
too well where Rebecca Mandel had grown up that I
couldn't associate my name with the pure, natural
products I was making!

I asked Archie, Joss and Charlie over to supper at
Munkyns to discuss the problem. As Charlie's shop was
near the quay, or the Hythe to give it its local name, he'd
bought fresh fish for us.

After the meal it was still light and we took glasses of
wine into the garden. I never tired of the view across the
fields to the water. We sat and chatted and then I told
them of my plan to try to storm the Knightsbridge store's
citadel, and that I wanted a woman's name for the
products, something that sounded sophisticated and
graceful.

'Well,' said Charlie, always the practical one, 'if you
want a graceful Christian name, why not call this mythical
woman "Grace"?'

I laughed. 'Great! That's fifty per cent of the problem
solved. I want the surname to sound European, but not
as if I was pretending to be French.'

'You started selling in Baildon. How about that for
a surname?' Archie said.

'Grace Baildon!' said Joss, appalled. 'Sounds like
someone who guts herring for a living.'

'Just a minute!' I was thinking back to the time I'd
spent with John in Paris. 'When we were in Paris there
was a little bistro we liked very much. We went there more
often than anywhere else. It was on the Rue de Lauré.
Supposing I dropped the acute accent over the "e" and
just made it Laure? Grace Laure — still pronounced in
the French way. What do you think?'

'Mmm. Grace Laure. Yes, I like it.' Archie raised his

244

glass. 'Here's to Grace Laure. May she one day be as famous as Estée Lauder or Elizabeth Arden.'

'Not to mention Helena Rubenstein,' added Joss.

And so we sat in the dying rays of the sun and raised our glasses to that newly born woman, Grace Laure.

'And are you going to be rich and famous, Grace Laure?' Stanley Upton-Smith asked.

'Well, to start with, I'm not Grace Laure. It's just a name. But I am ambitious. It isn't a male prerogative, you know,' I added, a little defiantly.

'Don't look so fierce. I never imagined it was.' He glanced at his watch. 'It's nearly one o'clock.'

'Oh, I'm sorry, I'm keeping you from your lunch.'

'That wasn't why I was drawing your attention to the time. I was about to ask you to lunch with me. There's a pub on the saltings at Castle Staithe that serves the best shellfish in East Anglia. I intend to take you there.'

I laughed. 'I can see why you're on the side of the pushy bastards! No "Will you?" Just "I intend to".'

'You look like the kind of girl who knows the difference between real and fake. I can't pretend to an effete manner I don't admire. I've asked you. A simple yes or no will suffice.'

I looked at his fine, intelligent face and remembered him saying that his childhood had been short of love. This was a young man who had made his own rules, realised his own talent and genuinely despised superficiality. I concluded that I liked him.

'A simple yes.'

'Good. I'll just lock up, then we'll drive over to the Staithe. It's about three miles to the coast.'

Five minutes later we were driving out of the village in an old estate car that was nearly as ramshackle as my van. On the way to Castle Staithe we drove through Heacham. I was looking out of the window at the countryside and was suddenly amazed to see what appeared to be acre after acre of dwarf lavender bushes. It was too late in the year for the lavender to be in flower but I was pretty sure what the bushes were. I asked Stanley about them.

'Oh, yes, it's lavender all right. The flowers are harvested in July and August. It's a wonderful sight just before harvest – a sea of hazy purple as far as the horizon. Let's make a date to see it next June.'

'I see. You *intend* to show me the lavender fields.'

He had the grace to laugh. 'I'd *like* to show you the lavender fields. Better?'

'Much!'

'Shall we make it a date then?'

'I don't really know where I'll be next June. I might be back home by then.'

'In the States?'

'Yes. Though now I come to think of it, I don't really have a home there. But I guess I'll go back, some day.'

We drove in silence for a few minutes and then Stanley said, 'What are you running away from, Beccy? Sorry! None of my damned business. But you are something of a mystery. Beautiful and expensively dressed young American women, who are trying to set up some sort of cottage industry in deepest, darkest East Anglia, do not arrive on my front doorstep very often. In fact, never before.' He glanced across at me. 'I don't mean to pry and I can see from your face it isn't something you want to talk about.'

I waited for a moment and then said: 'I don't mean to be mysterious or uncommunicative. It's just that the

events that brought me here are too recent and too painful
to talk about yet.'

'Especially,' Stanley added cheerfully, 'to a rude, glass-
blowing stranger. Come on, let's occupy our minds for
the last mile with thoughts of lunch. Delicious, mouth-
watering freshly cooked lobster? Cromer crab? Mussels
stewed in Norfolk cider? Home-made potted shrimps?
The humble cockle?'

'Stop it!' I laughed. 'You just made me realise how
hungry I am. I'll start drooling if you go on.'

An hour later, I leant against the back of the high wooden
settle on which I was sitting, totally replete. I'd had potted
shrimps served with mounds of home-baked bread and
farm butter. Then the most delicious, tender, freshly
boiled crab. Again, simply served with bread and butter
and freshly cut lettuce. With this feast from the North
Sea we had drunk a glass of locally brewed cider which
the landlady had drawn from an oak cask sitting on a
trestle behind the bar.

Before we drove back to Stanley's workshop we walked
along by the saltings. The tide was nearly out and layer
after layer of salt crust had been left. On the edge of the
marsh grew tall reeds. Stanley told me they were cut and
sold for Norfolk thatch. 'Although we don't call them
reeds around here. A true countryman from these parts
would call them windle-grass.'

We turned back and walked to the little pub's car park.
'I have enjoyed myself. I shall never regret that you
intended to bring me here. Thank you.'

'Will I see you again?'

I paused. 'As a friend?'

'No. I find you too exciting for that. As a lover.'

I shook my head. 'I'm sorry. Except for when I collect

the glass, I think it would be wiser for us not to meet again. Well, perhaps not wiser . . . fairer. I am sorry.'

'You're in love with someone?'

I hesitated, then: 'Yes, you could say that. I'm still in love with someone.'

He smiled at me. 'Don't look so sad. I shall wave you goodbye with the deepest, deepest regret. But I can't pretend that I could go on seeing you and not try to make love to you.' He sighed suddenly. 'Honesty is a curse, isn't it? I could have accepted your friendship then tried to seduce you . . . but I like you too much for that. Let's just say that if you ever fall out of love with my rival, I'd like to be the first to know!'

When I got back to Munkyns it was nearly six o'clock and the girls had gone home. I made myself a cup of coffee and sat at the kitchen table drinking it. I went over the day's events in my mind. Although Stanley was by no means good-looking, I had found him very attractive. I suspected that he would be a passionate and demanding lover, and a physical need, a longing to be loved again, briefly possessed me. But I knew that I still belonged to John and in a strange, perhaps twisted, way felt that if I sought sex without love I would be betraying him.

'But you can't be unfaithful to a dead man,' I whispered to myself.

I stood up abruptly and practically ran from the house, hurrying towards the path that led to the sea wall, and beyond that to a part of the shore I hadn't visited since I'd returned to Moreton.

I slid down the sea wall and then walked along the beach until I came to a part of the shoreline where the sand and shingle gave way to a sudden outcrop of rocks. It was just possible to climb over and around them and

I slithered and clambered across the rocks. On the far side I reached a little cove. It was sheltered by the rocks on one side and by a sandy promontory on the other. Rough marsh grass grew in tufts on the part of the beach rarely covered by the sea. Beyond the grass and small dunes rose the sea wall. Here it was very high and had been reinforced with slabs of concrete. It was virtually impossible to climb. The only way into the cove was over the rocks or from the sea.

John and I had seen it from the sea wall and had wanted to explore. And so the next day he hired a dinghy and we had sailed along the coast from Moreton Quay and then on into the estuary until we sighted the cove. We sailed further along the estuary to see if it was possible to reach from the land and had decided we would try to climb over the rocks.

We lazed away the rest of the day on the dinghy, returning to the rectory in the late afternoon. The evenings were still long and light until nearly ten o'clock. I suddenly had the idea that it would be fun to try to get to the cove right then. I was sure we'd find driftwood there and so I made up a picnic bag so that we could have a barbecue.

A childhood spent in the slums of New York had not exactly equipped me for the delights of open-air cooking. I could imagine barbecuing the steaks over a driftwood fire, but how to hold them in place? I took my problem to John. A great deal of his childhood had been spent on New England beaches and he knew exactly what to do. He found some chicken wire in the tool shed, cut it into shape with wire clippers and we had an instant and highly portable steak pan!

I sat on the beach, idly throwing pebbles at the sea, remembering that evening. I could almost smell the driftwood fire, hear the steaks sizzling. The cove that night had become our own enchanted kingdom and that was why I had never come back here. Now I needed to draw strength from my memories. I desperately needed to cling on to the love that John and I had felt for each other. I gave my mind, my whole being, to remembrance. And then, suddenly, it was no longer a memory. I was *there*. Time was suspended. I hadn't been to Castle Staithe that day. I'd been out on the estuary with John.

In the long, long golden and pink twilight that is so unique to England at that time of the year, we gathered driftwood, collected small rocks and stones to surround the fire, played Ducks and Drakes with pebbles, and generally behaved like two happy schoolchildren.

The water of the estuary was calm with just small sea horses on the waves further out where the river mouth widened to the sea. The water looked inviting, and as that part of the coast was totally deserted, I stripped off my old jeans, my panties, and cotton Breton jumper and ran into the water. The chill of it took my breath away at first but as I started to swim the water seemed warmer. John had taught me to swim a year previously and I loved it. I heard a splash behind me and knew that he had followed me in.

We swam for about ten minutes. There was a wonderful sense of freedom about swimming nude. The tide was turning and the water becoming a little more choppy. I dived through a wave, my body tingling with the exercise and the salt water. I let the next carry me back in towards the shore and suddenly I was in John's arms.

'Happy?'

'Wonderfully, crazily happy. And you?'

'Oh, my God, Beccy! There aren't enough words in the universe to tell you how happy I am with you . . . How much I love you.'

Suddenly he was no longer hugging me but kissing me passionately. Holding me close to him as the waves broke against our bodies. The buoyancy of the water was lifting me off my feet. John dived beneath the waves and I let myself lean back on to the support of the water and floated on my back. Then he was with me again. He dived beneath me and then he was pushing open my legs. His mouth, his tongue, were loving me. I gasped with pleasure. With desire. He twisted in the waves and was behind me, his hands caressing my breasts. He started to swim with me towards the shore.

When the water became too shallow to swim, John lifted me in his arms. He laid me on the sand where the waves just gently lapped against our bodies. He touched my wet hair. 'You look like a mermaid. I love you, Beccy. Oh, God, I must have you!'

I clasped my salty legs around his body as he entered me. I couldn't get enough of him. He was in me. Filling me. I shouted out my love, my passion, to the wheeling gulls. Then we lay in each other's arms and let the sea water cool our exhausted bodies.

Afterwards we let the warm evening air dry us as we lit the driftwood and watched the smoky flames leap into life.

I rose and walked to where we had built our barbecue. The winter seas had washed over the place time and time again. There was nothing left. And yet that evening held me still as firmly as if some ancient sorcerer had cast a spell over me. I knew beyond any doubt that I had been right not to see Stanley again. One day I would love again but for now I was still John's. I turned my back to the sea and started to retrace my steps, to walk back the way I had come. For the present there was room for only one thing in my life – my work.

At lunchtime on the day I'd waited to see the buyer, Mrs Blake, she came out of her office and glanced at me with irritation. Her secretary had already told me not to wait but I'd insisted that I hoped Mrs Blake could spare me just a few minutes. She left for lunch without coming near me. At two o'clock precisely she returned and entered her office without looking in my direction. Still I waited. I carried a presentation package. The cosmetics were in Stanley Upton-Smith's beautiful blue glass jars and bottles. We already had a brochure with a list of our products, but I'd had a high quality cover made up with our new logo, 'G.L.', on the front.

A couple of weeks earlier, my heart in my mouth, I'd carried out my plan to discover Mrs Blake's skin type. I'd scraped my hair back into a tight bun, the Plain Jane hairstyle John had so hated. Under my coat, I wore a neat white blouse and plain skirt. My shoes could only be described as 'sensible'. In my handbag I had a pair of spectacles, a notebook for taking shorthand and a well-sharpened pencil. I entered the store and went straight to the Kitchenware section, where I bought a large breadboard. This meant that I was given it in one of the store's big, distinctive carrier bags. Then I went to the ladies' cloakroom. I took my coat off and put it in the bag. By the rear entrance to the store there was a left-luggage department. Also a dog kennel, they thought of everything! I left the carrier bag there then took the lift to the third floor.

I knew I wouldn't be able to get through the main staff entrance, but I'd noticed that on every floor there was a 'Staff Only' door. I put on the spectacles and took out the shorthand notebook and pencil. I carried them in what I hoped was a purposeful, secretarial way and slipped through the staff door.

I made my way to the top floor where I knew Mrs Blake's office was located. This hadn't been difficult to find out. I'd telephoned her secretary and said I was arranging a delivery, which floor should I send the package to? I'd also telephoned the Personnel Department and pretended I was going to apply for a job. I now had the name of the senior Personnel Officer.

As I approached Mrs Blake's outer office I was so scared the palms of my hands started to run with sweat. If her secretary was in, I was going to say I was working temporarily at the store while the Personnel Officer's secretary was on holiday. I'd just have to pray that his secretary and Mrs Blake's weren't bosom buddies. To my immense relief the outer office was empty. I crossed to a door at the rear. It seemed reasonable to assume that this led to Mrs Blake's room. I knocked and walked straight in. The buyer was working at her desk. She looked up as I entered.

'Yes?'

'Mrs Blake?'

'Yes. Who are you? And what do you want?'

'I hope you don't mind my dropping in like this. You see, my sister wants to work in the Cosmetics Hall and . . .'

'Now come on, young lady, you know better than that. All applications have to go through Personnel.'

'Oh, I know, but . . .'

'But, nothing! Off you go, I'm busy. Shooo!'

'Right . . . sorry!'

I turned on my heel and left the office as quickly as

I could. It was all I could to do to stop myself running. But I'd discovered what I wanted to know: Mrs Blake's skin type. Now I could make up a personal range just for her.

Her skin type I'd recognised as very common. I know now it's referred to as a combination skin: dry skin on the cheeks and forehead, but with an oily panel down the nose and chin.

I'd selected a marsh-mallow night cream for use on the dry areas of Mrs Blake's skin. A rosemary lotion to put on the oily areas. Our thyme cleanser was gentle but slightly antiseptic and I knew this could be used on both the dry and oily areas. Similarly the moisturiser could be used on both areas as long as it was used sparingly on the centre panel of nose and chin. A parsley-based moisturiser that I'd developed since moving to Munkyns seemed to me ideal. A cucumber toner and the clove, apple and grape hand cream completed the pack.

I waited another two hours, then the door of the inner office was thrown open. 'All right. That's it. I've cracked! I'll see you.'

'Oh, thank you.' I rose, clutching the *G.L.* presentation pack as if it were a life-line. Perhaps it was.

'Come in. Now, what product are you representing?' She led the way into her office. I followed.

'My own. It's a range made entirely from natural ingredients – Grace Laure.'

'Very well, Miss Laure. I'll give you precisely five minutes to tell me why I should consider your products.'

It was the first time I'd ever been called Laure, but it was a natural assumption to make and I didn't want to waste my five minutes explaining that my name was really Rebecca Mandel. 'Rather than tell you about them, I've brought along some examples of our skin-care range.

You have a dry skin but with an oily panel down the centre.'

'Correct! It's damnably difficult to deal with.' She smiled ruefully. 'Even though I have the best beauty products in the world to choose from!'

It was such an honest thing to say I warmed to Mrs Blake. I set the lotions and creams in front of her. The blue glass with its gold lettering looked warm and elegant.

'Would you try using these for, say, four weeks?'

'Oh, now, really!'

'What have you got to lose? You've said yourself you find coping with your skin a problem. We use only the purest ingredients and a minimum of preservatives.' I quickly explained to her about the toxins created by using too much preservative, and that our skin-care range was designed to have a shelf life of only nine months.

'. . . That way the vitamins and minerals that occur naturally in the ingredients have a chance to work. Do, please, try them.'

Mrs Blake was watching me as I spoke. 'And do you use these products?'

'Of course! I have since I was a little girl.'

'Well, you have the most beautiful skin . . . Very good! No promises but I will give these a try. You're taking quite a risk, aren't you? I'm an influential woman and if they don't work . . .'

'They will!' I interrupted. 'Thank you for seeing me.'

'My dear, you looked such a cross between determined and lost, it was either see you or send you to Battersea Dogs' Home!' She offered me her hand. 'I'll be in touch.'

CHAPTER TWENTY

It was early evening on Friday. The girls who worked with me had gone giggling and chattering down the track on their bicycles. It would be at least another week before I heard from Mrs Blake – if, indeed, I heard from her at all. The telephone started to ring and I answered it. A craft centre further up the coast wanted to know if I could rush them more stocks. They'd practically sold out. I promised a delivery as early in the week as possible. Already we could hardly cope with demand. If we got a substantial order from Mrs Blake it would be both a blessing and a headache. I would have to commit myself to expansion. With the increased sales in East Anglia, that had been on the cards for some time, but I was nervous of over extending my resources. Most of my jewellery had been sold and to make the next step forward would take several thousand pounds. Well, I thought wryly, the coming weekend was definitely not the time to dwell on business problems.

I was going, for the first time, to D'Arcy House with Kit. It was his father's sixty-fifth birthday and the family were giving a ball. Kit and I had jogged along in an easy relationship. We had grown fond of each other. Sometimes I looked at his hard, young body and wondered what it would be like to lie in his arms. But I truly wasn't ready for a love affair and, since the night at Munkyns when he had hinted that we might become lovers, he hadn't pressed me, and for that I was very grateful. I'd occasionally see him out riding or at the village pub with a girl, but rarely the same one twice. I wondered about Kit's love life as I packed, then sternly reminded myself that his sexual adventures were none of my business. In any case, I was flattered that I was the girl he wanted by his side at D'Arcy House. Kit had warned me that it would be black-tie and very formal.

'That's okay! I haven't spent all my life as a country bumpkin, you know! I'll just have to shake out a lot of mothballs!' I'd laughed.

It seemed strange to take out the elegant, sophisticated clothes that had been so much a part of my life with John. I was going to travel in a gently pleated tweed skirt, with matching shawl. It was the softest Irish tweed, the colour of early heather. With it I wore a white fine wool polo-necked jumper. I tucked the jumper into the skirt and added a wide, soft leather belt that John had bought for me at Hermès. I pulled my hair back on to the nape of my neck with a large, tortoiseshell slide. I hoped I looked sufficiently 'country house' to make Kit proud of me.

He had arranged with his family that we would arrive after dinner, and so we drove up through the winding lanes of Suffolk at a leisurely pace. Rufus, as always, accompanied his master, stretched across the back seat on an old rug. He was happy simply to be near Kit.

We stopped for supper at an old, low-ceilinged, black-beamed inn then drove on to D'Arcy House. As we arrived the ancient house was a blaze of light. It looked heart-stoppingly beautiful.

'My God, it's lovely, Kit!' I said involuntarily.

For a moment, his face softened. 'Yes, it is.' Then his manner changed to his usual cynicism about his heritage. 'I just wish someone else owned the ruddy pile!'

Our car had been heard and the door was opened by an elderly butler. 'Welcome home, Your Lordship.'

It seemed strange to hear Kit addressed by his title. Over this weekend I would obviously have to get used to it.

'Thank you, Paget. This is Miss Mandel. Get someone to show her to her room, then guide her to wherever the family are holed up, will you, please? I'll go through to the kitchens, say "hallo", and get Rufus fed.' Kit turned and smiled at me. 'Paget will take care of you. I'll meet you in, say, fifteen minutes for a drink and introductions. All right?'

'Fine!'

Kit had carried our cases in from the car, so I imagined a certain amount of democracy existed at D'Arcy House. As he hurried off with Rufus, a young fresh-faced country girl appeared as if summoned by remote control. 'Russell will show you to your room, miss.'

'Thank you.'

Russell gave me an impish grin that was refreshing after Paget's starchiness.

'Miss Mandel is in the Rose Room in the East Wing, Russell.'

'Right you are, Mr Paget!' the maid replied cheerily. I swear Paget blanched at her easy manner, but I found it friendly and charming. I followed Russell up the magnificent carved oak staircase through the Long Gallery and then along a maze of twisting corridors. 'You will come back and find me, won't you?' I said. 'I'll never get back to the Hall otherwise!'

'Took me weeks to find me way about when I first come here. Like a blooming maze, it is! Here we are.'

She opened the door to my room and switched on the light. The incongruously feeble fitting in the centre of the ceiling barely illuminated the vast room. There was a four-poster with dusty-looking, and possibly priceless, tapestry drapes hanging around it. The room appeared to be clean but smelt musty from disuse.

'Cor!' said Russell involuntarily. 'Enough to give you the creeps, isn't it?' Then her hand went to her mouth as she repented her familiarity. 'Sorry, miss!'

I laughed. 'Don't apologise. I quite agree! Thank heavens it's only for a couple of nights.'

'I could light a bit of a fire in the hearth later. That should cheer things up.'

'Thanks, but don't bother. By the look of this room the chimney is probably blocked with old birds' nests. To say nothing of the odd bat!'

'Well,' said Russell dubiously, 'I'll leave you to have a bit of a wash and brush up, then after you've joined the family, I'll unpack for you. Bathroom's through there, miss.'

'Thank you. But there's really no need to unpack for me, I can . . .'

'It's my job, miss,' she interrupted. Then suddenly grinned. 'Old Paget'd have a blue fit if I let you do it yourself!'

'Okay.' I shrugged.

'Ta!' she said cheerfully, and headed for the door.

'Oh, Russell?'

'Yes, miss?'

'Do you mind if I call you by your first name?' I smiled. 'We Yanks get uneasy with too much formality.'

'It's Polly. Thanks!'

She left and I was alone in that miserable room. I crossed to the bathroom. It was nearly as big as the bedroom and even more bleak. Clearly the British aristocracy weren't strong on home comforts.

I washed, brushed my hair and freshened my make-up. About ten minutes later Polly returned and led me through the house. The family were apparently in the Little Parlour, a room which led off the Great Parlour where I'd seen the Munnings. The Little Parlour proved to be only marginally less magnificent than the Great Parlour! Kit explained to me later that in the Middle Ages a nobleman dined in a large Hall with his family, servants, henchmen, etc. During Tudor times manners changed and smaller rooms were built in the great houses where the family could enjoy their privacy. Thus the Great Parlour and the Little Parlour leading off the huge Banqueting Hall.

As I entered the room, Kit immediately came to me, took my arm and led me towards his family and their guests. I identified the Earl immediately because Kit was so like him. Kit's mother, the Countess, proved to be a thin, rather horsey-looking woman. Whereas the Earl was friendly, her greeting lacked any pretence at warmth. I'd no way of knowing if that was her usual manner or whether she'd taken an instant dislike to me. The Earl poured me a drink while Kit introduced me to the other guests. One girl in particular I noted with amusement. She was a very pretty young deb, Lady Ursula. I was fairly sure the Countess had invited her to distract Kit from paying me too much attention.

'Are you comfortable? Is your room all right?' he asked.

I hoped my face did not reflect my true feelings about the room in which I was to spend the next two nights.

'Perfectly, thank you,' I replied.

'Where has Paget put her, Mother?'

The Countess looked slightly uncomfortable. 'Er, I'm not sure, Kit darling. Get me another drink, will you?'

As he took his mother's glass, I said, 'The Rose Room, I think it's called. In the East Wing.'

Kit stopped. 'The East Wing? Good God, Mother, how could you let Paget put her there? It's like Dracula's Castle! It's virtually never used.'

'It's quite all right,' I said.

'It is not! I'll go and see the damn fool and get you moved right away.' Kit was really quite angry. I saw him glance at his mother with what could almost be described as dislike. 'I'll get your drink in a minute, Mother.'

He left the room and there was a moment's awkward silence. Then it seemed that everyone started to talk at once. Welcome to D'Arcy House! I thought.

As I dressed for the ball on the following evening I reflected on the change that Kit's angry outburst had brought about. I was now lodged in a delightful room in the West Wing. This room was large also but it had warmth and charm. It was panelled, the wood lovingly polished. The drapes and matching bedspread were in a beautiful flowery chintz. The bathroom was bright and relatively modern. There were magazines, flowers and a decanter of sherry on a table by the window. Everything the perfect hostess would supply for a welcome guest. I didn't want to jump to conclusions, but it seemed clear to me that I was not welcome at D'Arcy House, and my hostess had expressed her disapproval by putting me in one of the most dismal rooms in the establishment. She clearly didn't know her son very well if she thought she could get away with that!

My ballgown was laid out on the bed. Polly had ironed it for me and, when she'd brought it back, confided, 'Yours is the nicest of all the ladies who are staying.' I thanked her and took some comfort from that. I was sure the Countess would have liked nothing better than for me to look like Cinderella *after* the clock chimed midnight! Well, she was going to be disappointed. I had a beautiful gown. We'd bought it in Paris because we'd been invited to a ball given by one of John's wealthy French business associates. We were to have attended it just before we flew back to the States. Oh God, it still hurt so much. I still missed him desperately. 'Don't cry! Crying won't bring him back!' I clenched my hands until my nails dug into my palms. Slowly the moment passed and I was in control again.

There was a brief tap at the door and Polly entered. She'd come to help me dress. The gown was made of black lace. From a nipped waist, the skirt billowed out over a taffeta underslip. The neck was high at the front, but plunged practically to the waist band at the back. The bodice beneath the lace was very low cut but with the see-through black lace covering the tops of my breasts and shoulders. The sleeves were long and tapered to a point just below the wrist. I knew how lucky I was to have such a dress. It said everything there was to say about Paris and *haute couture* at its very best. I'd dressed my hair high to show off the back of the dress and taken from the bank in Baildon two of my last remaining pieces of jewellery — a pair of diamond clips. I put them in my hair. The dress really needed nothing else.

'Cor! You aren't half going to knock 'em in the aisles, miss,' Polly said appreciatively.

'Thanks, Polly. You've been so kind to me.'

' 'T'aint nothing! I've been pleased to look after you, miss. Not as I could say that for some of the stuck-up so and so's I have to deal with!'

There was a brisk knock at the door and Kit called out, 'Are you decent, Beccy?'

I laughed. 'Decent as I'll ever be! Come in.'

Kit entered carrying two flute-shaped glasses of champagne. 'I thought we could do with some Dutch courage . . .' he said as he entered. Then he stopped as he saw me. 'Christ, Beccy, you look beautiful!'

'I could say the same about you.' He looked extremely handsome in evening dress.

'Do you need me any more, miss?' Polly asked.

'No, thanks. But I am grateful for your help.'

'Yes,' Kit added, 'thank you, Russell.'

I burst out laughing. 'Oh, for God's sake, Kit. Her name's Polly!'

'Oh, miss!' Polly giggled.

'Yes, you're right. From now on it's Polly.'

'Oh, Your Lordship, what would Mr Paget say?'

Kit grinned. 'I really don't know. Perhaps I'll start calling him Fred!'

This was too much for Polly who collapsed into another fit of giggling and fled.

Kit handed me a glass of champagne. 'You're right, of course. D'Arcy House needs to join the twentieth century. A breath of the New World, that's what we need!' He raised his glass to me. 'You'd be good for us here, Beccy.'

Over your mother's dead body, I thought.

The ball was wonderful. I danced and danced. Mostly with Kit, who seemed impervious to his mother's frowns. I danced with the Earl twice. I gathered from Kit that this was quite an honour as his father loathed dancing.

'He thinks you're an absolute corker!' Kit laughed.

'A what? I mean, is that a compliment?'

'Pretty Wodehousian, isn't it? But, yes, to my father's generation it places you somewhere between an object of desire and a good sport. Praise indeed!'

'Oh, I see,' I said as Kit whirled me around the floor of the banqueting hall. 'A corker is someone you like . . . even after you've slept with her!' Kit's arm tightened around my waist. 'Got it in one.'

At eleven o'clock there was a splendid buffet supper served in the Long Gallery. Then the young danced on until a breakfast of kedgeree and Buck's Fizz at dawn. I thought about Kit saying that his family couldn't afford D'Arcy House. Well, the ball must have cost a fortune. Evidently our ideas of poverty differed considerably.

Polly woke me with tea at noon. In spite of the previous night's revelry, the family were still lunching at one. Most of the house guests left after the meal. Kit and I planned to leave at about four. He and his father went riding after lunch while I walked through the beautiful grounds. When I returned to the house, Paget approached me. 'Excuse me, miss. Would you join Lady Alice in her sitting room for tea?'

'Yes, of course. Thank you.'

He led me to the Countess's private sitting room on the first floor. Kit's mother was seated by the window working on a tapestry. A tray of tea was set on a table by the fire. As I entered the room she rose and crossed to the tea table. She indicated a chair nearby. 'Won't you be seated, Miss Mandel?'

'Thank you.' Her manner towards me had been so unfriendly the whole weekend there seemed little point in suggesting she called me by my first name.

'Milk or lemon?'

'Lemon, please. No sugar.'

When she had poured us both tea she sat down in an armchair opposite me.

'I'll come straight to the point, Miss Mandel. I shall

do everything in my power to stop you from marrying
my son.'

I was absolutely astonished. Kit had never even kissed
me. Why on earth should this forbidding woman assume
that marriage was a possibility?

'Lady Alice, there is not the remotest possibility of our
marrying. However, if there was, if I truly loved Kit, no
one — I repeat, *no one* — would stop me. I hope I make
myself clear!' I put down my tea cup and rose. 'Now,
if you will excuse me?'

'Please don't go, Miss Mandel! I realise I've been very
rude . . . unkind even . . . but I love my son very much.
I don't want to see him hurt.'

'Why on earth should I hurt Kit?'

'It wouldn't be you, my dear. He would hurt himself!
Sit down and hear me out . . . please!'

I hesitated a moment then nodded stiffly. 'Very well.'

'What I am about to say will no doubt make you angry.
I can only ask you to listen to it in its entirety and then,
I hope, you may find it in your heart to forgive me.'

'Yes?'

'When Kit started to write to me about you, then, on
his rare visits here, spoke about you with admiration, I
took it upon myself to . . . to . . . have you investigated.'

I suddenly felt sorry for this haughty woman. It was
clearly painful for her to admit that she had behaved in
a, by any standards, underhand way.

'I have no secrets from Kit. In fact, I have no secrets
from anyone. If you'd wished to know about my life,
you had only to ask.'

'Yes. Now that I've met you I think that's true. But
I wasn't to know that, was I? I'm afraid that the heir
to an Earldom attracts many . . . er . . . how shall I put
it?'

'Gold-diggers?'

'Ah, yes! Sometimes you Americans have exactly the right word. Believe me, please, when I say that it is not your relationship with John Kimberly, nor your impoverished background, that makes you unsuitable to be the next Countess. It is the fact that you are a woman of the world. A woman who, I assume, is sexually experienced. And, being so, would find it difficult to live without sexual satisfaction.'

'But why on earth . . .?'

'Kit needs to marry. He's our only son,' the Countess interrupted. 'But he needs a well-bred, dull English girl, who will not make a nuisance of herself. Will give him an heir and then turn a blind eye.'

I was by now thoroughly bewildered. 'A blind eye to what?'

Kit's mother sighed. 'Miss Mandel, my son is a homosexual.'

'What?' I rose abruptly and crossed to the window. 'I can't believe it!' But even as I said it, so much fell into place. Kit's anguish about his heritage. His easy acceptance that our relationship should be totally sexless. And yet, if it was true, how sad that he felt he must hide his sexuality . . . deny his instincts . . . suppress his natural desires in order to maintain the D'Arcy dynasty. How cruel life was! Then I thought, if the Countess was being honest, Kit had been less than fair with me. He had immense charm. He was great company. It would have been easy to fall in love with him. And then?

'If he were to marry a strong woman, with strong desires, I truly believe it would lead to a tragedy,' the Countess continued. 'In his late teens and early twenties there were one or two relationships. During the last few years I think he has been trying to fight against his natural inclinations. But it hasn't made him happy and I can't believe it will last. I'm sorry if my honesty has distressed you, but I hope you will come to forgive me. I want Kit to find a way . . . a path . . . that he can tread without too much unhappiness. He might think now that you could be his salvation but it would be desperately unfair on both of you.'

'Yes,' I said. 'You've been very wise. For all our sakes.'

The Countess smiled bitterly. 'Among the upper classes it is not an uncommon problem. Inbreeding. Our public school system. Whatever the reason, you have too much life, too much energy, to live a lie.'

'Would you excuse me now? I'd like to be alone for a while. Before . . . before Kit and I drive back.'

'Of course. But you do believe me, don't you?'

I looked at her sad, haggard face for a moment. The mask of hauteur was completely gone, leaving only an expression of despair.

'Yes, I'm afraid I do.' So saying, I hurried from the room.

CHAPTER TWENTY-ONE

The following week was hectic. On the Monday I engaged a lad from the village as van driver. It seemed a nonsense for me to take time off from actually preparing my skin-care products to drive all over East Anglia making deliveries. But even so, I was constantly taken away from the work in the kitchen to answer the telephone. Even without an order from Mrs Blake we would either have to expand or refuse new outlets.

I hadn't seen Kit all week. He seemed rather subdued on the drive back from D'Arcy House. I wasn't sure whether that was because we were both tired after an exhausting weekend, or whether he suspected his mother had spoken with me. I had decided not to mention the Countess's revelation. If Kit wanted to confide in me, so be it. I could see no reason why our friendship couldn't continue. But I knew I would be desperately hurt if he asked me for more than that. Of course, I was aware that some men, and for that matter women, are bisexual. But for me, personally, the idea of my lover being unfaithful to me with another man appalled me.

On the Friday evening Kit finally came to see me. I was sitting at the kitchen table, working on the accounts for the week, when I heard the sound of a car coming up the track. As I opened the front door, Kit was just parking. He got out of the car followed by Rufus who ran ahead up the front path to greet me. Kit carried a bottle of champagne. When he got to the door, he hesitated for a moment. 'We *are* welcome, aren't we, Beccy?'

'Don't be silly, of course you are! Come on in. But why the champagne?'

'Why not?' Kit said flippantly.

I shrugged and grinned. 'Why not, indeed! Come into the living room. The kitchen is knee deep in pots of cream and bottles of lotions, to say nothing of my accounts spread everywhere. There are some glasses in the corner cupboard. But you know that by now, don't you?'

While Kit got the glasses I knelt in front of the fire and lit it. The days were still warm, but the evenings were chilly and so I'd laid a fire ready in the hearth. The kindling crackled into flames and the logs started to catch. Kit had got me some cedar wood and the room was almost immediately tinged with its spicy smell.

He opened the champagne and handed me a glass. He raised his own. 'I give you a toast. To friendship, and an end to dishonesty!'

'Oh, Kit!' I put down my glass untouched. 'It's true then?'

Kit didn't answer at once. He crossed and sat in one of the armchairs by the fire, staring into the leaping flames.

'The truly, truly bloody thing is, Beccy, I don't want to be like this! I want a wife and family. Oh, nothing to do with the whole aristocratic inheritance rubbish! I desperately want to be . . . normal.'

He looked so utterly, infinitely sad. I crossed and knelt by him. Took his hand. 'Kit, dear Kit, it's nothing to be ashamed of. I guess we are as we are.'

'But why? Why? You slept with John Kimberly, didn't you? Desired him? Wanted him to touch you. To love you. Imagine if you discovered that that's how you felt about another woman. Wouldn't you be frightened, disturbed, and finally disgusted?'

'Oh, Kit!' I shook my head. 'I don't know what to say. How to help.'

'Just talking about it is an incredible relief. As to help . . . well! If I promised never, never to be unfaithful with anyone, in any way, would you still marry me? Who knows? Perhaps the best basis for marriage is friendship.'

'You don't really believe that, do you, Kit? Yes, I don't think any relationship can survive without friendship, but for me, even if it finally led to unhappiness, bitterness, I'd have to feel passion for the man I married.' I squeezed his hand, trying to lighten the moment. 'In any case, I'd be ridiculous as a Countess!'

'You're very wrong there.' He rose and fetched my glass of champagne. 'Here we are, my dear girl, drink up. Like so many things in life, once the bubbles go flat, it's not worth a damn!'

As I sipped my champagne Kit stood looking down at me. 'We can still be close, can't we, Beccy? I couldn't bear it if you despised me.'

I rose and hugged him to me. 'Oh, Kit, of course I don't despise you. I never will! You're my friend. You're one of the kindest, most thoughtful, dearest men I've ever met. If only . . .' I added softly.

'Yes,' said Kit bitterly. 'If only.'

Saturday, Sunday, Monday, I worked. Late in the afternoon on Tuesday, I got the call I'd been waiting for. Mrs Blake telephoned to say she was impressed with the skin-care range I'd given her. Could we meet and discuss her store stocking Grace Laure products? I put the telephone down and sat by it, stunned. Then I let out a yell that threatened to bring the dust of ages down from between the beams.

Ivy's daughter Peggy was the first to reach me from the kitchen, the other two girls close behind.

'Oh, my God, Beccy! What is it?'

I started to laugh with happiness.

'If it's a fit,' said one of the other girls helpfully, 'we ought to put a bit of wood in her mouth . . . stop her biting her tongue.'

This made me laugh even more. Finally, I started to hiccup. Peggy got me a glass of water. 'Can you tell us what's wrong?'

'I had an auntie took like this,' said the third girl lugubriously. 'Six feet under, she was, within the week!'

'Shut your mouth, you!' This from Peggy, tartly. Then to me, kindly, 'Come on, love. Have another sip of water. Try and drink from the other side of the glass. That usually does the trick with hiccups.'

Gradually the hiccuping slowed down, then stopped. I leant back in the chair, sighing with relief, then beamed at them like the Cheshire Cat. 'Is Alf back yet with the van?'

'Not yet, why?'

'Then have any of you got a parcel rack on the back of your bikes, so that I can ride pillion?'

'Yes. But why?'

I leaped up. 'Is the pub open yet?'

'Five-thirty. Opening about now.'

'Then come on! Everyone to their bikes. We're off down to the pub for champagne!'

The girls looked at each other, partly delighted, partly worried. 'You *are* all right, aren't you?' Peggy asked. 'Not sickening for anything?'

'No! We have just had the biggest, the best, the most

prestigious order you can imagine! AND WE'RE GOING TO CELEBRATE!'

The four of us dashed outside like crazy women. I climbed on behind Peggy, and then we bumped off down the track, shouting and laughing.

We attracted considerable attention as we thundered down the road to the village, a gaggle of cycling girls, Peggy bringing up the rear with me hanging on like grim death, my arms around her ample waist. All of us so young, so happy, so excited. Some villagers turned and stared, some laughed and waved because our mood was so infectious.

At the pub I emptied the contents of my purse on to the counter. 'When we've used up this, will you let me put the rest on the slate?' I asked the publican. He hesitated for a moment, then grinned. 'Right you are! I reckon you've been here long enough now to count as a villager.'

'Rubbish,' I said. 'That takes at least fifty years . . . but you can trust me to pay my debts! Champagne, please, landlord.' It was good of him to let me have credit, but I was enough of a realist to know that much of that was due to the fact that I had often been seen in the pub with Kit D'Arcy. In spite of centuries of misuse, the common people of England still trust a lord!

I'm ashamed to say I remember little of that evening. Except that, for the moment, I put problems of finance and expansion behind me and was happy. I gather Alf and Peggy took me home in the van at closing time, and Peggy put me to bed. And, as I suspect that they were pretty well as worse for wear as I was, it was lucky that the village policeman was drinking with us in the pub too!

CHAPTER TWENTY-TWO

The following Friday I had lunch with Mrs Blake. The order they were placing was indeed considerable. I saw no point in being anything but honest with her.

'To keep you supplied with the amount of product you will need once customers have tried our skin-care range will . . .'

'Now, just a minute, Miss Laure.' One day I would have to tell her my name was Mandel. 'You're being very optimistic here.'

'No, realistic! It has always taken a month, then demand takes off. I can't explain why four weeks is the magic time span, but I also cannot accept that London women are going to react that differently from their East Anglian sisters! I don't want an increased demand that we can't meet. If you will give me an order – in writing, of course – and six months to deliver, I can guarantee that we will have increased production sufficiently to meet demand.'

She thought about this for a moment. 'Yes. I can't see why not. But if we have to wait six months for the first delivery, I'm afraid I can't authorise any advance payments.'

'That's quite all right,' I said, with a confidence I didn't feel. Where was I going to get finance? 'The written order will suffice.'

That night at my account books I tried to figure the cost of expansion. There was a small factory unit on the industrial estate at Baildon that I already had my eye on. I could rent, not buy, that but would still have to pay six months in advance. The pots and bottles made up in blue glass would cost a little over three thousand pounds. Could I do a better deal with the glassworks than that? And wages! I would need at least five more girls to help with the making. Joss had settled in Baildon, and had bought a charming bow-fronted house on the Hythe. I very much wanted to ask him to join us, even if only part-time, but would never do so unless I could offer him a decent salary.

I finished my calculations and came to the gloomy conclusion that I would need, in total, at least six thousand pounds. I had a profit of seven hundred pounds banked. The remains of my jewellery – and, yes, I'd have to sell all of it – would fetch about two thousand pounds. I had approximately five hundred dollars remaining of the money that Briony had left me. That left a shortfall of a little over three thousand pounds. It was a hell of a lot but once I had the order from Mrs Blake, surely my bank would loan me the rest. But a chill voice inside said: 'Lend to a single woman? A foreigner who owns nothing.' What could I do but try?

I'd decided to sleep on it, but the next morning I received a cable that put all thoughts of business and of finance right out of my mind. It simply read, 'DOLL HAS DIED PEACEFULLY IN HER SLEEP STOP FUNERAL WEDNESDAY NEW YORK STOP THOUGHT YOU'D WANT TO KNOW STOP ALL LOVE MIKE'

I knew immediately that the first call on my finances was a plane ticket to New York. Doll, dear Doll, had been part of my life for so long. Had always been there for me. I think I loved her nearly as much as Mike did. It was unthinkable that I should not be with him at her funeral. I telephoned the one and only travel agent in Baildon. The first available flight was very early on Wednesday morning, but with the time difference between New York and London I should be able to get there.

I telephoned Mike's apartment in New York. No reply. I phoned all day Saturday and Sunday. I even tried his office. No reply. On Monday his secretary in New York said he was flying back from Los Angeles, but I might catch him before he left. In Los Angeles his secretary said he was on his way to New York. At least I found out where the funeral was taking place.

I flew economy and it was a long and wretched flight. I booked into a cheap hotel for the few hours before the funeral. It was pretty squalid but, even so, I bathed and then dozed for a couple of hours.

The flight, the hotel, everything was worthwhile when Mike saw me at the church. The Janowskis were Roman Catholic. The funeral was at Our Lady of Lourdes and St Vincent's. We put our arms around each other and our tears mingled.

'Jesus, Beccy, I'm so glad you came!' Mike was holding me, kissing my face, almost crushing me in his welcome.

'I tried to reach you. Let you know. How could you imagine I *wouldn't* be here? Doll was my grandmother, too!'

I felt that Mike was terribly near breaking down completely. That I had to be strong for both of us. It seemed that half the block was at the church.

'Come on, Mike. You know how Doll loved a party. Let's see her out in style!'

He held me close for a moment, then took a deep breath. Still holding me he whispered, 'I wish I could have given her a New Orleans funeral. A jazz band playing "When the Saints". That would have appealed to the trouper in Doll.'

I whispered back, 'When they're singing the Magnificat, in our hearts we'll be swinging "Dixie" with Doll.' My arms still around him I added, 'Come on, dear chum.' A silly endearment left over from our childhood. 'Come on.'

'I can't. I can't be brave, Beccy. She was the only family I ever had.'

'No, Mike, *I'm* family. Where we come from, family is more than blood. Come on, let's show the block this family knows how to have a funeral!'

And by God, we did! The service was beautiful. Doll was laid to rest with compassion and with honour. Afterwards friends and neighbours went to a small Polish restaurant. We had *schav* – a cold sorrel soup – *sholent*, *kugel*. And we drank to Doll. I was proud when Mike stood up and said, 'I loved my grandmother. Everyone on the block knew that Doll liked her gin. Well, there are worse things in life because everyone on the block also knew her as a good and loving neighbour, wise and caring. She sure as hell licked me when I was wrong, but she sure as hell gave me love. Her kind of love. It could be abrasive and sometimes hard to understand. But it was . . . Christ, I don't know. Just . . . there.'

When everyone had gone, Mike said, 'I have to be back in LA tomorrow. Will you come with me? Just for a few days.' Before I could answer he added, now in control but with such anguish in his voice, 'Please, Beccy, I'll go mad if I'm alone.'

I reached out and took his hand. 'Mike, dear Mike, surely we both know that for as long as we live neither of us will ever be alone.'

* * *

We flew into Los Angeles early the following afternoon.
It was hot. Very hot. The first thing that struck me was
the smell of gasoline. There was no smog, but the sky
was hazy with heat and the air oppressive. The
atmosphere certainly didn't live up to my idea of a
glamorous location, city of the stars and home to the
world's greatest movie industry.

Mike hadn't had time to find an apartment or house
to rent, and so had reserved a suite at the Château
Marmont on Sunset.

'You'll either love it or loathe it,' he said. 'LA people
think it mad to stay there, but New Yorkers and, in
particular, the Brits love it! It's a kinda cross between
Dracula's Castle and a Fairy Idyll. It's pretty camp but
it's genuine, and that's a rarity in this city.'

As it was my first time in LA, Mike got the cab to drive
via Beverly Hills. The smell of gasoline was forgotten as
we drove past the magnificent homes of the stars and the
movie moguls. Every style imaginable was there. One
house would appear to be a medieval English manor
house, its neighbour a Gothic palace. But one thing these
homes had in common was money. A lot of money. From
the security guards on the gates to the gardeners who
could be seen working quietly and methodically on the
landscaped grounds, everything reflected the wealth of
those who were top of the heap in Tinseltown.

When we drew up outside the Château Marmont I
didn't know whether to applaud or to burst out laughing.
It was utterly splendid. But although the original architect
must have had great flair and imagination, he certainly
lacked restraint. It was supposed to be a replica of a
French château and, I suppose, in a way it was. But it
had more turrets, more heavy oak doors studded with

square-headed, iron, blacksmith's nails, more ornate
arches, more heavily patterned tiles, more suits of
armour, more heavily carved pieces of Renaissance
furniture than all the châteaux on the Loire put together.
I simply loved it. It was a delight. A nonsense. A folly.
But it was joyous.

Mike had a suite of rooms on the second floor overlooking the garden and swimming pool. There were small
bungalows dotted throughout the garden and Mike told
me that many a good party had been given in them.

His suite consisted of one main bedroom, a small,
single bedroom, a splendid living room, a kitchen, and
a bathroom that looked as if it belonged in Pickfair, the
legendary home of Mary Pickford and Douglas
Fairbanks. There was a simply vast, claw-footed, cast iron
bath with handsome, old-fashioned brass taps, an equally
imposing wash-basin on a pedestal, and a lavatory that
made one realise why some of its kind had been
nicknamed The Throne!

'Okay, kid, let's get cleaned up and then I'll show you
the town! Beccy? Beccy! You hear me?'

I was standing in the archway that led to the kitchen.
It was spotlessly clean and well equipped, but there was
a simplicity about it that struck a chord in my memory.
I walked in and touched the scrubbed pine table, looked
at the gingham curtains. I could almost smell the food
cooking on the stove.

'Beccy?' Mike was by my side. 'You all right, kid?'

'Oh, yes!' I turned to him impulsively. 'Let's leave
seeing the town until tomorrow. Let's go out and get
groceries. I'll cook a meal and we can sit around the
kitchen table and talk, like the old days. It'll seem like
home.'

'Home?'

278

'Home . . . yes! Isn't that stupid? I wanted all my life, I fought, to get out of that ghetto. Now I'm calling it home!'

There was a pause. Then Mike said, 'I guess whatever we do, whatever we become, it'll always be part of us.'

'The worst part and . . .' I reached out and took his hand '. . . the best!'

He caught my arm and made me look at him. His expression was so gentle, so full of compassion. He held me for a moment, then leant forward and lightly kissed my lips. The action was affectionate, brotherly, but I saw regret in his eyes.

'Come on, kid. Let's shop!'

A couple of hours later, Mike and I were in the kitchen. We were like two kids playing house. Mike had his sleeves rolled up and was grating potato for me to make *latkes*, a kind of potato fritter. I'd made meat balls, and these were now cooking gently in onions and gravy on top of the stove while I made a cauliflower, black olive and pimento salad. As we worked, we chatted together like the old friends we were. And we sipped a stunningly delicious vintage Taittinger champagne. I'd nearly collapsed when I'd seen the price of it but Mike had been adamant.

'One concession I ain't making to this trip down Memory Lane is to drink root beer! Now take that look off your face, young Beccy. I can afford it!' He leant close to me and whispered in my ear, grinning as he did so, 'I'm a hot property in this town. For as long as my shows stay at the top of the ratings anyway! And top of the ratings means big bucks for everybody . . . me especially!'

And so he bought two bottles of champagne, and then selected a bottle of Californian Cabernet Sauvignon from

Martha's Vineyard, bottled by Joe Heitz of St Helena. Mike made his selection with such care and obvious enjoyment that my heart went out to him. I felt equal pride and pleasure in his success.

After a leisurely meal I told Mike he mustn't watch while I put together the pudding. Mike knew he was going to get a surprise because I hadn't let him watch me buy the ingredients in the supermarket. I mixed everything together in a tall glass, then carefully set it before him.

'There! A double nut chocolate sundae with maple syrup, heavy on the whipped cream.'

'What?'

'Don't you remember? All those years ago in O'Brien's drug store, you said when you had money in your pocket that's what you were going to order! Of course, you didn't say that you'd be eating it in Los Angeles, or that you'd drink vintage champagne while you ate! But, here's your reward for success!'

Mike laughed. 'My God, Beccy, fancy you remembering. Yeah, I remember too now. It was the day you used Doll's make-up and went to work in that hell hole of a sweat shop, ironing or something.' He laughed again. 'Christ, I'm glad the good old days are over!'

He reached up and pulled me down on his lap, still laughing. He kissed me, warmly, affectionately, then suddenly the kiss became passionate. His tongue entered my mouth. My need for him was as great as his for me. His hand undid the buttons of my blouse. My breast was his. His lips and tongue on my nipple.

'Oh, yes! God, yes!' Our young bodies were hungry for each other. Mike lifted me in his arms and carried me through to the bedroom. We tore at each other's clothes, matching passion with passion. As he pushed me back on to the bed I felt possessed by my desire for his forceful, demanding body.

'Beccy! Oh, my darling! Oh, Christ, I've never been so hard. Never! I love you!'

I caressed him, my hands glorying in his strength, his virility. My body was my mind. I gave myself up to feeling. The desire between my legs was nearly a pain. I longed . . . I ached . . . I needed him within me.

His hand was opening the rosy petals that guarded my secret place, my womanhood.

'I want you. I want you,' I heard myself cry out.

'Oh, Beccy, Beccy! My love. Forgive me, I can't wait! I want you so!'

He entered me forcefully, harshly. I shouted my joy, arching my body to his. He was thrusting ever deeper and deeper within me. I rose to meet his thrusts. We were one.

'Oh, my dearest, my dearest. Come with me. Come to me. Be mine. Always mine!'

We reached that little death, that wondrous moment when two bodies are as one together.

But the name I shouted, the man I called for as Mike's life force spilled within me, the man I still loved . . . was dead.

Afterwards Mike held me close and my tears mingled with our sweat. 'I'm sorry! So sorry! It was wonderful . . . wonderful! Why did I have to spoil it?'

'Hush, my darling! Hush.' Mike rocked me as if I was a child. 'I understand. The one thing we can't govern, Beccy, is our hearts. Sleep now, precious. Sleep. It's all right, I'm here.' He kissed me gently on the brow. 'I'm here. Sleep, baby, sleep.'

When I awoke the soft light of early morning was in the room. Mike was still holding me in his arms. He was sleeping deeply, peacefully. And I thought how young and vulnerable he looked in spite of his newfound success.

As I lay in the half light I reflected how ironic it was that he and I never seemed to be together at the right point in our lives. Before I knew that Mike loved me I'd met John. When he'd come out to France to care for me after the accident, I could only think about my loss, not of my future. I knew from last night that we could have a wonderful, exciting sexual relationship . . . but would Mike wait for me? Because, if I was really honest with myself, even without my realisation that I still longed for John, I had gone too far down the path of building a career. I wanted success too much and felt that, perhaps, it was at last within reach. I just wasn't ready to forsake everything I'd worked for . . . yet.

'Wait for me, Mike,' I murmured as I drifted back into sleep.

Later that morning I was relieved to find that Mike was totally easy with me. He was his old teasing, affectionate self and I was deeply grateful to him. Because he was telling me, in his own way, that last night had spoilt nothing between us. We could still be two lucky kids from the Lower East Side. We could still be friends.

Room service sent up the most incredible Californian breakfast. Freshly pressed orange juice. Scrambled eggs, brownies, ham, tomatoes, mushrooms, and a huge bowl of fruit. Plus toast, jelly and coffee. We were young enough not to have to worry about our waist lines and so we ate with enthusiasm.

'How would you like to go to a real Hollywood party tonight?' Mike asked, between mouthfuls.

'Oh, Mike, I've hardly any clothes with me! I was only expecting to go to New York.'

'Hell, clothes are no problem. You should see the shops

on Wilshire . . . on Rodeo. We'll get you something gorgeous. To be honest, Beccy, it's a party I can't afford to say no to and I'd feel great taking you on my arm.'

I didn't like to tell Mike that I just couldn't afford to buy the kind of dress I would need to go to a smart party. But before I could get the right words together, he said, 'What do you say, kid? Can I spend some of my dough on a beautiful girl? No, don't answer! Because whatever you say, I'm buying you a Tinseltown special. Something that'll knock them straight between the eyes. Okay?'

'Okay!'

Later, in the back of the chauffeured limo Mike had hired to take us to the party, I glanced out of the corner of my eye at him and thought how handsome he looked. Although he was only about five inches taller than me, he had a powerful presence. His hair hadn't darkened as he'd grown older and was still almost white blond. He was strongly built but not stocky, with broad shoulders and a frame that tapered down to a narrow waist and slim hips. Tonight he was impeccably dressed in black trousers, black tie, and a beautifully cut cream tuxedo jacket.

He caught me looking at him and winked at me. 'It's a long way from a shared lavatory on the landing, ain't it, kid?'

I laughed and squeezed his hand. I knew how important that evening was to him.

We were on our way to the home of Ira Schuman, a Hollywood giant. His studio, Artists International, was the only privately owned studio left in Hollywood. Ira Schuman was Hollywood. Now in his early seventies, he'd come West with Griffith and Sennett and Lasky. Mike told me that he'd always been an innovator, a leader rather than a follower, both commercially and artistically.

Age hadn't diminished his style and he was about to
become the first head of a film studio to go into television
production.

'He's the only one who's had the vision,' Mike was
saying, 'to see that television doesn't have to be a threat.
Sure, some movie houses will close down but a whole
new market is out there . . . television has *happened*!
You can't turn the clock back any more than theatres
could stop audiences going to see films. No! The thing
is to adapt, to go on making movies but to make them
for the small screen *as well as* the large. Ira understands
that.'

'And where do you come in?'

'I don't know for sure yet but I want to move on. I
want to produce more than just my own material. I want
to create, to set a style.' He suddenly grinned. 'I guess
I want to be a top cat!'

'And that's why you've been asked to the party
tonight?'

Mike shrugged. 'I just have a hunch something might
be on offer. But in any case, when you get an invitation
from Ira Schuman you don't say no. Not in this town!'

The limo turned into a driveway and stopped outside
vast, ornately worked iron gates. A guard stepped
forward from a gate house. Mike showed him his
invitation, the guard checked his list and we were waved
on through.

I don't know how many acres of Beverly Hills Ira
Schuman owned but, in a city where real estate was as
gold dust, the drive alone must have been worth a
fortune.

On either side of the driveway there were sweeping
lawns where the sprinklers can never have stopped, the
grass was so lush and green.

Then the house came into view and I caught my breath.
I was looking at a huge colonial mansion, straight out
of *Gone with the Wind*.

The limo stopped outside the graceful stone steps that
led to the impressive double front doors. As the car
stopped, a footman wearing full livery and spotless white
gloves ran down the front steps to open the door.

'Here we go, kid!' Mike said with a grin. 'Just
remember that Ira Schuman came from the same Hell's
Kitchen that we did!'

I looked up at the vast mansion, then slipped my arm
through Mike's, whispering, 'We've got a long way to
go before we catch up!'

'I've got a million-dollar girl on my arm, and that's
a start. You look stunning, Beccy!'

We'd bought my dress that afternoon, in a small but
incredibly exclusive boutique on Rodeo. It was a
deceptively simple black sheath. Deceptive because, for
all its simplicity, the cut was stunning. The dress itself
was strapless, but over the sheath I wore a loose chiffon
jacket. The whole effect was decorous but, Mike assured
me, incredibly sexy. My hair was piled high and to
complete my ensemble I wore a tiny pill box with osprey
trimmings. The owner of the boutique told us it was called
a cocktail hat and they were all the rage. It was a total
nonsense and utterly adorable.

We entered the hall, which seemed only a little smaller
than the auditorium at Carnegie Hall! Ira Schuman and
his wife, Wilda, were receiving their guests formally. As
we joined the queue to be greeted by our hosts, Mike
whispered to me that Wilda had once been a famous
silent-movie star. And that, incredible as it might seem
in the movie industry, she and Ira had been married for
over forty years.

As we drew nearer I studied the couple who were hosting this lavish, old-style Hollywood party.

Ira was about my height. His skin was tanned and very wrinkled by the Californian sun. He looked rather like a shrewd, old tortoise. But his eyes were lively and compelling. There were deeply etched lines of humour around them and I found myself drawn to this powerful man even before I shook his hand.

His wife, Wilda, was tiny and, even in her late sixties, incredibly pretty. While her husband was clearly a sun worshipper, her complexion was fine and very fair. Her hair, which was softly dressed into a knot at the nape of her neck, was glorious. It was truly white. Not grey, not faded, it was a halo of softness that framed her delicate features. If her personality matched her appearance I could understand why Ira Schuman had stayed married to this lady for nearly twice my lifetime.

Then we were being greeted by our host and hostess. Mike introduced me, and Ira Schuman smiled and asked, 'Is this your sweetheart then, Mike?'

'At the moment she thinks she's my kid sister,' Mike replied, laughing, 'but I'm working on it!'

'Have a good time, young persons. I'd like a word with you later, Mike.'

'Sure thing, Ira!'

'Enjoy yourselves,' Wilda Schuman added in her soft, pretty voice. And then we moved on to make way for the next guests on the receiving line.

The marvellous thing about the Schumans' house was that, although it was incredibly impressive, almost regal, its style was comfortable and casual. Here was a beautiful house that was also a real home.

The party was being held in a huge reception room that

overlooked the gardens and the pool, and beyond that an enchanting little Palladian folly.

One wall of the room was practically entirely made up of french doors. These were open on to the terrace that led to the gardens. The evening was warm and balmy but a gentle breeze cooled the room.

An army of waiters moved among the guests with champagne and, through double doors, I could see another reception room down the centre of which was a table about forty feet long. It was covered in spotless, starched linen and laden with a sumptuous array of food.

Although I had moved in very sophisticated circles with John, I simply couldn't believe the famous faces among the guests. Claudette Colbert, the James Stewarts, Greer Garson, the Fondas, Cary Grant, Fred Astaire and his wife . . . it was like a Hollywood Greats *Who's Who*.

'Just everyone's here!' I whispered to Mike. His arm slid around my waist and he held me to his side for a brief moment. 'Including us!'

The party was mainly made up of people from the movie business but, because of Ira Schuman's launch into television, there were some people that Mike knew from that world. He introduced me and we chatted and gossiped. I was having a marvellous time.

About three-quarters of an hour after we'd arrived, Ira Schuman's personal secretary, a young Harvard graduate whose engaging manner masked a fierce loyalty to his employer and, I suspected, a steely heart, approached us.

'Excuse me, Mr Janowski, Miss . . . Mr Schuman would be grateful for a few moments of your time in his study.'

Mike turned to me. 'Will you be all right for a while? I'm sorry but . . .'

'Don't be ridiculous. I'll wait for you on the terrace.

It's a lovely evening. Unbelievable after the chill winds of East Anglia!'

A waiter refilled my glass with champagne and then I wandered outside. I sipped my wine and leant against the balustrade that edged the terrace. I looked out over the impeccable gardens. A smoky, fascinating voice came from behind me.

'God isn't so damned fussy, is he?'

I turned and saw one of the most beautiful girls I'd ever laid eyes on.

'It should all be desert and scrub, you know. Or at best orange groves with dusty, dry earth between the trees. But that's reality, and they're not too hot on that in this town. You an actress?'

'No! I'm just visiting a friend in LA and he brought me to this party. Are you an actress? I'm sorry if I should recognise you but I've been living in the country for some time and I'm hopelessly out of touch.'

'I wouldn't call myself an actress. I'm a model, or I was. I'm just one of the hundreds of girls the studios are signing up to be the new Marilyn Monroe. First they killed her, then they want to find a replacement!'

'Killed her? I thought she . . .?'

The beautiful girl shrugged. 'There's plenty of rumours around that she didn't commit suicide. She ran with a pretty dangerous crowd. The Mafia, the Kennedys, the Rat Pack.

'But, no, I meant that the studio bosses made millions and millions from her films. Then when she needed help, understanding, they fired her. Still, I guess whatever they'd done, it would have happened some day. Not many people can take twenty sleeping tablets a day, wash them down with vodka, and live to a ripe old age.' She shivered. 'Jesus, I hate this town!'

'Then why stay?'

The girl laughed. It was a husky, throaty laugh with very little humour in it. 'I want to be rich and famous, don't I? Have my feet immortalised in cement and my face on a poster high above Hollywood Boulevard!' She smiled, then turned on her heel and walked back towards the party. She stopped just before the french doors and waved to me. Her face was lit up by another mischievous, enchanting smile. 'See you in the funny papers!' Then she was gone.

I found the encounter strangely disturbing. As if I'd turned over a beautiful stone and found something dark and frightening beneath. I tried to put the girl out of my mind as I walked further in the gardens. I reckoned Mike would still be with Ira Schuman and it was a lovely, starry night. I didn't think anyone would mind me wandering through the immaculate flowerbeds, around the pool . . .

I was nearing the folly when I heard footsteps on the gravel behind me. I wasn't concerned. I simply assumed that someone else was enjoying the night and the beautiful gardens.

Then I stopped and so did the footsteps. I waited a moment then walked again. The footsteps started again. Clearly someone was following me. I turned to see who it was. With so much security surrounding the Schuman home. I couldn't believe that it was a prowler.

A few feet away, hidden in the shadows, I could see the outline of a tall, powerfully built man. I was suddenly frightened. There was sweat on the palms of my hands, and my heart-beat quickened. Then the man stepped from the shadows and I sighed with relief. I recognised him as one of the guests at the party. He was a well-known movie star who specialised in playing dashing, swashbuckling heroes. Forever fighting pirates on the

Spanish Main with a sword in one hand and the swooning heroine supported by his other arm.

I wasn't sure, but suspected that that type of film was no longer as popular as it had been. Certainly Don Hayward was no longer the beautiful young athlete he once was. His waist had thickened and his handsome features were blurred from drink or drugs, or both. Even so, I felt I had no reason to fear him. Then he spoke and I realised how wrong I was.

'I watched you leave the party . . . I knew you wanted me to follow.'

'Don't be ridiculous! Of course I didn't want you to follow me. I'm simply walking in the gardens while my friend is talking to Ira Schuman. He'll be waiting for me now. Excuse me!'

I made to move towards the house but Don Hayward stepped forward and caught my arm. I could smell the drink on his stale breath. 'Regular little cock teaser, aren't you?'

I tried to stay calm, hoping to talk my way out of this situation. 'Please let go of me. I want to get back to my friend.'

'Oh, no! I don't think so. Not yet. I know women like you . . . say one thing and want another. I know what you want. I saw it in your eyes at the party.'

'Will you stop this? Your dialogue is as dated as your movies!'

'You bitch! You shouldn't have said that . . . or are you just trying to make me angry? Some women find that exciting. Is that what you want? A little excitement?'

He twisted my arm behind my back and I gasped with pain. 'Enjoyed that, didn't you? Oh, yes, I know your sort. You like a little pain with your sex, don't you?'

He jerked my arm again and this time I cried out. The

pain was excruciating. There seemed to be a hazy red mist before my eyes and I thought I was going to pass out. Then I heard my dress tear and his hand was on my breast . . . squeezing it . . . crushing it cruelly. Oh, God, I thought, he's going to rape me. I knew I was very near blacking out.

I summoned every last ounce of my strength and brought my knee up sharply between his legs. Now it was his turn to cry out in pain. He let go of me and staggered back, his hands going to his groin. I made to run past him, to get away from this drunken monster, but he reached out and caught me again. I screamed as he hit me across the face and felt myself falling backwards on to the gravel . . .

Then, mercifully, I heard Mike's voice and the sound of running feet. 'Beccy! Christ, where are you? I heard you scream!'

I think I must have called his name because within seconds he was by my side. He'd been followed by two other men who went to Don Hayward. One of them shouted angrily at the other. 'I told you not to let the bastard out of your sight!'

Mike's arms were around me, helping me to my feet. 'I'm all right. I'm all right.' I sank on to a garden seat. Mike swung around to face Don Hayward, hate and anger in his face. 'You scum!' He stepped forward and I think I heard myself laugh as one of the men called out, 'Don't hit his face . . . he's filming tomorrow!'

'Is he?' Mike shouted and crashed his fist full into Hayward's face. I winced as I heard the crack of bone, and blood spurted from my assailant's broken nose. Hayward put his hands to his face then straightened up and stared at Mike. 'You nobody! You're finished in this town — finished!'

Mike's voice was icy with anger. 'No, asshole, *you're* finished! You may have had a few days on a B movie tomorrow, but no major studio will touch you now!' Then he swung around to one of the other men. 'You're his agent, aren't you? I understand you've been trying to negotiate a television deal for this heap of human wreckage. Let me tell you something. From tomorrow morning, I'm the new Head of A1 Television, and I will personally see to it that your client never sets foot in a TV studio in this town!'

Mike tore off his tuxedo, now spattered with Hayward's blood. He wrapped it around my shoulders. I hadn't realised that I'd started to shake.

'Come on, darling, I'm here. You're all right now.'

Mike half carried me to the car. Suddenly I started to sob. 'I'm sorry, so sorry! I don't know why I'm crying. But I can't seem to stop!'

'It's shock. You cry all you want. I've got you. You're safe now.'

When we got into Mike's suite at the Château Marmont the telephone was ringing. He sat me down gently on the sofa, then went to answer it.

'Ira, thank you for phoning. Yes, she's not too bad now. Pretty badly shaken, of course . . . Yes!' Mike smiled grimly. 'I broke the bastard's nose for him . . . someone should have broken his neck a long time ago! . . . Yes, I'll tell her! It was very good of you to call.'

He hung up the phone. 'Ira and Wilda wanted you to know how sorry they are. They feel terrible that something like that should have happened at their home.'

'Oh, Mike, it was such an important night for you. And I ruined it!'

'Enough of that nonsense, kid! Come on, were going

to get you into a nice hot bath. Then I'm going to tuck
you up in bed with a large brandy.'

He ran a bath for me then bathed me as if I was a baby.
He put ointment on my cuts and bruises, and eased me
into bed. I sipped as much of the brandy as I could, then
Mike held me until I fell asleep.

I awoke briefly in the night. I suddenly found myself
smiling in the darkness. I remembered reading somewhere
that Don Hayward had won a blue at Oxford for boxing.
But he was no match for Mike. When we were kids, Mike
had been the best street-fighter on the block.

I slept late the next morning, nature healing my bruises
and my shock in the best way possible. A few times I
nearly surfaced then slipped back into a restful sleep.
During the moments that I dozed I could hear Mike
moving about quietly in the sitting room. Several times
the telephone rang but it was answered immediately, as
if he didn't want the sound of the phone to disturb me.

It was after noon when I finally awoke. I felt
considerably rested by my long sleep. I stretched, then
got out of bed, pulled on a robe and crossed to the door
which led from the bedroom directly into the large sitting
room. Mike was seated at a writing table working on what
I assumed to be a script. He turned as I entered.

'Beccy, how are you? I let you sleep, I thought that
was best.'

'I feel so much better. Bless you for looking after me
last night!'

'Think nothing of it. I'm just so sorry it happened. I
should've taken better care of you.'

'How on earth could you have known a guest at such
a high society party would behave like that?' I touched
his arm. 'You took great care of me. You always have.'

'Yeah, well, I guess I fell for the girl next door when I was about ten . . . I can't seem to break the habit!' Mike replied lightly. 'Now, come and have a look at your flowers. Ira and Wilda sent them.'

The most stunning arrangement of flowers was on the sideboard. Against it was propped a card, '*Do forgive us. And please come and see us again soon.*'

'Oh, they're beautiful! But they shouldn't have sent them. It was a very kind thought. I'll write and thank them.'

'They'd like that. Now, come and sit down and I'll make you some coffee.'

Mike fussed over me. Got me comfortably settled on the sofa. Insisted that I put my feet up. He hurried into the kitchen and I could hear him putting the coffee percolator on. 'I've got some bagels and some fruit. I'm putting them on a tray. And don't say "Don't bother" because I like to bother!'

I smiled and lay back on the sofa. Life had changed us both so much, but I guessed that I'd always be the girl next door to Mike. That bond, the shared knowledge of where we'd come from, how we'd fought to escape our environment, the will to succeed that had taken us out of the Lower East Side slums, was the rock on which our friendship was based. I could always be myself with Mike because he knew me through and through. The good and the bad. However much John had loved me, tried to understand me, he couldn't conceive of the life I'd lived before I met him. But Mike *knew*. He knew because he'd been there. He'd lived with the cockroaches, the smells and garbage.

Now Mike had been offered a powerful and important job. He needed to give himself to it totally. A wife, a home, and perhaps a family would be a distraction, and

I suspected that he knew that as well as I did. Well, I too had a new career. I wasn't ready for marriage, or for an emotional commitment. And as for any other relationship . . . I loved Mike too much and too well to keep him as a lover and lose him as a friend.

CHAPTER TWENTY-THREE

I stayed a few more days in LA with Mike, but we both knew that I would return to Munkyns. I briefly thought of stopping over in New York, then hiring a car to drive out to see Aaron, but decided against it. I had invited him to Munkyns during his successive holidays, but he always sent witty, charming notes explaining he was staying with friends, or his social life was too busy. It seemed that one day we would naturally come together again; until then he was best left to follow the life style that suited him. And, truth to tell, I'd been so busy I think he'd have been bored with both me and the countryside. However, I had written to him pointing out that he'd better not forget his studies. The trust fund saw him through to the end of his school education, but if he didn't gain a place at a college, both fees and allowance would stop.

My chief headache now was to raise three thousand pounds. Mike had asked me if my business was fully funded. Perhaps foolishly, I'd told him it was. I think I was anxious that sleeping with me shouldn't make him feel he was under an obligation to me.

A preliminary order had arrived from Mrs Blake. We had still to establish the price my skin-care range would sell for at the store. I'd kept the prices viable until then but on the low side. Now I was going to launch Grace Laure beauty care at a London store and in comparatively expensive packaging. I needed to think very carefully about the market I was aiming for, and the price that market could bear.

I telephoned first my bank manager and then Joss, and made an appointment to see them both the following day. If anyone could tell me about costing cosmetics it would be Joss. The firm he'd worked for had been expensive and exclusive.

I showed the bank manager my order and the work I'd done on the initial costing. I explained that I had a shortfall of three thousand pounds.

'Have you any collateral you can put up, Miss Mandel?' Why is it that banks are only really interested in lending money to people who don't need it?

'I'm afraid not. Beyond the order, and the accounts for the turnover of the business in the past ten months. We've gone from being a one-woman business based in a farmhouse kitchen to four of us working full-time, plus a van driver. Surely that impresses you?'

'It impresses me personally, my dear young woman . . .' his patronising tone put my teeth on edge '. . . but the bank can't go around lending money willy-nilly!'

I leant across the desk towards him. 'Mr Burley, I'm closing my account with this bank right now. And when my business is a success, which it will be, I shall make sure that every financial page in every major newspaper carries a story about your shortsightedness. And how your bank lost a potentially substantial account!'

'Now, look here,' he protested.

'But I thank you, Mr Burley, because I want that day to come so badly that I am now ten times more determined to be successful than when I walked through that door this morning. Good day to you!'

I rose and walked towards the door. To my

amazement, Mr Burley burst out laughing. I turned to look at him, to see if he was trying to put me down, but his amusement seemed to be genuine.

'By God, Miss Mandel! No one has spoken to me like that for years. Bravo!' He was still laughing.

'Look, getting my business started is no laughing matter to me! I've got an order here . . .' I waved Mrs Blake's confirmation in the air '. . . that companies would kill to get. And all you can do is call me a dear young woman!'

'Never again, Miss Mandel, never again! I recognise a chip off the old block when I see one.'

'A what?'

'Sorry, sorry! Probably you don't say that in America. It means genuine . . . tough . . .'

'Oh!' I said, enlightened. 'The real McCoy!'

'If you say so. Look my . . . er . . . Miss Mandel. I can't authorise more than one thousand pounds.'

'It's not enough.' Again I turned to leave.

'Hold your horses – and I can't imagine that the land of the cowboy doesn't know that phrase! Leave your paperwork with me and I'll take this up with the area manager. No promises, mind.'

'How long will it take to get an answer?'

'I'm lunching with him at the end of the week. Leave your telephone number with my secretary and I'll be in touch as soon as I get back to my office. Now, do we still have your account?' He kept a straight face but his eyes were twinkling.

I smiled and held out my hand. 'Well, at least until the end of the week!'

Joss led me into his incredibly neat, masculine sitting room. From the window there was a splendid view across the Hythe to the boats bobbing about on the water.

'Your dander's up, I can see that, Beccy! There's a spring in your step and a glint in your eye. Now, what have you been up to?'

'Fighting with the bank manager.'

'Excellent! And did you win?'

'Does one ever with banks? But maybe it was a draw. I'll know for certain at the end of the week.'

'Good! Now, how can I help you?'

'Well, you know the order's come through from Mrs Blake. I plan this to be a completely new range.' I smiled. 'The ingredients will be the same, of course. But now they'll be well presented in blue glass with the logo, and selling at one of the most exclusive stores in the world. I want to get the pricing right. The sort of customer who shops there will distrust anything cheap. On the other hand I want a good turnover. In short, Joss, I need your advice.'

'With pleasure.' He poured us both a dry sherry. 'What you have to remember is that for every item of cosmetics sold, the actual cost of the ingredients is only one shilling in the pound.'

'What?'

'Chilling, isn't it? But think for a moment. The store itself will mark up the price by at least one hundred per cent. If they sell for two pounds, you get a pound. Out of that pound, you have to pay for packaging, distribution, a roof over your head, wages. And at the end of all that,' he added dryly, 'I assume you want to make a profit!'

'That is the general idea, yes!'

'Then, my dear Beccy, you have some sums to do.'

I spent every evening with my account books. The blue glass containers were a major expense. On the other hand, they looked really beautiful, and would no doubt promote the impression that such lovely glass had to contain a worthwhile cosmetic. Finally I decided to err on the side of making the assumption that anything good was worth paying for. I priced Grace Laure in the Elizabeth Arden, Charles of the Ritz category, which meant it was cheaper than, say, Estée Lauder, but still at the top end of the market. I decided to wait until I heard from my bank manager, Mr Burley, before writing to Mrs Blake. If I didn't have the money to make the product in the first place, there wasn't much point in negotiating a price for it!

I hardly slept at all on the Thursday night. I worked with the girls in the morning, but when we broke for lunch I could no longer bear being indoors. I pulled on my coat and walked across the field to the sea wall. The tide was ebbing and there were sea gulls scavenging between the high water mark and the quickly flowing waters of the estuary. 'Is the struggle really worth it?' I wondered. I knew the answer almost before I formulated the question. For me, yes, it was. I don't know what drove me, but the need to achieve was desperate. Why I didn't know. Was it because of all those years of struggling? Of being the kike kid from the wrong side of town? Was it to compensate for the bitterness I'd felt when I realised that my race and religion would keep me in the store room of Kimberly's forever if I didn't fight against the system? 'After all, Beccy,' I thought wryly, 'settle for friendship and you could be a Countess one day!'

I wasn't even tempted. Not because I felt morally superior to women who married for a title, but because I wanted to be successful in my own right. To be successful in the way that a man is successful. To be known for my achievements rather than my husband's.

I had loved a man deeply, profoundly, wonderfully. I desperately hoped that I would again. But why should women have to choose between love and personal success? I wouldn't! I couldn't!

After lunch, every time the telephone rang I pounced on it. 'Leaping up and down like she's got a wasp in her panties,' Peggy said. Each time it was a call from one of our customers. Usually I'd be thrilled to be getting more orders, but on that day I just wanted to get them off the phone as quickly as possible.

At three-thirty, Mr Burley telephoned.

'Miss Mandel?'

'Yes.'

'It's Mr Burley. How are you?'

I interrupted him. 'Mr Burley, I don't want to be rude but please, *please* don't be polite. Yes or no?'

'Yes!' I heard him chuckle. 'That direct enough for you?'

'Yes! Oh yes! Oh, thank you!'

'There are certain provisos.'

'Yes?' I said cautiously.

'We would like to appoint an accountant. And we feel you should form a limited company. Otherwise my area manager and I . . .'

He talked on for some time about bringing a new business to the area . . . Local employment . . . Congratulated me . . . But I wasn't really listening. I felt numbed, almost exhausted, with relief.

'Are you still there, Miss Mandel?'

'Yes, of course!'

'Then I'll see you on Monday at ten-thirty. Well done!'

THE HERB

LADY'S MANTLE

'Our Lady's Mantle – the best friend to women'
Anonymous

THE WOMAN

PART FOUR:
LADY'S MANTLE
GRACE 1966–1970

'It seemed so great my happiness
That I was blessed and could bless.'
W. B. Yeats

CHAPTER TWENTY-FOUR

'At close of business today,' I said coldly, 'I expect you either to accept or reject my offer. If I have not heard from you I shall take that as rejection.'

'Now look here,' my antagonist interjected.

'No, Mr Kingly, *you* look here! You have factory space that I want. However, from the start of negotiations I made it perfectly clear that the space is the only thing I'm interested in . . . I have absolutely no desire to acquire an out-of-date assembly line. I have even less desire to incorporate your company's range of toiletries into the House of Laure. I'm tired of your prevarication, Mr Kingly. If you have a better offer, take it. If you wish to accept my offer, I shall be at my desk until 6 pm. Good day to you!' I hung up the phone.

I leant back in my chair and tried to contain my anger. Why is it, I wondered, that for a woman to succeed in business she has to be twice as tough, twice as hardworking, twice as ruthless as a man? I was tired of having to prove myself at every turn. But I was Grace Laure. The House of Laure was my creation and I was damned if I was going to pretend to be a wilting violet just to massage the egos of men I did business with.

We badly needed new factory space. I looked with satisfaction at the sales graph on my office wall. It showed a steady increase in business, but increased demand meant increased supply.

At the last directors' meeting, a board member, a bank

nominee, Charles Fairburn, had made a startling suggestion which I had rejected out of hand. He proposed that we extend the range of Laure products to include toiletries that were cheaper and easier to produce than the original herbal range.

'Do I understand you correctly?' I had asked. 'You actually think that we should use the Laure label on items that are not herbal and not from my original recipes?'

'My dear, young lady . . .'

'I may be comparatively young,' I snapped, 'but I am certainly not your dear, and I don't enjoy being patronised!'

'Very well. I shall come straight to the point,' Charles Fairburn had said coldly. 'The House of Laure is an expanding, successful business, and now is the time to capitalise on that success. Is it cost effective to specialise only in a range of products that use expensive, pure ingredients? I'm not suggesting that we bottle any old rubbish and plonk a Laure label on it . . .'

'I'm glad to hear it,' I said icily.

'I'm simply saying we should behave like businessmen and not indulge ourselves in some airy-fairy, back-to-nature crusade!'

'Mr Fairburn.' I did not feel inclined to be on first-name terms with someone so totally opposed to my concept of the House of Laure. 'Our products are a success because women know they can trust them. You may call the use of pure ingredients "back to nature", and you clearly mean it in a derogatory way, but I could give you a chemical analysis of the herbs we use. List the minerals, the vitamins, the medicinal properties. Explain why our products work. And they do work. That's why the House of Laure is a success. And you want to risk that success simply to make a fast buck!'

'All I'm proposing . . .'

But I pressed on: 'And as for your airy-fairy jibe, I take that to refer to my insistence that none of our ingredients are tested on animals.'

'Well, I for one won't lose any sleep because some poor little bunny has had shampoo sprayed in its eyes.'

'But I will! And this is *my* company.'

'Oh, yes! You're the majority shareholder, Miss Laure, but you need the continuing goodwill of the bank. Never forget that.'

'If that's a threat, Mr Fairburn, I would remind you that there is more than one bank in London!'

We moved on to other business but I was disturbed by my confrontation with Fairburn. Although my business was thriving, cash flow was always a problem – the gap between expenditure on the product and customers settling their account, a never-ending headache.

And I had an ambitious and costly plan that I wished to put into practice, and for which I would most certainly need the bank's funding and support. For a long time it had seemed to me ridiculous that we bought herbs from suppliers and didn't have our own farms. Now I had found land in Norfolk where we could grow lavender, and I had made an offer on a farm in Provence where, if my bid was successful, I would turn over the fields to the growing of herbs. I had been looking for about two years for suitable land. I wanted to grow herbs organically for use in Laure products, and both in Norfolk and Provence I had at last found land that had not been intensively farmed. Now Charles Fairburn's influence with the bank threatened the whole venture!

I wished Kit had been at the board meeting so that I could talk things over with him. But he'd been best man at a big society wedding that afternoon and so was unable to attend.

Kit, dear Kit, had been self-effacing as usual when I'd formed the House of Laure into a private company. 'Use my name on the notepaper if you like, Beccy, a title always goes down well with capitalists!'

He was right, of course. The bank had leapt at the chance of having Lord Christian D'Arcy on the board.

It was three years since Kit had proposed to me. Three years in which I'd struggled to establish the House of Laure. Three years of giving every waking moment of my life to my company. In those three years we'd expanded into Europe. We were on the verge of becoming an international company. But I was determined that we'd succeed by holding on to the principles that had established us: a pure product, honestly sold.

A few days after the board meeting I'd had a telephone call from the estate agent who was looking for new factory premises for us. I'd wanted for both sentimental and practical reasons to open a new factory within a reasonable distance of our existing one in Baildon. This would give a sense of identity with the company to the people who worked for us, plus help with the distribution of our products. The Kingly factory, halfway between Baildon and Colchester, was coming on the market. I knew the name Kingly. They manufactured shampoos, face packs, cold cream, deodorants and a range of toiletries for a mainly chain store outlet. I wasn't at all surprised to learn that the company was in difficulties. As far as I could see, the only thing their products had to recommend them was that they were cheap.

I made an offer for the factory which was very fair, even generous. I was surprised and annoyed when the agent came back and said that Kingly's wanted to sell as a going concern. Then Charles Fairburn's insistence that we expand to incorporate another range of toiletries came to mind. The timing of Fairburn's outburst, his threats concerning further financing from the bank and now the offer to buy out Kingly's seemed a little too opportune to be mere coincidence. But how was Charles Fairburn tied in with Kingly's?

I telephoned the agent. I wanted him to make it clear to Mark Kingly that I was only really interested in the factory itself. However, if he would care to give me a copy of his company's accounts and ledgers, I would give some consideration to his proposal.

It was a simple matter to check Kingly's board of directors. Charles Fairburn's name was not there.

I sat up late the night Kingly's accounts were delivered to me. Very late. At 2 am I stretched and finished a nearly cold cup of tea which was on my desk. As far as I could see, their books simply reflected the dismal story I already knew about Kingly's. A company that had not moved with the times and was now paying the price.

I was about to admit defeat and go to bed when I decided to try a different tack. I crossed to the drinks table and poured myself a whisky. As I added soda I thought wryly what a bachelor I had become. Taking my work home to an elegant but soulless apartment. Drinking the occasional whisky and soda in the lonely, early hours of the morning. Single-minded in my determination to win.

I sat at my desk again and picked up the Kingly books. Previously I'd been looking for financial irregularities. I'd found bad management but nothing worse. Now I was going to look for anything that struck a wrong note.

Another half hour passed. My whisky was finished and my eyes heavy with sleep. But suddenly I thought I'd found what I was looking for. Kingly's had a number of suppliers. The amounts bought by Kingly's from those suppliers were fairly constant and reflected the nature of the products they manufactured. Then why were supplies from one company out of proportion to both the turnover of business and what I knew to be the manufacturing capacity of Kingly's?

Is there such a thing as a sixth sense? Whatever the explanation, I just knew that when I went to Companies House in the morning, I'd find the name I was looking for on the board of the company oversupplying to Kingly's.

I looked at my watch. Ten minutes to one. Just time to take a leisurely walk from my office in Belgravia to the exclusive little restaurant off Hay Hill where I was lunching Charles Fairburn. I felt drained after my telephone call to Mark Kingly. I was chancing a lot by issuing an ultimatum that we close the deal by 6 pm that day or forget it. We badly needed that factory. But I also badly needed to know the loyalty, or otherwise, of my board.

The street outside my office was crowded. I was wearing a simple, cream Courrèges sheath dress. With it I wore white tights and cream court shoes with short, square heels. The hem was fashionably three inches above my knees. Which was about as short as I felt I could wear it and still be credible in the boardroom! The one concession I had made to the outrageous sixties was adding a pair of brightly coloured plastic earrings. The design was cubic and chunky and I absolutely loved them. My hair was still long but, like every other woman's on that street, it was worn straight. Since Vidal Sassoon had captured London, it was only elderly matrons who still had their hair permed and then tortured into rigid hairstyles. Between the 'Shrimp' with her long straight hair and Twiggy with her close-cropped Sassoon look there was no fashionable compromise. I suppose it was partly sentimental of me not to have my hair cut – John had so loved it long – but, whatever the reason, I hadn't joined most of the other young women in London and had my hair cut in a short angular bob.

Apart from an elderly lady with a pekinese under her arm, who was being helped by her chauffeur from the back of a Rolls, and a policewoman, everywhere I looked there were mini-skirts. The office girls hurrying to snatch a quick snack at the espresso coffee bars that had sprung up all over London were wearing them. Some of the skirts were so short there had been questions in Parliament about public decency! The young, married, affluent women hurrying to lunch dates in Mayfair wore them. The new breed of young businesswomen dashing between appointments wore them. London had discovered a style and vigour that was irrepressible. The city had thrown off the austerity of the late forties, the work ethic of the fifties and had discovered 'Youth' in the sixties. A new, immediate approach to fashion had been created in Carnaby Street and the Kings Road in Chelsea. Young men were also part of the revolution in the way we now looked. Even in Curzon Street I saw the occasional young man wearing a brightly printed loose shirt, with beads and long hair caught back in a leather thong.

Everywhere you could feel the vitality of the 'Swinging Sixties' and I loved being part of it. I was younger than, and, as yet, not as successful as Mary Quant or Barbara Hulanicki, who'd opened a marvellously innovative boutique, Biba, in Kensington Church Street, but I too felt the pulse of the city: the heady knowledge that if you dared to try to achieve, the one thing that *wasn't* going to hold you back was your youth.

I turned off Hay Hill and entered Stefano's. Ever since the success of La Dolce Vita in Soho, Italian-style trattorie had caught on. They reflected the informality that people were seeking in their approach to life. The food and wine were excellent but no one raised an eyebrow if businessmen dispensed with ties or women wore trouser suits. Even so, Stefano's was immensely fashionable. Kit had taken me to the restaurant one evening and since then it had become a firm favourite with me. That evening, among the ordinary mortals dining there, were Dusty Springfield, who'd been voted top female singer the previous year, David Bailey, the hottest photographer in town, Billy Wallace, Princess Margaret's old flame, and a striking young woman with a strong face, nearly very beautiful, nearly ugly, but arresting, who I couldn't place. Kit had told me it was Glenda Jackson, a young actress who had enjoyed a huge success at the RSC and looked as if she was moving on to great things.

As I entered the restaurant Stefano hurried forward to greet me. In spite of the success of his restaurant he never created the impression that his customers were lucky to dine there.

Charles Fairburn was waiting for me in the bar. 'I hope I'm not late,' I said, glancing at my watch.

'Not at all. I was early. I must say this is very gracious of you. It's not often an old fogey like me gets to be lunched by a beautiful young woman . . . or is that regarded as a sexist remark nowadays?'

'Not by me! I'm flattered.' At that moment the *maitre d'* offered us menus. 'Good afternoon, Miss Laure. Sir.'

'Good afternoon, Henri. Now, what do you have to

tempt us with today?' We discussed the menu pleasurably, then ordered. I often gave business lunches at this restaurant and the wine waiter didn't make the mistake of handing the wine list to my male guest.

'We're both having fish . . . I think a white burgundy, don't you?' I turned to the wine waiter without giving Charles Fairburn a chance to reply. 'A Château Fuissé, please. Not *too* cold or it loses its bouquet.'

Inwardly I grimaced at myself. I remembered my first meal with John, when he said how he hated wine snobs. Well, so did I, but lulling Charles Fairburn into a sense of security was the name of the game.

'I'm impressed,' he said, smiling.

'Oh, surely not? Knowledge is only a matter of application. As I'm single and entertain a lot, it seemed only sensible to learn. Of course,' I added wistfully, 'if there was a man in my life . . .'

Charles Fairburn reached out and patted my hand. The fish was taking the bait.

We were seated at our table and during the *hors d'oeuvres* engaged in small talk. When our main course was served I thought the time had come to show my hand.

'I talked with Mark Kingly this morning.'

'Good! I had rather hoped that the purpose of this luncheon was to . . . what shall we say? . . . resolve certain conflicts between us. Taking over Kingly's would be a golden opportunity, in my opinion.'

'Yes,' I said casually. 'I found your support of the Kingly expansion hard to understand . . . until I spent several hours reading their accounts.' I saw his hand tighten on his glass. His knuckles whitened. But he regained his composure quickly, and I saluted him for that.

'I don't think I follow,' he said with studied indifference.

312

'Well, of course, you're so much more experienced than me in matters of business. But isn't there what I think is termed a classic suppliers' fraud? A Director of company A does a deal with a Director and possibly the Purchasing Manager of company B. Two sets of accounts are kept, the false set showing a large order and a large payment. In fact the real order is much smaller and does not appear on the company's books. The fraudulent Directors of both companies A and B pocket the difference in cash. I gather it's a fairly common practice but, of course, criminal. Am I right?'

There was a pause. Then Charles Fairburn drained his glass. 'I underestimated you, didn't I?'

'That's not my concern,' I said briskly. 'All I'm interested in is getting the bank's backing to buy the land where I want to grow herbs. My concern is seeing that the House of Laure is not blackmailed into lowering the standard of its products!'

'Are you . . . are you going to the police?'

'No! Believe me, I have no wish to hurt you . . . I simply want what is best for my company.'

He briefly rubbed the back of one hand across his eyes. 'Oh, Christ! In so many ways it's a relief to admit all this . . . I've always thought of myself as an honourable man. I can't honestly think that, until now, I've done anything to be ashamed of. But now I *am* ashamed . . . bitterly ashamed . . . you seemed so young, you see, and I suppose I thought I could get away with it. I'm sorry.'

I beckoned to the wine waiter. 'Could we have two brandies, please?'

I sat silently, willing the broken man opposite me to find the strength to continue. Not for my sake, but for his.

The brandies came. Charles Fairburn drank deeply.

'I love my wife very much . . . very much. We've been married for nearly forty years. I respect her, like her, I can't imagine life without her. But . . .' There was a pause.

'Would it be impertinent if I said you no longer desire her?' I offered.

'It was a part of our life that was over, you see. Nothing was said, but sex seemed no longer to be important. We had the children, the grandchildren, and I honestly thought I didn't mind. Didn't miss it.

'Then I met someone. Someone who . . . Well, let's just say I met someone who made me remember that what was between my legs wasn't just for piddling! Forgive me if I'm being crude but . . . she obsessed me. Sex with her became like a drug. I had to have more and more. And then . . .' He trailed off.

'Then there was a price.'

'Nothing as obvious as money. Expensive gifts. A new car. Holidays that were supposed to be business trips.' He smiled grimly. 'There's no fool like an old fool!'

'I take it that's when Mark Kingly came on the scene?'

'Yes. When you put it like that,' he added slowly, 'it may have been a conspiracy. I don't suppose I'll ever know. But I needed money desperately, to keep her, to pay for my drug. What Kingly suggested seemed so easy. Fraudulent, but easy!' He shrugged. 'You know the rest. What are you going to do?'

'Nothing. And I ask you to do the same. If you truly think buying the land in Norfolk and Provence is a bad risk, then I don't expect you to recommend it to the bank. On the other hand, now that our cards are on the table, please don't stand in my way because Kingly is blackmailing you.'

There was a pause. Charles Fairburn looked wretched.

'He threatened to expose me if I didn't try to persuade you to take over his company as well as the factory.'

'Well,' I said briskly. 'I hope he's prepared to spend a very long time in prison. Because he'd get a much longer term inside for blackmail than you both would for a company fraud. Would you like me to speak to him?'

'Would you? Would you? I really don't deserve your help. I take it, of course, that you'll want me to resign from the Board?'

'Until now, you've been a good and active Director. Assure me that I can trust you and we'll forget all about this. I must warn you, though, if you try to betray me again I'll make a bad enemy!'

'You can trust me. I ask your forgiveness, and I'd like to give some advice . . . advice to a woman I respect. Don't give everything to the House of Laure. Leave something . . . something for life.'

Immediately I returned to the office, I asked my secretary to get Mark Kingly on the telephone.

'Miss Laure.' His voice sounded smug, as if he'd already won. 'I'm surprised to hear from you. Close of business today − wasn't that the game plan?'

'It *was*, but the rules have changed.'

He chuckled. 'Well, well! The ice maiden is a woman after all. And it's a woman's prerogative to change her mind. I take it this means you're prepared to do business my way?'

'No. It means I've had a long and very frank talk with Charles Fairburn. Good gracious, Mr Kingly, you've stopped chuckling.'

'You bitch!'

'Possibly. Now my offer still stands. The factory premises only. You have three hours in which to come to a decision. If I were you, I'd use those three hours to conjure up what it will be like being detained at Her Majesty's pleasure. Slopping out. Walking aimlessly around the exercise yard. Being locked up every night, year after year.

'If you decide not to sell your factory to me I shan't take any further action. It will simply be a matter of business between us. But if you try to harm Charles Fairburn, then I shall hand your company's accounts over to the Fraud Squad and I imagine blackmail and, possibly, conspiracy will be added to the charges. Do I make myself clear?'

A stream of abuse was hurled at me down the phone. All Mark Kingly got in reply was the click of my phone being hung up.

At five fifty-five that afternoon I had the Kingly factory.

But there was no time to gloat. There was a great deal of work to be done setting up the new premises. Increased supplies of ingredients. Increased packaging. Staff recruitment. I intended to ask Joss to take over the management of the new factory and to promote his assistant to run Baildon.

I telephoned Archie to give him the good news. I was by far the majority shareholder in the House of Laure with eighty per cent of the shares, but Archie and Aaron each held ten per cent.

When we'd set up the private company I'd wanted to give Archie a substantial holding. After all, it was he who had explored the question of preservatives in my products. But Archie wouldn't hear of holding a large stake in the company.

'My dear Beccy, all I did was look up a few books and make a phone call. Knowing you, I'm sure you'd have solved the problem yourself in time.'

'But *I* didn't, *you* did! And you've earned a part of the company. I won't stop pestering you until you give in.'

'Very well,' he'd laughed. 'Anything for a quiet life! But I definitely won't own more than ten per cent.'

After my call to Archie I wrote a brief letter to Aaron explaining my plans for the factory and for the purchase of land to establish herb farms in both East Anglia and France. I very much hoped that Aaron would join the company when he'd finished at Harvard and then, ultimately, be appointed to the board.

I'd formed a friendship with my brother again. Or, to be more accurate, and perhaps a little cynically, I'd consciously allowed myself to respond to his charm. I'd visited him twice while he was at the University of Southern California, then when he started studying at the Harvard Business School. He was competitive and successful, but part of me wondered whether the terms of the trust fund would keep him a scholar for the rest of his life!

It was seven o'clock and yet I could still hear my secretary at work in the outer office. Part of me applauded her ambition, but I also felt guilty that she stayed so late simply because I did. I was about to buzz through to her and insist that she go home when I heard the ringing of the office's main switchboard. A moment later my own phone rang. My secretary said, 'It's the Earl of Montacut . . . will you take the call?'

I'd found it difficult enough relating to Kit's title as Lord Christian D'Arcy but, since his father had died, I was always slightly startled to realise that the bearer of one of the most ancient titles in the Realm was an easy companion and friend of mine.

'Kit? Hallo! Where are you calling from? The ancestral home?'

'No, my club. I tried your flat first . . . I should have known better. Seven o'clock is much too early for Miss Laure to stop work!'

I laughed. 'Now, now. I don't hear you complaining when I announce profits are increased.'

'True. But then, we aristocrats love to grind the faces of the poor! Can I tear you away from the House of Laure for an evening? Are you free to dine with me?'

'Kit, I'd love that. When and where?'

'Mmm, let's see. How about the Caprice. Eight-thirty?'

'The Caprice? I hope *you're* paying?'

Kit laughed. 'Absolutely! I've got some great news that I want to share with you. Shall I pick you up?'

'No, it's just around the corner from my apartment. I'll meet you there. But what's the news?'

'All in good time. See you at eight-thirty!'

We had an exquisite meal, then went on to Winston's. Kit ordered champagne. 'You do realise I have to be at my desk at eight-thirty tomorrow morning?' I joked.

He looked suddenly serious and caught my hand. 'Is that all there is for you, Beccy? Grace Laure. No admirers? No lovers?'

'No admirers? How quaintly old-fashioned, Your Lordship. You'll be asking me if I have gentleman followers next!'

'Maybe the terminology is old hat but the sentiment is sincere. Don't be lucky at cards and unlucky in love, Beccy. I admire your success but worry about the way you drive yourself. Step off the treadmill occasionally.

'Kit, I thrive on the cut and thrust of business. I'm happy.'

'But your eyes are lonely!'

'Nonsense,' I said, briskly. 'Now, you've kept me in suspense long enough. What's your great news?'

Kit topped up our champagne. He raised his glass to me, sipped his champagne, then said, 'I have an heir. In fact, at the last count, I have seven heirs!'

'Kit, what are you talking about?'

'I've met someone, Beccy. Someone I really care about. Someone I want to spend the rest of my life with. I knew him at Agricultural College. I had no idea that he was . . . as I am. We happened to meet again at a point to point. Had a drink. We got on well together and arranged to meet again. There was no more to it than a couple of men who had the same interests, enjoying each other's company.'

'And then?'

'And then I realised I was attracted to him. I didn't do anything. Say anything. And then one evening he said that he'd hate me to hear gossip about him or for people to misunderstand our friendship, because he felt he had to tell me he was gay.

'My God, the relief, Beccy! My life suddenly made sense. I'd felt so wretched about my feelings for him. Ashamed, really. Then to discover . . . I tell you this because you've become my dearest friend. I do hope it isn't distasteful to you.'

'Oh, Kit, how can you say that? I've so wanted you to find someone you could be happy with.'

'I know. The thing is, we want to be together, spend our lives together. I've offered him the job of estate manager for D'Arcy farms and land. We'll be discreet. Our friends will know, of course. My mother might guess, but . . .' he suddenly grinned, '. . . we won't frighten the horses!'

'I'm not sure what this has to do with . . . what was it? . . . seven heirs?'

'I got to thinking how awful it was that I should make

some poor woman miserable just to bring another little earl into the world.'

'Your mother assured me that a lot of women will turn a blind eye for a title.'

'You wouldn't!'

'True but . . .'

'What you don't like to say is that you have too much pride, too much guts, to live a lie. I couldn't respect someone who married me for my title. And I can't bear the thought of deceiving some poor girl into thinking she's the love of my life.'

'And so?'

'And so I got on to Debrett's and engaged a first-class private detective to work with them. We traced a second cousin of my father's to New Zealand. He has two sons and four grandsons. Unless someone drops the bomb, in which case none of us will be worrying about our inheritance, the title is safe and I can settle down to being what the gossip columnists euphemistically describe as "a confirmed bachelor".'

'Well, Kit, dear friend,' I raised my champagne glass, 'I drink to your happiness!'

He raised his glass to me. 'And I drink to you *finding* happiness!'

Back home at my apartment I was restless. As I paced the sitting room I realised how lacking in individuality my environment was. I should have asked Bruno over to help me choose the furniture and decorations. Instead I'd simply been in a hurry to move in and to make the place comfortable to live in and elegant enough occasionally to entertain there. Always before I'd wanted to stamp my personality on anywhere I'd lived. Now, I simply wanted a place to hang my hat when I came home from building, ever building, the House of Laure.

I wandered through to my bedroom and undressed. As my evening with Kit was social and not business my skirt was much shorter than the one I'd been wearing during the day. The whole outfit had come from Biba — a very short silver sheath dress worn with shimmering silver tights, silver sling-back shoes with chunky heels, and really crazy, long, plastic silver earrings.

My apartment was serviced and, while I was out, the maid had come in and turned down my bed, had laid out my silk pyjamas with the monogrammed breast pocket, *G.L.* I turned from them and wrapped myself in the ageing dressing gown that John had given me. I briefly touched the monogram on that pocket: *B.M.*, Beccy Mandel.

I had thought Beccy Mandel dead. I had carefully and deliberately buried her when I had come to London. Then why did Grace feel so at home in Beccy's old robe? I no longer wanted to be Beccy. I wanted to be Grace: successful, independent, sophisticated. But deep inside me Beccy was still there: insecure, tremulous, desperately seeking the surety of love.

I wandered through to the kitchen and crossed to the ice box. I drank very little. Not from self preservation but simply because I didn't like it very much. And so it was unusual for me to take out a half bottle of champagne and open it. But that was the mood I was in. I needed a 'lift'. I needed something to *happen*.

My kitchen was all white. Stark. Almost surgical. I didn't really like it. I resolved that when I had the time I'd have it ripped out and then I'd replace it with a non-fitted kitchen. I wanted a dresser and a kitchen table. It would remind me of my mother's kitchen. Of Munkyns.

In the dining room I poured my champagne into a tall, fluted glass imported from Venice. I was going to take my drink into the sitting room but felt repulsed by its lonely perfection.

I turned instead to my small study. Here every wall was lined with Briony's books. A large, old walnut partners' desk was against one wall. I'd seen it in the antique shop in Baildon where I'd bought the Bristol glass étui, and knew it was exactly what I wanted to work at. From the kitchen at Munkyns, I'd brought up a comfortable Edwardian armchair. It was deep seated with a low back and scroll-shaped padded arms. True, it had seen better days, and a few of the springs had gone, but it was large enough to curl up in and small enough to be homely. It had a loose cover made of a flowery chintz which had been bleached by many washings and from drying in the salt winds that blew in from the estuary at Moreton. The expensive Mount Street interior decorator who had worked on my apartment had been warned, on pain of death, not to touch the study.

I curled up in the armchair and sipped my champagne. I suddenly wanted to listen to music. To drown in music. I glanced at my watch. It was after midnight and the BBC had closed down. I rose and crossed to the radio. I switched it on and tuned in to Radio Luxembourg. The haunting refrain of the Beatles' latest hit filled the small room. *'Eleanor Rigby picks up the rice in the church, where a wedding has been . . ..'*

A wedding has been . . . I'd desperately wanted to marry John. To bear his children. Would I ever marry now? 'Find happiness,' Kit had said. My business life was so enthralling, so fulfilling that I'd had very little time for my personal life.

'All the lonely people, where do they all come from?
All the lonely people, where do they all belong?
Ah, look at all the lonely people.'

It wasn't in my nature to be celibate. I'd had one or two brief affairs. Always with men I'd liked and respected but I'd not found anyone who inspired the love and passion I'd felt for John.

As I listened I felt Eleanor Rigby's loneliness. Her despair. I felt isolated by my success and not, as I usually did, sustained and buoyed up by it.

'*Father McKenzie, wiping the dirt from his hands as he walks from the grave. No one was saved . . . All the lonely people, where do they all come from? All the lonely people, where do they all belong?*'

As I crossed to turn off the song, the last lines mocked me. '*Ah, look at all the lonely people . . .*' I slammed down the 'Off' button. Silence. The room was quiet. Empty. I touched the well-loved books. 'Briony, I'm sorry. Give me the strength to be like you. Complete in one's self, strong enough to be alone and yet not be lonely.'

I fell asleep in the armchair I'd brought from Moreton. At 4 am I awoke stiff and bewildered as to where I was. '*All the lonely people, where do they all belong?*' 'Here!' I shouted at the deaf, unresponsive walls! Never again in the Lower East Side! Never again poor! '*No one was saved . . .*' Well, I'm saved. And Aaron is saved. Then why were my cheeks wet with tears? . . . '*Ah, look at all the lonely people.*'

CHAPTER TWENTY-FIVE

In the morning I showered, dressed, then had a light breakfast. I set out for the office, walking quickly, hoping that the keen morning air would blow away the mood that still persisted. I wanted to rid myself of a strange feeling of emptiness. I told myself sternly that I'd simply had too much champagne the previous night and it was no wonder that I felt jaded. I tried to concentrate on the day ahead, but the sad words of the Beatles song kept returning to my mind.

I needed a break, I decided. I'd go to Munkyns for the weekend. Walk the familiar footpaths. Sit and gaze at the sea. Relax. I still rented Munkyns from Kit but was finding it more and more difficult to get away from work and the office and to find time to get down to Moreton. But this weekend . . . Then I remembered that I had arranged to see a German entrepreneur who was flying in especially for our meeting. He wanted to manufacture the Laure range on licence. It was an interesting idea but I was worried that it would be difficult to monitor the quality of the product. Still, it was worth the meeting and, if all went well with the herb farm in Provence, I intended to expand even further into Europe. The German could be a very useful contact.

I'd walked even more briskly than usual and therefore was at the office earlier than my secretary. I picked up the mail and started to sort through it. One letter caught my eye and my heart stood still. In the top left-hand corner of the envelope was embossed the word *'Kimberly's'*. My hands were shaking slightly as I reached for the letter opener. I opened the envelope quickly, but took out the letter slowly. I don't know what I really expected. The images came tumbling into my mind as I held the folded notepaper. The staff entrance at Kimberly's . . . My first meeting with Briony . . . Drinking champagne with John in his grandfather's heavily panelled office . . . Then I unfolded the letter and saw the signature and the memories were no longer bittersweet, simply bitter. As bitter as aloes. John Kimberly Junior. I remembered his arrogance, his harsh words when he visited me at the clinic. If it hadn't been for his threat to drag John's name through the mud, I could have excused his behaviour as being caused by grief. But, in spite of his paying my hospital fees, I could not forgive. Well, the hospital fees had long since been repaid, as too had a good deal of Aaron's Trust Fund. But they'd been paid by Rebecca Mandel. John Kimberly Junior had no way of knowing that Grace Laure was one and the same woman.

I skipped through the letter. *'The House of Kimberly cordially invites . . . Prestigious store . . . Exclusive contract . . .* Oh, yes, John Kimberly Junior, Grace Laure would, after suitably long and difficult negotiations, allow you to sell her products – but at a price!

The launch of Grace Laure's skin-care range and cosmetics at Kimberly's was a very grand affair. My attorney had seen to that. After I'd opened our counter at the store there was a reception at The Plaza, a wonderfully elegant, old-style Edwardian hotel on Fifth at the edge of Central Park. Outside, horsedrawn carriages filled with tourists clip clop past the highly polished brass railings, on their way around the park.

I'd asked Bruno to escort me. Dear Bruno, with his bright ginger toupee precariously plonked on his head, was wearing a gaudily checked suit and a green shirt with a red tweed tie. I would have to admit the effect was startling and caused a few heads to turn. But I didn't care, it was my party, and I'd damn well bring who I pleased.

I'd chosen my clothes for the party very carefully. I'd noted that the fashions in New York were considerably behind London and Paris. The women were still wearing the neat, chic little dresses and jackets popularised by Jackie Kennedy. Their hair, too, was still back-combed and lacquered. I was astonished to hear that many fashionable restaurants banned women wearing trouser suits. David Frost had recently made popular the wearing of a silk polo-necked shirt with dinner jackets, but even he had been turned away in New York.

I wanted to look striking and fashionable enough to turn heads. I didn't want anyone to leave The Plaza that day without knowing who Grace Laure was. At the same time I couldn't afford to be outrageous or vulgar.

I got my secretary to check first that The Plaza allowed women to wear trouser suits. They did, but not in the main dining room. Well, so what? I wasn't dining there. I therefore chose a stunning outfit by Yves Saint Laurent. I wore very narrow black velvet trousers with a transparent blouse. Some very clever appliqué work across my breasts preserved my modesty. I had a green satin sash at my waist and my black velvet maxi-length jacket was lined with the same material.

Before I'd left London I'd had a fringe cut by Xavier of Knightsbridge. He was just as good a craftsman as Sassoon but without Vidal's desire for self-publicity. My fringe was long and straight in the style popularised by Jean Shrimpton and Audrey Hepburn. I'd known it would be difficult to find a hairdresser to wash and blow-dry my hair in New York and I certainly did not intend to spend hours under a dryer with my hair in curlers. I'd simply washed it in the shower and now wore it loose and straight down my back. My ensemble was completed by green satin evening pumps with low square heels and a simple Gucci shoulder bag.

'Love-a-duck, I've taught you well!' Bruno had said when we'd met. He took my hands and held me at arm's length, studying me. 'Can't fault it. You've come a long way, little Beccy.'

'Tonight, I'm Grace. In fact, I'm always Grace now, but especially when I'm going to spend some time with John Kimberly Junior.'

I'd met John Kimberly Junior on a number of occasions already. We weren't just launching the House of Laure at Kimberly's, it was also the start of a marketing campaign throughout the States, and there was a lot to be arranged. He clearly didn't recognise me. And why should he? He'd met a girl wearing a hospital robe, with bruises on her face and her hair pulled back in the simplest style imaginable. Why should he associate her with glamorous and successful Grace Laure?

On one occasion, he looked at me very keenly, then said, 'This sounds quite rude because how could anyone forget you, but I feel that perhaps we've met before.'

I simply replied, 'Oh, really?' Then smiled and added, 'Do you flatter all your business associates in this way?'

'Not many of my business associates look like you,' he flattered. I found it hard to keep my dislike of him from showing, and so I turned away and looked at the advertising proofs we were studying.

Now he was by my side. I introduced Bruno to him and we chatted for a while. Bruno's eyes glinted with such mischief I thought he was going to give the game away. I wondered why I didn't come right out and say, 'Yes, we have met before. I was your father's mistress.' But the truth was I liked my new identity as Grace Laure. It certainly made sense for the products and the woman who owned the business to have one and the same name. But there was more to it than that. As Grace I could be myself as I was now, without reference to my painful past.

Just as Bruno and I were about to move on to circulate amongst the guests, a good-looking man in his thirties joined us. 'Hallo, John. I should apologise for crashing in, but I'd be insincere, because I'm determined to meet the beautiful Miss Laure!'

He turned to me and held out his hand. 'My name's Paul, Paul Wingate. I demand to know why you're a beautiful young woman. Most *grandes dames* of the beauty business are overdressed, heavily made-up old hags!'

I laughed and shook his hand. 'I find that hard to believe.'

'It's true, it's true! This is ridiculous. I mean, you're not even covered in half a yard of diamonds!' He put his arm through mine and turned to Bruno and John Kimberly.

'If you gentlemen will excuse us, I'm going to steal Miss Laure for a few minutes.' And so saying he steered me away from them, through the room to a quieter area by the long windows overlooking the park. I was amazed that I allowed him to behave so outrageously. I was no longer used to being dominated by other men or women.

'Now, I'll let you go back to your party when you promise to have dinner with me.'

'I'll have dinner with you.'

'A quick and good decision. I can see why you're successful!'

'Yes, I can be decisive.' I smiled to soften the words. 'But be forewarned, I rarely do anything I don't want to.'

'I take note,' he said gravely, but his eyes were laughing. 'And I promise that when we dine, there won't be a bed anywhere in sight.'

I gave him my address and telephone number, I'd rented a small apartment for my stay in New York, and then went back to the party. But I was disturbed by the feelings that Paul had aroused in me.

I found him totally charming. He was tall, slender and moved with an easy grace. I wondered what his background was, what he did. Whatever it was he was obviously successful at it. His suit was well tailored and cut from expensive cloth. His glossy hair was dark brown and curled slightly at the nape of his neck. He was suntanned and looked very fit.

One of my guests was talking to me and I had to drag my mind away from Paul to try to converse intelligently. I saw Bruno looking at me with wry amusement. As soon as we were alone he said, 'Well, well. At last!'

'At last what?'

'At last you look like a woman who is about to fall in love again.'

The next couple of weeks were hectic. The launch of the House of Laure in New York looked as though it was going to be a success. The use of natural ingredients and the 'sell by' date on all the products seemed to have caught the New Yorkers' imagination. And our statement that none of our cosmetics had been tested on animals was ahead of its time. As I pointed out, there was no need to test on animals. The products had been used by humans for probably hundreds of years.

'Flower Power' and a return to a respect for the Earth's bounty and goodness was fashionable both in America and Europe. Bob Dylan was singing that the answer was blowing in the wind. In every way it was a time of change. The House of Laure was the first manufacturer to reflect that change in the cosmetics industry. We were in the right place at the right time.

I was also fortunate that I was young and that the image I had chosen to promote our products was natural, youthful, even wild. Three great women had dominated the cosmetics industry, one might even say created it: Helena Rubenstein, Estée Lauder and Elizabeth Arden. But they were all three in their late sixties or early seventies, and their advertising showed beautifully groomed young matrons, skilfully made up and formally dressed. Ours caught the mood of the late sixties – young, free-wheeling. The girls in our promotions were photographed against country backgrounds. A long-haired, natural-looking beauty walking through a field of wheat and poppies. A laughing young woman riding bareback along a seashore. A girl gathering herbs, her hair tumbling from a casually tied ribbon, and with a mongrel dog at her heels. It was romantic but it was fresh and, most importantly, new.

All these ingredients seemed to come together in New York and, as a result, I was very much in demand by the media. Glossy magazines interviewed me. I appeared on television. Did countless radio broadcasts. There didn't seem to be enough hours in the day. But, however busy I was, I made time for Paul.

After our first dinner date we met every day. For lunch, for dinner, for a late supper after I'd been interviewed or on the busiest days, for just a quick drink.

If I'd stopped to think I'd have realised that I was indeed falling in love again. But I didn't. Those first weeks back in New York were so heady. My business was a success, I'd heard from the London office that the bank had whole-heartedly endorsed my plans to establish herb farms in East Anglia and Provence, I felt at home with my metamorphosis from Beccy to Grace, and I had one of the most attractive men in New York dancing attendance on me.

For three weeks, beyond a fairly chaste kiss when he saw me home, Paul made no advances to me. I was beginning to wonder whether, in fact, he simply enjoyed escorting a successful and well-groomed woman around New York's more famous watering holes.

We got on famously. Argued, chatted, laughed together. But did he find me attractive? He must, I told myself, or why did he seek my company? But as the days went on I found myself longing for him to take me in his arms.

One night we were having a cocktail before going to the theatre. I was sipping a very dry martini, Paul a whisky sour. He suddenly put down his glass and said, 'You know, I want to sleep with you so desperately. Will you come away with me this weekend?'

I decided to match his cool approach and so replied casually, 'Do we have to go away? There are plenty of beds in New York.'

'Yes, Grace, we have to go away. Because, my darling, I'm not talking about a one-night stand, I'm talking about falling in love. And when we do make love, I want it to be somewhere romantic. I want time to savour the experience. Time to tell you what's in my heart as well as fulfilling my body's desperate, passionate desire for you. So will you come away with me?'

'Oh, yes, please!'

The following weekend Paul and I drove out of the city and along the Sunrise Highway on Long Island to Paul's weekend home situated on the very edge of the sea just outside Southampton. There the dunes sloped away from the house down to breakers rolling in from the Atlantic Ocean.

Paul's house was clapboarded and reminded me very much of East Anglia, which was hardly surprising as so many of the early settlers had come from those English counties. Even the county name of Suffolk had travelled to the New World.

Paul had telephoned ahead and a cold supper had been left for us: lobster, a selection of salads, a superb Chablis. I still knew very little of his background or his business affairs but his lifestyle spoke of considerable resources.

After our meal we strolled along the beach then returned to the house for a brandy. It was time for bed and I was suddenly nervous. As if I were a young, immature bride and not a confident, sexually experienced woman. Paul must have sensed my mood because he reached out and took my hand, and then, very gently, kissed my palm.

Then, very, very slowly he started to undress me. His actions were sensuous, not demanding or passionate. His hand would linger for a moment on my thigh. His lips briefly, too briefly, would touch my breast. He unpinned my hair and, for a moment, his tongue touched the lobe of my ear. Finally I was naked, every part of my body alive to his touch. I felt almost drugged with pleasure, with desire. I lay still, leaving Paul utterly in command of me.

'And now, my darling,' I heard him say, 'I am going to love you.'

He lifted me gently in his arms and carried me upstairs. He laid me gently on the bed and I heard myself moan my desire for him.

'Wait for me, my dear one, wait.'

Then he was within me. Taking me. Riding me. I cried out my love for him. I arched my body to his and clung to him. I couldn't get enough of him. Of his manliness. I think I screamed when I reached my climax. Paul seemed to be deeper, ever deeper, within me. As we lay back, afterwards, exhausted by our passion, I felt that he had made me totally his.

When I awoke I thought at first I was back at Munkyns because I could hear the sea. Then I remembered. I was in Paul's bed, in Paul's house, and he had made love to me.

I opened my eyes. The curtains were drawn, but the sun still crept into the room. It was simply but impressively furnished in Early American style. The bed was a mahogany half tester. A faded but exquisitely worked patchwork quilt and fine linen sheets covered my nakedness. My mind returned to the lovemaking of the night before and I stretched luxuriously, like a cat who has come in from the cold and discovered the warmth of a fire.

The bedroom door opened and Paul entered. He carried a breakfast tray and I could smell freshly ground coffee and newly baked bread.

'Good morning, sleepy-bones,' he said, smiling. 'While you've been a lay-a-bed, I've been for a swim, ground coffee, and warmed through a loaf of my housekeeper's home-baked bread.' He put down the tray and kissed me. 'You look beautiful!'

He pulled up a chair and we ate our breakfast together.

GRACE

My happiness was so great that it seemed almost a
tangible thing. Something to be touched, enjoyed,
treasured. I desperately hoped that Paul loved me, that
this wasn't just another affair for him, because I'd been
searching for another love for so long and this was
infinitely precious to me.

We had two more wonderful days and nights together.
I had to fly back to London on the Monday. There were
papers to be signed, details to be finalised concerning the
purchase of the farms. Things that only I could do.

As Paul drove me to the airport we were mainly silent.
The weekend was still with me and I hated the thought
of our parting.

Then, as the last call was made for my flight and I
simply had to go, he pulled me into his arms and said,
'You will marry me, won't you, Grace? Say you will,
darling.'

'Oh, Paul, my love.' I clung to him.

'This is the last call for Miss Grace Laure, a first-class
passenger travelling to London, Heathrow.'

'I must go.' I started to run towards the departure
gates.

'Darling, you haven't said yes.'

'Yes! Yes! Oh, yes!' I called back to him, laughing,
as I made the final dash to catch my plane. 'YES!

CHAPTER TWENTY-SIX

As I put the key into the door of my apartment, I could hear the telephone ringing. Please let it be Paul, I thought, as I dashed to the phone. It was!

'Hallo,' I said, a little breathlessly.

He simply replied, 'When?'

I laughed and said, 'Oh, as soon as possible, don't you think?'

'I most certainly do! I love you so much, darling. You look at your diary. Talk to your family. There'll be a lot of arrangements to be made.'

'Not really.' I realised that I'd told Paul very little about my background. 'I have no family except my brother, Aaron. As to the wedding itself, I take it that you're a Christian?'

'Agnostic Anglican would be an apt description, but the Wingates still get baptised, married and buried by the Church.'

'I'm Jewish.'

Did I imagine it or was there a slight hesitation before Paul laughed and replied, 'My darling girl, I don't care if you're a Zen Buddhist. I just want you to have a lovely wedding. After all, you're a beautiful, successful and wealthy woman and − well, I come from a very old family.'

Ridiculously the rhyme *'When Adam ploughed and Eve span, Who was then the gentleman?'* came into my mind again.

'Anyway, darling, the most important thing, the utterly wonderful thing, is that you've agreed to marry me. Nothing else matters but that.'

'I hope not.'

'Well of course it doesn't. Sleep on it, Grace darling, and we'll talk again tomorrow.'

'Can you phone me quite late? I've got meetings all day then a business dinner. Sorry.'

'Don't be sorry. A successful company takes a lot of running.'

'Ah,' I said jokingly, 'How do you know my company *is* successful? After all, our shares aren't quoted.'

Paul laughed and replied, 'Let's just say I have faith in you, darling. Sleep tight, precious. I'll call tomorrow.'

'Good night, God bless. *Whichever* God it is.'

I hung up and sat by the phone for a moment. Suddenly I shivered. 'You're tired my girl,' I thought. 'A hot bath, then an early night will do you the world of good.'

Then I looked at the pile of mail, neatly arranged by my cleaner on my desk, and knew there was no chance of an early night. By the time I'd bathed, had a sandwich and some tea, it was nearly 10 pm. I'd put on pyjamas and wrapped myself in the cashmere navy blue and gold robe that John had bought me, the one that had inspired the packaging. It was well worn now, but I couldn't bear to part with it. Before I settled down to my post I wanted to phone my closest friends and tell them about my forthcoming marriage.

No point in calling Aaron, he'd still be at a lecture. I tried Mike's number in Los Angeles. It would be two o'clock in the afternoon there. His secretary answered.

'Oh, Miss Laure, I have instructions always to put you through, but I'm afraid Mr Janowski is still at lunch with

Mr Schuman. I'll call the restaurant and ask him to phone you.'

'No! Don't bother him. Ask him to phone my London number when he gets back to the office. It's 10 pm here now. I'll be up for at least another four hours.'

'Very well, ma'am.'

'Thank you.'

Bruno would be at his shop for another three hours or so. I decided to ring Kit before it got too late. I telephoned his private number at D'Arcy House. It saved being vetted by the butler and then, if one passed muster, an interminable wait while Kit was tracked down in that vast old house.

'Kit, it's me. Am I phoning at a bad time?'

'Not at all, Young Laure.' Kit had found it impossible to cope with my dual role as Beccy and Grace, and so had invented the nickname 'Young Laure', which had stuck.

'My mother's in Scotland murdering poor defenceless birds and Harry and I are spending a splendidly quiet and pleasant evening in front of the fire with a good port and a good book. How are you? And how was New York?'

'A success, I think.'

'You only *think*?' Kit teased. 'That doesn't sound like the Young Laure I know and love.'

'All right, damn it, it was bloody marvellous! New Yorkers never do things by half, and we wowed them.'

'That's my girl!'

'As to how I am . . . Oh, Kit, I'm so happy! There's this dishy, charming, wonderful, sexy, dashing, intelligent man . . .'

'Sounds as if you like him,' he said, laughing.

'And . . . I'm going to marry him!'

In a moment his whole manner changed. He was no

337

longer teasing, flippant, but utterly and most touchingly sincere. 'Oh, my dear girl, I can't tell you how happy I am! I've so wanted your happiness. My dear girl!'

'His name is Paul Wingate and I'm so lucky . . . and . . . hell, I'm in love!'

Kit's manner suddenly became brisk. 'You will, of course, be married from D'Arcy House.'

'Kit, you can't possibly . . .'

'Oh, yes, I can! Aaron can give you away but I shall be *loco parentis*. I'm glad to say, not in years, but in my heart and in all matters practical. You will leave D'Arcy House on my arm and return a bride.' His manner suddenly lightened. 'Besides, what a wonderful excuse for a party! Start writing up your guest list and we'll liaise in a few days. This is great news, Young Laure.'

'Yes, isn't it? Good night.'

'Good night.'

Before Paul rang me the next day I had spoken with Aaron, Bruno and Mike. They would all come to my wedding. Mike had sounded happy for me but I found it a difficult conversation. He and Mrs Janowski were so much part of my younger self. The fact that for one wild moment we had been lovers, that all through our changing fortunes we'd remained friends, had never forgotten where we came from, had held on to some basic, almost tribal feeling for each other while we dared to dream . . . everything made us so close. And yet what lay unstated between us kept us at arm's length.

When we'd finished speaking, I sat for a while and wished that Mrs Janowski could have seen me wed. Since my mother died when I was twelve, she had been mother, grandmother, confidante and friend. Then it came to me. I still had her wedding dress. The dress that she had cut down for me so that I could go to the first night of *Sweet Bird of Youth* with John. I would wear it when I married Paul. I would wear it with love, and with pride.

While I waited for Paul's call the next evening, I couldn't help but be amused that following my confession that I was Jewish and had no family except Aaron, I was about to suggest that we be married from one of England's most famous stately homes. That one of my dearest friends was the Earl of Montacut who wanted to treat me as a loved and honoured member of his family. However, in spite of my love affair with Paul and my intense joy that we were to be married, it was impossible for me to banish thoughts of the House of Laure from my mind. That day I had signed the contracts of purchase for the new herb farms in Norfolk and Provence. I was well satisfied.

Because of our different faiths, Paul and I were to be wed at the register office in Colchester, in the presence of only close friends and relations. Aaron and Kit were to be our chief witnesses. Mike, Bruno, Paul's mother, sister and brother-in-law would complete the party. Afterwards there would be a reception at D'Arcy House. The Board of the House of Laure were to be guests, also Archie, Joss, Charlie and his wife. From Moreton, Kit and I had invited Fred, Eric, Martha, Lil, Ivy, and Peggy and Alf who were now 'walking out' with each other. I wasn't sure what Paul would make of such a motley crew but I couldn't believe that he wouldn't be as fond of them as I was.

Although Paul and I had spent the week before our wedding living quite openly together at my apartment in London, Kit had insisted that all the conventions be observed the night before the wedding. The bride's party, consisting of Aaron, Bruno and Mike were to stay at

D'Arcy House. Kit had booked the bridegroom's party into the D'Arcy Arms in the village.

We all dined in considerable style at D'Arcy House that night. Kit was an informal and gracious host, but it would be hard not to be impressed by the splendid Dining Hall with its oak panelling and vaulted, beamed ceiling from which hung a series of frayed but ancient and honourable banners.

My brother Aaron looked incredibly handsome in his dinner jacket and black tie, and I was so proud of him. I'd had little time to get to know Paul's family and wasn't sure whether or not I was imagining that they were a little cool towards me, or if it would just be a matter of time before we could become friends.

Bruno was his usual colourful, zany but wise self. Mike seemed to me to have grown in stature. He had the confidence of having found success in one of the most cut-throat and competitive businesses in the world – show business.

That night I lay in bed and found it difficult to get to sleep. Partly because I missed Paul's arms around me, and partly because I was so happy and excited. Everyone I held dear was going to be with me on my wedding day. Even Kit's mother, the Countess, was returning from Scotland and would be at the reception. I desperately wanted to get to sleep because I wanted to look my best in the morning, but sleep would not come. I turned on the bedside lamp and looked at my watch. It was thirty minutes past midnight. I decided to creep down to the Library and get a book, to try to read myself to sleep.

As I crossed the hall towards the Library I saw that there was still a light on in the Small Parlour. Then I heard voices – Kit's and Mike's. I'd been pleased and a little surprised at how well they had got on. It would be hard to imagine two men from more disparate backgrounds! I thought I'd ask them if I could have a nightcap with them. Chat for a little while. My slippers made no sound as I walked across the huge flagstones. I was about to put my hand on the door handle when Mike's voice stopped me.

'. . . he's gone through two family fortunes. I just hope Beccy's got enough money to settle his debts . . .'

'She's very much in love with him.' This was Kit.

'Yes,' I heard Mike sigh. 'Otherwise I would have tried to buy the bastard off!'

Horrified I turned away from the door. They could only be talking about Paul. But what they said made no sense. It was quite clear from his lifestyle that he had plenty of money. Ours had been such a whirlwind romance that I only knew that he had business interests that produced a handsome dividend. If I'd thought about it at all, I'd assumed that he had inherited money and had a share in a family business. I knew Mike too well to think that he would ever do anything to hurt me and so I couldn't believe that what he said was motivated by jealousy.

I walked slowly back upstairs and got into bed. I lay in the darkness thinking about what I'd overheard. True or false? Take 'false' first. Mike had simply got Paul muddled with someone else. But I knew Mike. He was a loving, caring man but he was also hard headed and, I suspected, ruthless. He just wouldn't make that kind of mistake.

He'd heard rumours, perhaps, about Paul when he was younger. It would be easy for a young, good-looking man from an old-established New England family to live the life of a playboy for a while, before he settled down and realised the harsh realities of life. Yes, that seemed to be the most likely explanation. Mike's information was simply out of date.

But I too was hard headed and perhaps a little ruthless. And if you're like that with the outside world, then you're also like that with your inner self. I told myself to have the guts now to ask the question 'True?'

I looked 'true' squarely in the eye and knew that, whatever the truth, I loved Paul too much to give him up. I could understand that pride would keep him from confiding in me that he had money problems. I remembered that he'd described me as a wealthy woman. I'd been so busy building up the House of Laure that my personal fortune, although immensely gratifying, wasn't really what motivated me. But, yes, I had a major holding in a company that was hugely successful and, more importantly, had great potential for expansion. At last sleep was claiming me. My limbs grew heavy and, as my eyelids closed, I knew that 'true' or 'false' mattered nothing to me. I wanted to be Paul's wife. I loved him, And surely I always would.

CHAPTER TWENTY-SEVEN

As I stood holding Paul's hand and watching the first of the herbs being picked at our farm in California, I had no regrets. We'd bought the land, a little to the north of the Napa Valley, soon after we'd married. It had been obvious that we needed to open factories in the States because demand for Laure products grew rapidly after our launch. But I wanted to establish the same principle as in England and France and grow as many of our own herbs as possible.

We'd been fortunate to find a small, family-owned vineyard that was for sale. The climate to the north of the valley was less advantageous for wine growing but perfect for the major herbs we used.

Now, we had rather sentimentally taken time off — time that we could ill afford — to witness the first harvest.

I thought of Martha and her 'afore noon' doctrine. All the herbs harvested were picked before the full heat of the noonday sun, and the pickers had instructions to treat the precious plants delicately and to avoid bruising them, thus damaging the essential oils.

I was clumsy as we walked along the gravel path between the beds of herbs. But my clumsiness was a joy, because I was heavy with Paul's child.

He'd been so loving, so caring of me during my pregnancy, that I could forgive him anything. For Mike had been right. Soon after our marriage Paul confessed to me that his business ventures had been a failure and that he'd made bad investments.

I had been shocked by the size of the debts, but determined that we should make a new start together. That Paul should have a second chance. The debts had been settled and I had given him thirty per cent of my holding in the House of Laure. This made him a major shareholder and I was therefore able to make his appointment to the Board comparatively easily. It meant that he drew dividends from his shares and had a Director's salary. I was happy with this arrangement because I didn't want Paul to be beholden to me financially.

Suddenly one of the pickers, an Hispanic, came towards me and pressed a large bunch of Lady's Mantle into my hands. She smiled and nodded towards my swollen belly as she did so. I spoke no Spanish and so could only smile and nod my thanks in dumb show. We used Lady's Mantle with buttermilk as a cleansing lotion for oily and spotty skins, but it was also used as a tea to ease the discomforts of pregnancy and aid recovery after birth. Once again, I wondered at the international language of herbs.

I felt tired but happy as we were driven to the airport at San Francisco where the private jet that Paul had hired was waiting. I'd hoped to have time to visit our newest factory, which was situated on the outskirts of Monterey, but we had to be back in London for a Board meeting.

I had a plan that I wanted to put into operation to extend the House of Laure and enter a new field. Ever since *Time* magazine on April 15th, 1966, had given over its cover and lead story to London and the 'Swinging Sixties', the cult of Youth had dominated that city. But there was more to it than the Stones, the Beatles, and Carnaby Street. There was an upsurge of interest in all things ethnic. In 'Health' foods and Herbalism. What I had in mind was a chain of shops called Body and Soul. They would be aimed at the younger buyer. The shops would combine selling a more cheaply packaged version of the Laure range, with running a juice and herbal tea bar. We would not only recommend skin care for specific problems, we'd offer teas, infusions and juices that could combat the condition from within. Also, I wanted to encourage customers to try out our products in the shop.

We had discussed my plan briefly at the last Board meeting and I'd realised that, quite simply, we had too many old men as Directors. They had no conception of what I was talking about. It was as if London didn't exist for them beyond the walls of the City and St James's Street, where the most old-established, prestigious gentlemen's clubs were.

Kit had sided with me in his wonderfully laconic way. 'Frankly, I know nothing about what is or is not "swinging", nor do I know anything about the problems of pimply youth. However, I do know that Young Laure here is no mean shakes at getting it right . . . and that's good enough for me!'

Now I had thoroughly researched the cost of establishing Body and Soul and had two potential sites lined up, one in Chelsea, the other just off Carnaby Street. I was excited about the project and determined to have my own way.

But, on the flight back to London, Paul and I were occupied with more personal things. As long as the House of Laure existed and expanded we would need to spend our time between the States and Europe. We had my apartment in London and had leased a town house in New York, but both environments were intensely cosmopolitan and once our child was born I wanted somewhere to create a home.

It had seemed to me for some time that the final cachet
the House of Laure needed was the establishment of a
salon. And, in spite of changing fashions, the only place
to do that was Paris. We had almost made up our minds
to make Paris our international headquarters, and to look
for a house in which to make our main home within
driving distance of that city.

But as we drove towards the House of Laure's London
offices, I could think only of the Board meeting ahead.
I knew I could count on Paul and Kit and possibly on
Charles Fairburn, although I certainly couldn't take that
for granted. That left three Directors who needed to be
convinced. Of course, I could call an Extraordinary
General Meeting of the shareholders and that would be
the end of the argument, because I was sure that Aaron
and Archie Crabtree would vote with Paul and me. But,
if that happened, there could be unpleasant consequences
with our bank. I simply had to carry the day.

The traffic was bad on the way into town from
Heathrow, but when was it ever any better? We were just
in time for the Board meeting but first I stopped off in
my office. There was something I hoped to find awaiting
my arrival. A letter. A very special letter. I read it through
quickly, then went into the Boardroom. We went through
the usual formalities, minutes of the last meeting and
minor matters, then we came to Body and Soul. I
presented the Board with my detailed figures, the
projected costs, and then my profit forecast.

'The House of Laure is rapidly becoming one of the
foremost names in the cosmetics industry. I know we have
a long way to go before we can catch up with Rubenstein,
Lauder or Arden. We do, however, have a healthy share
of the market. But our packaging, especially the blue glass
containers, is costly. There is a young and moderately

affluent market which we haven't tapped . . . Body and Soul can do that!'

'Miss Laure' — it was only in my private life that I was known as Mrs Paul Wingate — 'surely all this pandering to the young is just a phase?'

'Youth is always going to be with us. But, for the first time, they have a voice. I think we ignore that voice at our peril.'

'I for one cannot support such a risky venture.' This from the oldest and most experienced of the three Directors whom I'd felt sure would oppose me.

'I see. In that case, could we simply vote yes or no to Body and Soul. I've made my feelings known. I've given you facts and figures. Please, let's clear the air over this matter.'

It was at this point that I felt the first of the pains. Oh, please, no! My baby wasn't due for another four days. Surely not? I took my hands from the table and clenched the edge of my chair. Please, please, let the pain pass. . .

Kit and Paul were with me. To my intense sadness Charles Fairburn, reluctantly, was not. At least, I thought, it was an honest decision on his part, and it must have been a painful one to make because he was in my debt. I respected him for his integrity. The other three Directors were opposed to my scheme.

'Then, clearly, as you no longer have faith in me as Chairman . . .'

'Young Laure, no! You can't resign.' This from Kit.

Another pain, this time more intense than the first. My baby was telling me that he, or she, wouldn't wait another four days to enter the world. Fight the pain . . . Conquer the pain.

'I have no intention of resigning, Your Lordship.

However, with the greatest sadness, I must ask for the resignation of the Directors who have opposed me. If you have no faith in my judgement then *I* cannot keep faith with you!'

'Grace!' Paul exclaimed in warning.

'I must add my voice to Mr Wingate's,' said Henry Allan, the most influential of the Directors. 'I took the precaution of sounding out the bank about this madcap venture of yours. They are not prepared to consider it.'

'Because you influenced them against it!'

'They will call in the House of Laure's banking facility if you persist in launching Body and Soul. I think the commitment will be a little over one million pounds.'

Another pain. No doubt the Board thought I was pausing for effect. I was pausing to try to stop from crying out! Then I said, 'Very well. I will make arrangements for the full amount of the loan to be repaid to the bank. I shall be sad to bank elsewhere, because the branch in Baildon believed in me at a time when I most needed that. However, I do not need it now. I hope the gentlemen of the Board who will be resigning will soon find Directorships which pay fees as generous as those received from the House of Laure.'

There was a stunned silence. Paul and Kit looked at me as if I'd gone mad. I pressed on. 'I intend to take Laure products into the seventies and beyond, as an exciting, innovative enterprise. I do not intend to be held back by an "Old Boys" network that has no place in modern life. At least, not modern life as I perceive it.

'Before Paul and I flew to California I had a meeting with one of the oldest established merchant banks in the City. They may be old-established, but they are most certainly not old-fashioned. They will recompense what will be, from tomorrow, our former bankers and provide trading facilities of four million.'

The letter I'd received was confirmation of this.

At that point the meeting ended in uproar. Paul said indignantly, 'Grace! Why didn't you take me into your confidence?' Kit was congratulating me generously, so was Charles Fairburn. I deeply regretted that he'd sided with those who could not believe in Body and Soul.

'You could have trusted me,' Paul was saying. But now I had to give in to the pain. I grasped his hand.

'I'm sorry. I had to act as the Chairman of the House of Laure, not as your wife. But now, darling, please, get me to the clinic!'

I remember the pain of giving birth and yet have forgotten it. Because the moment when a healthy living baby is placed against a mother's breast transcends everything.

We had a daughter. I held her close to me and promised her that my love would always protect her. That she would never know squalor, or mean tenements, or what it was to be cold and hungry. I gave her my heart. I'd never known such happiness. I had Paul and now I had his child. We named her Sarah, after my mother.

She was nine months old when my world fell apart. We now had a beautiful home thirty miles from Paris but still had to travel a great deal. My baby came everywhere with me. I had a nanny, but I was determined that Sarah would always know that her mother was there, loving her. It became common for me to enter a business meeting carrying a brief-case in one hand and a carry-cot in the other.

Body and Soul had been a great success. We had opened branches in New York, Chicago and Los Angeles, as well as major cities throughout Europe. Aaron had joined the company and the Body and Soul chain of shops had become his special responsibility. He was appointed to the new Board, as was Joss. I wanted people around me who knew and cared about the company not accountancy. However, the House of Laure was still a private company. At the birth of our daughter I'd suggested to Paul that we both set aside five per cent of our shares for Sarah. He'd readily agreed. This meant that I no longer had a fifty per cent stake in my company, but I was still by far the majority shareholder and had no reason to believe that my husband and daughter would ever use their shares against me.

Now we were in New York and staying at our town house. We'd planned to spend the weekend at Paul's house on Long Island, where we'd first made love. He had gone up there at the beginning of the week to open the house and take delivery of a new sailing dinghy he'd had built. I planned to drive down with Sarah on the Friday evening. We hadn't been to Long Island for well over a year and both Paul and I were looking forward to a romantic, nostalgic weekend.

By Thursday lunchtime I was missing him desperately. We'd spoken on the phone every evening. He was his usual, loving self.

'I can't tell you how much I'm looking forward to Friday, darling. It's as if I've lost a limb when I'm away from you and Sarah.'

I buzzed through to my secretary and asked her if she could clear my diary for the following day. Sarah's nanny was to have the weekend off so that we could have a totally 'family' time together. I telephoned her to say that I was probably driving up to Long Island a day earlier and that she could have an extra day free.

By three o'clock my secretary had been able to

rearrange my appointments and my Friday was free. I was about to telephone Paul, then decided I would surprise him.

It was early evening when Sarah and I drove up to the house. The living room was at the front with marvellous views across the dunes to the sea. When the French doors were open on to the beach, the sound of the surf filled the room.

I suppose that is why Paul and the woman he was making love to didn't hear the car. I stood in the hall, looking through to the living room. There was only one lamp on but its light, together with that from the driftwood fire, clearly illuminated the naked bodies locked together in the act of love. I couldn't move. It was as if I was paralysed. I felt so agonisingly foolish, standing in the hallway, a bottle of champagne in one hand, Sarah's carry-cot in the other, with tears streaming down my face. Then I turned and ran. Ran away from the nightmare that was engulfing me.

I was half blinded by tears and blundered into the partly opened front door. I dropped the bottle of champagne, which practically exploded when it hit the tiled floor. I heard Paul cry out, 'Grace! Oh, God, no! Grace!' But I had to get away from that scene. From my faithless husband and his lover.

I got to the car and opened the rear door as quickly as I could, placing Sarah on the back seat. I was just getting into the driver's seat when Paul caught up with me. His handsome, suntanned body was completely naked. He caught my arm. 'Grace, please, this means nothing! Nothing! I love you!'

'Love me? Then, by Christ, we mean very different things when we say that. You bastard, let go of my arm!'

'Grace, please!'

In the back of the car, Sarah started to cry. It was more than I could bear. I tore my arm free, then clenched my fist and punched him with all my strength. Blood spurted from his nose as he staggered back in amazement and pain. I took my opportunity and leapt into the car. I drove away as if all the fiends of hell were pursuing me. I stopped a mile along the road. Taking Sarah from her carry-cot, I held her in my arms, soothing her, rocking her until she fell asleep. I'd forced myself to overcome my sobs, because I didn't want to frighten my baby, but as I held her my tears splashed on to her face. When I looked out across the ocean, I didn't see the majestic breakers and waves. I saw only a bleak, loveless future.

That night I booked into a motel. I longed to talk to someone about what had happened. But who? I realised I still felt a kind of loyalty towards Paul. I couldn't ease my anguish by confiding to a friend, however dear, that I thought my husband was a bastard. Mike was the only one I could have turned to, but he was getting married in two weeks' time. Dear God! Paul and I were invited. Had promised to be there. If I went alone Mike would be suspicious and I wanted nothing to ruin his wedding day. If I stayed away he would be incredibly hurt.

In any case, was I really going to break up my marriage? Perhaps Paul had been telling the truth when he'd said that sleeping with another woman had meant nothing to him. That he loved me. But I knew I could never reconcile myself to that way of life. Why should we accept that men are different, simply because they tell us so? I loathed the idea of being the kind of wife who turns a blind eye to her husband's affairs because 'he always comes home to me in the end'. To me, loving was a commitment. If I met a man I found attractive, I would deny myself the pleasure of a brief affair because I couldn't give myself to my husband knowing that I'd betrayed him. What the hell was marriage *for* if we just jumped from bed to bed without a thought for whom we were hurting? Perhaps even destroying.

Then I looked at Sarah. She was sleeping peacefully, clutching a well-worn, well-loved, toy koala bear that Paul had brought back for her from a business trip to Australia. She looked so vulnerable and so precious that I answered myself: 'This is what marriage is for.' Then I thought of my own life. I'd never really known my father. I'd longed to be like the other kids and have two parents. I remembered asking my mother when I was very small, 'Why haven't I got a pa?' and seeing the hurt in her eyes before she turned away without answering. Was I going to condemn Sarah, my beloved Sarah, to that? As the cold, icy fingers of dawn light crept through and around the thin blind of the motel bedroom, I knew that I was not. I'd also faced up to the fact that I was still in love with my husband.

Although, after what had happened, I found it difficult to believe that Paul really loved me, I knew without doubt that he adored his daughter. Once I'd dragged myself from my own pit of despair, I realised that he'd be distraught with worry as to what had become of us. I telephoned the beach house. There was no reply. When I telephoned our New York town house the phone was answered practically before it had a chance to ring. 'Paul?'

'Grace! Oh, thank God! Where are you? I've been out of my mind . . . are you all right? Is Sarah all right? Oh, Christ, Grace, I'll never forgive myself.'

'We're both fine,' I answered as levelly as I could. 'We're on our way home.'

'Darling, thank you. I'll never . . . never . . .'

'Paul, please don't make any promises now. We'll talk about it when I get home. Goodbye.'

Paul looked terrible when he opened the door of our town house. He obviously hadn't slept or shaved. He took me in his arms and hugged me to him. I didn't, couldn't respond to his embrace but neither did I pull away from him.

'Grace, I thought I'd lost you.' He let go of me and reached down to pick up Sarah. He cradled her gently in his arms. 'My two darling girls!' He turned to me. 'You *have* to forgive me, Grace. I couldn't live without you and Sarah.'

I climbed the stairs ahead of him to the first-floor drawing room. I slumped down into the deep-seated, imported sofa which faced the fireplace, utterly exhausted.

'Please don't let's talk about it now, Paul. Suffice to say, I've thought about it and I'm not going to leave you over a one-night stand. I take it this *was* a one-night stand?'

He sat beside me on the sofa, still holding Sarah. He shifted her gently on to the crook of his arm, then took my hand into his free one. 'Yes, it was. I was missing you like hell. I went down to the bar at the yacht club. Had too much to drink. I'd never even met the woman before. It just . . . happened!'

I turned and looked at him. His handsome face looked so haggard, so utterly dejected and despairing, that I knew I had to forgive him. I gripped his hand briefly.

'Let's just put it behind us, Paul. Make a new start. I promise I won't throw it in your face. Won't mention it again.'

'Darling, thank you.' Paul leant towards me to kiss me but I rose from the sofa and crossed to the fire. I looked down at the gas flames that licked around the imitation logs and thought how much I hated its phoniness. I suddenly remembered the open fire in John's apartment, and how the flickering light from it had bathed our naked bodies the night we first made love. I held on to the mantel and forced the memories from my mind.

'There are just two things, Paul, and please don't think I'm trying to punish you or be destructive. I never want to go to the beach house again as long as I live. And, just for the time being, I want to sleep alone. I need a little time. A little space.'

'I understand.' He laid the sleeping child down in the corner of the sofa, then crossed to me. I felt his hands on my shoulders. He turned me to face him and I didn't resist. He gently reached out and touched my face lightly with his hand, etching the shape of forehead, cheek bone and chin with his fingers. 'I love you, Grace,' he said, simply. And I believed him.

CHAPTER TWENTY-EIGHT

New Year 1970. We saw the new decade in at Munkyns. A year previously I'd finally persuaded Kit to sell it to us. I could never imagine a time when Munkyns, Moreton and Baildon wouldn't be part of my life. But with a toddler, a nanny and my longing for more children the old cottage was too small.

As soon as Kit had agreed to sell I'd sought the help of a brilliant young architect who fell in love with Munkyns and its surroundings the moment he saw it.

'Miss Laure,' he said sternly, 'I absolutely forbid you to touch this house! Its proportions are perfect. Originally a Hall House, probably thirteenth-century with a jettied cross piece added in, say, the late sixteenth century. Carry out further restoration by all means but change it? Never!'

'That's all very well but . . .'

'BUT! You have a large, oak-framed barn within a few feet of the main house. A single storey cow-shed linking the two would be quite acceptable.'

'To whom?' I interrupted.

The young man had the grace to smile. 'Well, certainly to a cow, as it will be timber-framed, insulated and lined with central heating! But if not occupied by a bovine friend, it would create an authentic-looking walk-way to an annexe that could provide a very large, galleried reception room, a kitchen, three bedrooms with bathrooms en suite, and there'd still be room for a playroom for your little girl!'

I smiled. 'When can I move in?'

The answer to that had proved to be just in time for Christmas. Not only had the barn been magnificently converted, the old house had been returned to its former glory. Timbers had been treated for woodworm and dry rot then sand blasted back to a rich warm oak. The tiny partitioned bedrooms I'd so disliked when I first saw Munkyns were gone. Upstairs we now had three large bedrooms and two bathrooms, which was ideal for Paul and me, Sarah and her nanny. The barn's bedrooms could be used for guests. I'd commissioned Bruno to furnish the barn and the house.

We'd kept most of the old, comfortable furniture which seemed to belong to Munkyns and had built around that. The eclectic, country-house look that I'd wanted to emulate in the apartment that John had rented for me in New York was now a reality. I'd played truant from the House of Laure for four whole days and Bruno and I had scoured East Anglia for antiques. I wanted nothing grand. Just good, solid country furniture.

Sometimes a glint would come into a dealer's eye. Here was a wealthy American and her interior designer just ripe to be plucked! Bruno would smile sweetly at them and say, 'Now take that look off your face, ducks. I know within a quid what I should be paying, so let's cut the bullshit and shoot crap, as we say in the good old U.S. of A.! No offence, sweetie!'

We found a huge carved oak settle that had come from a pub. This would stand next to the wood-burning stove we were having in the barn. Although the barn and the house were going to be centrally heated I couldn't imagine being in the country without a log fire. There was no fireplace in the barn but our problem was solved by importing a large, handsome cast-iron stove from

Norway. It created a focal point for the main reception area, which was a stunning galleried room open to the huge oak rafters in the roof.

Bruno nearly went crazy with excitement when we discovered an oak dining table with a matching set of ten dining chairs and two carvers designed by Ambrose Heal, just dumped at the back of a large warehouse at Long Melford. I thought he was going to murder the owner, a shifty-eyed, weedy-looking man, when he said that he didn't rate the furniture and was going to probably use the wood to 'bitser' other antiques!

We got the lot for £50 and when I protested afterwards that we'd been less than fair to the dealer, Bruno's face went nearly as red as his crazy toupee. 'Fair? Fair? Be fair to that ignorant, moronic, blockheaded, crass, unfastidious, barbaric, clod-hopping philistine! Words fail me!'

'You could've fooled me!'

In Norwich we found a seventeenth-century Dutch walnut and ebony armoire. At Thetford an early eighteenth-century oak chest with richly carved panels. Bury St Edmunds yielded a Jacobean foot stool, a Victorian walnut rocking chair, two Gustav Stickley slat-sided armchairs, a seventeenth-century oak gatelegged side-table and a set of Doulton nursery ware for Sarah. It consisted of a tea-pot, a milk jug and a cup and saucer, all designed and decorated by Cecil Aldin with studies of his famous dogs. I knew Sarah would love it.

At that point I had to return to London and my business, which was probably just as well for my bank balance! I left Bruno as happy as a lark in Bury. He'd found an old-established upholsterers and was incredibly impressed by the standard of their work. We'd agreed on warm earth colours for the barn and I knew I could trust Bruno to do a marvellous job.

A week before Christmas, Paul and I drove down to Moreton with Sarah for a final check that all was ready for the holidays. Ivy and Lil had come up from the village and had polished and vacuumed and scrubbed. A fire had been laid in the sitting room and in the kitchen range. Everything looked enchanting.

We'd stopped in Baildon and had picked up groceries. Earlier in the week I'd taken Sarah to the toy department at Harrods to see Father Christmas. Her little face was a picture of wonder as he'd sat her on his lap and asked what she wanted for Christmas. Then we'd bought crackers, a large cotton-wool-covered snowman whose hat lifted off to reveal a selection of little gifts, and a varied and wonderful collection of Christmas tree ornaments. I wanted Christmas at Munkyns to be totally traditional. The kind John and I had planned to have at the rectory all those years ago.

On the road to Moreton we'd stopped at a nursery and bought a holly wreath for the front door. I'd wanted to buy a Christmas tree but Paul was adamant that we'd get one later.

At Munkyns we toured the old house and were delighted with everything we saw. Bruno had found a magnificent carved oak four-poster bed and that now dominated the main bedroom in the cross-wing. How he'd managed to get it up the winding stairs was beyond me but there it was. It was hung with rich gold and cream damask from Gainsborough silks. The same material framed the view across the estuary at the front window and had been made up as a single curtain hanging from a walnut pole across the small window at the rear of the cross-wing.

Paul sat on the edge of the bed and smiled at me. 'This is going to take some living up to!' He reached out to me. 'You should sleep with an Elizabethan pirate in this bed. Nothing as dull as your husband.'

I laughed. 'You're not dull in bed, and you damn well know it.'

Within a fortnight of the incident at the beach house, the question of my sleeping apart from Paul had been resolved for us. We'd flown out to Los Angeles for Mike's wedding. He'd met us at the airport and told us he'd cancelled our hotel reservations and what did we think we were doing not staying with him?

'But your bride . . .' I started to say.

'Hell, kid, Julie and I have been living together for a year. It's a bit late to get bashful!' Mike replied. He was living at Malibu in a large, sprawling house built right on the beach. To take advantage of its position overlooking the Pacific rollers, the living areas of the house had been reversed. The ground floor was given over to bedrooms and bathrooms. On the first floor was one huge open-plan room divided into different living areas by the arrangement of the furniture.

Across the width of the room was a verandah. French doors folded back so that the room almost seemed part of the beach and sea. Mexican oak louvred doors at the rear of this amazing room led to a kitchen. It was crammed with every gadget ever invented. I wandered around, gazing in awe at the collection of appliances and kitchen aids.

Mike winked at me. 'Welcome to California!'

In the grounds at the back of the house was garaging for four cars and a staff cottage. An English couple took care of Mike and Julie. 'Bobby used to be butler to a real live Duke, no less. It took me all of four months to convince him he could call me Mike and I didn't want to call him Jenkins,' Mike laughed. He put his arms around Paul and me. 'Come on. Let's relax and drink to our good fortune. Julie won't be long, she's at the beauty parlour. She can catch up when she gets here.'

He led us through to the living room. 'Ever had a Bellini? Californian peach juice and champagne. I juiced the peaches myself this morning. Want to try it?'

I nodded and Paul said, 'Can't wait!' I watched Mike make the drinks and was happy for him. He wore his success and obvious wealth so easily and with such joy. I wanted to say, 'I wish Doll could have seen this,' but stopped myself because I wanted nothing to cloud the moment or Mike's obvious delight at having us as his guests.

We were sipping our second Bellini when Julie returned. She was small and stunningly pretty, like an exquisite Dresden doll. Short, blonde curls framed a heart-shaped face. Her eyes were a most astonishing cornflower blue. I wasn't at all surprised that Mike had fallen for her. But there was something about the set of her jaw that made me secretly think that appearances could be deceptive and that this lady could well be something of an iron butterfly. But she was an absolutely charming hostess. Bobby and Eve Jenkins cooked and served a delicious meal and Julie seemed relaxed and happy with us. Ready to accept Mike's friends as her own. She was an actress and was going to play the lead in Mike's new series. Her first starring role. We raised our glasses and drank to her success.

After dinner we chatted and played records. Sinatra had had a great hit that year with 'My Way'. Mike played it a couple of times and I teased him that he should make it his theme song. Then he played 'Gentle On My Mind', another huge success that year. I sat back, sipping my brandy, and let the music wash over me. The pain and hurt I'd been feeling the last couple of weeks seemed to slip away in the company of my dearest, oldest friend.

Mike suddenly looked at his watch. 'Hey, kids! What am I thinking of? It's after midnight and you've had a long flight today. Come on, I'll show you to your room. Bobby took your cases in and Eve's unpacked for you.'

We kissed Julie goodnight and followed Mike downstairs. There was no way I could ask him to give us separate rooms and so I followed him into the main guest suite. It was a lovely room, cool and spacious. The floor was tiled with blue and white Delft tiles. The blue in the tiles was the only colour in the room; everything else was pure white. Screens were pulled across the window to keep out insects but the french doors were folded back and I could hear the breakers as they hit the beach.

Mike indicated the bed. It was about eight feet wide and a heavy Mexican white wool quilt was folded back on it. 'That unzips to form twin beds, but I told Eve you guys hadn't been married long enough to want to use the zipper so it's made up as a double.' He kissed me. 'God bless! It's wonderful having you both here. See you in the morning.'

We were alone. Paul's pyjamas and my nightdress had been laid out on the bed. We'd booked a suite at the Beverly Hills Hotel, with two bedrooms and adjoining drawing room. I hadn't expected to be with Paul and so it was only by chance that I'd packed such an exquisitely pretty nightdress. Made by Dior, the palest apple green chiffon had been finely pleated and fell softly from the waist band. The top was of Brussels lace dyed the same subtle apple green. It was totally sheer.

Neither of us spoke for a moment. Then Paul said,

'Can you bear to sleep with me, just for a couple of nights? I promise I won't touch you.'

'I don't really have much choice, do I?' I replied stiffly. 'Now's hardly the time to tell Mike that we're estranged.' I quickly picked up my nightdress and went into the bathroom. I showered and towelled myself dry. Then, feeling ridiculously self-conscious, I put on my nightdress and went back into the bedroom. The guest suite had two bathrooms and I could hear that Paul was still showering. I got into bed and picked up a magazine from the side table.

After a moment he came back from the bathroom. His hair was damp and tousled from the shower and he looked absurdly handsome. We were both so awkward with each other that I nearly laughed. He climbed into bed and turned off his light.

'Good night, Grace.'

'Good night, Paul.'

I read for a while and then turned out my light. I lay in the darkness struggling with my emotions. The damnedest thing was, I still loved Paul. I closed my eyes, but sleep wouldn't come. Tentatively, I reached out my hand and touched him. 'Paul, are you awake?'

'Yes.'

'I want you.'

'Oh, darling! My darling wife.' And then I was in his arms . . .

I bent over Paul as he sat on the four-poster bed at Munkyns and kissed him lightly.

'Later!' he laughed.

Sarah was dashing around the bedroom, excited by her new surroundings. She was at that stage where her desire to walk and run was ahead of her legs and feet. This meant that if she wanted to get from A to B, she'd make an almost drunken-gaited dash across the room. Sometimes she'd make it, sometimes there'd be a wail as she landed on her bottom. I caught her and picked her up.

'Come on, little love, let's go and see the barn.'

As I reached the bottom of the stairs, Paul said, 'Why don't you and Sarah go and put the kettle on? I'd love a cup of tea.'

'I'd like to see the barn first.'

He grinned. 'Was it Noel Coward who said that women should be beaten regularly, like a gong? Go and put the kettle on!'

I shrugged and replied, 'Master, your word is my command.'

Paul went ahead into the barn and I carried Sarah through to the kitchen. I'd had a utility room with a sink, dishwasher and washing machine made at the back under the old catslide roof, but basically the kitchen was as when I'd lived here previously. A gleaming new cooker had replaced the primitive one I'd bought in Baildon but the big kitchen table where I'd sat to do my accounts when the House of Laure was a little cottage industry was still there. So was the big old dresser and the pine cupboards. I put the kettle on and then we joined Paul in the barn.

The moment I entered the galleried reception room I understood why he had wanted to go to the barn first. A huge Christmas tree, at least eighteen feet high and alive with hundreds of fairy lights, stood there. Sarah and I stared at it in wonder. Then she clapped her hands with joy. 'Pretty! Pretty!'

'It sure is, baby!' I said. 'Oh, Paul, how wonderful! How did you . . .?'

Paul laughed. 'Kit gave me Alf's telephone number.

After that it was a lot of surreptitious calls when you were out of earshot!'

That afternoon we unpacked the decorations I'd bought in Harrods and hung them on the tree. I'd also bought tinselled gold and silver paper chains and garlands and we hung these from the beams.

Bruno had done a wonderful job. A new floor had had to be laid and he'd chosen oak parquet. Some brightly coloured Indian dhurries had been thrown down on the polished wood. Opposite the wood-burning stove was a massive red leather Edwardian sofa. Bruno had telephoned me when he'd found it in a now defunct gentlemen's club. The leather was a little worn but not cracked and Bruno wanted to feed it and not re-cover. I was prepared to be guided by him and now saw how right he was. Although the barn was newly converted and furnished, Bruno had created a comfortable, homely atmosphere as if a family had been living here for years.

The barn doors had been replaced with a tall window, a copy of the weaver's windows you see in medieval houses in East Anglia. They were installed to give light for the weavers to work by when the wool trade had flourished in that area. They were much too big to curtain sensibly and so Bruno had had antique pine shutters installed at two levels. I closed the lower shutters against the darkening sky and then we had tea in front of the stove. I found a toasting fork by the sitting-room fire and we made toast and then spread it with Gentlemen's Relish. Sarah had fallen asleep on the red leather sofa amidst a clutter of baubles and garlands.

I was in a home I loved with my husband and my daughter. I thought that, perhaps, I'd never been so happy in my life.

*   *   *

The night before Christmas Eve we drove back down to Munkyns. I'd asked Sarah's nanny if she would like to go home for Christmas, and was very relieved when she said that she thought she'd have much more fun with us as her parents were Welsh Baptists and Christmas was usually a very gloomy affair back home in the Brecon Hills.

Lil, Ivy, Peggy and Alf had been wonderful and had seen that the house was ready and that my order for Christmas fare from Collins' store was picked up in Baildon. Ivy was going to pop in on Boxing Day morning to give me a hand with the lunch, otherwise I was on my own. I just hoped I could shed my mantle of high-powered businesswoman and become a high-powered housewife for the holiday period!

Bruno was flying in from New York and Aaron and his latest girl friend were coming from San Francisco, where he'd been setting up the opening of our latest Body and Soul shop. We'd arranged to have them met at Heathrow and driven down to Moreton as I knew Paul and I would need every minute of Christmas Eve to get everything ready. Kit and Harry were joining us for Boxing Day lunch and then coming back again for New Year's Eve. I'd asked Mike and Julie to join us for the holidays but their schedule at the studio was too tight for them to get away.

To my astonishment and delight the holidays seemed to go without a hitch. Unless, of course, you count my total inability to light the Christmas pudding. I seemed to have poured gallons of cooking brandy on it but the damned thing just wouldn't light. Bruno took charge and added so much vodka to my brandy that I was worried that if he did light it his toupee would go up in the towering inferno that would follow. But with a whoosh the pudding caught and we just managed to get it from the kitchen into the candlelit dining hall before it went out again.

When I look back those days of Christmas seem unreal, a fairy-tale idyll. We ate too much, walked along the sea wall, played silly parlour games, watched Sarah's delight in her toys and just had good old-fashioned fun.

Aaron had made me so happy on Christmas night. He'd followed me into the kitchen and put his arms around me. He'd never been very tactile with me and I was very moved. He hugged me to him and said, 'Now I know what's Yiddish for Christmas – Munkyns!'

Then came New Year's Eve. After lunch everyone wanted to go for a walk. Paul insisted that he'd stay behind and clear the kitchen. I'd protested but he'd said, 'It's the least I can do for you. Go on, shoo!'

I went into the hall and was about to pull on a warm jacket and boots to join the others when I realised that I was really quite tired. I asked if they'd mind if I put my feet up for an hour or so instead. I knew Sarah would be fine with her nanny and that Aaron and Bruno would take it in turns to carry her when she got tired. They all went off noisily and happily, Sarah insisting that she take along her new doll's pram. How they'd cope with that on the sea wall I'd no idea but the little girl got her own way.

The house was so quiet after they'd gone. I could hear Paul moving about in the kitchen and started towards it to join him. But I was tired and an escape from the chores for a little while seemed incredibly attractive. Perhaps I felt a little guilty about not helping him, and that was why I didn't tell him I hadn't gone with the others.

I wandered through to the barn and stretched out on

the red leather sofa in front of the stove. I felt warm and sleepy, but, oh, so happy.

The telephone woke me from a deep sleep. For a moment I wasn't sure where I was or of the time of day. I must have picked up the extension in the barn at exactly the same moment that Paul answered the phone in the main house. It was a woman calling. I didn't recognise her voice which was low and husky. An attractive voice.

'Paul?'

'For God's sake, Helen, I've told you never to call me at home. How did you get this number?'

'Simple, darling, I phoned the London flat. The answerphone had this number on it. Don't scold, if anyone else had answered I'd have hung up. Are you alone?'

'By chance, yes. Everyone's gone for a walk. But you took a terrible risk,' Paul chuckled. 'Then, you like living dangerously.'

I wanted to hang up. I didn't want to hear any more. Couldn't bear the note of affection in Paul's voice. But I stood there, frozen, holding on to the receiver.

'I'm missing you so, darling.'

'And me you,' Paul replied. 'It's only for a few more days now.'

'Can't you get away before that? Think of a reason to come to town. Even if it's only for a few hours. I'll make it worthwhile.'

'I'm sure you will! I'll see what I can do. But you must ring off now. Grace doesn't suspect and I don't want to hurt her.'

'Quite, Paul darling! Nothing must come between you and your meal ticket. You're a bastard, you know that? I can't think why I'm so in love with you.' Then there was a click and I realised she'd hung up.

I heard Paul put down the telephone and then I replaced the receiver on the extension. The room was beautifully warm but I shivered. Everything had been a lie. I'd been so happy since that night at Mike's house, and all the time . . .

I sank back on to the leather sofa and buried my face in my hands. Somehow I'd got to find the strength to play out the farce this holiday had become. To smile and be the perfect hostess and not let our guests know that inside I was dying. I realised that now I must recognise Paul for what he was: a charming, weak playboy who'd never stay faithful to any one woman.

So be it. I had a business to run and a daughter to bring up and I wanted my daughter to have a father. The tragedy was I'd just discovered that I'd never really had a husband.

I don't think anyone guessed how wretched and unhappy I was feeling. It was as if I was two people. There was a Grace who laughed and smiled and gave her husband and guests dinner. And there was another Grace. She stood apart and watched the whole dreadful charade. She was beyond crying. Even beyond recrimination. It was as if her life's blood had been drained from her.

Just before midnight Paul handed around champagne, a beautiful Heidsieck Diamant Bleu that he had chosen with care to see in the new decade.

Kit must have caught something in my eyes as I watched Paul hand around the drinks. 'Are you all right, Young Laure? You look tired.' Before I could answer Paul joked, 'It must have been all that fresh air. They all went traipsing along the sea wall this afternoon.'

'Not *all*!' Bruno said. 'Old Lazy-Bones put her feet up at home instead!'

Paul turned quickly towards me. His eyes asked the

question: Did I know? I nodded and then, as the clock started to chime midnight, I raised my glass to my husband and smiled. 'Happy New Year, darling.'

From now on I would give my husband what he had presumably always wanted. A marriage of convenience. Then the final chime. It was 1970! As everyone started to hug and kiss and cheer I thought that, no, that wasn't what Paul had always wanted. He'd wanted never to be found out.

Two weeks later I sat on a flight to Los Angeles. Alone. Paul and I had planned to go together. We needed to meet with the West Coast management team. The strategy for the coming year had been planned the previous Fall, but I believed in keeping in constant touch with the people now employed by House of Laure world-wide. Also, although I wouldn't admit it to him, I wanted to check that Aaron had chosen wisely the site for the new Body and Soul shop in San Francisco.

In the past few years San Francisco had become the home of the Flower People. 'Peace, Love and Understanding' was their cry. Although I could hardly see them flocking from their communes to Body and Soul, their movement had intensified interest in natural products. To have a shop at the heart of that movement, which was aimed specifically at the new breed of caring young people, seemed to make good business sense. It should also appeal to the hundreds of thousands of tourists who flocked to San Francisco, drawn by its new ideology.

Paul and I had not quarrelled. I was past that. Quite simply, once our guests had gone I packed our things, closed up Munkyns and, on our return to the London apartment, moved all of Paul's belongings to a guest

370

room. 'All I ask is that, for Sarah's sake, you are discreet about your affairs,' I had said.

'And will you guarantee the same impeccable behaviour, Grace?' Before I could answer he continued: 'But of course! The only big love affair you've ever had, or are likely to have, is with the House of Laure, isn't it?'

'You know how untrue that is, Paul. Let's not try to hurt each other. If you want a divorce I'll give you one, but we have a daughter who we both love very much. We're also partners in a multi-million-dollar international company. I suppose you could resign from the Board and I'd try to raise the money to buy your shares . . .'

'And face the future as the ex-husband of the brilliant Grace Laure? With money in my pocket but no career. No role to play in life. No, thank you!'

'You could always find another businesswoman with a thriving company and make her fall for your charms,' I said bitterly.

'Another businesswoman? Come on, Grace, there are not many women as successful as you are now! You're the tops, darling! Anything else would be slumming.' And with that, he'd quietly left the room.

And so we began the long lie that was to become our marriage. Paul and I had been going to stay with Mike and Julie. I cabled to say that urgent business was taking him to Paris and that I would be coming alone.

As I queued to go through US Customs, I was amused at the stir my appearance was causing. Once again, the States were way behind European fashion. Just when it seemed that skirts could get no shorter, designers plunged to the other extreme. They invented the maxi.

I was wearing a maxi suit made for me by a new young British designer, Jean Muir. The linen suit had a long, black skirt which reached to just above my ankles. The jacket was white with a dropped, soft waist and a loose belt made of the same material. The buckle of the belt, and the piping on the collar and sleeves of the jacket, were black. My shoes had a high, chunky heel, a softly rounded toe and a buttoned strap. I was glad to say goodbye to the mini. Although it suited me, as skirts got shorter and shorter it was difficult to look elegant. I felt much more convincing as the founder and Managing Director of the House of Laure wearing a maxi than I ever did wearing a mini. Also, I liked the softly romantic look that the style created. But from the stares I received from mini-skirted fellow travellers, it was obvious that the new fashion had not yet invaded America.

When I entered the main lobby of the airport I looked around for Mike, as he'd said he'd meet me. Instead, I saw a uniformed chauffeur holding up a card on which was my name.

'I'm Grace Laure.'

'Good afternoon, ma'am. Mr Janowski is sorry but he's been held up in a script conference. He arranged for me to meet you.'

'Thank you.'

The porter wheeled my luggage to the waiting car. Mike certainly didn't do things by halves, I thought, as I approached the sleek, black, stretch limo. This was endorsed when I got in. Awaiting me on the rear seat was a basket of roses, a note with them.

'*Sorry, kid! Hope you had a good flight. See you at the beach house later. P.S. Julie is away unexpectedly. Can you bear the company of an old grass widower? Bobby and Eve will chaperon!*'

The big, luxurious car turned north-west on to Lincoln Boulevard, past Marina del Ray with its thousands of yachts anchored on the blue waters then on to Route 1 for the forty-kilometre drive to Malibu.

Bobby and Eve Jenkins fussed over me when I arrived at the beach house. 'I expect you'd like a shower and a bit of a lie down, wouldn't you? You go and make yourself comfortable and I'll bring you a nice pot of tea,' Eve said, clucking around me like a mother hen. 'You're in the same guest suite as before.'

She led me into the suite where Paul and I had stayed. I fought to block out the memories of the passionate, love-filled nights we'd spent here.

'I'll unpack later. I'll only be a tick with the tea.'

Then I was alone. I was only going to be away for a week and it had seemed so unfair to subject Sarah to the long flights that would be involved, but I was desperately missing her. I'd phone her first thing in the morning.

I walked towards the bathroom to shower but the sound of the breakers was so inviting that I pulled on a bikini and walked towards the ocean instead.

The waters off the coast of California are rarely warm but the salt water refreshed and invigorated me as I dived through the breakers. As I swam I tried to cleanse my soul of the bitterness I felt towards Paul. I was young, not yet thirty. I was successful. I had a baby that I adored. Surely I could in some way build a life for myself without love?

Without love . . . what kind of future was I condemning myself to? A wave caught me off balance and I went under. I came up gasping for air. Without love. I dived through the next breaker and started to swim strongly out to sea. I trod water for a moment and looked back to the shore.

The sun was beginning to set and shadows crept across the beach. Lights were coming on in some of the houses.

It looked incredibly beautiful. Life was there to be lived. To be grasped. I'd achieved so much. If I had to make a new life for myself, I'd damn well do it! I'd lost my first love and been betrayed by my second. But I hadn't fought my way out of the Lower East Side only to have my life wrecked by a man, however much I'd loved him. Yes, I could go on. I struck out for the shore.

It was nearly nine when Mike got back from the studio. I'd showered, rested for a couple of hours, then dressed casually for the evening. I'd bought a pink, cotton jersey house dress when I was last in Rome. It seemed perfect for Malibu. Striking because of the vibrancy of the colour but casual and comfortable. With it I wore Ferragamo gold sandals. I was off duty and so I let my hair hang loose. I felt refreshed and renewed, both by my swim in the azure waters of the Pacific and my resolve to rebuild my life.

I was curled up in a large, comfortable armchair, sipping one of Bobby's impeccably dry martinis, when I heard Mike's car. Within moments he was entering the room with characteristic panache and vigour. He stood in the doorway briefly, smiling at me. Even at twenty feet one could feel the magnetism of the man. Mike wore success gracefully and with pleasure.

'Kid, you look a million dollars,' he said, opening his arms to me. He held me in a bear-like hug and I suddenly felt, 'Oh, God, this is where I belong.'

It was too late. Much too late. Mike had Julie and nothing must mar that happiness but being in his arms was like coming home for me. How could I ever have let Paul's smooth, up-market charm blind me to the worth of this man? Yet I knew it had been more than that. When I'd stayed with Mike at the Château Marmont and we had become lovers, I wasn't ready for a new relationship — partly because I was still grieving for John but mainly because of my ambition. Well I'd paid a high price for that.

'Come on, relax and have a martini before dinner. You look tired.'

Mike lightly put a finger across my lips. 'Shh! We're never tired in Tinseltown! You need talent but, by heck, do you need stamina!'

I took the jug of martinis from the ice box behind the bar in the living room and poured Mike a glass.

'After six hours arguing with the bastards at the Network, the temptation is to think, "What the hell? It's only show business!" and then give in. That's what the vultures are waiting for! Power, that's the name of the game. But I guess that's a lesson you've already learnt, kid.'

I smiled. 'Learnt and grown to like.'

He laughed. 'That's my girl! They always said I was the best street-fighter on the block, but secretly I knew that I could take lessons from you.' He finished his martini. 'Let's eat. I'm starving, and I know Bobby and Eve have cooked something really special for you. They really like you.' He slipped his arm around my waist. 'And so do I!'

Bobby and Eve certainly had made something special for our evening meal: mouth-wateringly light pastry cases filled with fresh, lightly cooked spinach and Stilton cheese, followed by a lobster and caviar salad. The cold lobster was served in a sauce of fromage blanc blended with mustard, lemon and fresh tarragon. The lobster was on a bed of red radiccio and garnished with asparagus, french beans and caviar. With the meal we drank a beautiful estate-bottled Californian chardonnay. To finish Eve had made an almond jelly served with small slices of fresh peaches. During the meal, or to be more accurate feast, I asked Mike how Julie was.

'Oh, great. Just great. She's in New York just now. She's been offered a part in the next Mike Nichols movie. She and her agent are in the Big Apple talking to him about it.'

'That's fantastic! But if she does the movie, will she still be able to star in your series?'

'No way! The movie's a six-month shoot and we're committed to twenty-six episodes a year. She's lucky. Her agent had been stalling on her new contract.' He shrugged. 'Now I know why.'

'You mean Julie didn't tell you she was up for the movie?'

'No, but I can understand that. If she didn't get the movie, there was still the television series. If she did, well . . . As an executive I should have insisted that she sign her contract weeks ago. As a husband I let it ride . . . now I'm paying the price.'

My assessment of Julie as an iron butterfly hadn't been far off the mark, it seemed. But I wished I hadn't been right.

'Mike,' I said gently, 'you gave her her big break. Surely she wouldn't walk out on it like that?'

'Kid, an actress would walk on her grandmother's face to get a lead in a movie. I accept that. I understand it. I loved Julie when I married her, but I didn't kid myself about her ambition.'

I noted that Mike used the past tense of love, but didn't want to pry further. How ironic. Here we were, each with our private grief, each putting on a front. I was tempted to reach out, take his hand and say, 'To hell with Paul and Julie, we've got each other.' But I held back. Partly because I assumed that Mike loved me now as a kid sister and not as he had when we were younger. Partly because I felt that our unhappiness was still too raw.

Later we walked bare-footed along the beach. The moon was low over the sea, its light catching the white of the surf as the breakers rolled in. We talked and laughed and teased. But, inside, I sensed that we were both empty.

I spent two more days at Mike's beach house. I'd planned to hire a car but he insisted on placing his driver and limo at my disposal. We had three outlets in LA that I wanted to check out. There was the salon on Rodeo Drive, a large counter in one of the most prestigious stores on Wilshire Boulevard, and our comparatively new Body and Soul shop on Sunset.

For the Body and Soul shop we'd taken over the premises of a famous Hollywood drug store. Once fashionable with young and up-and-coming stars, it had declined with the studio system. But the interior had been practically untouched since its hey-day in the thirties and forties and we'd simply restored it to its former glory. Where, so the legend went, Lana Turner had been discovered sipping a chocolate malt milk shake, Los Angeles' young now gathered to try our natural products before buying or sit and gossip while sipping herbal teas.

Our menus at the tea bar, and the information pack with each skin-care product, cross-referenced. Someone suffering from acne could try our lotion made from lavender, catnip and chamomile and then drink an infusion of basil, made from fresh leaves, to purify their blood. Someone with a dry skin could experiment with a range of creams and moisturisers mainly rich in essential oils, then have a cup of rose hip tea which is incredibly rich in vitamin C. We sold fresh salads which incorporated a wide range of culinary herbs, and a limited range of health food snacks from carrot and orange cake to caraway seed and dill biscuits. Plus a range of freshly pressed fruit juices and natural yoghurt shakes. The chain of shops had been a great success and I was very proud of it. Not simply because it swelled the coffers of the House of Laure but because it was a totally new concept, which a few years ago would have been denigrated as of interest only to cranks.

I'd given no prior warning of my visit to LA, not to snoop but so as to reassure myself that the staff I believed in could be trusted. There was more to the House of Laure than selling cosmetics. We had completely banished the idea of a beauty salon or counter being forbidding. The heavily made-up harridans of the cosmetic hall had no place in our concept. Our assistants need not be young but they must be sympathetic, helpful, knowledgeable. Not only be able to recommend a product, but also explain why the chemical and mineral component of every herb used contributed to its healing or soothing properties. And I loved to see how our assistants, with their casual but pretty cotton sprigged blouses and skirts, stood out against the pseudo-medical overalls worn by most cosmetics-counter assistants.

My last call on my second day was to the Body and Soul shop on Sunset. Aaron was managing that side of the House of Laure and I had no reason to doubt his flair. I'd simply wanted to call in on the premises while in LA.

As I entered the shop I was immediately enchanted by its Art Deco interior. Bakelite panels on which were mounted fan-shaped mirrors lined the wall behind the old soda fountain. The old marble-topped counters now carried our range of skin-care products. Apart from the high stools at the soda fountain counter, there was an area furnished with wicker tables and cream Lloyd Loom chairs. I was pleased to note that business was brisk.

I looked at the display of cosmetics for a while and was perfectly satisfied by the presentation. Then I crossed to the soda fountain counter. I was surprised and annoyed to see that one of the assistants had flowing, shoulder-length hair. It was a strict rule that anyone handling food or beverages should either wear their hair short or dressed above their collar.

'Excuse me, miss.'

A curt 'Yes?' greeted me.

'Which particular tea would you recommend for a dry skin?'

The assistant sighed. 'How the hell should I know? Can't you read?' She thumped the menu down in front of me.

'Perhaps I could see the manager.'

'What for?'

'Just fetch me the manager!' I could feel my temper rising but resolved to remain cool. Icy cool.

The girl shrugged indifferently then walked across to a door marked 'Private'. She opened it without knocking and yelled, 'Woman out here wants to see yer!'

After a moment a neatly dressed, hard-faced woman emerged. The assistant indicated me.

'Yes?'

'Are you the manager?'

'Yes, is there a problem? I'm very busy and I really can't . . .'

'Spend any time with your customers?' I interrupted.

The woman flushed. 'Spend any time with people who wish to make a nuisance of themselves. Now, what is it?'

'There's a notice over there. "Please ask for any assistance. Our trained staff will be only too willing to help.'' I asked for assistance. The reply was, ''How the hell should I know?'' You are therefore now looking at a very dissatisfied customer.'

'Look, lady, it's all written down. It's a matter of time. If everybody wanted to jabber about the products . . .'

' ''Expert advice and quality products, displayed in a relaxed and friendly atmosphere'' is the ethos behind this chain of shops.'

'Oh, yes? How the hell do you know?'

'Because they're *my* shops . . . I'm Grace Laure.'

The woman paled beneath her California tan. 'But . . . but . . . Mr Mandel . . .'

'Mr Mandel is answerable to me and to the House of Laure's Board of Directors . . . perhaps we could have a word in your office?'

The manageress led the way into her spacious office. She lit a cigarette and then paced up and down for a moment. I sat and waited.

'You see, I thought Mr Mandel had total control over Body and Soul. You can't buck the boss. Not if you want to keep your job.'

'First, let's get to the root of what's going on here. That girl should have been trained to answer my questions. She should have . . .'

'Yes, I know,' the manageress interrupted. 'But we've suspended the training programme.'

'You've done what?'

'We were doing so well, you see. Mr Mandel thought it a waste of money to have a girl on four weeks' pay just learning about herbs and stuff. I mean, business is just as good as when the assistants were trained!'

'For the moment. If I'd been a genuine customer and that girl had spoken to me as she did, I'd never have set foot in this place again.'

'Are you going to fire me?'

'What do you think?' I replied coldly. 'It's not just the matter of the way the business . . . *my* business . . . is run. There's also a criminal offence involved.'

'Criminal? I don't know what you mean?'

'Really? And you seem to be quite a sharp kind of woman! How much money have you and Mr Mandel been pocketing?'

The woman tried to face me out for a moment, then looked away. 'How did you know?'

'The profits for this branch have been pretty well consistent. The training programme costs the company approximately twenty-four hundred dollars a week . . . and you haven't been running the training programme. Need I say more?'

'Are you going to the cops?'

'No. I don't want the publicity. I'll pay you and that wretched girl out there three months' salary in lieu of notice, but I want you out of here within the hour.'

'Mr Mandel . . .'

'*I'll* deal with Mr Mandel!'

I went back into the shop, and as each assistant became free talked with them. Of the eight assistants on duty only two had done the training course. But apart from the girl I'd just fired, the other five seemed pleasant, bright young women. The problem was how to keep the shop running and get those five trained.

The first priority was to find out how many other Body and Soul shops had had their training programmes suspended. This would take at least twenty-four hours because of the time gaps between not only the West and East coasts but also the branches in Europe. I decided that I must take my personal assistant into my confidence. Amanda Douglas had started as my secretary and was now my right-hand man — although I applauded so much about the feminist movement, I found it totally ridiculous that I should be forced to describe her as a right-hand person!

I looked at my watch. 4 pm. Midnight in London. Amanda was an ambitious young businesswoman and I knew that she wouldn't resent a call from me, whatever the hour. I went into the office, mercifully the manageress had left, and put in a call to London.

A few moments later Amanda was on the line. 'Grace, how are you? What's wrong?'

I smiled. Amanda knew me well enough to know that I wouldn't have called her at midnight if it wasn't important.

'It's Aaron . . .'

I heard the sigh at the other end of the phone. Amanda wasn't surprised.

'The Body and Soul shop on Sunset . . .' I quickly explained all I'd discovered. 'But it's important that this should be kept between you and me, Amanda. No one else must know. Not the Board. Not Paul. Especially not Paul!

'I'll deal with my brother but I have to know the extent of the damage. Can you check directly with all Body and Soul shops as to whether or not their training scheme has been suspended? Positive ''No's'' I think, for the time being, we can count on. Any prevarication we'll have to investigate.'

'I'll get right on to it.'

'We also need a new manager here. I'll hold the fort for twenty-four hours but then I've got to get to the factory in Monterey. Check New York, Chicago, Dallas and Toronto to see if there's an assistant manager ready for promotion who is prepared to move to LA. Sorry, Amanda, it's a lot of extra work.'

'You know I thrive on it,' she said briskly.

After I'd hung up I sat for a moment trying to suppress the pain and anger I felt. The only possible course, it seemed to me, was to run the shop myself until I heard back from Amanda. Once we had a new manageress we'd take on extra staff temporarily to allow time for the untrained assistants to go on the course at the Monterey factory.

I telephoned Mike's secretary and left a message saying that I'd be at the Body and Soul shop on Sunset until closing time, 10 pm. Would she also ring Bobby and Eve and let them know I wouldn't be back at the beach house for dinner?

It was strange to be working in a shop again, but I found that I enjoyed it. About half an hour before we closed I was behind the counter juicing fruit when Mike walked in. He came straight over to the old soda fountain. 'Banana split, light on the cream, heavy on the chocolate chip topping, please, honey!'

I laughed. 'No way! How about a yoghurt and blackcurrant shake? Rich in vitamin C.'

'Uggh! What the hell are you doing here, Beccy?'

'Staff crisis. I'm hoping my assistant is sorting out the US Cavalry to ride to the rescue. In the meantime, I'm a shop assistant again!'

'What time do you close?'

'Another half an hour?'

'How about I take you out on the town after that?'

'Are you kidding? The store opens again at 8 am and I want to be on hand when the assistant manageress comes on duty! What do you say we stop at a deli and take home some cold cuts and pickles?'

Mike laughed. 'Okay by me. I gave Bobby and Eve the night off. Just never let them know we sunk so low as a deli!'

An hour and a half later we were having a picnic on
the floor of Mike's living room. He'd lit a driftwood fire
and the big windows were open to the sounds of the sea
and the night. We sat on cushions in front of the fire.
Mike had found a checked kitchen tablecloth and had
spread that out between us. On it was a selection of salt
beef, salami, smoked turkey, garlic sausage, coleslaw,
gherkins with dill, pickled red cabbage, beetroot with
horseradish and a really black loaf of rye bread.

'Boy, I'm enjoying this,' Mike said, slapping pickles
on an open salami on rye sandwich.

'Me too. I'd forgotten how great good deli food can
be.'

'I'd forgotten how great being with you can be, Beccy.'

'Oh, Mike, Mike! Say you love me. I need you. I want
you. I can't think about Julie. About disloyalty. I only
know I want you,' I thought.

Mike raised his glass to me. 'You're my best pal!'

I glanced down at my glass so that my eyes didn't give
me away. Then I looked up at him and smiled. I too
raised my glass. 'To friendship!'

At 3 am a call came through from Amanda. I'd only
been in bed for a couple of hours and was deeply asleep.
Mike tapped on the bedroom door.

'A call from London.'

'Oh, Mike, I'm sorry it woke you.'

'No problem.'

I picked up the extension by the bed.

'Grace? It's Amanda. Sorry to ring at this hour but
I thought you'd want to hear from me as soon as
possible.'

Mike mouthed, 'Is everything all right?' and I nodded.
He blew me a kiss and left me to my call.

'I'm pretty sure that all the branches of Body and Soul,

except the LA one, are running the training scheme. The assistant manageress in New York comes highly recommended and is ready for promotion. She also wants to go to California. She could be the answer to our problem. Shall I tell her to fly out?

'Apparently she's no ties, so long as she can get back to New York to sort out her apartment at some time in the near future, she can drop everything and be with you about 6 pm LA time.'

'Fine! Tell her to get on a plane and the company will cover all additional expenses. Thanks, Amanda. I'll stay in LA until tomorrow. I'll have to postpone the visit to the Monterey factory, and then I'm flying up to San Francisco to see Aaron. I don't somehow think he's going to be pleased to see me,' I added grimly.

A day later I was on a flight to San Francisco. The past twenty-four hours had been hectic. After Amanda's call I'd slept badly, my mind too active to allow me to relax. At breakfast Mike had asked me about the staff problems but I'd glossed over things and I think he accepted that I didn't want to talk about them.

To my intense relief the assistant manageress at the shop on Sunset seemed honest and capable and I truly believed that, although she knew the training programme had been suspended, she had not been part of the fraud involving Aaron and the manageress.

Mike's driver picked up the young woman from New York at the airport and drove her straight to Sunset. Ruth Del Rosso was a typical New Yorker. Very up front in her manner but with a great smile and a natural courtesy and warmth. We spent an hour in the office with the assistant manageress and I was sure I could safely leave the running of the LA branch to them. I'd booked Ruth into the Château Marmont as it was just across the street from the shop and assured her that the House of Laure would pick up the tab until she found her feet in LA.

Mike himself had driven me to the airport. When we said goodbye he hugged me to him, then held my shoulders as he looked down into my face. 'I know something's wrong, kid, and I know you don't want to talk about it. But if you need help, any time, any place, give me a call, eh?'

I longed to throw myself into his arms. To sob out my heartbreak, tell him about Paul and Aaron, be comforted. But I was no longer Beccy Mandel. I was Grace Laure, a successful, wealthy businesswoman. I had to live my own life. Fight my own battles. So I reached up and kissed him gently on the cheek.

'Thanks. When I need help, you'll be the first to know.'

'The last, you mean!' Mike said wryly.

'They called my flight again. I must go. Goodbye, Mike dear.'

I turned and walked briskly away. I didn't look back, but I knew that he stayed watching me until the very last moment.

At San Francisco airport I got a cab to take me to Aaron's hotel. I'd phoned ahead and made a reservation. The new Body and Soul was located downtown just off Union Square. It was in a fashionable shopping area with a number of big stores such as Macy's, Saks Fifth Avenue and Neiman-Marcus, and in the bustling streets around the square a good range of boutiques. Body and Soul was due to open in ten days' time and, during the run up to opening, Aaron was staying at the Four Seasons Clift on Geary Street. I could always rely on my brother, I thought cynically, to stay at the best, most exclusive hotel.

Especially when the company was paying.

I telephoned the new shop and after a moment Aaron came on the line. 'Grace! Where are you phoning from?'

'The Four Seasons.'

There was a slight pause and then, 'You mean you're *here*? Here in San Francisco?'

'Yes. Aren't you pleased?'

'Of course I am! I'm just surprised. I'd no idea you were in the States.'

'Look, Aaron, can we have a working lunch in my suite at the hotel? I need to talk to you. It's important!'

'Sure. I'll see you about one. Everything's going great with the shopfitting. Thought you'd like to know.'

'And the assistants? They're already on the training course?'

'Sure! See you later.'

I showered and changed then spent the rest of the morning making business calls. We were about to launch a new range of skin-care products using Jojoba oil. The research team at Monterey were very excited about the oil's properties and I'd very much wanted to see them and congratulate them personally. Damn Aaron and his stupid greed!

Just before one I phoned down to room service and got them to send up a selection of sandwiches and a large pot of coffee.

Precisely at one there was a brief tap on the door of the suite and Aaron entered. He didn't kiss me, just sat uninvited in a deep armchair opposite me.

I thought how handsome he looked. My love for him had been more like a mother's love for her son than a sister's. Ever since he'd stolen my few dollars' savings to shoot pool I'd known that he was a thief, but I'd let my love for him blind me to his true character.

'I phoned the Body and Soul shop on Sunset, Grace. There's a new manageress.'

'Are you surprised? You and the old manageress have robbed the company of several thousand dollars.'

Aaron sighed. 'Oh, Grace! You're rich. What the hell's a few thousand dollars to you?'

'It's not the amount of the money, it's the principle! I'm not going to ask why. There'll be no recriminations. You're a taker, Aaron, and you always have been. God help me, I love you. But I'll never trust you again.'

'Look Grace . . . Sis . . . I promise I'll never . . .'

'You don't need to promise. I'll see that you never have the opportunity to do it again. You have your shares, they pay handsome dividends. You're a wealthy young man. You can go where you like. Do what you like. But I'm promoting Amanda Douglas to run the Body and Soul shops.'

'You can't do that!'

'I can! Simply tell the Board that you want to explore your own business opportunities. No one need ever know the truth. I don't want the scandal, and I don't want your life ruined by prosecution. But I don't want you running any part of my company.'

'You're a tough bitch, aren't you, Grace?'

'Someone has had to be the man in our family. Unfortunately, that task fell to me. If I'm tough it's because life has forged me in that way. I hope I'm not a bitch, but if that's what you think of me, so be it. I'll never stop loving you and I'll never stop caring about you.'

'Always the big sister, eh?' Aaron sneered. 'Well, Grace, the House of Laure is all yours.' He rose and went to the door. 'I hope it brings you happiness.'

He closed the door quietly behind him and I was alone.

I felt drained and bitter. No, the House of Laure wouldn't bring me happiness in the lonely years to come. But it would fill my days and then, gradually, it would become my life.

THE HERB

RUE

'There's rue for you and here's some for me.
We may call it the herb of grace'
From an early ceremony preceding High Mass

THE WOMAN

PART FIVE: RUE

GRACE 1990

'Laurel is green for a season,
And love is sweet for a day;
But love grows bitter with treason,
And laurel outlives not May.'
Algernon Charles Swinburne

CHAPTER TWENTY-NINE

The dream was with me. I was not in my Paris apartment. I was still in that terrible, squalid place on the Lower East Side. I could feel it, touch it, smell it. I forced myself to accept the reality of the present. There were no rats, no 'roaches. No smell of unwashed bodies, sweating in the heat of a New York summer night. I could smell, very faintly, *Affaire du Coeur*, my favourite perfume and my latest success.

I'd supervised the blending myself. It was to be a perfume for a sensuous, sophisticated woman. A woman who liked to be loved but not to be owned. A woman of today. A glamorous, international woman who could hold her own in a man's world. In short, I had blended it for myself, and then I sold it to millions of women who wished they were me.

Affaire du Coeur. The kind of perfume that men buy for their mistresses, and wives buy for themselves. Wives buy it and hope that it will miraculously rekindle some spark that died after the children were born and they looked across the breakfast table and realised they'd seen the same face for too many years. I suppose those wives envied me my style, my success, my grooming. But then, they did not know about my dream. They didn't know the sacrifices I had made to that bitch goddess, Success.

I went to the windows and pulled back the drapes. The city was beginning to waken, and the pink light creeping into the sky foretold a beautiful day. It was September, but mild. I decided to wear my new red linen Yves Saint Laurent suit. If I was going to end the day defeated, I would do it in style.

I love Yves' clothes. They are chic but with a sense of drama that appeals to me. I crossed to my dressing room. The touch of a switch and the mirrored glass doors of my closet slid silently open. Row after row of couturier clothes were revealed. I laughed out loud and clapped my hands in pleasure, like a girl again. It was something I had never lost, my almost sensuous delight in having beautiful clothes, hand-made soft leather shoes and handbags, silk underwear.

When you have been poor, really poor, and you acquire great wealth, you either become austere about possessions or you embrace the life of the rich wholeheartedly and enthusiastically. There is no in between, no compromise.

I glanced at my watch. 6.30 am. Time for a leisurely bath before my housekeeper, Jeanne-Marie, arrived. I had no live-in servants, liking the freedom to make a spur of the moment decision to cook myself a simple meal or go out to dine, without facing the reproachful look of a butler who has been told that Madame will be dining at home that evening.

Paul and I rarely slept under the same roof. We were still married, but our marriage was a sham. But I had loved him. Why? I suppose because of his New England background I'd fooled myself that he was like John. I had also been completely his sexually. I thought back to the first time we had made love. He'd been so utterly in control of my body it was almost a seduction. Yes, I'd loved him. Loved him passionately.

And, as I thought that, I remembered vividly my saying to Kit D'Arcy: 'For me, even if it finally led to unhappiness, bitterness, I'd have to feel passion for the man I married.' How sad! How infinitely sad that those words had been so prophetic.

I was in the bathroom by now. As I stepped into the bath I caught sight of myself in the mirror. I was still slender, my body firm. I ran my hands over it and longed to be made love to again. Not the brief satisfaction of desire, but the loving union of two bodies. Passionate but with a selfless understanding of each other's needs. Where there is joy in giving as well as taking. It was a long time since anyone had loved me like that.

The House of Laure had taken everything. I'd lost Paul and I'd thrown away Mike Janowski's love. We were still close, but only as friends. He must have guessed the situation between Paul and me, but he never pried.

I'd had dinner with him three weeks ago on a business trip to New York. He'd flown in from LA for a meeting at CBS and I was there to launch *Affaire du Coeur*. We had both been tied up with meetings until mid-evening and so we met at Sardi's. As I entered I saw Mike standing by a table, bending down to talk to an extremely pretty young star and her manager. I felt a pang of jealousy, then chided myself. I had no rights where he was concerned. And however well groomed I was, however much I took care of my looks, I would be a fool to think that at forty-seven I could compete with a beautiful twenty-year-old.

Mike's marriage to Julie had been over for years. She was now an Oscar winner, a survivor, and although I couldn't forgive her for the pain she had caused Mike, I had to admit that she had matured into a superb actress. He'd never remarried but his photograph was often in magazines and newspapers, squiring beautiful young women to premieres, to parties, to film festivals.

Often I'd find myself longing to be in Mike's arms

again and curse myself for being such a fool as to put my career before my heart when I'd torn myself from him.

I stood for a moment at the entrance of the restaurant, feeling middle-aged, foolish and very vulnerable. All my sophistication seemed to slip away and I was as a young girl in love. I wanted Mike but knew it was too late. I took a deep breath and forced myself back into the role of Grace Laure.

Heads turned as I walked between the tables. I was famous. I was one of the Beautiful People. I was empty. Then Mike looked up and his smile of recognition warmed me. I wasn't only with the man I secretly still loved, I was with family. He hugged me to him, then looked at me closely. 'Hey, kid, you've got to start looking older or I'll suspect you've got a portrait in the attic, like that Dorian Gray guy.'

'Now let's not be cynical,' I laughed. 'Could it be that, just possibly, somehow in this age of falsehood and hype, my products actually work?'

Mike smiled at me. 'I've got a suggestion, kid. Sack your advertising team and put yourself on the posters. You'll double your sales.'

'Strange as it may seem, that would be a disaster. We can hardly keep up with demand as it is. Lack of preservatives are the key to our success and the stumbling block to further expansion. Sorry! Sorry! I am not – repeat, definitely *not* – going to talk business tonight. Let's just have damned, old-fashioned fun.'

It was a wonderful evening. We were so easy with each other. In Mike's company hard times simply became reminiscences. Past pain was soothed by his understanding and care. I was being offered, indeed had, his friendship. With a sad sense of what might have been,

I'd settle for that and try to put from my mind all those beautiful young women who clung to his arm and smiled into the lens of the newsman's camera.

Until a year ago I could seek consolation in the fact that I had Sarah. Then she seemed to change. I don't know why. Surely I'd shown her how much I loved her? I'd tried to keep her from the rich young crowd she ran around with. And perhaps rightly, she'd resented that.

But I was frightened for those young people. They treated the world as if it only existed as a playground for them. And I knew, because I'd seen the police reports, that drugs were readily available at the endless rounds of parties they filled their lives with. I had grown tired of buying off unsuitable young men who had slept with my daughter and then threatened to sell their salacious story to the tabloids. I had grown tired of getting phone calls at three or four in the morning from my attorney, telling me that the high-ranking police officer, who did very well from us financially, had tipped him off, yet again, that Sarah was at a party or a club under observation and did we want to get her out before the police raided? I'd warned her it must stop. That the next time I'd let her be arrested.

'Oh, for God's sake, Mother,' she had drawled. In spite of the fact that she'd been partying all night and well into the morning, my only daughter looked achingly beautiful. I couldn't let those looks, that shining promise, be destroyed. 'Don't be so damned heavy all the time!'

'You could go to prison, you silly little fool!'

'Oh, I don't think so,' she'd replied coolly. 'Not for possession. It's not as if I'm selling the stuff.'

I'd tried to reason with her. 'Look Sarah, you're not stupid. How many of your friends have you seen destroyed by drugs? Killed by drugs! I'm so desperately afraid for you.'

'Well, don't be. I can take care of myself.'

'Sarah, you're still so young . . .'

'When you were even younger than me you were sleeping with a man as old as Daddy. He told me. So I don't think you're in a position to preach! And don't start all that corny old rubbish about stopping my allowance because Daddy will give me anything I want. *He* loves me!'

'Loving doesn't mean giving someone everything they want, Sarah,' I'd said quietly. 'Loving means caring about someone's welfare. A family should . . .'

'A family!' she interrupted shrilly. 'You haven't cared about being a family for years. You drove Daddy away by your obsession with your bloody business.'

'Without my bloody business you'd have none of the creature comforts you regard so dearly. But there's a price to be paid for everything . . .'

'A price! Oh, really, Mother. Sometimes you sound so damned Jewish!'

I'd never in my life hit Sarah. But before I could stop myself, I reached out and slapped her face. I immediately apologised. Reached out my arms to hold her, to beg her forgiveness. She pulled away from me and ran from the room. A week had gone by and I'd neither heard from nor seen her. I'd written to her saying how sorry I was and asked her to meet me so that we could start to build some kind of bridge between us. But I'd had no reply. By losing my temper with Sarah, I'd played right into Paul's hands.

About a year previously I'd had a call from a representative of a huge Swiss pharmaceutical firm. He was flying to Paris, would I dine with him? He had a business proposition he wanted to discuss with me. I agreed to meet him. I couldn't see why I should not listen to what he had to say. I thought of the House of Laure so much as my company, that it simply didn't occur to me that his firm was planning a take-over.

We dined at the Ritz-Espadon at the Place Vendôme. It was a warm, balmy evening and I was glad that Monsieur Montaigne had booked a table outside. I had come to love Paris.

We had a beautiful meal and the evening passed pleasantly. While we were drinking our coffee I said, 'Isn't it time we discussed your company's proposition?'

'Of course, Madame.' He reached down to a briefcase that he'd brought to our table with him. He took out a large bound folder. 'Your company, past and present.' He indicated the folder. 'With predictions for future growth.'

'Apart from opening salons, my company has grown as much as it can. With our "sell by" date and the low use of preservatives, if we expanded any more we'd have a serious problem with distribution. Of course, we are branching out into the perfume market. But on the cosmetics side I feel we've gone about as far as we can go. Even so, it's an enormously successful business, you know.'

'I know! And that is exactly why my company wishes to propose a take-over. It will be an immensely profitable offer for all the shareholders.'

'But I've just told you . . . the business cannot expand further without increasing the amount of preservatives in our beauty products.'

'My company sees no harm in that.'

'No harm? We've built our reputation on natural ingredients that have a chance to work because of the low level of preservatives.'

'*Your* reputation would be intact. My company would use the Grace Laure name to market a wider range of skin-care products and cosmetics, with increased preservatives, which would be aimed at a . . . shall we say . . . less élitist consumer.'

'No! Definitely not! If you formalise your offer I shall, as chairman, have to discuss it with my board of Directors and the shareholders. But I'm convinced that the offer will be rejected.'

'Because of Mr Crabtree's ten per cent which will give you a majority.'

'My word, Monsieur Montaigne,' I said dryly. 'You have done your homework well.'

'Of course. Otherwise my company would not employ me.'

At eighty-four, Archie was too old and frail to come to a shareholders' meeting. But his mind was as alert as ever. I telephoned and told him of the offer, without indicating how I felt about it.

'My dear, I can't believe that you've spent your life creating a cosmetics empire you can be proud of, simply to let the product be ruined.'

'We're talking about a lot of money, Archie.'

'Good God, girl, I've more than enough money. I'm thinking about your heart being broken. I'll arrange everything through my solicitor. You have my votes.'

Because we were still a private company, the shareholders' meeting seemed dwarfed by the splendour of the boardroom. Paul, Aaron, Sarah and I sat at one end of the long mahogany table. As we discussed the take-over bid I thanked God for Archie's ten per cent holding and his proxy vote in my favour. Paul held twenty-five per cent of the stock, Sarah and Aaron ten per cent each. Without Archie's voting power I would have been outnumbered.

Sarah was totally indifferent to the bid and clearly longed to leave the dusty rooms of commerce and return to the playgrounds of the rich. It came as no surprise to me that Paul and Aaron seemed to feel no loyalty, no sense of responsibility, to the House of Laure and its employees.

At forty-four Aaron's playboy lifestyle was beginning to show. A certain puffiness around the eyes. A blurring of the jaw line. And, although I never saw him drunk, there was an edginess about him if a meeting kept him too long away from the drinks cabinet or, I suspected, something more potent and more dangerous.

As for Paul, there was no longer any pretence that he was involved in the running of the company. That was left to me.

The take-over would give them access to a very large sum of money that was in no way linked with the success or failure of the House of Laure. In other words, they would no longer be hostage to my success or failure in the business world. But, so far, my success had provided them with an enviable income and lifestyle.

As Archie and I were against the take-over and held the majority shares, there was no question of the bid going through. But, because Paul and Aaron had voted on the losing side, they had to offer their shares to me. I refused to buy them.

'Can anyone explain why I should raise money to buy shares that I *gave* you?'

'My dear sister,' Aaron said, 'you might as well consider our offer. Archie's an old man. Who knows where he's willed his shares? The next time there's a bid you might not be so lucky . . . And if you've voted against a company, they're hardly likely to retain you as Chairman, are they? Just think of it, the House of Laure without Grace Laure! So why not buy us out and be sure of your precious company?'

'Because I'm damned if I'm going to be blackmailed, Aaron! I don't understand you. You're my brother. Why are you doing this to me?'

'Has it ever occurred to you, Grace, I'm forty-four now, and for as long as I can remember I've been beholden to you!'

'I've never felt that you should be. I've always loved you, wanted to care for you.'

'Let's just say I want to be Aaron Mandel, *not* Grace Laure's brother.' And with that, he left the boardroom. Well, at least now I knew where I stood.

Some months later Archie had a stroke. I talked to his doctor and was relieved to hear that he was, at that time, in no danger. What I didn't know was that Archie's solicitor had advised him to give his nephew power of attorney. I'm sure, at the time, his solicitor did this in Archie's best interests. But a second stroke followed and poor, dear Archie hovered in that half world between life and death. That was when Aaron and Paul made their move. To be fair to Archie's nephew, he had no reason to be loyal to me. A great deal of money would be transferred to Archie's estate after the take-over. I assumed that the nephew was Archie's heir. I could understand that he was tempted.

The timing was too accurate to be a coincidence. A little after it was clear that Archie would be unable to make his wishes known in the matter, Monsieur Montaigne made a new improved offer and Paul called an Extraordinary General Meeting. It was that meeting I was about to go to. I was going to lose the House of Laure. I would be rich, but then I was already. What would happen to my employees?

Some of them had been with me since the company had started. The factory I'd bought from Mark Kingly was much bigger but we still had the original one at Baildon. Peg worked there. So did two of the other girls who'd worked with me at the beginning. Alf, who'd driven our first old van, had married Peg and was now in charge of the transport section for the factory. I still enjoyed seeing them, being with them. After the take-over, the new company wouldn't care about families and local employment. They would strip assets and 'rationalise' the workforce. It broke my heart to think of what was going to happen.

I was filled with despair that I was going to lose the company I'd given my life to. Today I faced the humiliation of being asked to resign from the Board.

Mike telephoned me just after I'd heard that Paul was calling a shareholders' meeting. 'Hi, Beccy, how are you, kid?'

I smiled. Only Mike could call a forty-seven-year-old woman 'kid'. Only Mike still called me Beccy. To Paul, I'd always been Grace. To Kit I was Young Laure. Even Bruno now called me Gracie. But always to Mike I was Beccy. I was so low I poured my heart out to him.

'Just get on a plane and come to me, kid. I'd guessed that things were bad between you and that son of a bitch you married, but I never thought he'd try to take your company away from you. Well, let him have it! Turn your back on the bastards and let me take care of you, my love.'

'Your love? I don't understand,' I stammered. As if indeed I was still young Beccy and not the sophisticated woman I had become.

'Oh, Christ, kid! For a woman who's the toughest businessman I know, you sure are dumb! I love you, darling girl. I always have and always will. Walk away from the House of Laure. Come to me, my Beccy.'

'Oh, Mike! You don't know . . . can't know . . . what hearing you say that means to me. But I can't walk away. I might lose − I know I *will* lose − but I want to see if I can get some sort of a deal for the people who work for us.'

'Well, you know where to find me.'

'Yes. Thank you, Mike. And God bless.'

I sat by the phone for a moment after I'd hung up. I felt sick with despair. The quest for success no longer stood between Mike and me. The gulf that separated us now was failure. I desperately wanted to go to him but never would if I felt myself defeated. As if we would only be together because I'd failed. He deserved better than that. And he would be less than human if he didn't question why I'd waited until this moment to tell him what was in my heart.

I dressed and carefully made up. I looked at my watch. It was time to go. Since Mike had called me the previous evening, my private telephone had rung several times. I'd left it unanswered. I knew it was Mike and I had nothing to say to him. To offer him.

As I opened the door to leave my apartment, the phone started ringing again. I was suddenly ashamed of myself for not answering. He was clearly worried about me. I hurried back into the bedroom and answered the phone.

'Miss Laure? I've been trying to reach you all night. This is Mr Crabtree's solicitor. I'm telephoning from Baildon.'

'Oh, no! Archie's died!'

'I'm afraid so. But, you know, it was peaceful and I don't think anyone who was fond of him would have wanted him to go on as he was.'

'No.'

'I cannot help but be aware of the take-over bid for your company. In the light of today's meeting, I felt you should know that on Mr Crabtree's death, the power of attorney was rescinded. Until the will is published, the shareholders will not be able to vote on the take-over.'

'I see.' But that simply postponed things and solved nothing. I was sure that Archie would have left his estate to his only nephew.

'Miss Laure, this is very improper of me but Mr Crabtree was very fond of you. I think you should know that he has left you his ten per cent holding in the House of Laure. At the next meeting you will be the majority shareholder. I'll be in touch. Good morning.'

I wouldn't only be the majority shareholder again. Because their offer to sell was in the minutes of the meeting concerning the first take-over offer, I had the right to buy Aaron and Paul's shares. The company would be mine and my daughter's. I still hoped for a reconciliation with my daughter. But in that moment of intense relief that the House of Laure would survive, I saw clearly the way ahead. I'd wanted success. The kind of success that a man usually achieves. Well, I'd had that. But what of me as a woman? Surely I hadn't forfeited my right to personal happiness.

I glanced at my watch. My secretary should be at her desk by now. I telephoned her and quickly explained the situation created by Archie's death. Would she telephone and explain to the other shareholders?

'And will you be in the office later, Madame?' she asked.

'I don't know, Paulette. I'll phone you.'

But I did know. I had control of my company again, and I'd never let it go until I'd found someone to care for it as I did. But I'd start looking for that someone immediately. I would no longer live only for my company. I wanted to love and be loved. I took my passport from the bureau drawer, put it into my handbag, and then took the lift down to the street.

My chauffeur was waiting. He held the door of the car open for me. 'To the House of Laure, Madame?'

'No, to the airport, please!'

I made one telephone call from the departure lounge then caught the first available flight to Los Angeles.

When I left the prefabricated chaos of Los Angeles airport, he was waiting. I saw him across the milling crowds and knew that wherever Mike was was where I belonged.

His hair was streaked with white now. He was still handsome, but a little stockier. His waist line had thickened slightly and there were fine lines on his strong Slavic face. Well, I was no longer a girl. I was a woman. A woman ready to be loved.

He saw me and his face lit up. 'Beccy! Beccy!' he called and then he opened his arms to me. The woman who ran to meet him was not Grace Laure, she was Beccy. I had come home at last.